RU**I**

W**I**LD

ALSO BY K.A. TUCKER

RUNNING WILD

a novel

K.A. TUCKER

ISBN 978-1-990105-20-3
ISBN 978-1-990105-18-0 (ebook)

Edited by Jennifer Sommersby

Cover design by Hang Le

Published by K.A.Tucker

Manufactured in the United States of America

To everyone who loves spending time in this world as much as I do, especially those willing to go into this story with an open mind and a soft heart.

PROLOGUE

August 2018

"I'm in love with you. Haven't you figured that out yet, you big dummy?" The stark declaration competes with the crunch of gravel beneath my boots as I trudge toward the steel-gray building. Nearby, an Otter's propeller hums, preparing for takeoff. At least the fog that stalled my flight from Anchorage this morning has lifted, but the sky is murky, and the drizzle has me squinting.

I release a shaky breath, my heart racing. Am I *really* doing this? After practicing some iteration of those words in front of my mirror countless times, will I *finally* work up the nerve to say them out loud to Jonah's face?

I've only been secretly pining for him for a few *years*.

Ever since that day I walked up to the red Cessna, my veterinarian bag in hand, to meet the bushy-faced pilot. I felt the spark instantly. There was no mistaking the returning interest in those stunning blue eyes, the color of an Alaskan sky on a cloudless winter's day. And, by the end of those two days, flying to remote villages to vaccinate and treat animals in need, all while contending with Jonah's piercing gaze, barking laughter, and flirtatious banter, that spark had erupted into a smoldering fire.

I knew I was in trouble, the diamond engagement ring heavy on my finger, outweighed only by guilt for my disloyal thoughts.

I said goodbye to my pilot and flew back to my side of Alaska, convinced myself that the attraction would dwindle, that what I was feeling would vanish. I already knew that was a lie, one I clung to for an entire year, while quietly falling in love with a man who *wasn't* my fiancé under the cover of providing philanthropic aid to the villagers and their four-legged family members.

The thing is, Jonah is one of the smartest men I've ever met, as well as the most perceptive. Deep down, he knows how I feel. He *must*. I've dropped enough hints over the years. All our late-night phone calls and days spent flying together. For God's sake, I *kissed* him once, that night so long ago, emboldened by liquid courage and the knowledge that he had hopped in his plane and flown *hours* over the mountain range to see me the *very* same day I told him I'd ended my engagement. As if he'd been waiting for his chance.

I didn't imagine the chemistry, either; it wasn't one-sided. I felt the way Jonah responded—those seconds that still burn in my memory, his lips eager against mine—before the worry of destroying our strong friendship ruined the moment.

He acknowledged his attraction to me. He told me he thought I was beautiful, kind, and brilliant.

And then we both agreed to put aside those feelings for the sake of our friendship. Just box them up, pretend the kiss didn't happen, and go on being Jonah and Marie. Best friends.

It's been years since that night, and I've honored that promise, gritting my teeth while watching him cycle through shallow relationships with women who never had a chance of keeping his interest. But my feelings have only grown stronger. Lately, they've become unbearable, bottled up like this.

Jonah is my person. I can read every glower, every smirk, every grunt. I can call him on his bullshit when he's being an ass and sink into his arms when he's showing his gentler side. He's the first one I call when I need to talk, the only one who knows me better than I know myself, the one I miss terribly whenever I'm not here.

He's the man I want to experience the rest of my life with.

He is *it* for me.

And after receiving the stomach-curdling message from Agnes about Jonah's plane crash, I decided it's time I said all this out loud. Maybe hearing it will make the brute finally put aside his fear and see what he'll be gaining rather than risking.

The aqua-blue Alaska Wild sign looks more vibrant than usual, but that could be the adrenaline coursing through my veins. Swallowing my nerves, I wipe away wet tendrils of hair that cling to my forehead and push through the door. The familiar and welcoming smell of coffee fills my nostrils.

"Marie!" Sharon shrieks, her hand on her swollen belly as she charges for me. I should have expected this greeting; I wasn't supposed to arrive until Monday, and I didn't tell anyone except Crystal, the local animal rescue group leader who lets me crash in her guest cabin while I'm in town.

Alaska Wild's pregnant receptionist seems to have doubled in size since I last saw her. I drop my bag, my attention stalling on her only for a split second before traveling beyond, to the brawny frame leaning against the reception counter, the grinning, handsome face I've been aching four long weeks to see. Except ... I frown. Jonah's wild blond mane and beard that I tease him about regularly have vanished, replaced by a tidy beard a fraction of its original size and shorter hair that looks styled with *product*?

Sharon throws her arms around my neck in a fierce hug. "Did you just land?"

"Uh ... yeah. Rough flight." I struggle to keep my focus on her, my attention veering back to Jonah frequently. What possessed him to do that? "Okay, first of all, wow, look at that belly! And it's only been four weeks since I saw you last."

"*Only*, you say." Sharon's hands slide over her stomach with a loud groan.

No longer able to ignore it, I march toward the counter. "And *you. What the hell*, Jonah?"

Not a beat passes before his strong arms pull me against his chest. I inhale the comforting scent of woodsy soap, relishing these few moments as I do every time we greet. If all goes as I hope it does this trip, maybe I won't be staying at Crystal's cabin anymore. Maybe I'll have a warm bed with an even warmer body next to me from now on.

"What the hell, indeed." His raspy voice is gravelly against my ear. "Hey, Marie."

With reluctance, I peel away, only to reach up and smooth my fingers over his groomed beard, the prickly ends tickling my skin. I've touched his beard before, usually with a teasing tug. It was always so scruffy. "I like it." I more than like it. I *love* this new look. It allows me to see so much more of that face I adore.

I'm temporarily distracted by the track of black stitches across his forehead, the only visible proof of his plane crash, and then Jonah moves away—too soon for my liking—to lean against the counter again, his attention shifting behind me. "I was the victim of a cruel and vicious prank." He chuckles. "I probably deserved it."

"Probably," a female answers dryly.

I turn toward the voice. I hadn't noticed the woman standing at the counter before, too enthralled with Jonah's new image. How hadn't I noticed her before? I can't help but gawk. She's stunning, her long, cinnamon-brown hair touched with flattering blonde highlights, her large hazel-green eyes lined with full, dark lashes that flutter at Jonah. She has flawless, glowing skin and an athletic figure—on display in a fashionable tunic and leggings.

The kind of body I know Jonah appreciates.

"This is Wren's daughter, Calla. She's here visiting," Jonah says by way of introduction.

"I didn't realize Wren had a daughter." Why hasn't Jonah ever mentioned her before? Why hasn't Wren? Jonah told me that his boss had been married once, many years ago, but that's all I've ever heard, and I've gotten to know the owner of Alaska Wild fairly well. He's a kind, quiet man. That he has never mentioned his own daughter seems odd.

I finally remember my manners, smiling at Calla as I reach forward. "First time in Alaska?"

Her hand is cold against mine, her manicured nails long and even and artificial. "Yeah."

"I picked her up from Anchorage last weekend. It's been … interesting, so far." Jonah's attention is locked on the beautiful face across from him as he flashes a flirtatious grin, and they share a secretive look.

An unpleasant feeling skates down my spine and settles in the pit of my stomach. Calla certainly doesn't seem like she's from around here. Those sculpted eyebrows must require meticulous grooming, but she looks like the kind of girl who sits in front of a mirror for hours each day, perfecting herself.

I've never been one to spend too much time fussing over my appearance, embracing a more natural, low-maintenance look that works well with my busy veterinarian practice and outdoorsy lifestyle. But suddenly, I regret throwing on the first shirt I pulled out of my dresser, and perhaps I should have made better friends with my hairbrush. Not that the rain wouldn't have undone that, anyway. But next to Calla—she's, what, in her midtwenties?—I look every bit the frumpy and weathered thirty-six-year-old.

It's beginning to make sense now. Calla must've had a hand in Jonah's new style. I can't imagine the conversation that led to that —or what it led to after.

"So, where are you from?" I hope they can't hear the strain in my voice.

"Toronto."

A city girl. Yeah, that explains a lot. "Oh, that's far." Thousands of miles away. Hours of commercial flying. A whole other country. Too far for Jonah, who isn't a fan of relationships of any kind, let alone long-distance ones. He wasn't willing to attempt it with Teegan, and they dated for months before she moved back to the lower forty-eight. "And how long are you here for?"

"Another week."

"Okay ..." Relief washes over me. A week. Barely more than a one-night stand for him. Whatever's going on here, it'll be over soon. Then I can profess my undying love for this man, and we can move on as if she doesn't exist.

"Unless I decide to stay longer," Calla says abruptly, her focus darting to Jonah, as if to check his reaction to that suggestion.

As if his response will be the deciding factor.

His eyebrow arches.

I know Jonah too well to mistake that look for anything other than excitement, anticipation.

Determination.

He *wants* Calla to stay. Quite badly, I'd guess. He can't even peel his eyes from her anymore. It's as if he's ensnared, and they're the only two people in the room.

And that expression filling his handsome face right now?

A numbing dread sinks deep into my bones. Jonah has *never* looked at me that way before.

CHAPTER ONE

Today

January

"Can we put this on my tab? Lori decided Christina needs braces, and she's hounding me to pay for them. I'm good for this, as soon as I get paid." Brad watches me with those expressive green eyes —eyes that I once found appealing.

"This isn't a bar. And you still haven't paid for Clementine's *last* visit."

Hearing her name, the wiry ferret clambers up his chest and lets out a distinctive clucking sound.

Brad winces. "But my ex ... you know what she's like, right?"

No, I don't, but I know him. Brad Garvis is a divorced, thirty-nine-year-old welder from Wasilla who rarely sees his kids and works a second job under the table so he doesn't have to pay more in child support. I know this because I made the mistake of dating him several years ago. He'd been brazenly flirting for months during a series of visits for his three sick ferrets. I thought him attractive, but he was a client, and besides, I was staying single until the moment Jonah realized he was madly in love with me.

And then Jonah started dating Teegan, a pilot with the coast guard. In a moment of weakness, tormented by mental images of them together, I agreed to a dinner date with Brad, followed by several more. I knew it would never go anywhere, but it was a suitable distraction for a time.

I *should* refuse him, but that eye infection is nasty, and it's Clementine who'll suffer if she doesn't get these drops. "I'll meet you out front in a few minutes with the prescription."

His shoulders sink with dramatic relief. "Oh man, you're the best, Marie."

Yeah, the best at being a sucker.

"I promise, I'll settle up by Friday."

"Uh-huh." Can he hear the doubt in my voice?

He's halfway out of the exam room when he stalls, crooking his head curiously. "Hey, you know, it's been awhile since we've hung out. I don't even remember why we stopped."

Because Jonah broke up with Teegan. But whatever existed between Brad and me had already run its course.

"What are you doing next weekend?"

"I'll be in the villages," I lie. I've started doing remote vet care through virtual consultations, especially through the winter months. Besides, my trusted pilot is currently in Hawaii on his honeymoon, cursing tourists and complaining about the humidity, if his latest text is any indication.

"Maybe another time, then."

I offer a tight smile. "Yeah, maybe." *No thanks.* I may be lonely, but I'm not desperate, and I'm *never* dating another client again. *Ever.*

Ten minutes later, I'm locking the door and flipping the sign to Closed, my three-hour Sunday morning clinic hours I offer once a month having flown by.

"You *should* have made him pay," Cory announces from behind the desk, her disapproval soaking her tone as she stares out the bay window. "He can afford it."

I watch Brad trudge down the narrow path—through snow I shoveled in darkness this morning—toward a new, freshly washed black Dodge Ram. She's right. That wasn't even an outrageous bill. I don't know why I always find myself in positions like this. Oh yeah, I do. Because I'm a chump who can't say no to helping an animal. "Next time he calls for an appointment, tell him he needs to settle up *before* you'll book him." And it'll likely be soon, because that bacterial infection is contagious, he has two other ferrets at home, and he gives them more attention than he does his human children.

"With *great* pleasure." Delight flashes in her large azure eyes as she reaches for a printout with one hand while typing on the computer with her other. In the next beat, she's up and sauntering across the room toward the filing cabinet, her wavy chestnut-brown hair a thick curtain reaching halfway down her back, her curvy figure moving with a blunt confidence I've always envied.

Cory has been my type A receptionist since my mother retired, keeping this place running far better than I ever could. Eight years later, she has earned her vet technician credentials but refuses to give up the office role, so she juggles both—booking appointments and running blood tests (and of course, accepting a larger paycheck) with proficiency. I'd be lost around here without her, and I will be should she ever leave. I'll need to hire *two* people to replace her.

My gaze wanders out the window again, to the cabin nestled among the snow-laden trees. It's a small, one-room structure, meant as a rustic, short-term guesthouse rather than the permanent residence I've turned it into. My father would crash there sometimes when this place was his and he didn't want to make the two-hundred-yard trek to our house on the other side of the property.

Sometimes I wish for more—more space, more privacy, more charm—but most of the time, I'm happy in my little home. Plus, can't beat free rent, and the walk across the parking lot to work is especially handy when I have a sick patient to check on overnight.

I've invested in it over the years, installing better insulation to cut the draft on the cold nights, a new red metal roof that pops against the crisp white backdrop, a kitchenette, a proper shower to go along with the toilet, and a small, screened-in porch where I spend many evenings, sitting in my Adirondack chair.

Decades ago, when my parents bought this parcel of land and opened this little clinic, Wasilla was barely more than a supply base for miners. People thought my dad was crazy. But then came the highway, and the city exploded with new development, turning the Mat-Su Valley into a viable and affordable suburb for commuters into Anchorage.

By the time my father retired and I took over, there were six other clinics around Wasilla and Palmer, all of them set up in shiny new builds as opposed to this old place that's required plenty of upgrades and fixes over the years.

But given where we're located, on the far western fringe of the borough, away from the busy hub and closest to Alaska's dogsled mecca, we've always had enough clients and patients to keep Cory and me busy. Sometimes I call my father in to lend a hand. I hazard Dr. Sidney Lehr appreciates venturing away from his *riveting* games of solitaire and Mom's fussing every so often.

Sure, the lobby could use a refresher—a coat of paint, brighter light fixtures, and more colorful lobby chairs, a new receptionist counter to replace the clunky one my mother sat behind with an infant me on her lap, and sturdier shelving for the small selection of specialty dog and cat food we carry—but I've focused my efforts on the back of the clinic, ensuring I have the latest equipment to do my job. Pretty chairs and freshly painted drywall don't save animals.

I check the clock. It's one P.M. on Sunday, the sun is shining, and there are no patients in the clinic to worry about. I have the entire afternoon to do ... *something* before dinner at my parents' tonight. Maybe I'll grab my cross-country skis and head up to Hatcher Pass to—

"Oh! Before I forget!" Cory beckons me to the computer monitor with a wave of her hand. "I'm going to print this out and put it up there." With a nod toward the clinic staff's photo gallery wall, she mutters under her breath, "To replace your mug shot."

I chuckle as I pass the picture in question. I'm grimacing more than smiling, my complexion is sickly thanks to my white smock and poor studio lighting, and my mascara is smeared from the downpour, but the photographer didn't tell me! Sadly, it was the best of the lot that day, and we chose it as a temporary joke that has now survived ten years.

I round the desk just as Cory's clicking on an email from Calla.

"I mean, you're beautiful, *anyway*, but this"—she gestures toward the candid shot of me in my black evening gown, standing on the frozen lake outside Jonah and Calla's house—"is incredible. Whoever they hired to photograph the wedding was, like, *amazing*. I need their number for Joe and me." She adds quietly, "If he *ever* gets around to proposing."

A twinge stirs in my chest as I study the genuine smile that crinkles my eyes. I remember when that picture was taken. I was watching Jonah shift from foot to foot as Calla strolled down the snowy path toward the red-carpeted aisle on the ice, as if he might implode if he had to survive *not* being married to her for one more second.

At that moment, I was *thrilled* for my best friend. Jonah has found the woman he's going to spend the rest of his life with—of that, I have no doubt. Those two couldn't be more different and yet more perfect for each other.

My happiness for him is what the photographer captured.

But I wonder … if that lens had snapped the center of my gaze, would anyone be able to decipher the mourning that still lingers deep within, over a dream long since proven a delusion, a fictional love story that will never evolve into reality? Jonah may have been *it* for me, but *I* am never going to be the one for him.

A soothing palm pats my arm, and I turn to find Cory's round face brimming with compassion. She knows this unrequited tale better than anyone. She's been here for its life span. I was dating Jonathan when Cory began working here. She squealed with excitement the day I showed up at the clinic with a ring on my finger. She watched me suppress my excitement every time I left for Bangor and ignore my conscience every time I returned. She knew I was going to end things with Jonathan before he did. My trusty employee has been through it all with me—the thrill and guilt of falling for Jonah, and the soul-crushing heartache of watching him fall in love with someone else.

"I am *only* happy for him. For *them*," I reiterate for what feels like the hundredth time. I even find myself liking my best friend's wife—God, Jonah has a wife! He's married!—more and more with each encounter, despite our differences in lifestyle and personality.

"I know you are. Because you're a decent human being and a *good* friend." Cory adds more softly, "But you *are* human, Marie, and you don't always have to be so composed and understanding. It's also okay to admit that it hurts. You were *in love* with him for years, and that's not a tap you can just turn off. You're not a kitchen faucet."

I snort at her analogy. "Yeah, well, the time for that hurt is long gone. Jonah's married, and he's too important to me to let it ever get in the way again. I've accepted that." A part of me recognized it long ago, in those months after Wren passed away and Calla left for Toronto, when I watched him drowning in misery. I could have attempted to fill the cavernous void in his heart with myself, with what I wanted for us. I can't lie—I considered taking advantage of his despair, tried convincing myself it could work, that I could be a suitable replacement.

But that voice in my head, the one that reminded me I would *never* be his first choice, was louder.

So, with a gnawing ache in my chest, I sent him a booking page for the next commercial flight to Toronto and told him he was an idiot if he let Calla get away without a fight. I had secretly hoped she would reject him, or that she wouldn't but what they had would fizzle, that Jonah's interest would wane, his goals in life pulling him in another direction. In *my* direction.

He ran to her and hasn't looked back since.

And aside from one moment of weakness that I still deeply regret, when Calla seemed miserable in Alaska and their priorities seemed too vastly different to find a path forward together, I have *never* considered telling Jonah how I truly feel about him again.

No, that door is closed forever. It's time for me to move on.

If I could only figure out how.

"Just know if you *ever* need a nonjudgmental ear, I'm here for you. And, you know, I'm also more than willing to set you up with one of Joe's friends."

My head falls back with an exasperated groan.

"I'm serious! He has a few cute, single ones. Are they the smartest? No. Are they relationship material? Also, no. But you'll have a *good time*."

My laughter drowns out the singsong lilt of her words. "Aren't they all his age?" Younger than Cory by two years.

"So?" She shrugs. "You're a youthful thirty-seven-year-old."

"I'll be thirty-eight next month," I remind her. "And I don't want a twenty-six-year-old *boy*. Even for *that*." Joe is a sweet guy, but Cory is the mature one in that relationship. Just being around him makes me feel old.

Knuckles rapping on the door makes us both jump.

Harry Hatchett and his mother Bonnie are huddled outside, a blonde husky dangling from Harry's arms.

"Speaking of annoying *boys*," Cory whispers. "He doesn't have an appointment."

"No, and I usually head out there." To the Hatchett property, halfway between Meadow Lakes and Fishhook, to their kennel of seventy-five sled dogs. That Harry showed up here now, carrying one of them, means something must be *very* wrong.

I move swiftly to unlock the door and get them out of the polar vortex that has gripped the entire Mat-Su region this past week.

"We were hoping we'd catch you," Harry says. He's a lean man who matches my height, with a trimmed beard that complements the mop of blond hair hiding beneath his winter cap. His baby-blue eyes and trademark playful grin have won plenty of female attention; the latter is noticeably absent.

I've known Harry for years, since I was fifteen and tagging along on clinic runs with my dad, and Harry was a rambunctious toddler, clambering onto his father Earl's sled to yell "Ready!" at an empty gangline. It's no surprise he grew up to become a competitive musher. He's a second-generation racer in the Iditarod, the historic thousand-mile dogsled race across two mountain ranges. It's in his blood. And while he hasn't won the Iditarod yet, he's determined to beat his father's record of five first place finishes.

It was always assumed that Earl and Harry would be lining up trophies next to each other for years to come. But three years ago, Earl suffered a massive heart attack while out training on their property. Their lead dogs brought the sled back without guidance, and without him. He'd collapsed on the trail.

By the time Harry and Bonnie found him, it was too late.

And Harry, only twenty-two, and an immature twenty-two at that, was left to take over the family operation.

"Dr. Lehr." Bonnie's pointy chin dips in greeting, and my skin prickles with awareness. She only uses my official title when they want something specific from me.

"Who's this?" I take in the dog's eyes—one a pale blue, the other brown. Apprehension fills them, but it doesn't make a sound. It's skinny and weathered, with oozing bite marks on its thigh.

It can't be one of theirs. Around here, the Hatchett name is synonymous with winning races, and breeding and keeping champion sled dogs. Between my father and me, we've treated the Hatchett Kennels for four decades, and they take exceptional care of their dogs.

"She wandered over from the old Danson place," Harry says with a sharp look.

"Right, your mother mentioned you had a new neighbor." A musher who moved here from somewhere abroad and bought the sizable property next to them.

"Look what he's done to her!" Bonnie shakes a gnarled index finger at the sad-looking animal in Harry's arms, her pinched face an odd mix of sympathy and triumph. This isn't the first time she's suggested that her new neighbor abuses his dogs, approaching me for help to expose him. But she's never had any evidence, only hunches.

Now, it appears she might have proof to back up her claim.

"I'll bet he's been using her to churn out litters of puppies." Harry bends his athletic body over to ease the dog onto the floor.

Her nose twitches, taking in the medley of antiseptic and animal scents as she looks around the lobby, searching for an escape, I'm sure.

I crouch to my haunches. "Hey, girl." I'd put her at about forty pounds. Not emaciated, but underweight for her size. She should tip the scale at fifty.

It's a long moment before she takes the few hobbled steps over to sniff my outstretched hand with a cautious pass of her snout.

From this angle, I'm able to see the loose skin and enlarged nipples on her underbelly. She's had puppies. Probably multiple litters, the latest one within the past six months. My nostrils fill with the smell of her fetid breath. "Have you met this guy yet?"

"Once. Mom and I headed over the week he moved in for a little meet 'n' greet. You know, the friendly neighbor thing to do. We ran into him halfway up his laneway. He didn't invite us to the house, and by the next week he had a gate up on the driveway and a dozen warning signs to keep people off his property. Seems weird, doesn't it? To be so unfriendly with your neighbors right off the bat, especially *us*? And in a tight community like this where people help each other out?" Harry shakes his head. "It's gotta make you wonder what he's hiding back there."

"He's doin' somethin' he doesn't want us to know about. That's the *only* explanation," Bonnie chirps.

"Definitely makes me wonder *something*," I murmur. The dog does another cautious pass before stepping forward, accepting a scratch on her forehead. Whatever she's been through, she's not aggressive. She lets me lift her lip to check her mouth. Her teeth look okay—not great—but her gums are a mess—an abscess is causing that foul odor. Aside from the obvious ailments, the dog doesn't appear sickly, though. Without doing a full exam and lab work, I wouldn't know for sure. "And you're sure she wandered over from this guy's place?"

"I followed the tracks to our fence line," Harry confirms. "Where else would she come from?"

"It's people like these who bring a bad name to mushing and give material for all those exposés. He has no business ownin' sled dogs or bein' anywhere near us. We need to make an example of him." Bonnie's jaw is set with determination as she looks at her son, goading him.

"Yeah, you need to help us with this, Marie." Harry's tone has shifted in his attempt to sound more commanding. "He can go back to Finland or wherever the hell he came from if he wants to treat dogs like this. I don't want him anywhere near *our race.*"

I bite my tongue against the urge to ask if they would be so adamant to stop their new neighbor from competing if there wasn't speculation that he's exceptionally skilled—enough to beat Harry, who came in second last year but has yet to win. I *also* don't mention the rumor that's been floating around about this new guy breeding and selling sled dogs to other mushers. I have no idea if that's wishful thinking or fact, but with a crop of dogs from Finland, that means fresh bloodlines, which means less risk of inbreeding. That concern has been cropping up more lately for dogs coming from Harry, who frankly doesn't know what he's doing in that department.

Not like Earl did.

But I don't miss the way Harry says *our race.* One might think he means Alaska, but I've experienced his entitled arrogance enough to know he means *his* race. The Hatchetts have positioned themselves as mushing experts within the community. With a multitude of Iditarod wins under their belt, they've earned notoriety. But without Earl, Harry is just an obnoxious, self-centered guy trying to fill shoes that will always be too big for him.

And of course, they'd want me, a veterinarian who has been volunteering with the Iditarod for the past decade and has personal connections with key people within the race, to be the one to raise the issue. It'll look better than a rival doing so.

Whatever the Hatchetts' motivation, there are clear signs of neglect here that concern me. If this dog is in fact their new neighbor's, this needs to be brought to the Iditarod Trail

Committee's attention immediately, and if I get my way, the guy will be disqualified from racing.

I read the clock on the wall. One ten. I guess I know what I'm doing with my afternoon now. "Cory, can you give Howie a call? If he doesn't answer his cell, try his home number."

CHAPTER TWO

"What's his name again?"

Howie eases his pickup truck to the end of the driveway, the passage beyond blocked by a metal farm gate. "Says here"—the animal control officer checks the paper file he grabbed from the office on the way to pick me up—"Tyler Brady. He applied for his kennel license last summer. Twenty-one dogs."

"That's all?" These competitive kennels normally have at least thirty, so they can select the best of the best come race time. Otherwise, they're leasing dogs from places like Harry's.

"Twenty-one dogs. Tami did the inspection and approved it."

"No concerns?"

"None. He was in the middle of a bunch of new construction for them, but he met all the basic needs. Food, water, beds, proper leads ... She didn't flag anything. Obviously didn't see this one." He peers over his shoulder at the dog stretched out in the back of the cab.

"And he's from Finland?" That's an awfully American name for someone who, according to rumor, moved here from the Scandinavian country last summer.

Howie drags a calloused index finger across handwritten notes on a separate piece of paper. "Yup. Finland."

A country with a robust dogsledding industry, with racers who regularly travel here to compete. So, what made him *move* to Alaska with his dogs?

"You sure you want to do this?" Howie studies me.

I consider his question for all of one second before nodding. "If what the Hatchetts say is true, then who knows what else is on that property. There could be more dogs like her. And if she escaped, he's going to want to get rid of any evidence of that before people start asking questions." Maybe I'm imagining worst-case scenarios, but all it takes is a visit to one poorly run kennel to make those horrific images live in your head. And with the state this dog is in, those images could be a reality here.

Howie scratches at his graying temples as he sizes up the chained gate.

"You have jurisdiction here." We're outside the city borders.

"Yeah, but that's not normally how this works." He chuckles. "This is gonna make for an interesting Sunday afternoon. But hey, what else did I have going on? You know, besides relaxing on my couch with a beer, watching a Giants' playoff game in a rare moment of peace while Debra takes the kids to her parents for the day."

I wince. "Isn't football over yet?"

He tosses the file onto the console between us. "Come on, for you, Marie? Of course, I'll do what I can. I mean, how often have you dropped everything to help us out?"

"Once or twice." I've long since lost count of the number of times I've been called in to treat an animal that Howie or one of the other officers has brought in on account of abuse. I've never minded, especially when it's Howie calling. He's been doing this job since I graduated from Washington State University with my veterinarian degree and returned to Alaska. The forty-four-year-old and I became friends long ago, the moment we realized we were kindred spirits where animals were involved.

His forehead wrinkles. "The office *really* should be phoning this guy to let him know we're coming."

"So he has time to hide what he doesn't want you seeing?"

"Yeah, makes you wonder, right?" He taps against the clipboard on my lap, holding the complaint form I filled out on the way here. A case file number is already scrawled across the top in Howie's scribble. "You done with that?"

"Yeah. Everything's there." All the facts provided to me—minus Bonnie's baseless accusations—after the Hatchetts arrived at my clinic.

"At least we're doing *some of this* by the book. You know it's already going to be a tough sell. And we can't just barrel in there with accusations. We don't even know if the dog is his."

"I know." She's not microchipped. I already scanned her.

"Okay, then. Let's go stir up some shit." He slides out of the driver's side and rustles around in the toolbox in his truck bed, pulling out his bolt cutters.

In his jeans and parka, with wisps of hair peeking out from beneath his knitted Giants cap, Howie cuts through the mushing facility's entrance gate—and nothing about this Sunday afternoon looks "by the book." But showing up here like two regular people who found a wandering dog, rather than an animal control officer and a veterinarian hunting for an abuser, might get us the information we need.

I shift my attention to our nervous passenger in the back, offering her a gloveless hand to sniff. Though skittish, she's beginning to warm to me already. I would have preferred leaving her at the clinic, if we're coming out here to accuse this guy of cruelty, we need the victim with us. "Don't worry, we'll get you fixed up, good as new," I promise.

A white lie. The dog's in rough shape. How rough, I can't say yet. Cory's running a few preliminary blood tests while the more

complex ones will have to go to a lab. I did what I could for the
oozing sores, cleaning and applying ointment, and dosing her
with a round of antibiotics. She'll need a special feeding plan to
put some meat on her bones, and the abscess on her gums will
require close attention.

In moments, Howie has cut the chain and pushed the gate
open, fastening it to a nearby tree to keep it that way. Tossing the
cutters back into his toolbox, he climbs in and throws the truck
into gear, and we're heading down the gravel driveway toward a
plume of smoke. The snowy Talkeetna Mountains cut into the
cold, crisp blue sky.

The spectacular view does little for the knots in my stomach,
as I wish whatever situation we're walking into could be over
already. I'm not made for confrontation. Not like Jonah, who
strolls headfirst into a tense situation and bucks around like a
bronco with a cowboy spurring its haunches. But I can dig up
courage when I'm protecting a helpless animal, and one look at
this dog draws searing anger to my tongue.

In the clearing ahead is a ranch-style house with a wrap-
around deck, designed to enjoy the view. Several outbuildings are
scattered throughout, their open doors revealing the various
storage purposes—wood, ATVs, tools. It's typical of any rural
Alaskan property I've ever stepped foot on.

What's not typical is the looming barn to our left, freshly clad
in vivid red siding that reminds me of the barns in Sweden I saw
many years ago as a college student backpacking across Europe
for the summer between first and second year.

"He's got a nice piece of land here." Howie parks behind a
side-by-side utility vehicle. "How many acres you thinkin'? A
hundred? Two?"

"The Dansons had horses, so a fair amount, I'm guessing." And
this Tyler guy is clearly using those stalls. Someone—I doubt the
Dansons—has spent a considerable amount of money, and not
just on the barn. Closed-panel fence boards that easily reach

seven feet high begin at the side of the barn and extend far beyond my view.

"He's got money to burn." Howie sizes up the new construction as well. "With the range and Little Su in his backyard, this guy must have paid a pretty penny to set up shop here." With a glance at the dog in his back seat, Howie cranks the heat and leaves the truck running as he exits. The slamming door earns a nervous jump from her.

"You stay here." I scratch her head and then climb out. The frigid air claws at me as I round the hood of the rumbling truck. My breath billows in a frost-coated cloud. "How do you want to do this?"

He scratches his stubbled chin in thought. "Here's how it's gonna go: We got a report of abuse that we're investigating. Even though this is a registered kennel, we're walking in here on the assumption that she's a pet and protected by those laws and *not* livestock laws, which don't always work in our favor."

Because sled dogs are considered "livestock" in the Mat-Su region—a classification that infuriates me to no end.

"As far as *I'm* concerned, this animal isn't getting adequate care, no matter what. From there, I'll see what kind of fines and whatnot I can ding him with." The look on Howie's face says he's not overly confident.

I grit my jaw with grim determination. "Get me proof that this guy is neglecting these dogs, and I'll take it to the ITC." We might not be able to shut down his kennel, but I can have him disqualified and banned from all future races.

"First, we need to see if he's home." Howie's head swivels, stalling on the olive-green pickup truck that sits nearby, wearing the eight inches of snow that fell overnight. The owner clearly hasn't taken it out, and I don't see any tracks to suggest there's a second vehicle.

But there *are* fresh tracks.

He drags his boot across the snowmachine trail that leads out into the woods beyond. "Someone's out and about today."

Everyone's out and about today, I want to say. It's a sunny albeit frigid day for playing in the snow, and with the days as short as they are right now, people are taking advantage. We must have passed a dozen sledders on our drive up here, speeding along paths and coasting over frozen lakes.

The barn's heavy door slides open and a head donning a fur-lined trapper hat pokes out.

"You Tyler Brady?" Howie hollers.

A dog barks in answer, followed by a second, and then a cacophony erupts from within the red barn and somewhere beyond as the dogs realize they have visitors.

From this distance and against the bright sun, it's hard to make out a face, but the guy looks young. Too young to own a place like this, all gangly limbs in his muck-covered navy ski pants and no coat to hide his skinny arms. The barn must be heated.

His head jerks from left to right as he frantically searches for something—or someone—but he doesn't answer.

Howie steals a curious look my way.

I can only shrug before calling out, "I think we found a dog that belongs to you."

That seems to trigger something in him. Reaching inside the barn, he produces a heavy winter coat and tugs it on before yanking the door shut behind him. He approaches us warily, his shoulders hunched, his Sorels dragging with each step.

The closer he gets, the younger I see he is. Late teens, maybe twenty. At almost thirty-eight, I'm finding it harder to pinpoint ages—teenage boys all look *so* young—but he has the sort of soft features that might still harden with age.

The boy comes within ten feet of us before stopping abruptly. His hat is pulled down low, hovering above large brown eyes.

"Hey, how are ya doin' today?" Howie asks cordially. That's

how he approaches every situation, no matter how volatile it might be. Of all the animal control officers at the station, Howie is the easiest to work with. He's also the most enthusiastic about his job and the most liberal with delivering fines.

The guy nods before stammering, "Good."

"Are you Tyler?"

He shakes his head. "No ... Tyler's, he's out."

Howie points at the tracks. "On his snowmachine?"

"Yes, sir."

Howie pauses as if considering how he wants to proceed. The guy keeps shifting on his feet and stealing glances toward the woods. He seems nervous. "You by any chance missing a female husky with one blue eye and one golden-brown? Blonde coloring?"

"Yeah. That's where Tyler is. I mean, he's out looking for her right now, over there." He throws a gloved hand in the direction of the trail. "Left awhile ago, right after we realized she wandered off."

Bonnie and Harry were right to come to me. If Tyler Brady is treating his sled dogs like this, he shouldn't be allowed near them.

The guy's furtive gaze darts to me. "So, you said you have her?"

I take a calming breath. "We do. She's in the truck, where it's warm."

"Oh. Okay." He rubs the back of his neck and then, after a moment, says, "So ... I can take her back now, then?"

Over my dead body.

"You have a way of getting hold of Tyler?" Howie smiles easily. "I just have a few questions about the dog—"

"Nymeria. That's her name."

"Game of Thrones fans?"

The guy offers a toothy grin that transforms his face. "Yes, sir. I am. Tyler said it's unoriginal, but he let me name her, anyway."

Howie chuckles. "*I* think it's a great name. And sorry, I didn't catch yours?"

"Reed, sir," he falters. "My name's Reed."

"Well, Reed, I think it'd be a good idea for us to have that conversation with Tyler before we bring Nymeria over. The truck's warm. She should be nice and comfortable in there while we wait."

Reed scratches his chin with a gloved hand. "What kinds of questions?"

"Just want to know a bit more about her. Like how old she is, where you keep her, what she's been eating, things like that."

"Oh." The guy shifts on his feet. "Is Tyler gonna be in trouble?"

"For what?" I blurt out, earning a warning glance from Howie.

Reed swallows hard. "He just figured he might be, if anyone ever found her here."

This kid is giving us all the information we need, I think with grim satisfaction. The asshole *knows* what he's been doing to that dog is wrong, and he's trying to hide it.

"We just want to talk to him for now. Learn a little more about this dog." Howie nods toward the barn, where a cacophony of high-pitched barks carry. "Say, how many puppies you got in there?"

"None."

Howie frowns with doubt. "*None?*"

"I mean, yeah, we got two, but we're not sellin' them, if that's what you're askin'. People keep comin' here, looking for puppies to buy, but we're not breedin' them for sale."

"Are you breeding them to race?"

"Yes, sir. We will. Those that wanna race, anyway."

My stomach tightens. "And what about the ones that *don't* want to race?"

My ears catch a familiar whir.

Reed's head jerks to the right, toward the growing sound. A figure on a snowmachine appears from the thicket of trees, moving at a slower pace, presumably to keep stride with the eight dogs running alongside him, tether-free. They move in unison, two by two, as if harnessed, their powerful legs charging through the snow.

"Damn." There's no missing the admiration in the single word as Howie watches the dogs. "Is that Tyler?"

Reed's head bobs.

"Okay, then. We'll just wait here until he gets home, and then we'll have ourselves a little chat." Howie rubs his gloves together, his gaze darting to mine, his eyebrow arching in a *let me do the talking* way.

They round the bend and the clearing. A male voice shouts something and then the snowmachine speeds up. Suddenly, it's racing toward us, the dogs chasing after, never breaking formation.

I straighten my back and ignore the urge to huddle within my heavy coat as the man pulls up and cuts the engine. His face is hidden behind a black balaclava and goggles. No helmet. There's no law requiring one in Alaska, but it tells me that on top of everything else, this guy has no common sense.

He throws a leg over the seat and climbs off his snowmachine. Meanwhile, Reed drops to his knees, calling the dogs to him by name with an ease he didn't have for us. They rush straight for his open arms, tongues lolling from their panting mouths.

Tyler Brady has beautiful sled dogs, I'll admit. Not the fluffy purebred Disney dogs that are great for tourism photo ops and leisure mushing. These are the typical leaner version of huskies that uneducated people mistake for underfed when they're consuming upward of ten thousand calories a day during train-ing. I can already see that malnourishment is not the case here, the dogs' winter coats thick and full, and marked in every shade of black, brown, and gray. There are a couple unusual ones in the mix, too—one has a curled tail and a wolflike appearance, its fur a mottled mix of silver and ash. A Siberian Laika, possibly.

While doing a visual inspection from twenty feet away doesn't tell me much, I can see healthy white teeth and pink gums, no limps, and no ghastly wounds like the ones on Nymeria.

But these are his racing dogs, I remember. He might treat them differently from the ones who won't take him across the finish line.

"Tyler Brady?" Howie asks.

"And you are …" The muffled question—a demand, really—is delivered with a brusque and slightly Midwestern twang. Montana or Wyoming. Certainly not Scandinavia.

"Howie Fulford. I'm an animal care officer for the borough."

Tyler's head swivels toward me, and though I can't see his eyes through the iridescent shield, I feel them weighing on me.

I clear my throat. "I'm Marie Lehr, a local veterinarian who sometimes helps out Howie."

"Helps out with what, exactly?" Tyler adjusts his stance and folds his arms across his chest. He's made no effort to remove his gear yet, and it's intimidating to face a masked man. "Cutting chains and trespassing on private property?"

Howie clears his throat. He also senses the tension radiating from this man. A man who stands a few inches over six feet, with a lean but sturdy frame. I'd hazard an athlete's body hides beneath that one-piece suit. Someone who can compete in—and win—a thousand-mile race.

But Tyler doesn't have the upper hand here, I remind myself. "Someone brought a female husky into my clinic this morning. They thought she might belong to you. Your—" I look to the young man scratching the head of one of the dogs. Is Reed his hired help? His son? Not likely, given he's only called him Tyler, but I have no idea if Tyler is old enough to have a son this age. He's still hidden from head to toe. "Reed confirmed that you're missing a husky."

"We are," he says slowly, evenly.

"Is she yours?" Howie pipes in. "One blue eye, one brown? Blonde fur."

Tyler is quiet for a moment, as if sizing him up. "Based on your description, sounds like her."

Two of the other dogs have grown curious and now approach us cautiously, their heads bowed as they sniff the air. They have little red booties on to protect their feet during their run.

Howie gives one of them—a black elkhound—a hand to sniff. "Okay, well, we have some concerns for her welfare that I'd like to discuss with you."

I brace myself for Tyler's claims that she's fine, well cared for. For us to mind our own goddamn business and get off his property.

He reaches up to tug off his goggles and balaclava, revealing a stony expression.

Despite my anger, my breath hitches. If I didn't want this guy arrested and thrown in jail—and fined so severely that his bank accounts are empty for the next ten years after he gets out—I would consider him attractive. He must be around my age—midthirties—with a full head of dark ash-brown hair and a few days of scruff coating a face cut in sharp angles.

He turns to Reed. "You okay? They didn't give you a hard time?"

"Yes. I mean, no, they weren't too bad," he stumbles over his words.

"Why don't you head back to the barn and take care of the pups. I got this." Tyler's voice is decidedly softer while addressing him.

Reed rushes to the red building as if he can't get away fast enough, calling to the dogs to follow. All trot after him except for the curly-tailed Laika, who seems more interested in us.

Tyler sighs heavily. "Let me guess, Harry Hatchett's the one who brought her in and told you she was mine."

"Does it matter?" I ask.

Piercing hazel eyes shift to study me. "One of my main competitors for a race with a half-million-dollar purse is trying to paint me an animal abuser so I get disqualified." A sardonic smile twists his lips. "Yeah, I'd say that matters, wouldn't you?"

"No one does the Iditarod for the money." And no *one* person gets that whole amount. Unless you slide in with a first-place finish—which most don't expect to have a chance at—you're losing money the second you sign up.

"Harry seems like the type to have money on his mind," he counters.

"Maybe he does," I acknowledge. He has bills to pay and an assumed reputation to bolster with trophies. Being rid of Tyler would even the odds for him. "It doesn't matter. What I care about is that dog in the back of our truck, and I've treated enough animals to know neglect when I see it." It feels like a knife wound to my chest every time.

"You automatically assumed *I* did that to her. You look around at this place, at my other dogs"—he gestures at his dog, with its lush fur coat and solid frame—"and you can't think of another reasonable explanation?"

"Do you have one for us?" Howie prompts.

Tyler peers off into the distance, as if weighing what he wants to admit. His hair is mussed from the balaclava, standing on end in every direction. "You're right. She *has* been neglected, by whomever owned her before I found her wandering in the woods."

Howie and I share a glance.

"So, now she's *not* your dog?" I press, my voice heavy with doubt.

"She wasn't, up until yesterday morning." He yanks off his leather mittens. "But she's my dog now, because there's no way in hell she's going back to the asshole who did that to her."

My mouth hangs open a beat, caught off guard by the venom in his response.

RUNNING WILD 31

He takes a deep breath as if to calm himself. "I tried to get some food and water into her, kept her in my house last night because she's too weak to be in the barn with the other dogs. We thought she would settle here. She seemed comfortable enough." He smooths a palm through his hair, as if trying to tame it. "And then Reed let her out this morning, and she took off. I knew she wouldn't survive another night out there, so I went looking for her. I followed her tracks all the way to the Hatchetts' fence."

I steal another glance at Howie. Is Tyler telling the truth, or is this a cover to save his own skin?

Howie gives me a one-shouldered shrug and a look that says he's inclined to believe Tyler's story of rescue.

Given the shape of the other dogs I've seen so far, I'm leaning toward the former as well. It wouldn't be unheard of for someone to abandon an old dog that is no longer of use to them. Hell, people are vile enough to toss puppies into garbage bags. "She needs medical attention."

"I'm aware of that—"

"I've started running tests already, but she's going to need dental work and a special diet—"

"Sounds expensive." Tyler smirks. "Have you tallied all that up yet? Got the invoice for me ready?"

I falter, taken aback by his insinuation. "This isn't about me making money. It's about what she needs."

The grim amusement slides from his face. "I'm taking her to see Frank Hartley in Palmer first thing tomorrow morning. *He'll* tell me what she needs."

I can't help the snort that escapes. "And you're accusing *me* of seeing dollar signs." Frank is a money-hungry ass who runs unnecessary tests to pad his billables and has misdiagnosed more than one animal.

"Hartley's my veterinarian. He's already treated the whole kennel, and at a better rate than I was quoted by others. Seems like a decent enough guy."

The only reason Frank might have given Tyler a deal is because he wants his clinic's name tied to a champion musher. Secondhand notoriety.

Tyler studies me a long moment before shifting his attention to Howie. "You can follow up with him if you want, but I promise, she'll get the care she needs from a vet who *isn't* on Hatchett's payroll."

My indignation flares. "I'm not on *anyone*'s payroll!"

"Aren't you his veterinarian?"

"Yes, but—"

"She only got away a few hours ago, which means he called you and you dropped *everything* on a Sunday afternoon to trespass onto my property so you can build a case against me and take my dogs away. Do you do that for *all* your customers, or just the ones who have decent competition living next door?" His eyebrows arch in mock question.

I set my chin. "I take *every* report of animal abuse seriously."

"That, she does," Howie pipes up. "Marie's got a bit of a reputation around here as a crusader. I swear, if she collected a buck for every time she helped someone out for free, she'd be flying around in her own private plane by now. Ask anyone, and they'll tell you there's no one more generous in all of Alaska."

I flash an appreciative smile to Howie for his kind words, even as that term pricks at my chest. *Crusader.* That's what Wren Fletcher used to call me. Sometimes I still have to remind myself that the kindly owner of Alaska Wild is gone.

"So, if I called up Dillon Wagner and asked him, he'd tell me that same thing?" Tyler asks.

"You know Dillon?" Howie's voice is laced with surprise.

Wasilla's chief of police.

"Yeah, we go *way* back. Same with Marshall Deeks. What about him? Would he say the same about your little crusader here?"

Marshall runs parks and rec for the Mat-Su Valley. I can't

believe this asshole is name-dropping, a not-so-subtle way of letting us know he may have just moved here but he has connections.

He's not the only one. "Maybe we should call Wade Phillips to see what *he* thinks about this entire situation." The race's chief veterinarian and the man I did my surgical residency with. "Or Grant McManus. How about him?" The race marshal for the past seventeen years and one of my father's best friends. "I've got him on speed dial. Should I call?" I slide my phone out of my pocket to make my obnoxious point.

Tyler pauses, his eyes skating across my features. There's a haunted—almost sad—quality to them. "*Marie Lehr*. I know that name. You volunteer at the race."

"A lot of veterinarians do." It'll be my tenth time doing it, and I've done everything from prerace dog prep to working the drop dog hubs to checkpoint care. Unease slips down my spine with the sudden recognition painted across his face, and where this conversation is likely going.

"I hear Skip Haygert would've won last year, but *you* made him withdraw to give Hatchett a chance."

"I did *not* do that for Harry." I feel my cheeks flush. "Skip's dogs had a virus. They were ready to collapse. Two were dehydrated, one had frostbite. They needed to be pulled, so I pulled them." Leaving him with only four dogs. Mushers need at least five running to the finish line.

Skip, a small-minded, fifty-year-old veteran of the race and three-time winner, did not agree with my assertion, especially not when he was leading with only seventy-seven miles left to Nome. As far as he was concerned, I had no business telling him how to run his team. But he didn't win that fight. Harry couldn't make up the time, though, and finished second.

After the race, with the backing of a veterinarian who happens to be a Haygert family friend, Skip filed a formal complaint, accusing me of being hostile and inexperienced and making bad judgment calls. He demanded I be removed from future race checkpoints.

Unfortunately for Skip, Wade sided with me.

Tyler tosses his gloves and balaclava onto his snowmachine's seat, seemingly unbothered by the biting cold. "You were quick to make the call, weren't you? A lot faster than some, from what I hear."

"Some don't have the guts to do what needs to be done," I snap before I can stop myself. I've heard the odd rumor of volunteers "suggesting" a dog be pulled but not making note of it in the race log for fear of backlash in the community. "Plenty of dogs dropped in that race. Over *two hundred*." For everything from exhaustion to injury to pneumonia. In most cases, it was the musher making the call for their dog's sake.

Skip should have dropped his dogs without question, without argument. He *should* have slid into the checkpoint already aware that they were struggling. Good mushers are skilled at watching for the signs. But I know his type, and he would've kept them going the last seventy-seven miles.

If I had my way, he'd be banned from ever racing again.

Tyler reaches down to scratch the top of his dog's head. "What do you think, Tank? Is someone getting defensive?"

I *am* getting defensive. I can't help it, though. The fact that this guy—an outsider who moved to Alaska from a foreign country within the last year—has heard this story means Skip and his fanatical fan base are smearing my name around town.

"And now, here you are, trying to take out Hatchett's competition for him again." Tyler's lip turns in a thoughtful frown. "Did you already call the ITC on me, or is that your next stop?"

I shake my head at this idiotic accusation. "I don't care who wins that stupid race. All I care about are the dogs." Animals who aren't protected well enough by the state that lauds the sport they're bred and trained for, who are deemed "lesser than" in the world of animal statutes.

Tyler's expression tightens. "*Stupid* race, huh? I wonder what the committee would say if they heard how one of their volunteers *really* feels."

I grit my teeth. He's *trying* to get a rise out of me.

The secret truth is, despite being born and bred in Alaska where dog mushing is the state sport and to many, part of its identity, I've struggled to embrace the race itself. Sure, when I'm in the thick of the clamor, surrounded by enthusiastic volunteers, fans, and mushers, and witnessing the genuine excitement of the dogs, the thrill of the race can be captivating.

But there's a reason these long-distance races are considered the most extreme in the world, with the Iditarod at the helm of that label. The dogs are running a hundred miles a day. They're running in bitter temperatures, through blizzards and biting winds, along craggy hills, ice bridges, and through gorges. While they're conditioned for the cold, and they tug at their harnesses with anticipation to run every day, they're all frayed by the time they rest, curling up on their pile of straw to recuperate. Many don't finish, arriving at checkpoints with issues from exhaustion to dehydration, frostbite, and injury.

When I treat those dogs, I hear the voice in my head that asks if they would sign themselves up to spend days running across our frigid state if they had another choice.

I'm not the only one conflicted. Mushing is a sport plagued with controversy. Fervent activist groups have made it their mission to raise alarms about the bad actors who use harsh training methods and culling practices, and the lack of state regulation that allows for some of this behavior to continue—an ugly side that makes my heart ache and my vision turn red with anger.

They've latched on to the worst of the worst in the community and amplified the horror stories, which are difficult to brush aside as one-offs, no matter how much a person may love the sport. Because one story of dead sled dogs found in a pile is enough for most people.

If they had their way, these anti-mushers would demolish the entire commercialized industry and bring an end to dogsledding. The reality is, there is too much love and too much tourism tied to this sport for that to happen. But their efforts haven't been for naught. The Iditarod is a costly race to hold every year, and major corporate sponsors have been pulling their support in droves—whether because of the pressure or the economy, it's hard to say. Likely a combination.

It's not just the activists who are raising alarms. There is plenty of strife within the community itself, with mushers speaking out against those who give credibility to the horror stories, who they claim are willing to do *anything* to win. Some of the top mushers—labeled world-class athletes—have been called out as the worst perpetrators for harsh training methods, the overbreeding, and inhumane treatment in their bid to produce the best racing teams in the world. They're criticized for running kennels that look more like farms, with over a hundred dogs and a revolving door of handlers to manage them, but little evidence of the musher's daily involvement.

It makes plenty of people ask: In a sport where the relationship between the musher and the dogs is said to be "everything," what kind of bond can these mushers have with their dogs?

The accused mushers vehemently deny the allegations, insisting their dogs are their family, that they're being targeted by sour mushers and disreputable activists with an agenda. Maybe that's true. Animal control officers like Howie, upon visiting the kennels, haven't been able to find proof that matches photographic and video evidence floating around social media. These mushers keep going, with plenty of fans to charm and sponsors to help pay their bills.

But the mushing community has been pulling back the curtain in recent years, speaking out against unacceptable practices and demanding change. And while state laws are slow to respond, Iditarod organizers have made efforts to rewrite race rules to try to appease the concerns of everyone involved—activists, mushers, and fans.

And me? All *I* can do is make sure these dogs have an advocate and proper care. That's why I've volunteered two weeks of my life each year for the past decade, so I can ensure the dogs aren't suffering because their mushers have their sights set on the finish line. That's why I'm standing on Tyler Brady's property today.

My priority will always be the dogs, never the humans. If I had my way, all these kennels would go through more rigorous inspections, with fewer laws to protect the humans and more laws to protect the dogs. I would have the authority to walk into any of these places and walk out with whatever dog I felt would be better off elsewhere.

And secretly, if the Iditarod were canceled, I can't say I'd be upset. The annual event may have started in honor of the great dogsled relay of 1925, a race to get serum to Nome to save children dying of diphtheria, but it has since turned into a media-heavy, high-stakes competition with plenty of prize money up for grabs.

But I know to keep that opinion to myself and my focus on the dogs. Neither the ITC, nor the mushing community, some of whom are my clients, would be too eager to have a volunteer veterinarian with such apathy for their beloved race.

I adjust my tone and meet Tyler's stare. "I'm here because I care about the animals. The *decent* mushers appreciate my concern." An unspoken challenge. *Are you decent, Tyler?*

His jaw ticks. "There's no need for your concern here. You'll never see dogs better cared for than mine."

"You sound pretty confident."

"Because I know it's the truth. I'd give you a tour, but I have better things to do." A smug smile touches his lips. "And you need to run on over to report into Harry."

"I'm not going to—" I cut off the denial. I don't have to defend myself to this asshole.

"Yeah, sure, you're not," he mutters, his amusement slipping away, replaced by a hard, cold glare. "Now give me my dog back and get the hell off my property before *I* call the ITC and tell them you're trespassing at my kennel and harassing me and my family." He nods toward my boots. "See? Tank agrees."

I look down in time to see the dog with its hind leg lifted and a stream of urine shooting out onto my pants. The scent of ammonia hits my nostrils a second later.

It's not the first time a sled dog has peed on me—some of them can't seem to help themselves—but that couldn't have been planned more perfectly.

Howie, who has remained more of an observer up until now, sidles up to me, turning his back to Tyler. "We don't have much of a case here, Marie," he whispers. "Not unless we can prove this guy's lying, and something tells me he isn't. Meanwhile, we cut his chain and trespassed without any proof that the dog was his, besides Harry's claims. This guy could be a *real* dick if he wants, and it sounds like he wants to be."

"I know." Getting fired from a volunteer position with the Iditarod would not only be embarrassing but it would also limit my access to animals who need me.

"I can stop by Frank's next week and poke around a bit if you want? Make sure he's treating her."

"That would be helpful. Thanks, Howie." Frank and I don't agree on a lot of things—namely all the pro bono stuff I do that he says makes other vets look bad, and all the price gouging he does that infuriates me. He'd *never* give me details on Tyler's dogs if I asked.

"Okay, so I'm gonna do us all a favor and hand the dog over to him, and consider this matter investigated and resolved." Howie saunters over to the rumbling pickup to open the back cab. "Attagirl. Come on down." He hauls the dog out and sets her gently on the ground.

Tyler fishes a treat from his pocket and whistles for her. She limps over, her tail wagging. She doesn't seem afraid of him, at least.

"You have yourself a good Sunday afternoon there, Tyler!" Howie slides into the driver's seat with a wave, as if he's bidding farewell to a friend.

He leaves me standing in the cold with dog pee on my pants to face this guy alone. Thankfully, Tyler has all but dismissed me, dropped to his knees, a gentle hand on Nymeria's head while he murmurs something that I can't hear. At least he's capable of kindness to someone.

The dog he called Tank hovers around them, sniffing the female with interest.

With one last glance around the property—is there a *Mrs.* Brady here? She wasn't listed in the kennel licensing paperwork, from what I saw—I convince myself that I've done all I can. For now.

"I started her on amoxicillin. Tell Frank to call me if he has any questions or wants the test results." No point running the same tests twice, even if Tyler deserves to pay for them. Though, knowing Frank, he'd bill Tyler, anyway.

I turn to head back to the truck.

"Not even an apology, huh?" Tyler calls out.

I pause, the thought of uttering those words sour on my tongue. But does Tyler deserve to hear them? "I don't take kindly to being accused of ulterior motives," I say instead.

"Probably as kindly as I take to being accused of animal abuse."

"I never accused you." Not officially. "Besides, I won't apologize for looking out for these dogs." That's the only reason I'm here. *Someone* neglected this poor girl, even if it wasn't him.

"Did Harry mention that he showed up here when I moved in?" Tyler's fingers stroke behind Nymeria's ear. "He came to tell me not to bother starting up any kind of touring or breeding business, seeing as his family has cornered that market around here."

"He didn't mention that, no." Friendly meet 'n' greet, my ass. What was Harry thinking?

Tyler smirks. "He's lucky I have no interest in a bunch of strangers traipsing all over my property and near my dogs. But do me a favor, will you? When you stop by his place to give him the good news, you know, that he'll still have to lose to me in March—"

I roll my eyes.

"Let him know that I wasn't planning on breeding to sell, but you've helped me change my mind. Tank here would love to see some of his pups in the Iditarod one day." He ruffled the dog's head. "What do you think? Will mushers around here want my dogs?" The haughty smile that curls his lips tells me the question is rhetorical.

I don't bother feeding his ego with an answer, turning on my heels to walk away.

"Can't wait to see you on the trail!" he hollers after me.

Yeah, can't wait.

The truck's cab is warm when I climb in. That knot in my stomach that I arrived with has dissolved, only to be replaced with general unease.

Howie backs the truck far enough to turn. "Can't say I've seen you so ruffled before. You're normally the levelheaded one."

I realize I'm scowling. "He's spiteful."

"What do you expect, Marie? You showed up here with a spike for his head, and he knows it."

"I guess I did."

"If the guy takes care of his dogs as well as he says he does, he's gonna take offense to this. It's like accusing a parent of abusing their kid." Howie smooths his palm over his face. "We should've handled this differently. Let's just hope he's all talk. That last thing I need is to be on the police chief's shit list."

And the absolute last thing *I* need is another formal complaint to Wade.

I steal one last glance in the side-view mirror as we head down the driveway. Tyler is walking toward the barn, Nymeria hobbling beside him.

CHAPTER THREE

"I asked my cat what's two minus two." My father pauses for effect. "She said nothing."

A medley of laughter and exasperated groans greets me as I shake off my snow-covered boots at the door and stroll into the familiar living room. This is the only home of my parents that I've ever known. Aside from updated pictures within the frames and a growing collection of trinkets, nothing has changed. It still smells the same—of burning wood, apple-cinnamon potpourri, and a well-used kitchen. Even the three twin beds in the loft room that my sisters and I shared as children are the same.

"Grand*pa*," Tillie moans. "You don't even have a cat."

"*She* liked my joke." Dad gestures at Nicole, who's rolling around on the rug, laughing hysterically. Beside her, Bentley reclines on his side, unruffled by her theatrics. No one would ever guess the black-and-white husky spent years racing across the Alaskan terrain in subarctic temperatures with the way he basks in the warmth from the woodstove.

"That's because she's *five* and she laughs at anything. She can't even do math!"

"*Oh.*" His blue-gray eyes flicker to me, amusement in them.

"Well, maybe I should tell the joke to your aunt Marie and see what she thinks—"

"The nine-year-old is right. It's terrible, Pops." I lean forward to press a kiss against his forehead.

"Ha!" My precocious niece grins, victorious.

"Jeez. Tough crowd tonight, huh, Yukon?"

The golden husky who's never more than five feet from Dad rests his chin on my father's arm, earning himself a head scratch. Somewhere in the house, there's a smaller, female version of him named Aurora, who I rescued from an unsavory owner with Howie's help. She's skittish and likely hiding upstairs until the pint-sized people are gone.

I hug the girls. "Where is everyone?"

"Where else? Hanging out in the kitchen while they've left me with these two wolves." My father adjusts his wire-rimmed glasses and then smooths a hand over his belly to fix his button-down shirt. He has always been a tall, slim man, but retirement and age have softened his body and slowed his walk. Neither have kept him from his regular hikes, though, where the seventy-four-year-old will spend hours during the summer months, his trekking poles gripped for balance and the dogs at his side. But even with that activity, my father has developed various health issues over the last decade, with type 2 diabetes being the most surprising and concerning.

"Okay, Tillie, grab those cards over there for me, will ya?"

"What for?" She collects the deck and trots over to hand it to him.

"Seeing as you're *so* grown up, it's time I taught you how to play poker. That way you can take all your daddy's money."

Nicole bursts with another round of roll-on-the-floor laughter. "Grandpa Jokey, you're *so* funny."

Tillie is right, her little sister finds *anything* my father says amusing, even when she has no idea what he's talking about.

I chuckle as I head toward the voices. Sidney Lehr may be

known around these parts as an exceptional veterinarian, but I've never seen anyone prouder to wear the title of "Grandpa Jokey."

The smell of pot roast, potatoes, and roasted root vegetables —a typical Sunday meal in the Lehr household for as long as I can recall—hits me as I stroll into the kitchen.

"... maybe she's changed her mind about having kids. She's always on the go with work."

"Oh, *come on*, Mom. We all know she wants a baby. She's almost thirty-eight. Does she realize how hard it can be to get pregnant in your forties?" Liz's back is to the door, her lengthy golden-blonde hair worn down today rather than in a ponytail. She's perfectly positioned to block my mother's view of me behind her. "And all because she had to spend years chasing after that bush pilot who wasn't interested in her. Now she's alone, with no prospects."

My ears burn as I listen to my sister critique my life choices and check the ticking clock on my womb between sips of chardonnay. *Also* a typical Sunday event in the Lehr household, it feels sometimes.

"Well, I don't know what to say—Marie!" Mom pulls a pan of sizzling vegetables from the oven, offering me an exaggerated smile and then Liz a scolding glare as she hip-checks the door closed. At five foot one, it's a struggle. "You're later than usual."

"Yeah, busy day."

"Hey, Mare." Liz doesn't have the decency to look sheepish at getting caught gossiping about me, but she's never done ashamed well. "How was your weekend?"

"Oh, you know." I grab a bottle of beer from the fridge, twist off the cap, and take a big swig. "Just out there, *somehow* surviving life without a husband."

Liz's eyes narrow. It's my subtle dig at her, and we both know it, but she deserves it after what I just walked in on. Liz doesn't know how to be single. She's had a boyfriend since she turned sixteen and was allowed to date. When one relationship ended, it wasn't more than a week before she was locked into a new one. She met Jim when she was twenty-four, married him at twenty-six, and was pregnant immediately after. Now they live in a beautiful modern house near Eagle River, close enough for an easy commute to Anchorage where Jim is a partner in his father's accounting firm.

"Where is everybody else?" The pot roast is already plated and wrapped in foil.

"Jim's working late tonight."

"Oh yeah? How's his football team doing?" Another subtle dig because I can't help myself. No doubt he's skipped family dinner to stay home and "work" in front of the television. Not that I'm complaining. Conversations with my brother-in-law always lead to talk of money—namely, how much I *should* be making at the clinic. He's my accountant, an arrangement my father made and I abhor but have honored thus far to avoid family strife.

"Vicki and Oliver will be here any minute." Mom wipes her palms across her apron and slips off her glasses to clean them against her shirt. "They were putting together the crib this weekend. Well, *Vicki* was putting together the crib."

I chuckle. We all love my little sister's husband, but instruction manuals and Allen keys have never been Oliver's forte. He'll be the first to admit it. "They must be getting excited." The baby is due in two weeks.

Liz sniffs. "Are you kidding? More like anxious. Swollen ankles, eight pounds sitting on your bladder, seventy-two pillows just to try to get comfortable? That last month is *hell*."

Not that you would know, I hear tacked on to the end. But that's just my sensitivity talking. Liz isn't outright cruel, she just speaks without thinking. Often. And ever since she had Tillie, she is the self-proclaimed expert on all things pregnancy and baby related.

"Could be any day now. The baby's dropped." Mom pauses to look around the kitchen as if to take stock of what still needs to be done for dinner. Her teal-blue eyes—a perfect match to mine

—land on the harvest table. "Would you mind setting that for me, Marie? For eight tonight."

I collect a stack of plates from the cupboard and set to task, happy to have something to do.

Liz, who has never been the first to volunteer when I'm around, remains where she is, leaning across the counter. "*So*, I ran into Jonathan at Target yesterday."

That explains the conversation I walked in on.

"He looks *really* good."

"Yeah. I heard he's taken up running." Though Jonathan *always* looked good.

"And he's engaged. Her name's Carrie. She seems nice. Pretty."

"They've been together for a while." Almost two years, I think. I saw them once, as I was pulling up to the grocery store and they were walking out. She's petite and dark-haired and, I've heard from mutual friends, allergic to dogs. It's like Jonathan was following an "opposite of Marie" checklist when he started dating again.

I'd been expecting a run-in, eventually. It's impossible to not cross paths with your ex when you live within five miles of each other, but I've succeeded in avoiding any close encounters so far. That day, I waited in my truck until they were gone. I heard they bought a house in a new subdivision in Palmer, so the likelihood of a grocery store meeting has diminished considerably.

"She's pregnant."

"Oh yeah?" I swallow my surprise with a swig of my beer, feeling an unexpected twinge at that news. Predictable, though it must not have been planned. Jonathan was always adamant that the wedding comes before the baby.

"She's due in March. A boy. He told me its name, but I can't remember—"

"Clancy," I finish. After his grandfather. Jonathan has had that name chosen for years. It was just the mother of his son who he had to swap out.

Liz is observing me as if I'm a bug beneath a microscope. I know what she's doing—searching for proof that I regret handing back that diamond ring. She never understood why I would. Jonathan is husband material on paper—handsome, smart, faithful, successful, well mannered. And to be fair, there was never anything wrong with him, nothing concrete that I could add to the cons column for why I shouldn't marry him other than "doesn't make my heart race like Jonah does."

Liz and Jonathan got along famously. At one point, I thought she might have had a secret crush on him. She has never met Jonah, but I know she would never approve of him. She approves of very little in my life lately.

It wasn't always that way. Liz and I are sixteen months apart —I was born in February and Liz the following year in June. Growing up, we had people convinced we were legitimate twins because we looked so much alike, and we were inseparable. I can still remember sitting on the clinic floor with our legs stretched wide to form a makeshift pen for the litter of sled dog puppies our father had rescued from being culled. We laughed as they stumbled around, unable to control their bladders, peeing all over. It didn't bother us any. We had grand plans to take over Dad's clinic one day, working side by side as Dr. Lehr and Dr. Lehr.

But then something shifted in Liz. She stopped coming around the clinic to help with the animals, and she no longer wanted to hang out. The usual sisterly spats turned into major blowouts, and what used to be friendly teasing morphed into vicious competition. It upset me until my father sat me down and explained that for all our similarities, there were glaring differences. Namely, how easily my grades came to me while Liz struggled for her mediocre ones. Playing pretend veterinarians was one thing; getting into a veterinarian school was another. Liz was beginning to see the reality of that, and she has never handled jealousy well.

The tension eased by the time we reached our twenties, once I left for school and Liz seemed content in her receptionist position at a car dealership in Anchorage, "running the office," as she claimed. But the bond we once had has never returned, and that sense of rivalry still lingers.

Honestly, I'm not sure if my sister is bringing up Jonathan's pregnant fiancée now because she's genuinely curious where my head's at, or if she sees it as a chance to feel superior. Liz, the happily married Lehr sister with two beautiful kids and a smart, successful husband.

Marie, the lonely, childless Lehr who still spends her days getting peed on by dogs.

I keep my fears to myself, but sometimes, late at night, when the rain beats against my cabin's tin roof and I'm unable to sleep, I *do* question if I made a horrible mistake. I wonder how different my life would look had I chosen the other path, the one where I married Jonathan. Would I be happy *enough*?

I never wonder too hard, though, because if I'd truly been content with him, I wouldn't have been so easily swayed by that hairy-faced bush pilot's charm.

But I'd be lying if I said I haven't thought long and hard about whether that choice tucked my desire for children into a sturdy coffin. I always assumed I would be a mother one day, once my career was established and the time was right. Longed for it. Nobody has to remind me of my climbing age and the challenges it might present, especially given our family's history—the two miscarriages Mom had between Liz and Vicki, the one Liz had between her two girls. I remind myself of it every time I see a pregnant woman walk down the grocery store aisle or hear a baby's cry.

Lately, I worry that I've already missed my chance and I just haven't realized it yet.

I can feel Liz's gaze boring into the back of my head as I set the last plate down. "I guess it's good I never married him, then."

"And why's that?"

"Because he'd never have had a chance to name a son Clancy." It's the running joke in our family that to be born with a Y chromosome, you have to be canine. Mom has three sisters, three daughters, and two—soon to be three—granddaughters.

The door to the kitchen swings open and a gust of cold air sweeps in. "We're here! We're here! Don't start without us!" Vicki waddles in, her cheeks puffy, one hand on her swollen belly, the other on her back for support. She looks as wide as she is tall. Of the three of us, she's the only one who inherited our mother's petite stature.

Oliver follows closely after, his lanky arms saddled with bags of empty Tupperware containers that Mom will gleefully refill for their freezer. Having children who still need her in their twenties and thirties keeps her young, she always says.

The smile that fills my face when I see my twenty-nine-year-old baby sister is genuine. "You look good."

"I look like a beached whale. Get this thing out of me already!" she wails.

Liz's snicker vanishes in her glass of wine.

———

"Whatever happened to that guy you were seeing?" Vicki looks ready to explode in her chair, her cheeks flushed, her palms rubbing over her enormous belly in a futile effort to help digest her meal. "What was his name, Tom or Cody, something like that —thanks, babe."

Oliver collects Vicki's empty plate and gives her shoulder a comforting squeeze. I'd label him a doting husband to his uncomfortably pregnant wife, but he has *always* been that way, catering to Vicki's every need.

In contrast, my other brother-in-law has never once put his own dishes into the dishwasher, let alone anyone else's.

"Toby." I pass my plate to Oliver's waiting hand and nod my thanks. "It didn't go anywhere."

"Why not?"

"I don't know. He's a *really* nice guy. He's just not for me." As I knew would be the case when I agreed to dinner with Jonah and Calla's neighbor and friend.

"Oh." Vicki's brow furrows with disappointment. "That's too bad. He seemed like your type."

I laugh. "You've never even met him."

"Well, yeah, *I know*, but you said he was big and burly and … and …" Vicki searches for words, settling on "*hairy*." She caps that with a burp that earns giggles from Tillie and Nicole.

He sounded like Jonah is what she's saying. Unlike Liz, Vicki *has* met my best friend before, and even though she married a man who couldn't be more different—a gangly, baby-faced sweetheart with a total of four chest hairs (Vicki has counted)—she immediately saw Jonah's rugged appeal.

But Toby is nothing like Jonah.

There is *nobody* out there like that guy.

"What about Cook?" Oliver chirps from the kitchen sink where he's already scrubbing a dirty pot.

"Who, *Steve* Cook? Your boss?" Vicki's face scrunches up. "Isn't he living with someone?"

"Nah, they broke up. He's single again. I think he's, like, forty-two? Maybe forty-four?"

"Oh." Vicki ponders that a second and then shrugs as if to say, *Why not?* "Yeah, you should try Steve."

As if he were a pair of socks to test out.

Being the perpetually single Lehr sister—and the oldest, at that—for the past few years, I'm used to this. Every family dinner inevitably veers to the topic of my love life … or lack thereof. It's usually Jim throwing out single friends' names, though. Oliver must feel like he has to fill the void.

I tap my foot beneath the table as I finish off the last of my beer. Are all families like this or just mine?

"Anything exciting happen at work this week?" My dad changes the topic, saving me from more matchmaking.

"Not until today. You almost had another dog."

"Don't you dare bring any more animals into this house!" Mom protests, collecting the last of the dirty dishes before heading to the dishwasher, pausing long enough to toss scraps of meat to Yukon's and Bentley's waiting maws. "I thought I was done running a rescue house when your father retired."

Dad and I share an amused look. All three dogs currently living under this roof are here because Mom offered to foster them and then wouldn't give them up.

"And what was this one's story?" he asks.

"On that note ..." Vicki eases out of her seat to waddle toward the living room. Though she can't resist a box of kittens, she was never bitten by the veterinarian bug and finds our chatter "depressing."

Dad collects a toothpick and leans back in his chair, readying to hear my tale. By the time I'm done recounting Harry's visit and everything that followed, including the accusations Tyler made about my motivations, Dad's expression has soured. "Sounds like a real son of a—"

"*Dad.*" Liz gives a pointed look toward the girls, but their focus is riveted on the heaping brownie sundaes in front of them.

He offers a sheepish smile. "Is this new guy breedin' those dogs he brought over with him?"

"That's the thing." I repeat what Tyler claims Harry did. "He made it sound like he will, just to spite the Hatchetts."

Dad whistles. "Sometimes that family leans too much on their history around here. Things have changed, especially with Earl gone. It was foolish of Harry, trying to tell this man what he can and can't do. Then again, Harry's always been a fool."

"Especially a guy like this one." Who doesn't seem like he'd back down from a fight. "Just wait until people around here see those dogs race. I'm telling you, Dad, they are impressive. The way they ran in formation, untethered?" I understand why Harry, a competitive guy by nature, would be nervous. Keeping a sled team is costly—thousands of dollars spent a year on a balanced diet of kibble, meat, and fish, housing them against the elements, outfitting them to race, bringing in veterinarian care for the revolving door of issues that arise from all those dogs together. It's not unusual for a musher to spend thirty grand a year to prepare a team, and that's not even considering the race fees, which are in the thousands themselves.

The Hatchetts pay for it by relying on sponsors, hosting tourist tours during the off-season, leasing dogs, and by breeding champion sled dogs for mushers. It's an art form of sorts, pairing the right mix for speed, endurance, and attitude. Earl had a knack for it, his lines producing competent racers time and time again.

There have been plenty of doubts about Harry's skills.

"So he thinks he's gonna give Harry a run for his money at the race, huh? As a rookie in the Iditarod." Dad's skepticism is obvious.

"I don't know, but he certainly thinks highly of himself."

"Part of me would like to see that kid's ego get knocked down a few pegs. He needs that before he loses whatever good grace being Earl's son has afforded him. But the Hatchetts are also good for the sport. The fans really like them."

Harry's considered a local celebrity and media darling. He's young, he never balks at giving an interview, and he has a face that female race fans flock to. But these fans haven't met Tyler yet. What's he like when he's not being accused of abusing dogs? Does he have what it takes to charm the crowds?

Will they react to that ruggedly handsome face the same way I did?

Liz sets a bowl in front of Dad.

He examines the brownie suspiciously. "Has the warden approved?"

"Yes, it's Liz's *special* recipe." Mom emphasizes *special* with a stare, which means it's made with beets or cannellini beans or something equally unappetizing that the children are oblivious to and that won't spike Dad's blood sugar levels.

He hasn't been able to eat a meal without Mom's approval since his diagnosis. Fortunately for him, Liz can make even vegetable-laced brownies taste good, something we all appreciate.

The usual family dinner chatter takes over while we clean up. Then Liz bundles the girls to get them home for bath and bedtime and Vicki moans about her aching back as Oliver helps her pull her coat on.

Soon, it's just Dad and I in the kitchen, with Yukon curled up next to Dad's feet as he savors the last of his dessert.

"Jim called me yesterday. Told me to get you to increase your fees."

"Really? He's going to you now?"

"Because you won't listen to him."

"I *did* increase them."

"That was three years ago, Marie."

I've already had this conversation—twice since the fall. "Maybe Jim should *decrease* his accounting fees."

Dad snorts.

"I'm fine. Overhead was a bit higher this year, and I have a few outstanding client bills that will get paid. But I'm *fine*." I haven't been flying out west nearly as much. I don't have a mortgage to worry about, but there's always something to repair or replace. Next up is my ultrasound machine, a fossil that needed to go five years ago. I could buy a new truck with what it's going to cost, and the bank isn't keen on lending me more. Thankfully, my father is willing to cosign for the loan.

Growing up with a veterinarian for a father, I was well versed in the realities of this career path before I submitted my application to vet school. I knew I wasn't getting into this business for the paycheck, especially where I live. Still, sometimes I look at my life—at the amount of schooling I needed and the exorbitant debt I accumulated, at the nights I've spent curled up next to a sick patient I didn't want to leave alone—and wonder if I would've been better off going to med school.

A job as a family practitioner might have been easier. It certainly would've been more lucrative. Here, I do it *all*—diagnostics, surgery, medicine, dental care—rather than simply write a referral, and I can only charge what people can afford. In the world of animal medicine, there is no government assistance, and few have insurance.

But humans have never interested me, not like animals do.

And when I watch those humans waffle about paying for treatment to help their pet, or when they tell me I'm wrong, or when they decide they don't want to be in the room while I euthanize their family member and I'm the last face it sees ... those days dealing with humans are especially frustrating.

"I'm not gonna tell you how to run your clinic," Dad adds quietly, "even though it was *my* clinic and I ran it well for *many* years. But you are a highly skilled veterinarian, Marie. A certified *surgeon*. You could be working in the hospital in Anchorage, charging three times as much with all the education you've accumulated. No one's going to think less of you for charging enough to cover your bills. And maybe doing less of the things you don't get paid to do, like freezing your butt off in a tent for two weeks every March."

"My sleeping bag is quite warm, actually," I counter. And I'm usually sweating as I run around, tending to the dogs that come through the Iditarod checkpoints.

My dad groans at my flippant answer. "At least I can tell Jim I tried."

My thoughts drift back to my day, that twinge of worry

lingering. "So, what do you know about this musher, anyway? What have you heard?" Dad's still well connected around the borough and the sled dog community. Aside from his long-standing friendships with Wade and Grant, he plays poker on Thursdays with Bill Compton, who writes feature stories for the Mat-Su Valley paper. And there are still plenty of mushing families who call his home number for a second opinion from time to time.

"This new Finnish guy?"

"He's not Finnish. He's American. Lower forty-eight." Did Tyler grow up in Alaska and move away, only to move back? That's what Jonah did. Or did he come for a visit and decide to stay? He wouldn't be the first to do that.

Dad pushes his empty dessert bowl away. "His family in Finland is well known in the industry over there, mushers themselves. They have a reputation for taking good care of their dogs."

"That would've been helpful to know before I went there," I mutter.

"It would've been helpful to *ask* me before you went there." He flashes a scolding look. "He won the Finnmarksløpet last year."

I'd heard about his racing—and winning—Europe's longest dogsled race. "So he knows what he's doing."

"Oh, I think he knows." Dad chuckles. "Bill wanted to do a little exposé on him for the paper, help drum up excitement. The guy wouldn't answer any questions. He said he doesn't like the spotlight."

Interesting. Usually mushers are all over any chance to talk about themselves and their dogs, hoping to attract local sponsorships to help cover the steep costs of running a team. Harry posts videos on social media at least once a week of himself "educating" people on the world of mushing. He knows a lot about the sport, I will give him that. It's his delivery that sometimes ruffles feathers.

"It was just him and that kid, Reed, from what I could see.

Hard to run a competitive team without more help than that." Mushers rely on their family, friends, and community during racing season. They need help in Nome, at the end of the race, and someone back in Anchorage, ready to collect dropped dogs. A guy with Tyler's experience would know that.

Dad collects his spoon in a futile attempt to find any missed crumbs. "He must know someone around here."

"He was name-dropping the police chief and the head of parks and rec, but I can't see them playing handler. Maybe he was just bullshitting to try to scare us?"

"Who knows." Dad tosses his spoon into the bowl with a yawn, giving up.

"I should head home. It's getting late." I reach down to scratch Bentley's head. "What do you think? You want to come with me?" Sometimes I borrow him for the night. As much as I would love to come home to a dog every night, my lifestyle doesn't allow for that.

Dad sighs, and I know he's about to unload heavy thoughts. "Look, Marie, I know you're doing what's right, but you need to be more careful. You can't have mushers going to the ITC about you. That mess with Skip last year stirred up a lot of noise for Wade."

"He agreed with me."

"Yeah, but he's also gotten a lot of flak for it from a couple of the veteran volunteers who thought you were too hard on Skip."

"One of Skip's dogs developed pneumonia after the race." It recovered—thank God—but maybe it wouldn't have had it run those last seventy-seven miles.

Dad raises his hands in surrender. "Wade agrees, and he wants veterinarians like you there to make sure those dogs stay healthy. But there have been complaints—"

"From whom? More than just Skip?"

"One or two folks, saying you favored the Hatchetts. It's baloney. *I* know you didn't. Wade knows you didn't. But Harry has rubbed some people around here the wrong way, and they're looking for any way to hit back. You're his vet."

"I'm also Jed Carling's and Darlene Wilcox's vet." Though they don't show up at my clinic demanding I pull strings and pay visits. No one is as big a pain in my ass as the Hatchetts are on the regular, but no one else makes me as much. Their kennel is a busy business, and it pays well to be at Harry's beck and call, as much as I despise it sometimes.

Dad lifts his hands again. "You asked what I heard, so I'm passing it along. Don't shoot the messenger."

"Those people can shove their accusations up their asses."

"Funny, isn't that what you told Skip to do?" Dad chuckles. "Wade took you on as a rookie, and he's thrilled to have you back every year. But he's been doing that job for more than two decades, and it's getting harder, with the sponsors dropping and all this noise from these activists. He's not going to be doing it for much longer, and I know you'd be *really* unhappy if the person who replaces him doesn't call you back."

And there are enough veterinarians applying. People come from all over the world to volunteer.

"*A lot* of people still live for this race."

"I know, Dad." Tour companies that charge thousands per person to give tourists "the Iditarod experience," villages that swell to two and three times their regular population, restaurants that earn a hefty share of their annual revenue in the first two weeks of March ... they'd feel the absence of the race not just in their spirit but also their wallets.

"Locals are fed up with these anti-musher folks in their tiny New York and LA condos tellin' Alaskans how to live. Now, if they start hearing that one of their own is sabotaging and threatening mushers, well ... that could hurt you."

Dad has always been keen on protecting our reputation, even more so as each new veterinarian moves into the valley.

I weave my fingers through Bentley's mane, the simple effort soothing. "I think that guy's threats were empty." I hope they are. "He was just angry with how it all went down."

"And how high was that horse you rode in on?"

"*At least* ten feet tall." I should have treated the dog and brought her here, and then relayed Harry's claim to the ITC and let them take over. I overstepped boundaries, allowing my anger to cloud my judgment. And if what Tyler told me is true, and he is rescuing—and treating—a wandering old dog that will be of little use to him, then maybe he isn't so bad after all.

"Did you at least apologize to him?"

I give Dad a look.

"You know, sometimes you have too much of your old man's pride. I wish you'd taken more after your mother."

"Mom would have told him off." Especially if he displayed that smug smile.

"Probably." He scratches his chin in thought. "But you'll likely be crossing paths with him at the checkpoint when he rolls in with his team, so maybe you should consider going out there and smoothing the waters. It's better to be on good terms than the ones you left on."

He's right, but it doesn't settle well with me. "Just the thought of going back out there makes my blood pressure spike."

Dad gets that twinkle in his eye. "Hey, well, if you have to go to the doctor about that, make sure you bring a red crayon."

I groan, my voice monotone as I deliver his corny punch line, "So she can draw my blood?"

He chuckles. "I guess I've told you that one already, huh?"

"Suck it up, Marie." I take a deep, calming breath as my truck comes to a sliding stop at the end of the driveway. The sky is murky with no mountain range in sight. Today's forecast is calling for upward of eleven inches of snow beginning this after-noon, but already, large flakes float through the air.

I spent the entire night and morning mentally preparing myself to face Tyler Brady again, but the farm gate blocks any hope of passage, a new chain hanging from the post.

"You don't waste time, do you?" It's a relief, though, because it means I don't have to face him in person.

I slide out of the driver's seat, the handwritten note that took me four attempts held tight in my mitten so as not to blow away with the breeze. It was a "just in case the gate is closed" letter, but also a way of sorting through my thoughts before I said them out loud. I'm not sure if any of those thoughts could be called an apology, *exactly*. More like a truce, with mention of how healthy his sled dogs looked while running yesterday. Either way, it's the right thing to do. I'll feel better after delivering this small olive branch.

My hand is on the door to the mailbox when I spot a new sign mounted on a tree just below the bright yellow No Trespassing warning—a large rectangular piece of plywood with fluorescent orange spray-painted letters that reads, "No Crusaders."

"Oh, you *child*." My cheeks burn as I march back to my truck, the note crumpled in my fist. I toss it to the floor of my passenger seat, throw my truck in drive, and pull away.

CHAPTER FOUR

March

The evergreen branches sag beneath the layer of freshly fallen snow as I coast up the driveway. Jonah's hangar looms on my left, but Archie, his orange-and-white Piper, is already on the private airstrip, waiting for takeoff.

Jonah crouches in front, inspecting one of the skis. He's wearing navy arctic overalls to keep his lower half warm while his parka hangs over the open cockpit door.

My heart squeezes as it does every time I see him, in that split second before I take a deep breath and remind myself that it wasn't meant to be, that I'm happy for him.

Thankfully, as the months go by and reality settles in, the sadness isn't so much a deep ache as a dull and lingering disappointment. I'm waiting for the day that fades, too. That's when I'll feel like I've truly moved on.

I hop out of my truck and holler, "Wishing you were back in Hawaii yet?" I've only seen him once and briefly, right when he and Calla returned a month ago. The deep golden tan he was sporting is long gone, leaving him with his typical olive complexion.

"When I can be flying bales of straw and pork belly around Alaska instead? You kidding me?"

I laugh as my boots sink into the snow. He meets me halfway, enveloping me against his broad, warm chest and a soft flannel shirt that smells like Irish Spring soap. His stylish beard could use a trim, but it's nowhere near the blond bush of pre-Calla days. Sometimes I miss it.

"How the hell did you rope me into doing this again, Marie?"

I savor his warmth for only a second—he runs hotter than the average human—and then I pull away, hyperaware that anything longer might be construed as beyond friendly on my part. "Because it's winter, you're bored, and frankly, it's *really easy* to rope you into *anything* to do with flying."

And the Iditarod needs volunteer pilots as much as they need veterinarians. Every year, at least thirty pilots step up to join the Iditarod Air Force, otherwise known as the IAF. They're the ones hauling supplies and volunteers into the twenty-six—give or take, depending on the year—checkpoints, most of those locations only accessible by air. They also fly media around and take the dogs dropped along the trail back to Anchorage.

Jonah may be volunteering, but there is long-term opportunity, which is how I hooked him. Fans and tourists come from all over the world, eager to witness the race. They pay pilots a lot of money to fly them around, and as a flight charter company owner always looking for business, it's an opportunity for Jonah to get involved, make himself known.

"Yeah, yeah." Jonah grins sheepishly. "It's been a few years, though. I forgot how much work it is." He stretches his left arm out in front of him. "I've been hauling fifty-pound drop bags for two weeks."

"Is it bothering you?" He shattered that arm in a plane crash last summer, the second time Jonah went down in two years.

That was one of the scariest nights of my life, waiting for a phone call from the rescue team, fearing we'd lost him for good.

"Nah. Just whining for the sake of it. Did you go down to Anchorage to watch the big dog-and-pony show?"

"Don't you mean the dog-and-reindeer show?" The weekend before the Iditarod is always a big one, with a ceremonial start for the teams in downtown Anchorage before the mushers and their dogs are shuttled up to the official race start in Willow. The days are filled with media interviews and spectators cheering for their favorites as they set off along the eleven-mile urban stretch. It's such an important event for the sport, the city, and the entire state that they'll do *anything* to make sure it happens. One March, due to an especially mild winter, organizers hauled in a train's worth of snow from Fairbanks to build up the track so the teams had something to slide across.

The ceremonial start is capped off with a herd of domestic reindeer running down the streets.

I shake my head. "Too busy. Prerace checks and all that." The last step in a month-long process ahead of the Iditarod, where mushers are required to prove their dogs are fit to race, undergoing a battery of tests, deworming treatments, and veterinarian approvals. "Plus, I didn't want to see Skip's smug face as he waved at his *adoring* fans." One of whom I suspect left a scathing review of my clinic online. I don't have anyone named Shanna on my client roster, and her accusations about the service were vague. They seemed a personal attack on me, even going so far as to mention the Iditarod in her comments.

Jonah's heavy brow furrows. "Is that guy *still* giving you problems?"

"I guess we'll see."

"You want me to pick him up on the trail and drop him off somewhere where no one will ever find him? 'Cause I'll do it. Don't worry, I'll make sure the dogs get home safe."

I laugh. The IAF has been known to answer distress calls from mushers who scratch along the trail—they may get disoriented in a whiteout, or injured, or decide they can't go on any farther—and need a ride back to safety. While Jonah's all talk on leaving a man to die in the Alaskan tundra, knowing him, he will make Skip's life hell if their paths should cross.

"Let me get back to you on that, but I think Skip'll stay away from me this year." If anything, I should be more worried about a run-in with the Iditarod's shiny rookie, whom I've heard more than a few excited whispers about.

True to his word, Howie stopped in at Frank Hartley's the week after our confrontation and confirmed that Tyler had brought Nymeria to the clinic for treatment. The bill was enormous, and Tyler covered it all without complaint. And because Howie is Howie, he followed up *again* a month later, and Frank confirmed that she's spayed, has put on almost ten pounds, and looks like a whole different dog.

Tyler hasn't even run the race yet, and his name is already casting a warm glow on spectators and the community alike. Even Wade made mention during a casual chat with my father that Tyler's dogs are some of the fittest they've ever seen, and he wouldn't be shocked if he placed high. And apparently, there're whisperings about the Leonhard Seppala Humanitarian Award, handed out by the veterinarian team to the musher who demonstrates exemplary dog care during the race, based on the little of Tyler and his team that people witnessed this weekend.

Jonah's ice-blue eyes study me for a moment. "Something buggin' you, Lehr?"

Besides this gnawing feeling on my conscience that I allowed the Hatchetts to play on my vulnerability, that my behavior that day was *far* less than exemplary? Wouldn't that be something, if word got around that I accused this guy of animal abuse, only to have him win the humanitarian award a month later? Skip would have a field day with that.

I should have at least been the bigger person and left that note in his mailbox.

I push my regret aside. "I'm fine. Just tired. I had a lot to do before I could leave." Volunteering at race checkpoints means time away from earning money and tending to patients. Cory is holding down the fort, and my father can step in for emergencies, but it's still a long time to shut down. Thankfully, Jonah's offered to fly me out, saving me from hitching a ride a day early with the other veterinarians from the crew.

"Don't worry." He drops a heavy hand on my shoulder. "You can catch up on your sleep at the checkpoint."

I laugh. "Jerk." I'll be stationed at two this year, both remote locations, without even a village for supplies or running water for a hot shower. The first, Rohn, a cabin nestled between two mountain ranges and where two major rivers converge, could see fifty-eight teams and upward of eight hundred dogs come through within a thirty-hour span. Some will stay for only a few minutes, others for a few hours. A few might decide to make the checkpoint one of their mandatory rest stops.

From there, an IAF pilot will fly me five checkpoints down the trail to Cripple, a ghost town from the days of the gold rush and the official halfway point on the route, where I'll do it all over again.

It'll be a cold, challenging week, and I'll contemplate my life choices at least once a day, usually when I'm struggling to crawl out of my sleeping bag.

"You ready to get a move on soon?"

"Yeah, stuff's loaded. You need help with yours?"

"Nah. I'm good. I don't have much." A subzero sleeping bag and mattress pad, and a duffel bag of warm layers to cycle through. And, of course, my medical bag that I never go anywhere without. "Where's Calla?" She never misses seeing Jonah off before a flight.

"She had to stop by the cabin to help the renters work the coffee maker, but she should be here soon."

I peer across the frozen lake, though the derelict little shack they turned into an Airbnb cabin rental can't be seen from this angle. "You guys getting a lot of bookings?"

"*Solid* since the honeymoon. Who knew?" He shakes his head. "I thought she was crazy for wanting to sink all that money into that place, but she was right."

"She's right about a lot of things." And while Calla was resistant to move to Trapper's Crossing, she's made what was once a rustic and trash-filled log cabin into a cozy paradise.

"Don't tell her that. She'll use it against me in our next fight." He tosses a tool into the box and reaches for his coat.

I'm trekking back to my truck when I catch the faint buzz of a snowmachine. By the time I've hauled my belongings from the back, Calla is coasting up.

Her eyes sparkle as they size up my loaded arms. "You look like a Sherpa."

"I feel like one." *And you look ready to grace the cover of an outdoor magazine.* She's picture-perfect as always, her long, caramel-colored hair framing her face, the fur pom-pom on her black knit hat dusted with snow. It's hard to pinpoint what it is, but Calla has a look about her that can make even a pair of jeans and a plain white T-shirt look stylish. I met her mother, Susan, at the wedding, and it's clear Calla inherited that flair from her. I'm not sure there's a room Calla walks into where she doesn't draw attention, without even trying.

There was a time when I was jealous of her for that, and for everything else she is that I'm not—namely, Jonah's first choice. His only choice. I'd lie in bed at night, itemizing all the ways I'm better suited to Jonah, reasons why he should pick me. I wished she would be another Teegan, an interest that faded with time and distance. I cursed myself for not letting Jonah know how I felt sooner, as if that might have made any difference.

None of it mattered.

I wish I could say I was above the bitterness and envy, but as Cory has reminded me on more than one occasion, I'm only human. I have a heart that aches when dreams are shattered, and emotions that can pull a river of tears when hope proves false.

Just have hope.

Don't stop hoping.

If you believe in it long and hard enough, it will happen.

What a foolish and dangerous notion for a person to cling to.

Hope is what broke my heart. Not Jonah, and not this city girl from Toronto who showed up in Alaska unannounced.

"Jesus, Marie. Why are you so damn stubborn? Here, give me some of that." Jonah sounds annoyed as he yanks the bundles from under my arms, leaving me with nothing but my black veterinarian's bag. "You get everything sorted over there?" he throws over his shoulder to Calla, already on his way to the plane.

"Yeah. All good." Calla climbs off her snowmachine, her white bunny boots sinking into the snow. We fall into step with each other, trailing Jonah, our breaths billowing ahead of us. "I hear your first stop is the Rohn safety cabin?"

"Yeah. You know it?"

"We've been there a couple times. Stayed overnight once." Her smile is secretive. "Are you sleeping in the cabin?"

I laugh. "God, no. They use that for meals and for the mushers." There'll be bodies everywhere, wherever someone can fit a sleep pad down to grab an hour of rest. "I'll be in a tent."

She grimaces.

"Don't knock it. They're *way* more private, and they have stoves in them. Ask Jonah. He's stayed in one with—" I cut myself off before I make the mistake of saying Jonah stayed in a tent with me for a few nights the last time he volunteered with the IAF. We weren't alone, and nothing happened, aside from me stuffing my ears with plugs to drown out his reprehensible snoring, but the prick of warning along my spine says that might not matter.

Calla and I seem to be on good terms now, but it's taken time and several bumps along the way to get here. I think she saw through me that very first day we met at Alaska Wild. She's always suspected my feelings for Jonah weren't platonic, that I would gladly take her place. And while she's never questioned or accused me to my face, there were some moments last year when I waited for a confrontation.

Jonah and I have a history and a close friendship, and I'll be the first to admit I held—still hold—a possessiveness over it. But I wanted more, and she knew it. I saw it every time she looked at me, her pink lips pinched into a tight line. I heard it in her unspoken words when she tried setting me up with Toby. *Find your own man, Marie. This one's mine.*

If the roles were reversed, I can't say I would act any differently. Her wariness was understandable, just like my envy was for what she had with Jonah. Calla picked up her life and moved to another country for him, to a home that was so vastly different from everything she'd left. They faced a wave of growing pains in those first months, and here I was, that female "best friend" racing over every time Jonah needed an ear to vent to.

I can't say whether my not-so-secret feelings for Jonah were the linchpin in her distrust, or if she would've felt that way about me regardless, since I had something with Jonah that she didn't: a past.

I suspect they fought over me, but Jonah never revealed it.

I have no doubt he defended me; it's just who he is.

But there was a stretch there where I held my breath, expecting her to give Jonah an ultimatum, and I was *terrified* of what his answer would be. I'm *still* afraid because I know who Jonah would choose.

But things have shifted since last summer, with Calla finding her own way in Alaska. The two of them are married, and she seems to have made peace with my existence in his life. Maybe one day we'll consider each other friends. Until then, I'm not about to poke a charred log to see if it still smolders by bringing up memories of her husband and me sharing a tent.

"Hey, babe!" she hollers after Jonah. "Did you mention Bandit already?"

"He's *fine*," comes his gruff response while securing my luggage into the plane.

"Why? What's wrong with him?" I ask.

"He's been sleeping a lot more than usual and eating less."

"It *is* winter still." Not that raccoons hibernate, but they do tend to hide in their hovels during the colder temperatures. I'm no expert on raccoons. I know they don't tend to live more than a few years in the wild, but Bandit leads a cushy life, complete with daily feedings and a well-insulated chicken coop that their neighbor recently built for them.

"Yeah, maybe. He just seems ... I don't know, depressed."

Jonah snorts. "A *depressed* raccoon?"

"I think he needs a friend."

"He *has* a friend. Zeke."

Calla glares at Jonah. "I mean another raccoon. I was hoping he'd find one when we moved here, but I haven't seen any around." To me, she asks, "Does anyone ever bring strays in to you?"

I falter. "Stray raccoons? Well, *no*. There really aren't any in Alaska." There's the odd rumor that they lurk in the southwest and on the islands, but the rest of the state is inhospitable.

"What do you mean?" she says slowly, genuine confusion furrowing her brow. "What about Bandit?"

It dawns on me then. I look to Jonah's broad back, incredulity in my voice when I ask, "You never told her?"

"It never came up."

"*What* never came up?" Calla looks from Jonah to me.

I shake my head at my friend. "We flew down to Port Angeles

for the weekend to pick up some equipment I needed for the clinic, and you know how Jonah never closes his duffel bag all the way? He always leaves it open, like, six inches?"

"Yeah …" I can see the wheels turning in Calla's mind. Maybe she hasn't ever noticed that little habit of his.

"Well, Bandit crawled in when we were loading the plane to come home." He didn't make a sound the entire trip, not once during any of the fuel pit stops. He must've slept the whole way. I chuckle as I recall the moment we discovered him. "We were back at my place, and Jonah was dumping his clothes onto the floor. You should have heard him scream when the little black-and-gray furball tumbled out."

Calla still looks confused. "But my dad said you found him under your porch …" She scowls as her voice trails off.

"'Cause that's what I told him," Jonah says.

I laugh. "Wren knew you were lying!"

His eyes shine with amusement. "He told you that?"

"Yes! He let you stick to that story so Max and the other pilots wouldn't tease you, and because he knew you were terrified that you'd be the guy who brought a plague of raccoons to the state." People have tried to import the creatures here, but they've never flourished. Jonah was convinced that this time, they'd succeed in becoming a regular nuisance. As if Bandit would somehow multiply like a gremlin when wet.

"He always was good at coverin' my ass for me." A wistful smile touches Jonah's lips, as it always does when we reminisce about his old boss. His would-be father-in-law now.

"You should've seen him, though, Calla. Jonah was *so* afraid Bandit wouldn't survive, and he didn't want to leave him, so he spent an entire *week* at my place, feeding him with this *tiny* little baby bottle." I hold my hand out in front of me in a cup, mimicking how Jonah held him. "And he'd wake me five times a night so I could check on Bandit—"

"All right, all right, story time's over." Jonah smirks.

"I wanted to murder him, I lost so much sleep that week." The truth is, being shaken awake at three A.M. by a panicked Jonah was not enjoyable, but I didn't want to murder him. Quite the opposite. Watching him fawn over a tiny, helpless animal like that? The whole experience only made me love him more.

And the moment I take in Calla's face, I realize my mistake.

"Anything else *I* should know about that hasn't 'come up'? You know, seeing as I'm your *wife*." There's a distinctive annoyed edge to her tone as she levels Jonah with a steely look.

Maybe I'm just overly sensitive, but I hear the unspoken words that go along with that question. *Is there anything else Marie knows that I don't?*

And here I was, trying my best not to stoke any territorial fires.

"Ready to go?" Jonah slams Archie's back door shut, sparing a second to shoot me a wide-eyed "thanks a lot" stare.

I offer Calla an awkward smile and then dart to my side of the plane to climb into my seat, silently cursing my best friend. As much as I love him, he has many flaws.

Calla's irritation is splayed across her features as Jonah closes the distance. I can't hear their conversation, but I can imagine it. Both of them are headstrong, unwilling to back down in an argument. It can be entertaining, watching them banter back and forth like opposing players on a volleyball team. Most of the time, Jonah will say something highly inappropriate and obnoxious, and it either defuses the situation or detonates a nuclear bomb.

But their fights can also be tense. I only hope my name isn't in the mix. So far, neither have glanced this way, which is a good sign.

The corners of Calla's mouth twitch before curling upward. She shakes her head at him. She may still be annoyed, but he's melting her anger quickly, enough that he must feel comfortable leaving. He checks his watch and then pulls her into his arms.

I turn away as they kiss, letting my gaze settle on the frozen lake, the tree line, and the mountain range that I know is in the distance, obscured by the clouds.

And I breathe.

Will I ever have what they have?

I can't picture it anymore.

It's a few minutes before Jonah hauls his big body into his seat and sets to flipping switches on the cockpit panel. "Okay, let's get this show on the road." His mood hasn't soured, so I assume all is well in the world of Calla and Jonah.

I fit the headset over my ears. "For the record, you're an idiot."

"It never came up!" he exclaims in defense, but then adds in a mutter, "Yeah, I know."

CHAPTER FIVE

It's almost seven P.M. when Keenan hollers, "I see a head lamp!"

Every volunteer—eighteen of us in total, with three veterinarians besides myself, two vet techs, two people handling communications, one person to care for return dogs, a race judge, and eight volunteers handling everything from recording musher times to cooking meals—rush for his vantage spot where we can watch the mushers coast in.

The Rohn checkpoint is just under two hundred miles into the race, but the stretch they need to navigate to get here is the highest on the thousand-mile trail, the elevation over three thousand feet in the Alaska range. And once they pass that, they face the Dalzell Gorge, which, depending on the weather, can be either a delightful excursion or a white-knuckled ordeal. More than one musher has arrived at this stop with broken sleds and injuries—everything from bloodied foreheads to fractured ankles.

Fortunately, the weather has cooperated this year, and the snow bridgeways the trail crew built over the creek have held.

"Who do you think it is?" Keenan, the big-bellied man who has been running the checkpoint for the past two decades, asks no one in particular, squinting past the spruce trees and into the murky distance. It'll be pitch-black soon; the gift of a full moon is useless behind the thick ceiling of clouds.

Each sled has a GPS tracker pinned to its front that tells fans following along exactly where the racers are and how fast they're going, but out here, where there's only a small generator to keep the communications team collecting and sharing race data, information is sparse and spotty. Besides, it's more exciting to find out in person.

"My money's on Hatchett," Marty declares. "He was the first to Rohn last year."

"Skip has been training hard," Roger counters. "I'll bet it's him. In fact, I'm betting he wins this whole thing."

I school my expression. I've worked with all these volunteers before, so I know them well. Roger's a helpful and kind man, his only fault being his taste in mushers.

For my sake, I hope he's wrong because Terry, the head checkpoint veterinarian, assigned me to the first team in.

"Look! There's another one!" someone else hollers, pointing to the light trailing not far behind.

I huddle in my parka and watch the teams approach through the thicket of trees, mentally preparing myself for the steady stream of dogs arriving between now and tomorrow morning. The more competitive racers will be in first and gone quickly, while the teams racing simply to say they finished the Iditarod will trickle in through the night and rest for five or six hours. But short of any issues, they'll *all* roll out of here by tomorrow night.

Once mushers clear the mountain range and begin taking their required twenty-four rest stops at a checkpoint of their choosing, the stretch between the first and the last racer at a checkpoint expands. I expect to have teams in Cripple spreading over three days.

The volunteers tasked to record entrance times prepare, and the round of cheers and applause collect in the deep, silent valley between the looming peaks, the checkpoint marked with battery-operated lights, fires for warmth, and a banner to welcome them.

"It's Skip!" someone declares, at the same time I make out his round face.

Tension stirs inside me. I shift my focus to the dogs charging in, watching their gait. He still has all fourteen, and I don't see lameness in any.

With a deep breath, I step forward.

"Boyd? Why don't you take this one?" Terry declares, jerking his head toward Skip. "Marie, get the next." His blue eyes say nothing and everything as they meet mine. I'm no fool. Wade told him to run interference. I'm fine with that, as long as whoever's checking Skip's dogs is doing their job.

Boyd marches for the sled team, tugging his trapper hat low on his head. They've parked in the short-term area, meaning Skip plans on leaving shortly.

Thank God.

I wait patiently for the next musher, ignoring the trickle of reporters snapping pictures of Rohn's first arrival.

Two minutes later, Harry slides in.

I smile at the dogs, their tongues lolling, as volunteers descend on the team. I know each one by name, and have treated all of them from birth. There's an unmistakable wave of relief as I count fourteen, all strong on their legs without a hint of stiffness or struggle.

"Glad to see a friendly face, Doc!" Even bundled in layers and furs, Harry's cheeks are rosy, windburned.

"Hey! What's that supposed to mean?" Peter declares in mock upset, his clipboard out to mark down Harry's exact time in. "We're *all* friendly faces around here."

Harry grins. "Fine. A *pretty* face."

"Can't argue there." Peter gives his straggly, snow-coated beard a stroke.

I ignore the flirtation—Harry's made comments like that in

the past, but it's all for show and empty of meaning. I'm about fifteen years too old based on the girls I see him around town with. I trail him as he directs the dogs to another short-stay lane, securing the sled with his snow hook.

By the time I've reached him, the photographer has snapped their shot and I can do my job. "All good out there?"

"It's been better, but it's been worse, too. A lot of icy spots." He hops off his sled and digs out his dog team diary to hand to me. "They built those bridges narrow this year. I thought I was gonna slide off one, for sure." He drops to his knees and strokes Bowser's and Sheeba's napes. "These two kept that from happening."

"Any concerns?" I quickly scan the notes from the veterinarians at the previous stops.

"Nope." Harry punctuates that with a head shake. "They're running like a well-oiled machine."

"Good." And, unlike Skip, I know Harry will be watching his team intently. I've had to put down dogs for him before. He's held their head and cried every time. For all Harry's faults and ways in which he annoys me, I will be the first to defend his love for his dogs.

I nod toward the safety cabin. "Keenan's got a pot of his moose chili on the stove."

"Nah. Wanna put some more distance between me and the others." His gaze flitters toward Skip before he looks over his shoulder, down the trail. "Saw someone not too far back but couldn't tell who it was. Hopefully not that asshole Brady."

Harry was not happy when he called for an update on Nymeria and I explained the situation. He was clearly pinning his hopes on a different outcome. "You *really* that worried about a rookie?"

"No," he scoffs. "This is my fifth time running this race. I'm gonna win this year, you watch." He pulls a pack of frozen salmon from his sled and doles out a snack to each dog. "I don't get why everyone's making such a big deal about him, anyway.

His dogs are nothin' special. I'll bet he's getting a rude awakening about what Alaska's really like, after coming here and thinking he's hot shit."

He's not the only one who thinks he's hot shit. Harry's used to having more than his share of the spotlight—being a Hatchett, being so young. He doesn't like that there's someone else who might be getting more attention. "Forget about your neighbor and take care of your dogs."

"I always take care of them." He rubs Comet's hind leg, the one that has caused her issues in the past. "You got my back for the Leonhard Seppala, right?"

I stumble on a suitable response. It's the most prestigious award, next to winning the race. What is he asking me to do?

"Relax, I'm just kidding." He smiles coyly—as if that could win me over. "You done after this stop?"

"No, they need me in Cripple next."

"Perfect." He drops his voice and looks around. "I'm doing my big rest there."

The mushers keep their game plan close to their chest while race fans spend countless hours speculating on where they'll rest based on the supply drops at the various checkpoints and previous race plans. Stopping in Cripple means he's pushing on past McGrath and Takotna, where most mushers take their required twenty-four-hour stop.

Twenty-four hours dealing with Harry Hatchett? Not *perfect.*

"You're going for the gold, huh?" The first musher to the checkpoint gets $3000 in nuggets, in honor of the old gold rush town. One of many baiting prizes along the trail.

"'Course I am. I need everything I can get. Running this kennel is … expensive."

It seems he was going to say something else—hard? Impossible?—but decided against it. Would admitting either of those things feel like failure to him?

My dad and I have both often wondered what the Hatchetts'

financial situation looks like now that Earl is gone, how they're managing. Harry's coat still wears the embroidered stitching of his sponsor—a construction equipment supply company that has operated in Alaska for decades and was willing to support the sport when Earl was alive. Are they as willing now?

This is the part of this race—and this industry—that raises alarms in me. Harry may care deeply about his dogs, but when prize money and prestige dangles ahead and financial burdens weigh on his shoulders, will his ego let him make the right choices? That, I'm not so sure. "Don't push the dogs too hard."

His expression turns sour with annoyance. "How about I leave the vet stuff to you, and you leave the racing stuff to me, 'kay?"

I force a polite smile.

Ten minutes later, I'm happy to be watching the back of Harry's navy parka vanish into the night, the dogs barking excitedly as they pursue Skip's team.

From there, three more teams arrive in tight succession, keeping the Rohn crew busy as we do our best to welcome and care for each. Not all mushers are in a rush to keep going after such an arduous trek through the pass. A couple spread straw for their dogs to rest and retrieve the drop bags that hold snacks and meals, gabbing and laughing with volunteers who mill around, helping where needed.

Two hours later during a lull, Keenan bellows, "Two coming in!" followed by a perplexed, "What in Sam Hell?"

I navigate around piles of dog poop to join in his watch. Ahead of us, two head lamps approach, moving slower than the usual six to seven miles per hour, one after another, the musher in front turning back frequently to check over their shoulder.

They're twenty feet out when I realize one of them is Tyler. I recognize his jawline, covered in a short layer of scruff and set with grim determination.

He eases his team to a halt before dropping the snow hook to keep them in place and hopping off his sled. "We need help over here!" he hollers, guiding the team behind him in with a soft *whoa*.

The other musher is hunched over the front of his mangled sled, blood trickling down his forehead. It's Larry Reese, a veteran racer and another contender to win, having placed in the top ten a handful of times.

"Get Monica out here!" someone calls as volunteers charge forward, followed closely by the photographer and news reporter.

Within moments, the checkpoint race judge is charging out of the cabin, tugging on a hat over her graying hair and wiping a palm against her mouth to catch any residual chili. "What happened?" She inspects Larry with a worried frown.

"I'm not sure. I heard the dogs and saw a faint light, *way* off the path. Looks like he took a bad spill in the gorge. I found him unconscious, with his dogs tangled up in a fallen tree," Tyler explains, pausing long enough to scowl at the photographer who just blinded him with a flash. "He came to shortly after I arrived, so I got him up and his dogs unraveled. He didn't want to call in for help, so I hung back to make sure he got here okay."

Because activating his emergency transmitter for help would mean an automatic withdrawal from the race.

Larry may be conscious now, but he doesn't seem completely aware of his surroundings, squinting against the spotlights. Still, he tries to wave it off. "I'll be fine. I just need a few hours to regroup." He steps off his sled and his legs wobble, forcing Monica and Tyler to dive for him.

I've seen mushers roll through checkpoints with scrapes and bruises. I've heard stories of veterinarians stitching up gashes for them on their way through. After months of training and thousands of dollars to keep a team, no one *wants* to withdraw from the race. But it doesn't take a doctor to see that Larry knocked his head hard in that fall, and likely has a concussion on top of whatever else. Plus, his sled is mangled, beyond a quick patch job.

If Larry's not smart enough to make the right call to scratch, Monica had better withdraw him.

In all the commotion, I hear myself ask, "What about the dogs?"

Tyler's head snaps to me, and he falters, as if shocked to see me there. He shouldn't be; he knows I volunteer on the trail.

"Did you notice if any of them were hurt?" I didn't get a good look at them running in.

"One of the wheel dog's hind legs is bothering her. The one on the left. But otherwise, they're all fine. I've already checked."

I'll be the judge of that.

As the others deal with Larry, I head straight for the dog in question, a beautiful blue-eyed husky with deep caramel markings. A quick examination tells me she's not cut by branches or ice, but she has injured her hind leg. No matter what's decided, she's gone as far as she can go in this race.

I shift to the other wheel dog for an inspection, earning a lick against my cheek for the attention. From there, I slowly move through each dog, who seem in fine spirits despite their ordeal.

"An Iditarod rookie, and you're already playing Good Samaritan," Terry declares, his booming voice dividing my attention from my task.

Tyler has left Larry to the others and is now tending to his team, handing Terry his dog diary. "I'm just glad I was there to help." He pushes back the hood of his red musher's down jacket, revealing a black knit cap that hugs his head and shows off his pleasing side profile.

A visceral reaction—that same instant admiration for a handsome face that sparked when I first met him—stirs in my stomach. It's quickly quelled by the reminder of his abrasive personality. But he can't be all bad. If Larry was as far off the marked trail as Tyler claims, he *could* have claimed to not see him

and sped past. Not that I know a single musher—including Skip
—who would consider doing something so callous. Still …

"He wouldn't be the first one. That stretch can be a nightmare.
Claimed more than one musher's hopes over the years." Terry
reviews the notes with an intense frown. "Your dogs sure looked
real good coming in, though."

"As they should. They're the best team here, and they've been
training hard."

I fight the urge to roll my eyes at his arrogance.

"They all run in the Finnmark race with you?"

"All of them." Tyler yanks off his gloves and leans down to
massage one of the wheel dog's front legs.

I note the various badges sewn into his sleeve. A common
practice for both mushers and volunteers who don the various
emblems to highlight previous races they've participated in, clubs
they belong to, their kennel, even sponsors. A black-and-white
patch that's larger than the others sits prominently on his shoulder, of a musher's sled and the words "Team Mila" below it.

"How is she?"

I realize Tyler's talking to me. Even in the dim night with
nothing but the overhead spotlight, I can make out the pretty
hazel of his irises.

He must be asking about the injured wheel dog. I find my
voice quickly. "Likely a sprain. She'll heal, but she's done for this
race. The rest of them look okay so far." I offer a head scratch to
the mottled beige husky I'm inspecting.

He shifts his quiet focus back to his own dogs, murmuring
softly to each.

The reporter comes around to ask a few questions about
Larry's accident, which will surely front all the Iditarod-related
news tomorrow, but Tyler dismisses him after ten seconds,
claiming he needs to focus on his dogs.

"You're a bit of a mystery around here," Terry says, shifting
from dog to dog.

Tyler chuckles. It's a deep, unexpectedly pleasant sound. "I'm not very interesting, and I've never been one for cameras. I like to keep to myself."

"You're in the wrong sport, then, champ. Especially in Alaska. Where you from again? Finland?"

"That's right." Tyler gives the blond husky a head scratch and then moves on to the next.

"And before that? Somewhere in the lower forty-eight, I'm guessing."

My ears perk up for his answer, my curiosity overpowering my contempt for the man.

Tyler pauses, as if considering answering. Clearly, Terry has disregarded the *keep to myself* comment. "Montana, originally. Near Whitefish."

Terry makes a sound. "Been there! Drove through one summer with the wife, back in '92, on our way to Yellowstone. Beautiful area."

"It is. But so is Alaska." There's a pause and then Tyler asks, "You ever been, Marie?"

"Huh?" I feel like I've been caught eavesdropping.

He smirks, like he was aware I was listening intently. "Whitefish, Montana."

"No. Never made it that far." I shift back to Larry's dogs.

"So Montana to Finland to Alaska. That's quite the route," Terry says. "How'd you end up in Finland, racing sled dogs, anyway?"

"It's just where my path led me." Tyler crouches in front of a lean black husky. "How is my team?"

"They look good!" Terry signs the diary and hands it back. "I know things got kind of scrambled with all the chaos comin' in. Not sure if Peter asked if you're gonna rest here?"

Tyler juts his chin in answer, to the dark stretch leading out of the checkpoint. "I have some ground to catch up."

Terry chuckles. "You've got at least seven days to make up the time, but you can grab your straw over there." He directs Tyler to the bales with a pointed finger and a "good luck" before strolling away, heading toward the warmth of the cabin.

"Do you want to check over my dogs for me?" Tyler asks suddenly. "You know, make sure they have *your* approval?"

I set my jaw. I'm guessing that's some sort of reference to last year's debacle with Skip. "Nope, sounds like you're good to go."

"Are you sure?" he frowns. "Because you seemed to be watching that veterinarian *very* closely."

It wasn't Terry I was watching, not that I'm going to admit that.

Tyler shrugs. "And you said you don't trust the others, so—"

"*I never said that!*" I hiss, glancing around to make sure we're not within earshot of anyone. Despite the cold, my cheeks burn. The last thing I need is that rumor flowing through the volunteer crew. Finishing my examination, I climb to my feet, intent on calling the other volunteers over to look after Larry's dogs while they sort out what to do about Larry, so I can get the hell away from Tyler. I assume the state troopers have already been called in to provide a medical check and evacuation, if required.

"I'm serious," he calls out, his tone shifting to a more somber sound. "That guy seemed more interested in me than he was in my team. I don't know how thorough he was with my dogs, and I wouldn't want them to suffer because of it."

Despite my annoyance, the genuine concern in his voice stalls my legs. "That's just Terry being Terry. He'll talk your ear off, but he's one of the good ones."

"Maybe. But that gorge was more challenging than I expected." His gaze wanders behind him, back toward the trail, pitch-black now. "Tank injured his leg last spring. He looked good running today, but I'd still like a second look at him from someone I trust. If you wouldn't mind."

I can't keep my jaw from gaping. Someone he *trusts*? Is this a joke? "Why? So you can accuse me of sabotaging you if I find something wrong with him?"

A pained expression flickers across his face. "We got off on the wrong foot. Harry pissed me off, and I took it out on you. But I think you'll agree I'm not one of the bad guys, and *I* know you were only looking out for Nymeria."

That sounds like an apology, or as close to it as I'm likely going to get. Oddly enough, it's in the same vein as the hand-written note I *didn't* deliver back in January.

I clear my throat. "How is she, by the way?"

"She's doing well." A slow, amused smile touches his lips. "I'm assuming you already know that, though, seeing as your friend was by Frank's twice, asking. What? You didn't think Frank would tell me?" If he's at all irritated by that—or by my feigned obliviousness—he's hiding it well. He shifts his attention to the curly-tailed silver-and-ash dog at the head of the pack who watches us quietly, as if understanding every word. "I'd appreciate your help with Tank now. I need him with me to the end."

Tyler has already figured out how to play on my weakness.

With a glance over at the cabin to make sure Terry isn't around—what would he think if he knew I was rechecking a dog, especially after what happened last year?—I abandon my escape plan and march for the left lead dog, crouching in front of him. "Remember me?" I whisper, scratching behind his ear.

He licks his lips in answer, his breath skating across my face.

"Yeah, of course you do. Don't pee on me again," I warn, listening to his breathing and measuring his pants across my cheek before I check his gums and the skin on the back of his neck for any signs of dehydration.

The whole time, I feel Tyler watching me closely, that pene-trating stare unsettling.

"How old is he?" I ask.

"Nine, next month."

"Wow. I wouldn't have guessed that." Though there's intelligence in the dog's eyes that only comes with age.

"It's his left leg that was the problem."

I gently palpate it, looking for any bumps or bulges, anything that might stir a flinch. "There's nothing here. And no signs of muscle loss." I finish off with my hands on his other joints, looking for any problems that might come with a nine-year-old dog. "No dehydration, no overheating, no aches." I cap off the declaration with a pat before climbing to my feet. "He looks perfect. Ready to run another eight hundred miles. With adequate rest," I add, my tone warning.

Tyler nods. "You got it, Doc."

In the distance, a head lamp glows faintly and volunteers are already moving into position, preparing to deliver another hero's welcome. Only fifty-something more times to go.

"I guess I should get moving." Tyler tugs his gloves back on. "I know you didn't do that for me, but thank you, anyway."

"No problem." Without that layer of animosity—that his apology seems to have chipped away in an instant—I can already feel my unease around this man fading.

"You checkin' out now, Brady?" Peter marches forward, his clipboard at the ready.

Tyler pulls his hood back up, the fur ruff framing his face. "Ready." His voice is barely above conversation, but the dogs hear the command all the same. They bark and tug against their harnesses, excited to get going.

I move backward, out of his way.

"Is this your only checkpoint?" he calls out, peering at me from behind his cowl.

"No, I'll be in Cripple, day after tomorrow."

"Then you can hand me my gold."

I can't help my laughter at his brazen confidence. "I guess we'll see." Not that a veterinarian would be the one handing out the prize. The sponsor has a rep for that honor.

"Why? You don't think I can do it?" His voice holds a challenge.

"You've never run the Iditarod before. Others have." I shrug. "And you won't be the only one racing for that prize."

His eyes narrow. "So Hatchett's going for it too, huh?"

"I have no idea what Harry's doing." I keep my voice even. Harry told me that in confidence. And that Tyler's shooting for the gold means he's planning on resting either at Cripple or even farther, at Ruby.

Twenty hours with Tyler Brady. Doesn't stir the unpleasant reaction I expected.

His smile is crooked, but it makes his already handsome face impossible to turn away from. "Right."

I struggle to stop the responding smile.

"See you there, Crusader." With one last pensive look, he shifts his attention to the distance, a steely expression taking over his face. There are two hundred and forty miles of remote Alaskan tundra between here and the next time I'll see him. He releases the snow hook. "Let's go." Another soft command, but that's all it takes.

I watch the number on the back of his bib fade into the darkness.

Maybe Tyler Brady isn't so bad after all.

CHAPTER SIX

"Marie?"

"Yeah?" I croak, burrowed deep in my sleeping bag, like a caterpillar waiting for my metamorphosis.

"We've got our first team coming in." I hear the apology in Karen's voice.

Already? "How long have I been asleep?" Surely, my head just hit my mat.

"I reckon you got almost two hours." She snorts. "More than me!"

I don't doubt it. Karen, a loud and tiny grandmother from Fairbanks, was busy heating soup and assembling sandwiches for the trailbreakers coming through on their snowmachines when our plane dropped us off early this morning. She's been running the Cripple checkpoint for longer than I've been a veterinarian, and she does it all. If she's not out at the greeting point to cheer on the mushers, she's cooking in the checkpoint's "headquarters"—a hut with plywood walls and metal shelves that are brimming with everything from paper plates to propane canisters and Coffee-Mate—all supplies Karen personally arranges to bring in every year.

Normally a two-hour power nap is all I need, but after the two-day whirlwind at Rohn, my body aches. Or maybe I'm getting too old for this.

"Lord, it's hot in here. I wouldn't put so much wood in that thing."

I tug my cover down to confirm that the glow from the wood-stove burns bright, illuminating the yellow walls of the arctic tent. "Tell Terry," I mutter, unable to hide my annoyance. He stoked the tent stove with so much wood this afternoon that it was almost too warm for even base layers by the time I settled in. He must have snuck in and added *another* log while I was sleeping.

No wonder sweat is building around my shirt collar.

"They're maybe a mile and a half out," Karen warns.

I do the quick math. A mile and a half at six or seven miles per hour ... "I'll see you outside in five. Ten, tops."

"Don't make me drag you out of your bag." She chuckles, but from what I've heard of Karen, the only thing she takes more seriously than her kitchen is a proper greeting for the teams, especially the first one in.

"Wait!" My eyes peel open, the sleepy fog lifting. "Do you know who it is?"

"I hear it's that handsome rookie from Finland. See ya out there!"

There's only one person she can mean. Tyler did it. He's going to get his gold nuggets.

And Harry is going to be *so* pissed.

My soft chuckle carries through the tent.

———

Cheers and applause explode as the silhouette approaches through the stunted black spruce that dapple the otherwise empty, flat tundra. Tyler's red musher's jacket and the dogs' matching red booties and coats provide a picturesque contrast to the sea of snow in the waning daylight. A trail photographer on-site for the grand entrance takes full advantage, snapping as the team slides in.

Tyler eases his sled into a long-term spot and drops his snow hook, then steps off. He pushes back his hood, revealing a few more days' worth of growth across his jaw. Eyes that look like they haven't shut for more than an hour at a time for days—they probably haven't—scan the various functional sheds and arctic tents that make up the isolated checkpoint, now bustling with excitement from volunteers and media personnel who've been waiting for this monumental arrival.

When his tired gaze passes over me, it doubles back quickly. He offers me a lazy smile that seems to say, "Told you so."

I smile back.

And maybe it's because we're both exhausted, but our eyes hang there, fastened on each other for a long moment.

"So? You gonna take the TV or the gold?" the prize sponsor rep, a burly man bundled in a parka, drops his beefy hand onto Tyler's shoulder and then turns to pose for a semi-candid shot. Hopper, the race judge at this checkpoint, hovers beside him.

"I can get a TV anywhere," comes Tyler's wry response.

"That, you can." The rep's laughter booms in the vast, empty wilderness. "How about we head over there for the little ceremony?" He gestures toward a table nearby where the trophy and gold await.

Tyler rubs a palm across the stubble on his cheek. "Can I take care of my dogs first?"

The rep holds his hands up in surrender. "Fair enough. You do what you gotta do. I'll be inside, where it's warm." He lumbers toward the hut.

Tyler's shoulders seem to sink as he heads for the straw—the first step in a lengthy process of caring for the team before he can even think about a moment's rest for himself.

"Well, kid?" Terry sidles up to me, his attention on the dogs ahead. "How are you feeling? Good nap?"

I grunt.

"You shouldn't be so tired. You're half my age."

"More like two-thirds. And you got way more sleep than I did last night." The fifty-nine-year-old veterinarian vanished at nine P.M. I found him snoring in his sleeping bag, with no request for a wake-up call. He had no intention of getting up until his alarm went off this morning.

"True," he admits with a chuckle that slips away as quickly. "It's just you and me till Sam can catch a flight in the morning."

"Yeah, I figured." Sam, the third veterinarian assigned to this checkpoint, left here yesterday morning to cover for an ill veterinarian in McGrath. Coordinating all the flights—of dogs heading back to Anchorage, of volunteers and media moving between checkpoints—is a monumental task that requires a lot of flexibility, especially when juggling the unexpected.

So right now, it's just me and what I'm beginning to think is my assigned babysitter, care of Wade.

"The tracking report says Skip's about two hours out if he keeps his pace, and Harry's not too far behind him. We might have as many as four more teams rolling in overnight. So why don't I steal a bit of sleep now while you take this one?" He nods toward Tyler's dogs. "Then I'll look over Skip and Harry while you get a few more hours' rest. Sound like a plan?" He's already making his way toward the yellow dome.

"Don't put too much wood in!" I holler after him.

"It's the stove!" he counters.

"No, it's definitely the operator."

Tyler is already spreading a thick layer of straw for his dogs and doesn't seem to notice me approaching.

An unexpected spike of nerves stirs in my stomach as I watch him. "I guess your goals weren't too lofty."

"Hey, Crusader." He looks up briefly and meets my eyes,

allowing me to see the heavy bags under his. "I told you I would make it here first."

I ignore the nickname, crouching to greet Tank with a head scratch. His panting is hot against my cheek. "What are you going to do with your big prize?"

"I promised it to Reed."

I can't keep the surprise from my voice. "You're giving Reed $3000 in gold nuggets?"

"Yeah. He deserves it." A curious frown touches his brow. "Why?"

"No reason." Reed probably does deserve it. He must spend a lot of time with the dogs. "So is he your nephew or cousin?" Tyler referred to him as family.

"Brother."

They must be fifteen to twenty years apart. "Wow, that's a big age difference between you two."

"Yup." He drops the last pile of straw beside me for Tank. The other dogs have already settled in their spots, waiting for their meals. "He's a good kid."

"He seems like it." A bit nervous around us but at ease with his canine companions. And I sense that's all the information I'm going to get about Reed.

"So, how'd we look coming in?"

I've never been this close to Tyler. Now, I admire his features. The bridge of his nose is perfectly straight and ends in a pointed tip that flatters. The painful-looking crack on his chapped lips doesn't detract from their fullness.

He's staring at me.

Waiting for my answer.

"Good. You look good," I mumble. "I mean, *the dogs* look good."

"Good." Yet *still* he hovers there.

It's another long second before I realize he's holding out the dog diary, waiting for me to accept it. That's why he's looking at me like that.

"Oh! Right." I snatch it from his hand, my cheeks burning as I bury my head in the pages of veterinarian notes. "You still have your full team."

"And it'll stay that way, if they can handle it."

"Really? You're not going to drop any near the end?" Even the top mushers will leave a few dogs in that last stretch. Fewer dogs means less time taken out of the race to care for them when every minute counts.

"Not if I can help it. They've all worked hard, and they all deserve to finish the race." He scratches the jet-black dog's head on his way past.

We work quietly as we get the team settled. I focus on my routine examination, pulling my stethoscope out to check each dog's heart and lungs, gums, paws, and joints, earning myself plenty of licks in the line.

Tyler is busy rubbing down each dog's muscles and smoothing ointment on their paws to keep the pads from getting chapped. "So, I've always been curious, who was it that cut through my gate? You? Or your animal control friend?" He fastens the insulated jacket on the blond husky again.

His tone is casual, but his question makes me wary. "Why? You want to send a bill?"

"Relax." He chuckles. "I'm just wondering how far past the line Marie the Crusader is willing to go for the sake of an animal?"

I shift to the black swing dog, pressing my stethoscope to his chest. "As far as I'm concerned, there is no line."

Tyler's silent for a moment and I feel him watching me, but I keep my focus on my patient.

"I think I like that answer."

"Enough to take down your stupid sign?" I quip without much thought.

His lips part, but he falters on his words. "How do you know about that?"

"I *may* have driven out to your place to apologize the next day."

"Really? What happened? You forgot your bolt cutters?"

An unexpected laugh slips out, and it earns me his crinkly-eyed smile.

"Better yet, you decided I didn't deserve an apology."

"Something like that." I lift the dog's lip to check his gums, and he snarls.

"Airi, settle down," Tyler warns, adding, "He likes to make noise. Especially when he's hungry."

"I don't blame you, Airi. I get grumpy when I'm hungry, too." I stroke his neck.

"You should stop distracting me, then, so I can hurry up and feed them." His gaze skates over my face, stalling on my mouth. I see raw curiosity, interest.

Is Tyler flirting, or is he this way with everyone? I don't know him at all.

But a part of me admits that I want to.

I take my time with my medical checks to make sure they're thorough while Tyler shifts to food preparation, examining the kettle he set up to melt snow for water and then hauling his weighty drop bag of food to his sled.

The dogs whine and bark as they watch him pour kibble into fourteen identical red bowls and mix it with chunks of meat and warm broth that he prepared in a cooler. Only when each dog has a bowl in front of it does Tyler step back and take a breath. The fur ruff that protected him from the harshest elements is frozen, caked with snow and ice.

"Tired?"

"Exhausted," he admits. "I can't wait to sleep."

Which he'll get to do soon, based on how all the dogs are inhaling their meals. With full stomachs and beds to rest, they can easily log eight hours without stirring. "Your team looks healthy."

He nods, his shoulders sinking with relief as if he was anxiously waiting for me to declare that. "Good."

The checkpoint is buzzing again as volunteers spill out from the communal hut.

"Skip must be almost here." I do a poor job hiding my disdain. It's time to wake up Terry, before I get stuck facing off with the old musher again.

"I was hoping it was Hatchett."

"He's not far behind." I scribble my name in Tyler's dog diary. "Go get some sleep."

"I plan on it. As soon as I see the look on Hatchett's face when he rolls in." He grins as he collects the book from my grasp, our fingertips grazing in the exchange, stirring something inside me.

"I'm sure you'll find it gratifying." Harry was that kid who threw baseball bats across the base in a fit of frustration when he struck out. After how obnoxious he was in Rohn, a part of me wants to watch this showdown unfold, but then I'll be stuck playing his sounding board, and I'm not choosing sides in this neighborly spat. "Have a good night." I pull my gloves back on, savoring that lingering spark against my skin as I walk away, accepting that, despite our rocky introduction, I'm attracted to this guy.

"Hey!"

I turn back—too fast and too eager for my liking.

"For what it's worth, I met Skip at the drawing banquet, and he's a fucking idiot. I don't doubt you made the right call."

Another apology of sorts. And something I needed to hear Tyler say. Whether ingrained through my father or simply the way I am, my reputation as a veterinarian has always been important to me. To a fault sometimes.

The last dribs of our terrible first impressions of each other seem to be melting away in the frigid cold.

He watches me quietly, waiting for my response.

"Of course I did." I walk away, not giving him a chance to ruin the moment.

Tyler's soft chuckle follows me toward the tent.

And thoughts of him take up residence in my mind as my body sinks into a peaceful slumber.

CHAPTER SEVEN

An alarm pulls me from a deep sleep. It's a soft, repetitive chime, like that of a watch.

At first, I ignore it, because staying burrowed in your sleeping bag and ignoring everything around you is the only way you can get a decent rest while working these checkpoints. People are always filtering in and out of tents and cabins, finding any little spot they can.

But the alarm continues to ding, and so I unfurl from my arctic cocoon to investigate.

And come face-to-face with Tyler.

He's lying directly beside me on his back, our sleeping pads butted up against each other. His chest rises and falls in a slow, rhythmic wave as he sleeps soundlessly, tucked into his sleeping bag, oblivious to his alarm.

I went to sleep thinking about Tyler Brady, and now he's lying here. I frown, wondering for a moment if I'm awake or dreaming. It's like he materialized from my thoughts. But what the hell is he doing in this tent? The mushers have a tent where they can crash. This one is meant for the veterinarian volunteers.

Did no one direct him?

How long has he been here?

I push those questions aside as I study his form in the dull glow of the woodstove. His features are relaxed and innocent, his lips parted slightly. He peeled off his outer clothes and hung them on the line to melt and dry out, and then crawled into his sleeping bag in his base layer. The collar of his fitted moisture-wicking shirt frames a long, columnar neck, just below a sharply jutting Adam's apple.

I could admire that face for hours, but Tyler has an alarm set, which means he wants to rise. He *needs* to rise to care for his dogs. And he's not so much as twitching. I've always thought these competitive mushers are a crazy lot for what they put themselves through. After days of catching an hour here, an hour there, bundled and lying on straw among his dogs in the wilderness, his body has said *no more*.

I check my watch, and gasp when I see that it's almost five A.M.

I should have been up hours ago. Why didn't anyone wake me sooner? The flames in the stove are fading, no fresh logs added in some time, which means Pyro Terry hasn't snuck in to cook us out. The air is on the cooler side, though still comfortable enough.

I hesitate for only a second before I whisper, "Tyler."

He lets out a soft, guttural sound but otherwise doesn't stir.

"Tyler." I place a hand against his shoulder, his body firm and hot beneath my palm, and shake him gently.

He shifts, slipping his arm from deep within his sleeping bag. His fingers weave through mine to clasp my hand. He pulls my knuckles to his mouth.

I giggle, even as my stomach stirs with the feel of his lips against my skin. He must have slathered on ChapStick or Vaseline before he went to sleep because they're soft and sticky and warm, and such a contrast to his bristly jaw.

A part of me isn't in a rush to ruin this moment by waking him, but I know I have to.

I pull my hand from his grasp. Before I have the chance to call his name again, he's rolling onto his side and reaching for me, his hand sliding over my hip, over my back, to collect a fistful of hair at my nape as his face burrows against mine. The softest murmur of "love you" escapes him, and then he's pressing his lips to mine in a sleepy but intimate kiss that deepens by the second. His weight shifts onto me as he works to get closer, until I'm half pinned beneath him.

My heart races as I find myself responding.

He's clearly used to reaching for *someone* in his sleep. At this moment, every physical inch of my body wants to be her.

But those words aren't meant for me.

And when that truth registers in my head, I break free from the kiss and say loudly, "Tyler. It's time to wake up."

He stirs with a sharp inhale, as if startled awake by a dream. Or a nightmare.

Time in the cozy, dim tent seems to hang for several beats, both of us frozen, inches apart, staring into each other's bewildered eyes, equally confused by the current situation but surely for distinct reasons. I feel the tension radiating through his body as he processes the reality he woke up in.

Finally, he releases me and rolls off, settling onto his back. "Christ," he whispers under his breath, rubbing his palms over his unshaven face. With a quick tap of his finger, he quiets the alarm on his watch, and then sits up and looks around. "Where is everyone?" His voice is groggy and deep, his hair a wild mess.

"I don't know."

He stares at a spot on the tent wall for so long that I wonder if he fell asleep with his eyes open before leaning over to collect a piece of wood. "This needs another log," he whispers, more to himself.

I admire the way his clingy shirt stretches over his cut arms and the web of muscle across his back. Not until he shuts the stove door do I ask, "What are you doing in this tent?"

He groans as he flops back, his arms stretching over his head. "Fucking Hatchett."

Of course. I should have known it had something to do with his nemesis. "What did he do?"

"What *didn't* that idiot do? I was asleep in the mushers' tent for maybe two hours when he came stumbling in with his shit and dropped his sleeping pad *right beside me* so he could be close to the stove. He stepped on me, *twice*. Don't even try to tell me that was accidental because I caught his smile the second time."

I wince. These mushers bank on their twenty-four-hour rest to catch up on much-needed sleep so they can make it to the finish line.

"And then he jammed the stove with so much wood, he turned the tent into an oven. I was sweating so bad, I thought I'd have to strip down."

My gaze flitters over his torso. *Yes, that would have been terrible.* "Are you sure it was Harry who did that?" Because it sounds like someone else I know.

"Yeah, I watched the prick do it. I went outside to cool off. Both literally and figuratively, because I was ready to choke him —" His jaw ticks with tension. "I ran into Terry, and he sent me in here. I couldn't see who was in the bag next to me. I didn't know it was you." He opens his mouth as if to say more, but no words come out.

Uncomfortable silence hangs in the tent. That mistaken kiss seems to have left both of us off-kilter.

I try to shake it off. "Did Harry say anything to you when he arrived at the checkpoint?"

"No." After a moment, a slow smile spreads across Tyler's handsome face, blossoming into a grin. "But he showed up just in time to see them hand me my gold and take a picture with my trophy, and he looked a little stiff."

I chuckle. "He is *very* competitive and convinced he's going to win this year." But would Harry disrupt another musher's much-needed sleep like that on purpose? Yes, now that I think about it, I wouldn't put it past him, especially where Tyler is concerned.

What an asshole. It reeks of unsportsmanlike behavior, and yet it's not blatant enough to get him kicked out of the Iditarod.

Tyler stands with a stretch. "I better get out there. The dogs have been sleeping for almost eight hours. They'll be up again soon."

I try not to stare as he dresses but fail miserably. I've only ever seen Tyler in bulky outer clothes but now, in his fitted base layer, with the fresh log aglow, its steady burn illuminating the tent, I have a prime view of his fit, athletic body.

And thanks to the snugness of his long woolen underwear, little is left to the imagination, both from the back and when he turns around.

I close my eyes and listen to him slipping on his ski pants. I don't need these visuals burned into my brain while I'm still reeling from that kiss.

"You on duty soon?" he asks, drawing my eyes open again, just in time to see him tug his wool sweater over his head.

His question reminds me that I'm not here to make out with and ogle mushers. "Yeah. I should have been out there hours ago. Terry was supposed to come and get me." I peel myself from my cozy sleeping bag and reach for my own ski pants.

"The last I saw him, he was heading into the hut." Tyler's attention drifts over my wool leggings and shirt, stalling on my chest for a brief second before he ducks his head to pull on his boots.

We finish dressing in awkward silence, like two people who woke up next to last night's drunken mistake and are attempting a swift exit.

He pulls on his knit cap. "Will you do rounds of the teams again?"

"Yeah, I'll check them out to see how they're holding up." If I can read Tyler at all, he'll go straight to his dogs with nothing more than a quick stop to the outhouse—or a snowbank—to relieve himself. "Do you want me to grab you a coffee? I'm sure there's a fresh pot brewing." It's a guarantee. Karen's militant volunteer schedule requires it.

"That would be great. Black, please." His hand is on the zipper to the door when he stops. "And about earlier ... I didn't mean for that to happen—"

"It's fine. You were asleep. And ... confused." And I let it go farther than I should have—I enjoyed it *way* too much.

His head turns halfway toward me, showing off the rigid line of his tense jaw. "Yeah."

I hesitate, unsure how to word this. "Is there anyone who would be upset if they heard about it?" A girlfriend, or *wife*, who will accuse me of trying to move in on her territory? I've had enough of that.

He opens his mouth but then falters on his answer. "No. There's no one."

A wave of relief hits me, followed quickly by a surge of anticipation. Regardless of who he might have been saying those words to, Tyler's just confirmed he's single.

He pauses. "What about you? Am I gonna have someone showing up at my house, threatening to beat my ass?" He studies me over his shoulder, his expression oddly somber for his words.

"No, no one like that."

His gaze drifts over my bundled form before settling on my face. "Good."

Good that there's no one—that I'm single—or good that he won't have to deal with an angry boyfriend?

Tyler chuckles as I work through possible meaning in that single word, as if able to read my inner turmoil. "See you out there." With that, he ducks out of the tent.

And I take a few minutes to calm my heart and my burgeoning hopes.

———

Steam rises from the paper cup as I trek along the path from the hut, my head lamp guiding my way through the darkness. It's eerily quiet with only the odd crackle from the blazing firepit and my own boots crunching through the snow to keep me company. But Rick, the guy manning the kitchen while Karen rests, confirmed that along with the twenty or so volunteers on-site, sixty-seven dogs and their mushers are asleep here tonight. The next team is expected to arrive in a few hours with the dawn. Thankfully, Skip came and went, aiming to get to Ruby for his big rest and the cash prize.

The closer I get to the glowing light in the distance, the more the flutters in my stomach stir. I haven't felt this sort of reaction to someone since … well, Jonah.

Tyler already has his cook pot going when I reach him. The dogs are up and stretching their legs as far as their lines will allow them, eager for their second soupy meal of kibble, meat, and broth, before they curl up for another eight-hour stretch of sleep. They're the only ones who eat and sleep well during this race, the mushers and volunteers running ragged at their beck and call.

Tyler looks up at the last minute, his eyes far more alert now than they were in the tent, but still lined with bags. He accepts the coffee from my mittened grasp with his bare hands and a murmur of thanks. "Did you find Terry?"

"Yeah, he decided to let me sleep and then crashed in your old spot." Rick confirmed that he went down right after the last check-in a few hours ago. "He likes an uncomfortably hot tent, too, so it's a win-win for all of us."

"He can spoon with Hatchett if he wants." Tyler takes a long draw from his cup.

I can still feel those lips against my knuckles. And my mouth. "I doubt he'll get as good a wake-up as *I* did, though."

Tyler coughs on his coffee. "So that's where we're at? Joking about it already?"

I feel my cheeks flush. "What *else* are we supposed to do?"

"Good question." A secretive smile disappears behind another sip.

What I would do to read his thoughts at this moment.

I shift my focus to one of his wheel dogs, straddling her body so I can stroke her front legs the way mushers often do, warming up and loosening her muscles. She thanks me with a swipe of her nose against my chin.

"You have a team?" Tyler asks, tearing open the bag of kibble and pouring it into the lined-up bowls.

"Of sled dogs?" I chuckle. "I can't even commit to a goldfish, let alone a pile of dogs."

"You seem to know what you're doing."

"Well, yeah. I grew up in the sled dog capital of Alaska with a veterinarian for a father. *Of course* I do. But I've never been interested in the racing side of it. Just the athletes." I give the gentle husky one last scratch before shifting to the next.

"You've gone mushing, though, right?"

"A few times. Short runs, usually once the snow is on the ground and the dogs are starting their seasonal training, so I can watch them move."

"Let me guess, with *Harry*?" He says that name with scorn.

"Yes, with Harry. With his father, Earl, before him." He was a nice man.

Tyler makes a noise. "How do you put up with that arrogant little punk, anyway?"

"I've known him forever, and he's not *all* bad. And the Hatchetts have been loyal clients to my family for decades." I hesitate.

"Plus, I have a lot of bills to pay, and he has a lot of dogs." It feels like a betrayal to my profession to admit that I'm with him, in part, for the money, but it's the truth. And the way Harry has been behaving, it's becoming the only respectable excuse. "I'm sure Frank Hartley would go out on the trail with you for the right price."

"Yeah, I'm noticing he likes to nickel and dime, but you already knew that, didn't you?" he says dryly.

"It's not my fault you didn't do your research." I give Tank my bare hand to sniff, but he dives for my glove instead, nipping at the thumb. I manage to pry it from his teeth with a soft scold. It's always a good sign, though, to see a sled dog's playfulness.

From the corner of my eye, I feel Tyler watching me.

"Maybe I should switch veterinarians. What would you think about that?"

I think that would be a *huge* problem for my steadfast commitment to *never* date a client again. I school my expression. "You'd have to make sure your new veterinarian can handle having you on her roster. She might be too busy."

He ladles hot water into the dishes. "She wouldn't be too busy for me."

I chuckle. "You sound pretty confident about that."

"Am I wrong?"

I search for the right answer. How hard to get should I play? Who am I kidding? I don't have time for games. "No, you're not wrong."

He smiles as he passes the bowls out to the dogs. Tank abandons all interest in my gloves. "Seriously, though, you should try mushing. There's nothing like being in the wilderness, just you and your dogs."

I shift out of his way, collecting my coffee from its perch on his sled. "I'm sure it's an experience." My attention wanders over the frozen tundra before us. I can't see much in the dark, but I've seen it in the daylight, and I know there's a whole lot of *nothing* between us and any other living person.

"Come out with me when I train for next year's race, so you can see what I mean."

"You haven't even finished this race, and you're already planning the next one?"

"As long as this team wants to run, I'll keep them running." He pats each dog's head as they dive into their meals.

"I'll think about it."

"I hope you do. My runs aren't short, like Harry's, though. I go all night."

I wasn't expecting that, and I choke on my coffee, coughing and sputtering.

My shocked reaction earns a chuckle from Tyler as he leans down to shift two bowls apart, separating the dogs. He meant *exactly* what his words imply, and I'm not sure we're talking about him hiring me as his veterinarian anymore.

Blood rushes with the knowledge that this exploding attraction isn't one-sided, not in the least. Whoever would've thought the angry, spiteful man I met in January would end up being someone I might be attracted to?

Definitely not me.

The sky is murky with predawn light when bundled bodies begin emerging from tents with more frequency, some heading to the outhouse, others to the hut, where a hearty plume of smoke billows from the pipe. Tyler's team will be ready to settle into another long stretch of sleep when they're done eating.

And I've lingered around one musher's team for too long to not stir a few whispers, if anyone's paying attention. Thankfully, Harry must still be asleep. I'll have to deal with him at some point, but I'll happily avoid him for as long as possible.

I brush off the snowflakes falling from my forehead. "They'll have a stack of pancakes ready in there, if you're hungry." While the mushers all have a supply of vacuum-sealed pizza and burritos in their drop bags to sustain them, checkpoint volunteers like Karen take pride in offering a hot meal.

"Starving." Tyler kneels in the snow, investigating his runners. Deciding what needs fixing later, after the dogs wake up from their second sleep. If these mushers aren't fussing over their dogs or catching up on rest, they're tinkering with their sleds. Some send an entire new one to a checkpoint ahead of time so they can swap out. "I'll be there in ten. Save me a few?" He caps that off with a wink.

"You'll be fine. Karen rations." I catch myself smiling as I head for the hut, my heart and mood light despite my frozen cheeks and rumbling belly, and I know that grin is one hundred percent because of the rookie musher from Whitefish, Montana, by way of Finland.

On my way, I slow to scan Harry's team without getting too close to disturb them. They're asleep on their straw beds, banks of snow beside them to cut the wind and jackets to keep them insulated. All sleep soundly, their noses tucked beneath their tails.

I still remember first learning about sled dogs sleeping out in the cold. It was at the Hatchett Kennels and I was seven. Earl Hatchett was three weeks out from the Iditarod and doing overnight training runs to get his team up to top condition, camping in the woods. I couldn't comprehend how any living thing could withstand minus-twenty-degree temperatures. Iggie, a pointer my father had rescued, spent his evenings sprawled on the kitchen floor by the woodstove, waiting for scraps. He'd be shaking within five minutes of stepping outside.

Earl being Earl, he was happy for any opportunity to educate how sled dogs are different from other dogs, how they not only tolerate the cooler temperatures better thanks to two layers of fur, but they also prefer it.

I had a tough time buying into his sermon, but in the years since I became a veterinarian and volunteered for this race, I've seen the truth in his words. With their heavy winter coats, spending too long indoors makes them uncomfortable. When allowed inside, it's not uncommon for these dogs to pace by their owner's door, panting, asking to be let out to cool off. Iditarod races during mild winters—still cold by human standards—see mushers forced to rest their teams for long stretches during the day and a record number of dropped dogs due to overheating.

Only when I confirm no signs of discomfort in the dogs—shivering or ice on their coats—do I feel comfortable moving on.

Lynn Corball, a musher from Seward who came in while I was sleeping, nods in greeting as she ladles broth into a dog dish. Rick said she checked in three hours ago. She should have her dogs sorted and be resting herself by now.

As if she can read my mind, she laments, "He didn't eat much earlier." She throws a flat look toward her sable-colored lead dog, who waits eagerly, his tail swishing. The other dogs are curled up on their straw beds but watching their musher intently.

I offer her a sympathetic smile. "At least he looks hungry now." Otherwise, as a veterinarian, I'd be concerned.

"You gave him too many snacks on the way in!" Harry calls out behind me, appearing from the shadows. His boots crunch in the snow, a hot coffee in hand. "Now you're gonna have a tough time settling them down again if you don't feed them all."

At that moment, Harry sounds like Earl. But, unlike Harry, Earl knew when *not* to share his wisdom.

Lynn shoots a glare his way before shifting back to her task. I'm sure she's none too pleased to be schooled by a musher half her age.

I'm equally displeased. I didn't want to deal with him yet. Why is he awake?

Harry, oblivious or not caring that his expertise is unwanted, shifts his attention to me. "Where were you last night when I rolled in? Didn't they tell you I was coming?"

"I was catching some sleep."

"Yeah, well, you're *my* veterinarian. I expected you there for my dogs." There's no mistaking the displeasure in his tone.

"I'm here for *all* the dogs, as a *volunteer*, and I can't do my job if I'm dead on my feet," I snap, my anger flaring.

"Whoa." Harry has the nerve to hold up a hand, to look taken aback by my reaction.

I inhale a deep breath to collect my composure. I'm hungry, and my patience is paper-thin. "What are you doing up? Couldn't you sleep?"

"I slept okay, except Brady decided to get up and make a bunch of noise just as I was settling in." His eyes wander past me to where Tyler's sled and team are resting, and they narrow. "If I hadn't gotten hung up in Ophir fixing my sled, that gold would've been mine."

"That's all part of racing, right?" It's a complex chain of speed, timing, and intuition, all of which can be derailed by countless variables, some manageable and others impossible to predict.

"Still, you should have seen the smug look on his face when I checked in. He was waiting to accept the trophy until I could get here, just so I could see him do it."

"He had to take care of his dogs first." Though I can't confirm that Tyler didn't take his time doing it.

But Harry's not listening. "He didn't leave that far ahead of me. Had to be pushing those dogs hard. You should check them out, make sure they're fit to race."

"I *did* check them when they came in. They were all fine."

"Well, you need to check again—"

"I *did*, just *now*, and they're *fine*," I say through gritted teeth. I know what he's doing. "How about I leave the racing stuff to you, and you leave the vet stuff to me, 'kay?" I throw the words he said to me in Rohn back in his face.

He works a retort around in his smarmy mouth, but when he meets my challenging glare, he seems to think better of it.

"I'm going to grab a bite—"

"Man, that last stretch coming in here last night was rough," he cuts in, taking a sip of his coffee. "There were a bunch of markers missing."

At least he's attempting a normal conversation. "It happens. Those things aren't permanently affixed to the ground." It's a monumental task every year to set some twelve thousand fluorescent-orange-tipped lath markers so the mushers don't get lost, especially if caught in a blizzard. "You told the crew so they can go out and fix them, right?"

"Yeah, yeah, of course. And sounds like people made it through fine." He pauses in thought. "Skip said they were down when he went through, too. Makes ya think, doesn't it?" He glances in Tyler's direction again. "It's like someone kicked them over."

There's only one "someone" that could be.

I realize which angle Harry's working, and my disgust swells. Not only is he arrogant enough to think he can manipulate me like this but it's beyond poor sportsmanship. "So, first, you accuse him of pushing his dogs too hard to get here ahead of you, and now you're saying he took time out of racing to sabotage you? A guy who went out of his way and put himself in danger to help Larry Reese in the gorge? Who stayed with him the whole way to make sure he made it in?" That story is circulating through all the checkpoints, earning Tyler prominence among both volunteers and mushers. "Harry, if you start going around accusing him of things without *any* proof, it's going to look bad, and not on him. On *you*."

"I didn't say it was Brady," Harry stumbles as he backpedals over his allegation.

"He was the first one through. Who else do you think it could be?"

"Yeah, well ... How is that possible, anyway? He's a rookie. How's he in the lead?"

"Maybe he's just that good, Harry."

He sneers as if tasting something sour. "Whose side are you on here?"

I've run out of patience. "The dogs' side. *Always* the dogs. Now go and take care of yours. I'm sure they're as hungry as I am." I move to leave.

"Wait, Marie—"

"And don't lecture Lynn again, unless you want to get strangled in your sleep." The list of potential assailants is growing by the minute. I'm ready to add my name to the page.

I march for the hut, not waiting for his response.

CHAPTER EIGHT

Laughter spills out with the warmth as I slip into the hut, shutting the door quickly behind me.

"… thought there might be a critter hidin' up in there, but there was nothing! And he spent half an hour barking at the damn tree before he'd run again!" Gary slaps his thigh as he chortles. "I sat there on my sled, freezin' my nuts off. I swear, he's the sweetest boy, but he's got bricks for brains."

A few volunteers are awake at this hour, and three of them are cramped around the table, holding paper plates for Karen to fill and sharing stories while they mentally prepare for the day. Most of these people just love the sport and the dogs, but some, like Gary, are recreational mushers themselves, and a few have tackled the two- and three-hundred-mile races—snack-sized qualifiers for anyone running in the Iditarod.

"Look who decided to join us!" Karen flips a pancake on her propane griddle. "I heard Terry burned the midnight oil and let you log in a few extra. Hope it helped?"

"It did. I'll have to thank him for that." *And* for sending Tyler to my tent. I hang my coat on a bent nail—a makeshift hook—by the door. The woodstove is kept blazing in the hut, and most people need to escape to the outdoors for relief. Sometimes I think that's by design, so no one lingers too long inside.

"Annie's about five miles out." Karen checks the watch strapped to her sturdy wrist. She's down to her base layer and an apron while she cooks. "After that, we likely won't see any new teams rolling in until the afternoon. So, you might be able to get a little more rest."

That depends on where Tyler is. He'll grab a few more hours once his dogs are settled, and I can't see myself getting a second of sleep, no matter how tired I am, if he's lying beside me.

Hopper reaches for another helping of pancakes.

"That'll be your fifth and final one," Karen announces with a warning stare.

The race judge drops his jaw in mock shock. "Who decides on these portions?"

"My wrists do! And my balance!" She looks pointedly down at the wooden crate she's standing on. More than one person has offered to saw inches off the legs to lower the counter-height table, but she insists this height is best for the masses. "I've got twenty volunteers to feed, plus all the press coming through, *plus* hungry mushers who could use a warm meal."

The sixty-one-year-old grandmother of three runs a kitchen in a greasy diner in Fairbanks. I'm sure she's used to having four skillets and countless spatulas going at once. Maybe not while standing on a box.

"Fair enough, but look at me!" Hopper gestures at his tall, beefy frame. He stands at well over six feet and looks like he hasn't missed a meal in his entire life plus a few extras on the regular. "Five pancakes won't get me through the morning!"

"And that's why you also get a sausage." She taps the pan that holds the lean red reindeer meat links before slipping her spatula under another pancake. "Marie, dear, grab yourself some food while it's hot. You barely ate last night."

I help myself and shift into a free spot, balancing my plate on one palm while I press my fork through the fried batter to try to cut it. "Does anyone have an update on Sam's flight here?" With the steady stream of mushers and their teams coming through beginning this afternoon, some staying to give their dogs a rest, other's plowing through in minutes, the more veterinarians for the task, the better.

"Not yet, but they'll get her here in time, don't you worry. It's supposed to be a sunny day."

I sense Hopper looming beside me. I look up to find him staring at my plate.

"You gonna eat *all* those?" he asks, earning my laugh. It's all in good fun, and yet Karen hops off her wooden crate and chases him away with her spatula and "Get outta here!" like he's a stray dog.

He scuttles out the door, snatching his winter coat on the way.

My breath catches as Tyler passes him on the way in. He gets more attractive every time I see him.

"The man with the gold has come for breakfast!" Karen exclaims in the same singsong tone she used for me.

"I heard there was a hot meal in here." Pretty eyes drift over faces, stalling a few extra beats on mine.

I feel a stupid grin forming, so I shovel in a forkful of pancakes to quell it. Only it's too much food, and I'm left struggling, pretending that my mouth isn't full. This *can't* be an attractive look.

"Hungry?" Karen asks, already loading up a plate.

"Not as hungry as Marie, from the looks of it." Tyler's smile is sly as he shucks his coat and hangs it.

I focus on chewing and marveling at the way Tyler moves, remembering what's under that thick wool sweater and ski pants.

"Ration's five pancakes and a sausage link. Two for you, because you need your strength." Karen winks as she hands him his plate. "Just don't tell Hopper."

"Your secret's safe with me." He sidles in beside me, though there's more space on the other side. "Good?"

I moan in answer, unable to manage a coherent word.

"I'll take that as a yes," he murmurs, digging in.

"You've surprised a lot of people, rookie." Gary shuffles over to pour himself more coffee. "You're a real contender now."

"As opposed to before?" There's a hint of arrogance in Tyler's tone, but in this case, it seems warranted. He *did* win the Finnmark race.

"Alaska's its own beast, as I'm sure you've already learned. Hope you got a few hours of decent sleep last night."

"Started out rough, but I definitely didn't want to leave my bed when I woke up."

I keep chewing, hoping my flushed cheeks aren't too obvious.

"Yeah, I'll bet a warm tent is better than a bale of straw out in the snow." Gary sets the empty pot back on the machine.

"You empty it, you brew it!" Karen chirps, not even turning from her griddle.

"Jeez, you got eyes on the back of your head, woman?"

She responds with a raucous cackle. "Sure do. And that thing takes twenty minutes, so you better get started."

Gary smooths fingers over his graying mustache while he studies the machine, a perplexed frown on his face as he lifts a flap and tests a few buttons. "This is different from mine."

"Here. I got it." Tyler shifts past me, his hand brushing my thigh in the process—whether by accident or intentionally, I can't tell—and sets his plate down to free his hands.

Another plus for Tyler: Doesn't balk at stepping in where needed, even for something as trivial as making coffee. My brother-in-law Jim would not have budged.

The list of appealing qualities grows.

Saves neglected animals, check.

Helps injured people, check.

Incredible kisser, even while unconscious. Check, check.

Gary moves out of the way to watch Tyler measure the grinds. "You got some good-lookin' dogs there."

"Thank you," Tyler says smoothly. "They come from strong lines of distance runners." A practiced response that he's probably given countless times.

"Oh, no doubt! Winning that big Finnish race, now makin' good time in the Iditarod as a rookie. There's talk you might win this. Wouldn't that be something? It's been decades since a rookie won." Gary's voice brims with approval. "You planning on breeding any of those dogs for sale? 'Cause I know of a few people already askin'."

"I'm considering it. To the right people." Tyler sets the brewer, collects his plate, and shifts back to his spot beside me.

Gary's momentarily distracted by a question from the other volunteer, and I'm guessing that's fine with Tyler because he doesn't seem overly interested in continuing that conversation.

I've finally swallowed my pancakes. "I didn't think you were serious about breeding them." I thought he said that in a moment of spite.

"I wasn't. But I also was." He carves into his sausage link. "The idea's growing on me."

"Hey, you're out near Fishhook, aren't you?" Gary suddenly asks. "Near the Hatchetts?"

"*Right* beside them," Tyler confirms, his tone flat as he mumbles, "unfortunately."

I give him a gentle elbow followed by a warning look. "Behave," I whisper. Gary's wife and Bonnie volunteer together at the Trapper's Crossing Christmas party and talk often.

His heated gaze flitters to my lips before it flips back. "Or what?"

My mouth goes dry as I search for a suitable answer.

"Well then, you best be careful with those dogs of yours. There's a thief in your area."

Gary's caution grabs my attention. "What do you mean? Someone's *stealing* sled dogs?"

"I guess you didn't hear the crazy story Jody Snyder was tellin' back at the hotel during registration." Gary dumps Coffee-Mate to his cup and stirs. "His uncle had a dog stolen right out of his kennel."

"Jody Snyder." That name rings a bell. "His uncle is Zed Snyder." A two-time Iditarod champion and well known in the community. Last I heard, he'd retired from racing and was doing tourist excursions.

"That's the one."

Beside me, Tyler chews quietly, seemingly indifferent to this concerning story.

"What happened?"

"Well, accordin' to Jody, Zed fed 'em their evenin' meal and they were all there when he went to bed. The next morning, he was short one."

"Maybe it broke off its chain?"

"No, ma'am. The chain was fine. The collar was hangin' off it, as if she slipped out. And the door to the enclosure was sittin' open to make it look like Zed forgot to close it, but he says he didn't forget to close that door. It looked like someone tried to cover their tracks, scrapin' their boot prints out of the snow with a shovel. But the trail led up to her house. He swears someone came right in and took her."

This is troubling. "Why her?"

"Not sure. She was up there in years, but she's produced some nice racers. Tom Scalding and Kerry Rice both have sled dogs from Zed."

I know both mushers. They've finished in the top ten in the Iditarod previously.

"She was a pup from one of Zed's favorite lead dogs. A pretty blonde with one blue eye and one brown."

An eerie prickle of familiarity trickles down my spine.

Beside me, Tyler shifts in his boots.

"Where'd you say Zed lives again?"

"Out his way—" He juts his chin toward Tyler, who seems intently focused on his plate of food. "Near Fishhook, on the Wasilla side."

I concentrate on my breathing as I process this information. If Nymeria is the dog they're talking about, that means Zed Snyder, a world-class musher back in the day, did *that* to her.

But Tyler's story doesn't line up with Gary's. Did someone steal the dog and let it loose in the woods? Or was Tyler lying to me? Did *he* slip onto Zed's property and take the dog right from beneath Zed's nose while he slept?

And what about all the other dogs? "Wouldn't Zed have heard the commotion?"

"That's what *I* said! 'Cause no one's walking into my kennel at night without stirring up a heck of a lot of noise. But he takes his hearing aids out at night. Didn't hear a damn thing." Gary waggles his index finger in the air. "Either this person knew that, or they got some big brass balls to be strollin' into a man's kennel."

"Strange that I haven't seen anything in the newspaper about it. Seems like a story the community would jump on," Tyler says casually. Too casually. "He must have reported it, right?"

Gary frowns. "You know, now that you mention it, I'm stunned I didn't read about it in the paper. Jody said his uncle was talkin' about retirin' her soon, but a man's property is his property, no matter what, so why wouldn't he go to the cops?"

"Good question." Tyler collects his remaining sausage in his fingers and tosses his plate in the bin on the way to the door. "Thank you for the hot meal. Much appreciated."

"Oh, you're so welcome, darlin'." Karen beams. "Now you go on and get some more rest before you're off again."

I watch Tyler's back until the door shuts behind him, my mind reeling with questions.

"He's a quiet one, huh?" Gary sips his coffee. "Likes to keep things close to his chest."

Karen cackles with laughter. "Don't know, but he's definitely a handsome one." She waves her spatula at me. "You two seem friendly. What do you know about our rookie?"

"Not much." How good his mouth feels against mine. That's about it, apparently.

"Heard he refused to give any interviews on the opening weekend," Gary says. "Not a one."

"He doesn't like the attention," I hear myself say, and it feels like a defense.

Karen snorts. "Well, I'm sure his neighbor stepped in to fill more than enough time slots."

That stirs Gary's laughter. *Everyone* has an opinion about Harry, and it's usually not flattering.

The volunteer standing next to him—a trailblazer named Eric, I think—pipes up. "I think he's racing his wife's dogs."

My teeth are halfway into a bite of sausage when my stomach drops to the plywood floor. "His *wife?*" He's *married*?

Eric winces. "Not anymore. She died. A few years ago, I think? I was reading some old articles online about him. Finnish news. She's the one who got him into mushing. Her family has a kennel in Finland. They're big into racing."

Of course. There must be write-ups on Tyler there, given he won their big race. Why hadn't I ever looked him up? My father mentioned relatives in Finland, only he thought it was Tyler's family. But if he married her, then they've become his as well.

"Some of those dogs were hers, I think."

My mind drifts to that badge on his sleeve.

Team Mila.

I'll bet that's not a sponsor.

I'll bet that's his late wife.

"Do you know how she died?" She had to have been young. Cancer? Car accident?

Eric shakes his head. His frown says, if it was mentioned, he doesn't remember.

I chew my food without tasting it as I replay that moment this morning with a new understanding. That's who Tyler was reaching for in his sleep. That's who he was kissing, professing his love to.

His dead wife.

And then he woke up to a harsh reality.

To me.

My appetite has all but vanished, but I don't dare toss the rest of my sausage link in the trash in front of Karen. Copying Tyler's move earlier, I shift for the door, tucking it between my teeth just long enough to pull on my jacket and hat. "Thank you for breakfast."

"Uh-huh. Lunch is chicken noodle soup and ham sandwiches, and we've got moose chili for supper."

I duck out the door as I'm mentally tallying the nights I've had chili so far. It's been *all* of them, except for that one night someone made moose *stew*. The roadkill lottery has been generous this year.

I spot Tyler right away, perched on a stump stool beside the blazing fire, stitching poly rope for his gangline. He looks up to see me but then shifts his attention back to his task—no smile, no beckon. Nothing to suggest he wants to explain himself.

He *must* realize that he'll need to. At least to me.

I gather my thoughts as I approach, deciding how to broach … what, exactly? Which topic is less icy to tread on: His status as a widower or dog thief?

"I thought you'd already be asleep." I settle down on the log next to him. There are eight stools around the fire—hunks of a giant hardwood, hauled in by snowmachine or ATV from a terrain where more grows than these spindly black spruces.

"Soon."

I watch the flames dance and listen to the fire crackle as I consider that day we met. The more I think about it, I already know the answer. Reed said they'd get in trouble if anyone found that dog on their property. At the time, I assume he meant because she had been neglected, but that wasn't it.

It's because someone stole her from Zed Snyder.

Tyler chuckles. "You like to choose your words before you speak, don't you?"

"I'm not usually one to blurt something out, no. Not unless I'm *really* upset."

"And are you? Really upset?" He studies me.

I consider that question. I assume he means about Nymeria and not the whole mistaking-me-for-his-dead-wife bit. He doesn't know that I know, and it's not like there has been a reasonable—or expected—place for him to bring her up. "No. I don't think so." I pause. "But why?"

"Besides the obvious?"

He hasn't denied committing the crime.

He peers over his shoulder, scanning our surroundings that brighten with each passing minute ahead of an impending sunrise. Everyone is busy with tasks or huddled in their warm tents, resting. "I was in Wasilla, meeting with some friends in a pub. Zed was there. He sat down to shoot the shit for a while, and I overheard him talkin' about a dog he was set to retire. The last litter she gave was small, the puppies not looking like good sled dogs. She'd made him a lot of money over the years, but she'd hurt her leg in a fight with another dog recently, and it wasn't worth spending the money to get it fixed. She was eight. He figured it was time for her to go."

My teeth grind. "And by 'go,' you don't mean adopting her out to a good home."

Tyler shakes his head. "Wouldn't even consider it."

Fucking Zed Snyder. He's clearly of *that ilk*, the type of musher who thinks it's reasonable—humane, even—to put a dog down when they're no longer "working" for him. They draw a solid line between a sled dog and a family pet and are adamant the two can never wear the same label. My parents have three retired sled dogs who prove that isn't true. In Nymeria's case, at eight, she could still have another six years of a happy life in someone's loving home.

Fortunately, this type of musher is few and far between nowadays. Unfortunately, they do still exist. And worse, there's no way to stop guys like Zed from "retiring" their dogs when they're no longer of use, no state law to protect dogs like Nymeria.

This is at the very root of the issue I have with the sport in our state.

"So you, what, followed Zed home from the bar?"

Tyler's bare hands work smoothly over the rope, as if the cold doesn't bother him. "I didn't need to. It's easy enough to find information around here."

"Oh right, your police chief buddy. He's willing to bend rules for you?" Or outright break them.

"Speaking of friends who bend rules, how's your animal control officer doing?"

Touché. "He's great. Thanks for asking."

Tyler smirks, but his amusement slips quickly. "I was still thinking about the guy and the dog a few days later. Couldn't shake it for some reason. I started thinking that I should take a trip over and see if she was still alive. And then I wondered what I'd do if she was. I knew he wouldn't give her up. That kind of guy is set in his ways." He collects another piece of poly rope from his box. "I saw Zed's hearing aids. I knew he'd likely take them out at night to sleep and probably wouldn't hear anything if someone were to go in there. So I decided to risk it. And when I saw her, when I saw how she'd been kept ..." The muscle in his jaw ticks. "I *wanted* him to hear the dogs barking, I *wanted* him to come out and explain himself to me. I would have ..." His voice drifts, the words left hanging.

"So you took her." A risk, given he wouldn't know if she had been microchipped.

"Yeah," he admits. "Brought her home, tried to make her comfortable. Called Frank to tell him I'd found an injured dog wandering in the woods who needed care. It was Saturday night, though. Couldn't get hold of him."

"Yeah, Frank doesn't give out his home number, even for emergencies."

"And you do?"

"For my patients? Of course." Sometimes I regret it, especially at two in the morning when I get a call because a cat is hacking on a hairball.

"The rest happened like I said it did." He tosses the rope into a crate. "But now she's doing well. Her leg is on the mend. She's putting on pounds, getting used to our dogs and her new home. Her new life."

Surely, she would have been dead by now. If not by the end of Zed's gun barrel—because he'd be too cheap to pay for a needle—then from festering wounds. "What about the other dogs in the kennel? How were they?"

"I did a quick once-over because I needed to get out of there, but they seemed fine from what I could see. Someone should pay a visit, though."

And someone named Howie will. I'll make sure of that. "You basically trespassed and stole a dog that was on death row."

"Not basically. Exactly. And if I had to do it again, I would, a hundred times over." His smile is soft. "There is no line."

A shiver runs down my spine as he echoes my words from earlier. How can I fault him for doing what he did? What *I* would do, if I had the nerve. I can't. I can only like him *more* for it. If I have a weakness for anything besides an injured or scared animal, it's for the man who's willing to swoop in to save it.

Really, there's nothing I find more attractive.

But worry gnaws at me. "The Hatchetts know about the dog.

If they hear Jody's story, they're going to put two and two together and Harry is, well, feeling threatened by you." That's becoming clearer with all his pathetic accusations and conjecture. "He won't be quiet about what he knows."

"The only people who know the truth are you, me, and Reed. As far as anyone else knows, I found a neglected dog wandering in the woods and brought her home." He shrugs. "And if Zed or Harry wants to stir up shit, let them try. I have all Frank's reports on her condition when I found her, and I'll make sure those newspaper people write about how an Iditarod champion abused one of his dogs. A dog whose pups a few of these mushers around here are racing now. My guess is Zed was afraid of how it'd look if people tied her to him, and he didn't want to risk stirring up attention. Probably been tiptoeing on eggshells."

And the Hatchetts wouldn't want that kind of attention, either. Earl bred a few of his dogs with Zed's. Plus, any negative news against a musher is bad for the sport overall. While Harry might have seen Tyler as a threat worth going after, Zed's crimes would only hurt the Hatchetts' kennel in the end.

Tyler has given this serious thought.

"Don't worry, your secret's safe with me."

"What kind of secrets are we tellin'?" The snow crunches beneath Hopper's heavy boots as he storms up to the bonfire, lifting his arms over it as if to collect some warmth. "You whisperin' sweet nothings to our beautiful veterinarian, musher?"

"That's what I was just telling her, actually. How beautiful she is." Tyler's eyes roam my features, and I see appreciation within.

I'm caught off guard by the blatant compliment, even if it's just a cover for our conversation, and I feel my cheeks flush.

"We got a team comin' in." Hopper abandons the fire. "Number forty-two!"

"I guess that means I'm back on duty." I peer over my shoulder toward the trail, and then at the bodies on the move, readying to greet them. They'll be here in minutes. There's no sign of Terry.

He must still be in the tent. I'll let him sleep, seeing as he was kind enough to do the same for me last night.

"You planning on greeting number forty-two with that?" Tyler nods to the half-eaten reindeer sausage I still have within my mitt.

In the depth of our conversation, I'd forgotten it. I laugh, shove it into my mouth, and stand, stretching to rid myself of the chill of the hard surface against my backside. The move does nothing for my reluctance. "You should get your sleep while the dogs are resting," I say between chews. Because he'll be lucky to get one or two hours over the next several days that it'll take to get to the finish line in Nome.

He tosses the line he was working on into the crate. "I will."

Will he still be sleeping later when it's my turn to nap? If I lie down next to Tyler, will I catch a repeat of this morning?

The practical side of me asks if I want that, without learning more about this guy. But now is not the time to ask about his late wife. I wouldn't even know how, anyway. But he's been flirting with me all morning, so he must have made peace with the loss.

He just told me he thinks I'm beautiful.

"Hey, Marie?"

I stall, happy for any excuse to linger. "Yeah?"

"If I'm not up by noon, you mind waking me?"

It's not uncommon for a musher to ask a volunteer for a wake-up call. It's on our list of duties. And yet nerves stir in my stomach. "No problem."

"Just, you know," he peers at me from below that thick fringe of lashes, "give me a kick, or something."

"A *kick*?" I echo. "Is that what you want?" That isn't what I had in mind.

He bows his head for a moment and when he lifts it again, he's grinning. "Or something."

The volunteers are beginning their celebratory cheer as the

dogs charge forward, tongues lolling. It's time for me to go, though I want to follow Tyler back to the tent.

"Don't worry, I'll make sure you're up." I march away before he can see the color in my face that isn't caused by the cold. I'm halfway to the checkpoint entrance when I can no longer fight the urge to peek over my shoulder.

Tyler is still sitting on the stump, watching me, his expression pensive.

CHAPTER NINE

"I'm starvin'." Jonah rubs his stomach. "What do they got here today?"

"Soup and sandwiches, Karen said earlier."

Hopper, within earshot, corrects, "*A* sandwich." He drops a hand on Jonah's shoulder. "Not nearly enough to feed men our size, my friend. Not nearly enough."

It's true that they're both big men with appetites, though where Hopper's parka stretches across a bulbous midsection, beneath Jonah's down coat, there's nothing but flat muscle.

"How big are these sandwiches?" Jonah squints at the hut. The sun has climbed high in the sky, and its reflection against the blanket of snow is blinding without sunglasses, which he must have left in his plane when he arrived at the checkpoint with Sam.

As thrilled as I was to see the familiar orange and white plane, I can already hear the complaints brewing on his tongue. Jonah gets cranky when he hasn't eaten—worse than me. "Don't start whining."

"Shut up." He gives my shoulder a playful shove. "You hungry?"

"What time is it?" I ask casually. As if I haven't been acutely in tune with the minutes and hours passing since I parted ways with Tyler, obsessing over how soon I can slip into my own sleeping bag under the guise of a nap. But I haven't had a chance. Annie swept through and dropped two dogs in our care before she continued on, both sweet girls showing hints of a tendinitis flare-up. And then the buzz of the approaching plane announced Sam's arrival, who happened to be catching a lift with Jonah, and ... here we are. I'm equal parts exhausted and wired.

Jonah checks his watch. "Quarter to twelve."

My heart skips a few beats. "I'm actually gonna try to get an hour or two of sleep before the afternoon rush." Several teams are on their way here and, with the *balmy* minus-ten-degree weather, they'll be resting their dogs for a few hours to keep them from overheating.

He grimaces and looks around. "Am I gonna have to deal with that idiot?"

It's my turn to reach out and shove him. I don't have to ask who he means. Jonah has heard me gripe about the Hatchetts enough times to have made up his mind about Harry without even meeting him. "He's sleeping." *Thankfully.*

Jonah grunts in response. "Fine. I'll get your sandwich for you."

I bark out a laugh. "Bullshit, you'll *eat* my sandwich for me."

"You know me too well, Lehr." He winks.

I *do* know Jonah too well, and he'd give me the boots off his feet if I needed them. "Don't leave without saying goodbye!" I watch his back as he veers off, sauntering to the little hut that will surely feel smaller with his larger-than-life presence in it.

My stomach is a ball of tension as I approach the yellow tent, toying with the idea of turning around and coming back in fifteen minutes, when it wouldn't seem like I'm angling to pick up where we left off.

The tents are spread out, away from the cook hut and the dog teams, guaranteeing some degree of quiet. I'm careful as I draw open the zipper, hoping the sound of it sliding against its teeth doesn't disturb Tyler. Inside, the air is on the verge of being too cool, the wood in the stove nothing more than glowing embers.

Tyler sleeps on his back like before, his arctic bag pulled to his chin.

I admire his still, handsome face for a moment before turning away. I shuck my outer clothes and boots, hanging them on the line next to his, thankful for the stop Terry and I made in McGrath on the way here yesterday morning to shower at the laundromat. By the time I catch a flight home, I'll smell as bad as the sled dogs I'm treating.

My attention gets caught on the black-and-white badge on Tyler's sleeve.

Mila. Am I right? Was that his wife's name?

Is he wearing her name on his sleeve in her honor?

His heart on his sleeve?

What has this man been through?

There's so much about Tyler that I don't know, and yet here I am, eager to hear him tell me how beautiful I am again, hoping this time he'll roll over to kiss me and it *won't* be a mistake.

"It's not noon already, is it?" Tyler's sleepy croak startles me.

"In another fifteen minutes. I'm sorry, I thought I was being quiet enough."

"You were." He smooths his hands over his face. "It's me. I've been drifting in and out."

"That's not good." I step over him to stuff a log into the stove and then I make my way around to slip into the warmth of my sleeping bag, adrenaline racing.

He rolls onto his side. "Is something wrong?"

I realize my flurry of thoughts sits plainly on my face. "I was looking forward to kicking you awake, is all."

His crooked smile may as well be an accusation of my ulterior motives. "I can close my eyes and pretend to be asleep so this plays out." Our mattress pads are still butted against each other. He's lying *so close* to me.

"My plan has already lost its luster." I pray the cold air hides the flush from my reddened cheeks.

"I should have kept quiet, then. I'm not always a smart man."

I shift to face him. "Wow. I never thought I'd hear *you* admit that."

"I have moments of weakness." His voice has turned raspy. "This is definitely shaping up to be one of them."

The silence in the tent is palpable as I study the tiny golden flecks in his irises and the deep green ring that surrounds his pupils. I sense him shifting ever so slowly toward me, and my heart rate races with anticipation.

But then a troubled expression fills his face, as if he's remembering something that perturbs him.

"Is something wrong?" I echo his question of a few moments ago.

"No, nothing. Just ..." Turning onto his back once again, he studies the tent's ceiling, his breathing measured and slow. "I should get up. I have a long way to the finish line, and my dogs need *all* my focus."

As opposed to giving some of it to the infatuated veterinarian who is eager to climb onto your lap.

I smile, even as my discontent stirs. "You're right, they do." We can always pick this up back home, after the race. "Get out of here already and let me sleep."

He climbs out of his sleeping bag with a stretch.

I watch him as he collects his bedroll and sleeping bag, securing them to tuck back into his sled. Too fast, he has all his outer gear on and is pulling on his hat.

Is it just me, or does he seem eager to get away?

He's peeling back the zipper when Karen's reedy voice carries. "You've already had your ration, Hopper!"

She must be chasing him out of the hut again. It makes me laugh, despite my disappointment.

Tyler watches the debacle outside unfold. "Any idea what's for lunch?"

"Soup and a sandwich."

"That sounds perfect."

Not as perfect as if Tyler turned around and slid into my sleeping bag for a few hours. "I'll see you later?"

He falters. "You know where to find me." With that, he's gone, shuttering the tent and leaving me alone.

Sleep evades me.

———

The cacophony of dogs barking and tugging on their harnesses has the nearby teams howling in protest. They *all* want to run, but after a full twenty-four-hour rest, Tyler's dogs are heading toward the trail.

Tyler and my paths danced around each other all afternoon without ever crossing. Or maybe it was my path that weaved in and out, looking for a reasonable opportunity to cut in while he toiled away on his sled, replacing the runners, tightening bolts, taking full inventory and rearranging. I never did find the right time, wanting to respect his space while he prepared to leave.

But now he's about to take off, across the tundra and along the Bering Sea, and I feel the overwhelming urge to speak to him one more time before he leaves.

"Counting down the minutes?"

"Basically." He checks his watch, his mood subdued. I guess mine would be, too, if I had days and another four hundred miles ahead of me.

My gaze floats off into the waning sun. There's a lot of nothing out there. Anywhere from ten to thirteen hours of snow and stunted trees, depending on how fast he travels until he reaches the next checkpoint in Ruby. Hours of just him and his dogs and his drifting thoughts. Some mushers have claimed traversing those flat plains are the most challenging.

Gary is heading this way with a clipboard to take down information to feed into the official race, which means Tyler's time at this checkpoint has come to an end.

"Good luck, stay safe, and call me when you're back in town. We can grab a coffee or dinner or something." It's as overt an invitation as I can collect the nerve to offer.

"Yeah …" The smile I get back is not the playful smirk I was growing used to. It's sad and full of resignation. "I think we might have gotten off on the wrong foot. *Again.* This was fun, Marie, and you're an incredible woman, but I don't want to make it more than it is."

An uncomfortable, cold feeling washes over me.

Tyler searches the expanse of wilderness. "I can't get into it because I'm about to go out there with my dogs, and my head has to be one hundred percent focused on them, but the truth is, I was married once and now I'm widowed, and my life is the way I want it. Uncomplicated."

I force a wide smile. "Well, if you change your mind, you know where to find me." How else do I respond, after that shutdown?

What the hell happened?

"I won't change my mind. Not about this." His intense eyes lock on mine. "But friends, I can do. I'd *really* like to do. I think you're pretty cool."

"Friends. Great."

Friends.

Great.

He tugs on his fur-lined mittens. "Come by the kennel sometime. I'll give you that tour I didn't want to give you before."

I can't tell if he's serious or if it's a vacant offer—I don't have his number to call ahead so he'll unlock the gate—but I nod, anyway.

"Ready." The sled jerks with the dogs' wild jumps at that softly spoken command.

Gary saunters over. "Okay, musher number ten, looks like you're off?"

"I am."

Gary scribbles down the time.

Tyler's jaw is set with determination as he releases the snow hook. His sled speeds away with a round of cheers from the volunteers. He throws an arm up to wave but doesn't look back.

CHAPTER TEN

A deep rumble sounds in Bentley's chest, his rapt attention on my laptop monitor as fourteen dogs run toward the Burled Arch, their path lined with cheering fans and bright spotlights to cast out the darkness.

"You remember that, huh?" I stroke the husky's fur with my fingers, comforted by his warmth next to me as we watch the livestream of the Iditarod from my bed. "I'll bet you miss it." It's been five years since Bentley was retired from his racing team, and while the dog never crossed that finish line in first place, he completed the grueling journey to Nome enough times to be considered a world-class canine athlete by many in the mushing community.

It feels good to be home, and yet the sudden and complete silence after so many days of people and planes and hoopla is at the same time disconcerting.

Jonah and I landed in Trapper's Crossing early this afternoon. My truck was waiting for me where I left it, cold and buried under a foot of snow.

After a lengthy scalding shower to soothe my aching muscles and a touch-base call to Cory to learn all that I'd missed in my days away, I swung by my parents' place, collected a dog and a plate of lasagna, and came back to my little cabin in the woods.

All day, I lectured myself about how I didn't need to lose another moment of sleep over dogsled races and mushers, how I needed to get back to regular programming. And yet my carefully laid plan of passing out from exhaustion was foiled the moment I knew Tyler was going to win the Iditarod.

He took the lead after Unalakleet and has held it, growing it by the hour as he raced along the coast, whipped by high winds across Norton Bay near Shaktoolik and then narrowly escaping a snow squall before White Mountain that slowed several other mushers.

They've been preparing for his grand entrance for hours in Nome, and now, after nine days and ten hours of racing crossing the Alaskan wilderness, I'm watching Tyler cross the finish line.

I could lie and say my only interest is in the dogs—like it was when I stayed up to watch Harry cross last year—but I wouldn't be fooling anyone, including myself.

Still, I let my attention shift to the dogs for as long as possible. There's nothing in their gaits to suggest Tyler worked them too hard, but I already know he wouldn't. The veterinarians handling the finish line won't find anything worrisome with any of them.

The team passes under the mammoth carved wooden archway, and Tyler pushes back his hood. My excitement and disappointment war inside, constricting my chest. He's achieved something no one has since 1975: he has won the Iditarod as a rookie.

And he did it with his entire team of dogs crossing the finish line. Another rarity.

Based on the GPS tracking, Harry will come in fourth, behind Skip and last year's winner, Jessie Schwartz from Seward. But he's a good seven hours behind. Tyler will be snoring in a warm bed by the time the next racers slide into town.

For a man who was so convinced this was his year to shine, Harry is going to be *furious*.

Reporters flock toward Tyler with their cameras and microphones angled as he throws a hand up to the crowd. The commentator, a man with a deep, buttery voice, interprets the scene—the chaos, the excitement, the adrenaline that must be coursing through Tyler's veins.

Tyler looks rough. More than nine days without a shave or a decent sleep, beyond the one he had lying next to me. The ruff around his hood is iced over, his skin is wind-burned, his eyes red and drawn.

But a serene look passes over his features, overshadowing all those other details, and when he tips his head back toward the night sky, it's as if I can feel his triumph radiating through the screen. It gives me a small reprieve from the awkward exchange at our parting, a moment where I can be happy for him and his accomplishment.

It doesn't last long, though, as he flaunts that devastatingly handsome smile at the crowd and cameras flash, capturing the moment.

My stomach sinks with the bitter heaviness of regret. How did I misread everything so epically ... *again*? I was *so sure* there was something more between us than friendly banter. But did I imagine everything? Was he leaning in to kiss me, or was it *me*, leaning into *him*? Was his comment about me being beautiful just innocent flattery? Jonah has told me I'm beautiful before, too, and look where that ended.

I'm thirty-eight years old. I can repair torn ACLs and clear blockages from intestines, reconnect nerve tissue, and, when necessary, amputate limbs, but I can't accurately decipher when a man is flirting with me?

I didn't understand how much I was hoping for this thing between us to be real until Tyler told me it wasn't.

The rest of my time at the checkpoint was a blur. I threw

myself into my task, focusing on the teams coming through to keep my mind from wandering, working until I slumped into my sleeping bag, my eyelids shutting almost instantly.

Tyler drops his snow hook and is off his sled, heading for the dogs with a bag of pork belly, their tails wagging. Meanwhile, the race officials rummage through his sled, ensuring he has all the mandatory gear as required by the rules, including the dog diary I signed, before they can officially declare him the winner.

It's difficult to see through the crowd, but he pauses long enough to hug an older gentleman. No one I recognize. His father, maybe? I never asked Tyler if he had someone waiting for him at Nome, but it would make sense. Most mushers have a handler lined up for when they arrive in the city, so the dogs can be properly cared for while they rest.

From there, it's an assembly line of procedure—Grant McManus introduces Tyler to the crowd as the champion before shuttling him over to hand him the oversized prize check for photo ops, and then beyond to a slogan-laden presentation of a pickup truck from the sponsoring dealership. Finally, they head to a table, where Tyler sits with Tank and Nala, and the officials place yellow rose garlands around the lead dogs' necks.

I smile as he ropes his arms around them, pulling them tight to his side, his grin for the cameras genuine and wide.

Reporters converge with microphones and questions, and I strain to hear his answers around all the background noise, hoping to glean a bit more insight on a man who avoids talking about himself.

"You were living in Finland before you moved to Alaska last summer. And you raced and won the Finnmarksløpet, the longest dogsled race in Europe, a year ago at this time. How would you compare these two trails?" a female reporter, unseen on the screen, asks.

"They're both incredibly challenging. The Finnmark is a bit shorter at 750 miles, but with strong winds across the fells and the temperatures, it can get treacherous. I'd say finishing either is a great feat, no matter whether you're first or last." His eyes dart to the camera before shifting to a spot on the ground

"Did you grow up mushing?" a man asks.

"I didn't. I discovered it a few years ago, when I moved to Finland from Montana and fell in love with it immediately."

"You say you've only been doing this for a few years, and yet here you are, a world champion of the Finnmarksløpet and now the Iditarod."

"Maybe *more* than a few years." He grins sheepishly. "And I had good training. Tero and Anja Rask, of Rask Huskies in Finland, have been mushing their entire lives. Tero has raced and won the Finnmarksløpet three times. They're both here, actually. Right over there." He points somewhere beyond the camera and throws up a wave, I assume, to them.

I mentally take note of the names, intent on searching them once I can peel my gaze from Tyler's face. That answers the question about the man he hugged.

"You were married to their daughter, Mila Rask, also a competitive musher in Finland. Is that how you were introduced to mushing?" another male voice asks. They're firing questions at Tyler from all angles, as if armed with them ahead of time. I guess that makes sense. No one has been able to pin him down until now, and people watching want to know about this year's champion.

The muscle in Tyler's jaw ticks. "Yes, that's right. My wife's family are big into mushing and when I met her, I fell in love. With everything, I guess. Her. The dogs. The life."

My heart squeezes, hearing him so candidly admit that.

"Mila Rask was a top-five finalist in the Finnmarksløpet in previous years and expected to win one day, until she tragically passed away during childbirth just under two years ago, as did your son. Did you …"

The reporter's question fades with the blood rushing to my

ears, my horrified focus on Tyler's face as it takes on a stony expression. This reporter clearly dug into Tyler's personal life in preparation for the interview. Why would he mention that on a livestream as Tyler's celebrating his win, though?

No wonder Tyler avoids interviews.

My stomach churns as I wait for Tyler's answer to the insensitive ass's question—whatever it was. "That's right. This is Mila's team." His attention shifts to Tank, his hand scratching the dog's chest. "She always talked about racing the Iditarod, and so it was a no-brainer that I would do it for her now that she can't. This race, and this win, was for her."

"And a monumental win it is! A thirty-seven-year-old rookie crossing under the Burled Arch with his full team ..." The questions drift into another direction—about the race's challenges, about what his postrace routine looks like, about next year—and I only half listen.

Tyler would have been about thirty-five when he lost his wife. Not just her, either. A son, too. How did it happen? Did he drive her to the hospital, their hands clasped, their senses buzzing with excitement and nerves, and all the possibilities for years to come, of a full life together?

Only to drive home alone?

Mila's bag in the trunk, empty car seat in the back.

No wife.

No child.

What would she say about all he's accomplished in her honor?

How often does he think about her?

I can't imagine the pain that must consume him from the moment he wakes until he drifts off at night.

How do you get over something like that?

Not in two years, you don't.

Possibly never.

My life is the way I want it. Uncomplicated.

Our last parting is beginning to make more sense. Maybe I

wasn't imagining everything after all. Maybe there *was* a spark of interest there, at least a physical one, but it's clear he's still living for his wife.

For a ghost.

I can't compete with a ghost.

I'll never win.

I don't even want to try.

CHAPTER ELEVEN

June

"Linda told me they were interested, but that was back in January." Harry scowls at Ginger, an aptly named husky with tawny fur, but his thoughts are not on the dog.

"Then give her a call."

"I did. *Twice.*" His eyes cut to me. "Left a message, too. She hasn't called me back yet. Same with Sam, and he was talking about taking a couple."

I know he's hoping I'll have an explanation to ease his worries. This is what happens during my visits to the Hatchetts' kennel—Harry unloads his problems and looks to me for answers and reassurance. "She did scratch in this year's race, and she's getting up there in age. Maybe she's thinking retirement soon, which means it doesn't make sense to bring on a new dog. She's raced, what, nine or ten times?"

"Twelve."

"There you go. That's a lot for anyone."

Harry works his jaw over his brooding thoughts. "Yeah, maybe you're right."

I collect my black medical bag and begin heading toward my truck. My job here is finished, and my afternoon is full of appointments at the clinic.

Harry lumbers beside me. Clearly, he's not finished yet. "And Gary was talking about signing up for the next Iditarod and taking Dodger and Sailor, but I haven't heard from him, either."

"Gary Seymore?" The volunteer from Cripple?

"Yeah. He did the qualifiers with the two of them and made decent time."

The two huskies in question are standing on top of their respective houses, watching Harry's hired help—a twenty-one-year-old named Benji with aspirations to race the Iditarod one day—check water dishes. They're solid lead dogs. Obviously not Harry's best, which he uses for his own team.

"I agreed to give him a referral and everything." Harry shrugs, like he doesn't understand what else could be stopping Gary from racing next year.

"He has time to commit. And four grand just to sign up is a lot. *Plus* your fees for those two."

He smooths a hand over the back of his neck. "What am I gonna do, if I keep breeding and training these dogs, and no one wants them?" He sounds less like the cocky ass who grins at spectators and more like the gangly boy who used to trail around Earl, hanging on to his every word.

"I think you're getting ahead of yourself," I say calmly. "You have great sled dogs, and everyone knows that."

"My father never had this issue. People were lined up for our dogs when he was alive." His eyes drift over the property. "If I'd won this year's race, this wouldn't be an issue. I *should* have won. I don't know what happened."

Tyler beat him. That's what happened, plain and simple. And in the months that have followed, I've heard Tyler's name on more than one musher's lips, along with questions about what the champion's "stock" is like and whether he'll be breeding or renting out his dogs.

It wasn't only Tyler who beat him, though. Harry didn't come in second. He came in fourth.

The truth is, Hatchett Kennels still produces top talent sled dogs—Harry knows how to train them—and many of the best mushers have lineage from here, but people have been lured away by the new and shiny—the Iditarod champion who relocated to Alaska with dogs of fresh lineage.

But I'm not about to point that out. I have things to do, and Harry no doubt already knows.

Now I just need to get out of here before Bonnie Hatchett arrives to complain about something. "I have to get back to the clinic. Bottom line, Ginger looks good, and I've given all of them their shots." I nod toward the sizable kennel where the older puppies roam, untethered, curiously watching. They're too young for training yet, still months away from mingling with the older dogs and learning the pecking order. "Change the bandages on Motto's paw tonight before bed and use the ointment." The dog got a big thorn stuck between his toes during a run that Harry couldn't extract. "The usual deal with the bill okay?"

Unlike Bradley Garvis and his ferrets—who never paid his bill and hasn't been back since—I never worry about Harry paying. Cory will invoice him tomorrow, and he'll swing by to settle within a day or two.

"Yeah, about that." His forehead puckers. "We need to come up with some kind of arrangement."

Unease slides down my spine. "What kind of arrangement were you thinking?"

"I've been goin' over numbers, and my vet bills are *high*, Marie."

"Well, yeah, you have seventy-five dogs." It seems like I'm out here almost every week.

"I get that. But my family has been loyal to your clinic for years. Decades, actually. Like, I crunched the numbers." He pulls out a small notebook from his back pocket and flips through to show me a mess of hand-scratched calculations. "You've made *a lot* of money on us, especially over the last few years since my dad died."

"Because you've called me out here a lot." Earl had years of experience. He knew how to pull a thorn from his dog's paw and when to have it treated by a professional. "And you've gotten *a lot* of personalized veterinarian care during that time." Where is Harry going with this?

"Right, but am I paying what I *should* be paying? I mean, I've always been good to you, but business is business." He falters. "I'd hate to have to look elsewhere."

I bite my tongue, waiting for him to continue.

He adjusts his stance, pulling his shoulders back, and says firmly, "You need to do better with your rates and your service. That's what I'm saying."

I struggle to keep my jaw from falling open. Does he realize how good *I've* been to *him* over the years? How many times I've prioritized his kennel over my other clients, dropping everything to race out here when he's called? He already gets a discounted rate as it is. Hell, I don't charge him a home visit fee or for my travel out here!

But losing the Hatchetts' business would be a significant loss of income. It wouldn't completely ruin me, but it would hurt. The question is—what's more important, my business's bank account or my pride?

I tamp down my shock and frustration and clear my throat. I need my father's advice. "I will evaluate my costs and fees and get back to you. How about that?"

"That sounds reasonable, Marie. I know you'll come up with a plan. And, make no mistake, I appreciate you." I sense triumph in that look. Like he assumes he's won.

I grit my teeth as I climb into my truck. With a standard wave out the window—I'd prefer to flash a middle finger—I edge my truck along the pothole-riddled driveway. It's in desperate need of some fresh gravel. The property has fallen into disrepair since Earl's death. I don't know if that's Harry's inability to focus on more than the dogs, or if the money situation is worse than I suspected. Given this rehearsed speech he just delivered, it could be money related, but it could just as easily be Harry's ineptitude.

I'm fuming by the time I reach the end of their driveway. The fastest way to the clinic is to my left.

I turn right instead, hoping the extra fifteen minutes I've just tacked on to my drive will clear my head.

The driveway one over from the Hatchetts' looks the same as when I last stopped with a handwritten letter in my grasp, only without the blanket of winter to veil the bramble on either side of the gate. I'll bet that barrier has proven more useful with his newfound fame. The trespassing signs still hang prominently from the trees.

But the personalized one for me has been taken down, I note, as I slow to a stop in front of the lane.

It's been three months since the race, and I've done my best to push out all thoughts of Tyler.

After spending several days scouring the internet to read everything about Mila Rask and Tyler Brady's life together, of course. It wasn't hard to find information and pictures. Rask Huskies has an entire section dedicated to Mila—to her life, her achievements, which were impressive in the mushing community. She was gorgeous. Tall and slender, with sharp cheekbones, brown eyes, and jet-black hair rather than the more common to Scandinavian blue eyes and blonde hair. She styled it in various lengths, from pixie cut to a chin-length bob. And their life together looked perfect, living in Finland's northernmost region of Lapland, on the family's farm with a full staff of handlers and two hundred sled dogs trained to run tourist expeditions in the arctic wilderness.

The disappointment that overwhelmed me when Tyler and I parted still lingers, a dull nuisance that reminds me every so often of those brief moments at the checkpoints—the looks, the smile, that kiss. All parts of a man who is still very much in love with his dead wife.

If he wasn't, it might have gone somewhere.

I would have at least liked the opportunity to find out.

I throw my truck in gear and continue, rounding the bend in the dirt road.

A lone figure approaches, jogging in the middle of the road. These roads are so seldom used, it's not surprising that a jogger wouldn't use the shoulder, but the man isn't making much effort to move, shifting only a few feet to his right, forcing me to slow to a crawl.

I'm twenty feet away when I recognize Tyler.

A curse slips out even as my heart races, my eyes sizing up the soft gray T-shirt that clings to his torso, and the simple black track shorts that highlight lean but muscular calves and thighs.

A second curse slips when I realize he's recognized me, and he's coming to a stop.

"Thought that was you," he says through pants, giving his sweat-soaked T-shirt a tug away from his stomach, drawing my attention to cut biceps. "Here to see Harry?"

"I was. I'm on my way back to the clinic now."

He points in the opposite direction. "Isn't it that way?"

"I have a stop to make," I lie smoothly. He knows where my clinic is, which means he must have looked it up. I push aside the little spark that pricks me with that awareness. "Congratulations. You know, on winning."

He nods but doesn't say anything more. Is this as awkward for him as it is for me?

I swallow against this uncomfortable feeling that swells in my chest, torn between wanting to stay but then remembering our last exchange and thus desperate to leave. "So, what have you been up to? Besides polishing all your trophies." It wasn't enough that Tyler won the race and the purse that comes with it, and the halfway gold nuggets, but he also walked away with the Rookie of the Year, the sportsmanship award for helping Larry in the gorge, and the coveted humanitarian award.

He offers a lazy smile. "You gave me one of those, didn't you?"

I shrug, though he likely already knows that the vote by the trail veterinarians for the Leonhard Seppala was unanimous this year.

"I heard an animal control officer did an inspection of Zed Snyder's kennel and jammed him up with a bunch of fines. Not having up-to-date rabies vaccinations, that sort of thing."

Good ol' Howie. "That's unfortunate."

"It is." He studies me. "You haven't come by to see the kennel at all. Why is that?"

"I've been busy."

He reaches up to wipe a smear of mud off the top of my side-view mirror. "Really? Couldn't come by once in three months?"

"You have a gate."

He smirks. "That's never stopped you before."

"I'll be sure to bring my bolt cutters next time I'm out this way, then."

His eyes narrow on the empty road. "Or you could just follow me back now."

His offer is tempting, for all the wrong reasons.

Far too tempting.

But what am I even doing? What's the point? I already know where this leads—grave disappointment. "I can't. I have a patient waiting." That I'm already going to be late for.

"Maybe some other time?"

"Yeah. Maybe." It comes out flippant, not at all convincing.

And he must pick up on that because he backs away a few steps. "You're angry with me."

"I'm not," I counter.

"You're definitely less friendly than you were." He folds his arms over his chest, drawing my focus to the thick pad of muscle the cotton clings to. "Is this because of Cripple? Because I was honest with you?"

He's blunt, like Jonah is blunt. That's always been an attractive quality to me.

In this case, it's annoying. Tyler needs to be *less* attractive, not *more*.

"No. I appreciate honesty, actually. I don't like wasting my time." I already wasted five years pining over a man I'd never have.

"So, you're saying friends are a waste of time. *Wow*. I wouldn't have expected that from you, but good to know." There's discontent in his voice.

I sigh. "That's not what I meant."

"Then what did you mean?"

I wouldn't know where to begin to explain myself. Furthermore, I have no interest in trying. A truck is approaching from the opposite direction. A good enough excuse for escape as any. "I have enough friends, is all. And I have appointments to get to. Take care, Tyler." I throw my truck into gear and ease away. Leaving on a sour note is for the best.

I fight the urge to check my rearview mirror until I lose.

Tyler is still standing in the middle of the road, watching me go.

CHAPTER TWELVE

"God, Earl sure loved those dogs." Dad's aged blue eyes are on the hang glider as he sails past us. "I was afraid Harry would start mucking things up around there. He's just too much like Bonnie, if you ask me, and she doesn't have Earl's way with people."

Harry's father was much like mine—boisterous and easygoing, always one to share a joke or story. His mother, on the other hand, has always been the serious sort, fretting over things she can't change and searching for problems in every situation so she can claim she saw them coming.

I step over a fallen rock on the worn trail that rounds Summit Lake, watching Bentley and Yukon as they explore, their snouts to the ground. We left Aurora at home. She gets agitated in public parks. "Harry's not a bad guy. He's just had everything handed to him, and now he's having to work to keep it. And it doesn't help that Bonnie has convinced him that he can do no wrong." She has always been one of those parents who can find fault in those around her child but never her child. Harry struggled in school? It's because the teachers were inadequate in their jobs. Harry didn't make a sports team? The coach couldn't see real talent if it slapped them in the face. A girl doesn't want to date Harry? Clearly, she's a dimwit.

He can't afford to pay his bills?

It *must* be because his veterinarian is gouging him.

Bonnie didn't do Harry any favors with her brand of parental cheerleading. He's grown up in a cloud of entitlement, his ability to blame others for his failures almost an art form. And that failure hits him hard. I've had to give more than one pep talk over the years, including one after this year's race.

"She always did call him God's miracle. Remember, they had a hard time having him. It took years. She was in her early forties when he came along. They'd all but given up on the possibility by that point." Dad whistles and the dogs turn from their exploratory wanders to rush back. They're not supposed to be off leash anywhere within the park, but Dad's never been good at following rules, and walking dogs born and bred to pull as soon as they're tethered is as easy as herding a pack of feral cats. It's quiet in Hatcher Pass this early in the morning, so we're not likely to offend anyone.

"Earl would be rolling in his grave if he knew about this." Dad shakes his head. "Has Harry paid his latest bill?"

"Cory hasn't sent it yet. I wanted to talk to you first. See what your gut says." I've been sitting on it for three days.

"Oh yeah?" Dad cocks his head. "What does *your* gut tell you to do?"

I expected as much from him. "My annoyed gut tells me to send him the invoice and tack on a home visit fee. My sensible gut says I might want to look at what he spends in a year and then charge him a monthly average rate with a modest discount, so he feels like he's getting *something* from me."

Dad makes a sound. "Two stomachs, Marie. You should get that looked at."

I snort at his lackluster joke. "Really helpful."

"You want my advice? Well, if we're talking in digestive

systems …" Dad watches as a marmot darts from a boulder and Bentley gives chase. It slides under another crop of rocks to safety. "The first one might make you feel good in the short run, but you're gonna suffer down the road. The latter one sometimes makes things harder to digest in the short term, but in the long run, it usually works out better."

"So, sensible is the way to go." Honestly, it's what I would have chosen in the end. That's me— pragmatic Marie. Except when it relates to men and love, apparently.

"As tempting as it is to tell that twerp where to stuff it, because he would deserve that, he won't go anywhere. He has an overqualified veterinarian catering to him. He'd have to be a damn fool to not see that." Dad pauses, studying the expanse of bush-dotted knolls that make up Hatcher Pass. We've hiked this treeless area together for years—at first, with my younger sisters in tow, and then, when their love of the outdoors took a back seat to other things, just Dad and me.

I won't lie—I prefer this. Secretly, I think he does, too.

In summers, we'd climb up to April Bowl, a shallow, turquoise-colored tarn, and beyond, traverse the ridge to Hatch Peak; in winters, we'd navigate the trails with snowshoes and avalanche transceivers strapped to our bodies. My mother was never keen on those excursions.

My favorite time to come, though, is the fall, just before they close the summit for the winter, when the bushes are tinged with burnt red leaves and the peaks are coated with crisp white snow, and there isn't a soul in sight for miles.

Our adventurous treks were put on hold about five years ago when I brought home a silver husky named Aspen. She was thirteen, and while she loved the hikes, she couldn't manage the climb. So we kept to easy trails, circling Summit Lake, collecting blueberries and fireweed, and looking for marmots and ptarmigan.

But then Aspen passed, and my father didn't push to resume

our more adventuresome hikes. He'd find excuses to avoid climbing to the ridge. "Next time," he'd say. Or, "I can't shake this leg cramp."

The truth was my father had aged. It'd happened unbeknownst to me, somewhere in the seams of my busy life while I was so focused on what lay ahead for me in five, fifteen, twenty years. Sure, the birthdays passed and the years accumulated. I wasn't blind to that. But my father was still here, as he had always been—a constant. The reality that he wouldn't always be lingered in the recesses of my mind, but it was somewhere in the distant future.

And then Wren Fletcher died—too young and too quickly—and I came home from Western Alaska after that funeral, after watching Calla bury a father she'd only just reconnected with, and Jonah say goodbye to a man who'd treated him like a son, and for the first time, I truly noticed how white Dad's hair had gotten, how wrinkled his hands were, how his gait was no longer that of a sturdy man but of a man who feels every step in his joints.

That's when I started looking at the future in smaller increments. How much longer will I be able to bend my father's ear for advice? Five years? Ten?

Will I be standing in this spot in a year's time, talking out loud to myself, wishing he were around to tell a terrible joke?

"Looks like messy weather moving this way." He nods toward a thick band of dark clouds moving in over the far ridge. Turning on his heels, he whistles to the dogs once again and begins heading back toward the road and parking lot.

But his pace is meandering, slow. Always a sign that something weighs on his mind. "Marie, you know how proud we are of you. Keeping the clinic going the way you have … Well, it's made me so happy to be able to look out our kitchen window and see patients coming and going still, after all these years."

"That's why I took it over." Even when I was doing my

surgical residency with Wade Phillips in Anchorage, I saw myself coming back to work with my father. When his health problems kicked in, and he started talking about retirement, we struck a deal over apple pie and Coors Light, sitting at their kitchen table. I'd take over and pay my parents rent to cover their bills so they could stay in their home, my childhood home. It was a win-win for all.

"And I know Jim has been riding you a lot about the accounting side of things, but he does mean well. And money is something he understands."

"Believe me, if there is something Jim is good at, I know that it's counting *every* penny." That and shifting all responsibility for his children to his wife. "But I don't tell him how to run his accounting business, and I don't need him telling me how to run my veterinarian business." Sometimes I wonder if he's sizing up the clinic's earnings for my sister's inheritance.

"See, that's the thing. There's always been two sides to this business. The animal care part, which no one's suggesting Jim knows anything about, but then there's the other side. You know, all the money stuff. And *maybe* it couldn't hurt to have someone who knows that side well step in."

"We're doing fine. I have Cory."

Dad gives me a guarded look. "Marie, you're a brilliant veterinarian, but I've seen the numbers."

I shrug. "I'm getting by!" Sure, the chunk that goes to my parents and to my student loans is considerable, but I don't have much else in the way of expenses. "I live rent-free, and my debts could be worse but aren't, thanks to you guys. I'm doing okay."

"You could be doing *more* than okay if you weren't such a bleeding heart. Don't get me wrong, I'm thrilled that you give so much of your time to helping, even when there isn't a price tag attached to it. Liz could stand to have a bit of that rub off on her." He says that last part more to himself. "But getting paid for your hard work doesn't mean you don't care about these animals. You care too much sometimes. Why else would you be wasting your talents here? You could be working with Wade down in Anchorage. He'd still hire you on—"

"But it's not what I want. I like being my own boss. I like having flexibility." Not that Wade would ever stop me from volunteering at the Iditarod. I've already accepted my invitation for next year's race.

Yukon and Bentley take off after another marmot, ignoring Dad's commanding whistle.

"These dogs," he mutters, stepping over a crop of stones, the leashes dangling from his grasp. "How many years, and they haven't figured out that they'll never win against those little rodents—"

The stones roll beneath his boot, and my father loses his footing. He falls to the ground with a sickening crack.

"Dad!" I rush to him, collecting his wire-rimmed glasses off the ground, my adrenaline kicking in. His grimace of pain only amplifies my fears that it was no ordinary tumble. "Your ankle?"

"My leg," he forces out between gritted teeth, tugging on his pants to ease up the hem.

"Oh, Dad." I grimace at the ghastly display. His tibia has snapped like a twig, one end of it broken through his skin. Blood streams down his leg.

"I can't see a thing." He collects his glasses from my grasp and slides them back on, fussing for a moment to adjust before realizing that the frame is bent and giving up. "Would you look at that."

"This is a bad break. We need to staunch that and get you help." I check my phone, even though I know there's no signal up here.

He winces as he shifts, unbuckling his belt and tugging it free. "I knew I wore my good leather one for a reason today." He loops it around his thigh and fashions a tourniquet to stem the blood flow.

The dogs have abandoned their hunt for rodents and trotted to sit by my father's side. Yukon whines, his nose dipping toward Dad's leg.

"Oh, so *now* you two decide to come," he grumbles but spares a moment to pat each of them on the head. "It's not your fault. It's mine. Seventy-four years old and I've forgotten how to walk."

I peer behind us, toward the road. We're half a mile away. Too far for an injury like this unless there's no other choice. "I'm going to get help. Someone will drive by soon enough." I fasten the dogs to their leashes and then loop the handles around my father's fist. "Just stay here. And keep your hands off it," I warn. My father's been known to skip medical professionals and stitch himself up from time to time, but there's not a lot he can do out here.

"I'll try my best," my father says, a joking lilt in his tone, despite his grimace.

———

With mounting frustration, I check the time again. I've been pacing this desolate dirt road for fifteen minutes without a single vehicle passing. Most days in June, I'd be complaining that it's too busy.

All I need is one car. One person to drive by.

If I'd just started walking toward the parking lot, I'd have reached my car by now. From there, it's a short drive to the lodge and help.

Regret burns inside as I contemplate standing here any longer until I decide I can't wait for someone. I'm about to head to the car when I spot a familiar white-and-green pickup truck in the far distance, creeping along the winding road. It's a park ranger. Even better than a random tourist. Relief envelops me as I jump and wave frantically. It's already heading in this direction, but I need it to move *faster*.

The park ranger vehicle eases to a stop—there's little room to pull over.

The man driving hops out.

My jaw drops as I take in Tyler's face. "What are *you* doing here?"

He smirks. "I would've thought the truck and the uniform are pretty self-explanatory."

"Yeah, but ..." I take in the standard khaki-brown and green ranger uniform, the bulletproof vest, the sidearm strapped to his hip. He's wearing a baseball cap rather than the broad-rimmed campaign hat, with State Park Ranger stamped across it in yellow lettering.

I guess this answers the question of what Tyler does for money if he's not running sled tours through the summer. A lot of mushers work seasonal jobs, taking on as many hours as they can with fishing charter companies or other tourist-type work, or in construction, before they start their rigorous fall training schedule.

But no ... "Over three million acres of park land in this state, and you have to work *here*," I mutter under my breath.

"I'm sorry, what?"

"Nothing."

He frowns. "You were waving me down. Is there a problem?"

"Oh my God. *Yes.*" My momentary shock over seeing Tyler here disintegrates as I explain the situation and my father's compound fracture.

I've barely finished talking when Tyler's reaching for his radio. He calls in to dispatch as he calmly strolls back to the truck.

I don't think a park ranger uniform has *ever* fit someone so well, but I shift my gaze—and my thoughts—to more pressing issues.

He climbs in, throws his hazards on, and pulls over precariously close to the narrow, shoulder-free edge before stepping out again. "An ambulance is on the way."

My pace is brisk as I lead Tyler toward my father, an uncomfortable silence sitting on my shoulders, interrupted only by the occasional buzz of his radio.

"Slow down, Marie."

"He's been sitting out there alone for almost twenty minutes. He's diabetic, and he has high blood pressure." Not to mention the bone sticking out of his leg.

"I get it, but the ground is uneven, you're panicking, and we don't need more than one broken leg today."

"I'm not panicking. I don't panic. And I've been hiking here since I was five. I know how to walk—ahh!" The stones beneath my hiking boots roll, much like what caught my father off guard, and I lose my balance.

Before I tumble to the ground, Tyler is there, his viselike grip locking on my biceps while his other arm loops around my waist. I feel his strength as he hauls me back to my feet. "You good?"

I test my ankle. "Yeah. I'm fine." I falter on a thanks, stealing a glance upward to find sincerity in his eyes. His hands are hot against my skin, even through my shirt, and a pleasing masculine scent of cedar and citrus peel teases my nose.

He shifts away and opens his mouth, but promptly shuts it before a *told you so* comment escapes.

Good. He has *some* restraint.

"So ... is this a seasonal thing? This ..." I wave a hand at Tyler's uniform as we continue at a slightly slower pace. It must be. There's no way he can carry a full-time job *and* train his dogs for the Iditarod.

"Yeah. Started back in April."

"Those positions are hard to come by." I remember Howie saying that his friend had been applying religiously for years and couldn't get so much as a toe in. He ended up going down to the lower forty-eight.

"They are. Luckily, I know a few people."

"Like the head of parks and rec," I answer for myself, recalling that name-drop way back when. "Is this something you've done before?" Specializing in law enforcement, too, based on the vest and gun.

"I *am* qualified, if that's what you're asking."

"Oh yeah? How?"

He smirks. "Do you want to see my résumé?"

"Maybe." There are so many things about this guy that I still don't know. "Who takes care of the dogs while you're here? Your brother?"

"Reed. Yeah."

"How old is he?"

"This feels like an interrogation. Is the crusader worried that my dogs aren't well cared for during the off-season? Do I need to bust out that humanitarian trophy *you* gave me?"

"I'm beginning to regret that vote." It's the second time he's brought it up. "He just seemed a little *young.*" I spent ten minutes with that kid, and while he was at ease with the dogs, that's a lot for *anyone* to handle.

"He'll be twenty-one in the fall, and yeah, he is, in some ways. He can be *painfully* shy, especially around girls, but I've never seen anyone more in tune with those dogs." Tyler hesitates. "Reed is my wife's half brother. Her parents split when she was about ten. Her dad married an American and moved to Montana, where they had him. They have a mushing tour company down there, so he's grown up around sled dogs. When I told him I was moving here and bringing her team with me, he asked if he could move, too."

I don't miss the way he refers to her as his wife. Not his *late* wife.

"And you just took him in."

"Of course. He's family. Plus, he's a good kid, I trust him, and I like having him around." He nods ahead. "Yours?"

Yukon and Bentley trot toward us, their leashes dragging behind them.

"Yes." Panic surges. While the pass is a wide-open space, the knolls and low bushes make it easy to miss someone who might be sitting on the ground.

Or lying there, unconscious.

We pick up the pace and while I'm normally coolheaded in emergency situations, now I'm holding my breath while my mind churns through terrible worst-case thoughts.

We crest a hump and find Dad where I left him, fiddling with his glasses in an attempt to bend the wire frame back. "Is that you, Marie?" He slides his glasses on. "Oh, there you are. I was starting to think you'd abandoned me."

I drop to my knees next to my father, my relief bringing a cold sweat to my skin. "How is it?"

"Still broken." He offers Tyler a wan smile. "I supposed that's not what you guys mean about leashing your dogs, is it?"

"No, but I think we can let it slide this time." Tyler crouches on the other side of my dad, examining the protruding bone. "That's a good break, all right."

"I've been called an overachiever from time to time."

My dad's quippy humor is kicking in strong, which means he's in a lot of discomfort and is trying to overcompensate.

"Help is a few minutes out. Luckily, they were in the area."

"I hope that help is strong." Dad scowls at the path to the road. "I *tried* to get up, but—"

"You *didn't*." I spear my father with a scolding glare before inspecting the wound more closely. The tourniquet seems to have done its job with stemming blood flow, but I'm more worried about infection the longer he's sitting out here in the dirt. "At least you didn't try to put it back together." Stubborn old fool.

"Thought about it. Then I remembered that I'm better at

setting bones on dogs than I am on humans, so I talked myself out of it."

"That's right. Marie told me you're a veterinarian, too." Tyler's gaze flickers to me. "Like father, like daughter."

"Once upon a time. Now I leave the animals to Marie. She's far better at it than I ever was." He waggles a finger between us. "Why do I get the feeling you two know each other?"

"Dad, this is Tyler Brady. He won the—"

"Iditarod! That's right! Of course, I've heard that name. Both Wade and Grant talked nonstop about you."

A genuine smile fills Tyler's face. "You know Wade and Grant?"

"I do. They're good men. *Terrible* card players, but good men."

Tyler's chuckle is deep and soft. "Small world, I guess."

"Wait until they hear about this." Dad nods to the uniform. "Looks like you lead a busy double life."

"I have a few things on the go, yeah."

"Well, what a day ... Marie never told me you two were friends."

"Oh no, we're definitely *not* friends. Marie has made it clear that she doesn't need any more. She has too many. No time for more, I guess," Tyler says dryly.

I roll my eyes, even as my cheeks flush.

"Oh yes, she's a regular butterfly, that one." But my dad frowns curiously at me. He knows better than anyone that my calendar is always kept open for animals and my friend circle is tiny. Almost nonexistent, it feels lately.

And now I look like an ass, but it's better than having to explain why I'm unwilling to play friends with a man I'm attracted to ever again.

An ambulance siren carries in the distance, saving me from that conversation.

"Sounds like the cavalry is here." My dad tries to shift and winces. "Good thing. My left butt cheek is asleep."

"How long do you think it'll take them to make it down?" I ask, worry tugging at my nerves.

"Not long. Hang in there." Tyler pats my dad on the shoulder before standing. He starts back in the direction of the road, radio in hand.

My father's focus trails after him. "So, that's the one who saved the dog from Zed Snyder's rifle?"

"Dad!" I hiss, glaring at him. I told him that in strict confidence, never to be repeated. It'd be bad enough if the mushing community found out about his gallant dognapping. Now that I know what his off-season gig is, what would his boss do if he found out?

"Don't worry, I haven't said anything to *anyone*. What is he? Thirty-five? Thirty-six?"

"Thirty-seven. Why?"

"No reason. It's just … that's a good age. He saves animals and people. Not squeamish. And he sure is a handsome fellow. Polite. Nice teeth."

I groan. "Not you, too—"

"I just don't see why you can't be friends."

"It's complicated."

"Probably not *that* complicated."

"It is. And we're not doing this now." Or ever. It's bad enough I'm constantly badgered by my sisters and brothers-in-law.

"Can't a dying father share his last wish for his daughter's happiness?"

"Oh my God, stop it!" I can't help my laughter. "You're *not* dying."

He winces with pain. "I might, after your mother finds out about this."

Fear that my father might say something highly inappropriate in front of Tyler urges me to explain in a whisper, "He lost his wife and unborn son two years ago."

Dad grimaces. "Oh, now that you mention it, I do remember Grant telling me that."

"So he's *nowhere* near dating anyone, anytime soon."

"Here!" Tyler hollers, waving. Two male paramedics are making their way down, a stretcher in hand.

Yukon and Bentley take off toward the newcomers, barking.

Tyler's sharp whistle reins them in.

"Oh, would you look at that," Dad murmurs as we watch Tyler collect their leashes and give them each a friendly pat. "Dogs know the good ones, Marie. Dogs *always* know."

———

The sight of my father lying in the back of an ambulance brings both relief and anxiety. "I'm going to take them home and then I'll meet you there, okay?" I holler as the paramedic is about to shut the door.

"Tell your mother it's too late to get a refund on me," he calls back, his voice strained.

The paramedic chuckles as he closes them in.

I shift out of the way, hugging myself as I watch the ambulance driver maneuver the wide switchback in the road so he can turn around and head toward the route to the hospital in Wasilla.

Tyler smiles. "He's a funny guy, that one."

"He can be."

The dogs are testing Tyler's grip on their leashes, but they've settled with each command from him.

"Here. I'll take them. Thanks." I reach for the leashes, grabbing them below the handle to avoid any contact. Simple hand grazes always seem to be my undoing.

Tyler watches Bentley with interest. "They were sled dogs?"

"Yeah. Retired. The owner wanted Yukon to be a sled dog, but he had other plans. Didn't you?" I scratch his chin. "I should get them home and let my family know what's going on." I begin backing away. "So ... thank you, for your help."

"Just doin' my job." He lifts his hat off his head, only to put it back.

I stumble over a step.

Jonah does that *all the time*.

In fact, so many things about Tyler remind me of Jonah. He's nowhere near as brash as Jonah can be, but there's that quiet confidence and a deeply ingrained integrity that screams of always doing the right thing and helping where he can.

"What's wrong?" he asks, and I realize I'm staring.

"Nothing. I'm sure I'll see you around." Seeing as I can't seem to avoid him.

"I was hoping to talk to you, actually." He steps forward, his focus drifting along the shallow valley, the result of a glacier wearing down rock between the ridges. "I'm looking for a new veterinarian."

"Frank's not working out?" I already suspected that would eventually be the case, given our conversation at the checkpoint.

"No, Frank and I are *not* working out. Our personalities don't mesh, and the fucking guy won't pick up his phone."

"Never would have guessed that."

"So, do you know of any good ones?" He's watching me carefully, the fringe of long, dark lashes making his irises pop.

I think I know what he's asking, but I could be wrong. I've misunderstood Tyler before. "What *exactly* are you looking for?"

"I want someone available to me when my dogs need them. Within reason, of course, but I want someone who's going to answer their phone when I call, give advice when I need it, and come out when they need to. Someone I can trust to do what's right by my dogs, always."

Tyler calling me at all hours of the day and night?

Something tells me he'd be calling me a lot. Possibly more

than Harry. With Harry, it's because he's young and inept. With Tyler, it's because he appreciates a professional opinion.

It'd be a healthy income, I'll admit, having two teams—one of them an Iditarod champion. Except Harry would lose his mind if he found out.

But then I'd be spending more time with Tyler, and he's already managed to creep into my thoughts too much when he's not in my life at all.

Yukon tugs at his leash, reminding me that we're standing on the side of the road and my father is on his way to the hospital. I have priorities, and Tyler is not one of them.

"You should give Don Childs a call. He's in Wasilla, near the old Sears. Just off the highway. Let him know I sent you."

Tyler's shoulders slump. It's not the answer he wanted.

But it's the only one I can give him.

"Thanks again for helping." I rush out of there without another look back.

CHAPTER THIRTEEN

"Grab me one of those, too, would ya, Marie?" my dad calls out around a bite of mashed potatoes.

I reach for the fridge handle to fish out a second bottle of Coors Light.

"Don't you *dare*," my mother hisses, her palm pressed against the door.

The moment she turns around, I flash Dad a sheepish smile and mouth, *Sorry*.

"I think I liked the hospital more." He shoots a sullen look toward my mother's back. "My nurses were a lot nicer."

"That's because you listened to them," Mom answers crisply, filling a tall glass with water from the Brita. She sets it and a glass ramekin in front of him at the dinner table.

He glowers at the litany of prescribed pills in the little dish, as if deciding how much of a fuss he's going to make. For a man so well-informed about the benefits of modern medicine, he's never been good at taking a doctor's advice.

With a heavy sigh, she pleads, "Come on now, Sidney. Don't be difficult tonight. *Please*."

It's been two weeks since my father's fall in Hatcher Pass, and *everyone's* tired. He spent six days in the hospital. According to the doctor, as far as "bad breaks" go, it was a "good" one, and his leg should heal nicely with time. But it still required pins and a cast to just below his knee, and eventually, physical therapy.

He's been home for more than a week, and the days have worn on both my parents—my father, because of discomfort and limitations; my mother, for playing nursemaid to a frustrated old man, twenty-four hours a day.

Liz has found an excuse almost every day for why she can't make the thirty-five-minute drive over to help—Tillie's ballet, Nicole's art classes, Jim's workload—and Vicki comes when she can, but with a fussy five-month-old baby attached to her, her help is divided and short-lived.

So it's mainly been my mother, and me whenever I'm not working. "Remember when I suggested we skip Sunday dinner this week?" Liz spears Mom with a knowing look as she drops a spoonful of stemmed broccoli onto Tillie's plate.

My niece's mouth opens, disgust etched into her face.

"Do *not* start. Not one word of complaint, or no dessert. Both of you," Liz snaps, dumping a helping in front of Nicole, too, who looks equally displeased. "Would you pass the salt, hun?"

On the far end of the table, Jim eats his dinner, tuning out everything and everyone around him, including his wife.

Don't strain yourself, Jim. I reach across the table and hand it to her.

"But if you didn't come, then I wouldn't get to see my two favorite people, would I?" Dad steals a glance to make sure my mother isn't watching and then, with a wink at his grandchildren, tosses a chunk of beef to Yukon's waiting maw.

The girls erupt in laughter, and their giggles help douse the growing tension in the kitchen just as Vicki and Oliver emerge from the living room.

"Perfect timing." Mom takes her own seat.

"Yeah, we'll see how long it lasts." Vicki sinks into her chair across from me, checking the buttons on her shirt as if to make sure she didn't stroll in with a breast hanging out.

Molly has been a tough baby—first with colic, and lately with a string of recurring ear infections that will require ear tube surgery in a few weeks. I've never seen my little sister so tired before. She's normally the one with fresh highlights and a well-chosen outfit. Now, her blond ponytail is frayed and sloppy, her oversized plaid shirt one of her husband's.

"How's work, Oliver?" Fishing charter season is in full swing again, and he's gone from morning until night, seven days a week. This is the first time he's made it to Sunday dinner since April.

"Man. *Busy.*" He stabs two slices of beef with his fork and drops them onto his plate. For such a lanky guy, he can eat more than anyone at this table. "My boss said we're booked solid until September. All day, every day. It's good, though. We need the money."

I don't doubt it. Oliver's the only one working right now. Vicki has spent the better part of the last decade figuring out what she wants to do by process of elimination—three years waitressing before she moved to real estate, where it took her three years to decide that selling houses wasn't for her; a year working in a health store while considering a naturopathic career; one semester in a college fitness and health program with her sights set on a degree toward becoming a personal trainer. She even did a brief stint behind the desk in the clinic when Cory took a few months off to travel across Europe. The place has never been more disorganized than during that time.

Last year, Vicki announced over Sunday dinner that she'd been hired to work reception in a local salon and had enrolled in a hair design program. It's the most excited she's ever been about anything … and then she found out she was pregnant.

She's completed two-thirds of her state-required education hours. We're all hoping she'll go back to it soon.

"Did you mention it to her already?" Vicki elbows Oliver, her voice soft. "You know, about Steve?"

"Well, not lately. I brought it up before, though, remember?" he says, equally soft.

As if no one can figure out where this is going.

I stifle my groan.

"Hey, Marie, I think you and Ollie's boss would hit it off. He's big on the outdoors. Hiking and hunting. And fishing, *obviously*. And he's good looking. Here, you have a picture, don't you?" She holds her hand out for Oliver's phone. "A bit more gray than I like, but a full head of hair."

"Hey!" Jim chirps, glaring at Vicki as he smooths a hand over the bald spot on the back of his head.

"Doesn't hear me asking him to pass the salt, but *that*, he hears," Liz mutters to no one in particular.

Vicki ignores them both—as she often does, she's never been a fan of Jim's—and holds up Oliver's phone to show me a candid picture of a man in waders, standing in the middle of a river. "He's forty-two. No criminal record. Smokes, but he's trying to quit. One eighteen-year-old kid. So, proof that his plumbing works—" She waggles her eyebrows. "His ex is *way* out of the picture. She's already with someone new."

I make a sound that might be agreement as I chew. The truth is Steve sounds more ideal than any of the guys Jim has tried to set me up with. He's handsome enough, in a rugged, outdoorsy way, his hair wispy at the ends, and his face coated in graying scruff. He's older than I am. Maybe that's been my issue all along —chasing after younger men.

But is this what my dating life has come to? My siblings taking secret shots of unattached associates at work and presenting their vices and sperm count to me over a platter of slow-cooked beef?

"Oliver already showed him your picture, and he's *definitely* interested."

"*Which* picture?" I give my brother-in-law an exasperated look. "*Why* do you have a picture of me?"

He shrugs. "It's the one Vicki sent me."

"The one from the clinic," she clarifies.

"The one *on the wall*?" My jaw drops a second before I burst out laughing.

"God, no! That would have scared him away." Vicki giggles. "No, the one on the desk. You're wearing a black dress."

"Oh, right." From Jonah's wedding.

"Well, he liked it, and he wants to meet you. So, what do you think?" she asks, pausing with a mashed potato-laden fork in the air, eager for my response.

"I'll *think* about it."

Jim sets his cutlery down with a clatter and leans back in the chair to rub his belly. "That was fantastic, as always, Eleanor." He's *always* the first one finished. He's also always the first one up from the table, leaving his dirty dishes for his wife—or anyone else—to collect.

But tonight, he settles in with a toothpick. "I gave my buddy a call. The one in real estate I told you about?" His attention is on my father. "With the house and the clinic, plus that cabin, he's saying you could get at least five hundred. Maybe more. The market around here's hot right now."

Jim's words take a moment to process, and when they do, they don't make any sense. "What's he talking about?" I shift my gaze from my dad to my mom, back to my dad. "What's he talking about?"

"Goddamn it." Dad tosses his fork on the table. "I didn't have a chance to bring it up yet."

"*Oh.*" Jim cringes at Liz.

"Bring *what* up?" My stomach sinks as it all becomes clear. "You want to *sell*? You said you'd never sell."

"*Never* isn't realistic, Marie." Liz's tone is patronizing, like an adult lecturing a child.

Dad opens his mouth to speak, but he can't seem to choose his words. "We're just talking ... we haven't ..." He ends his attempt with an annoyed glare at Jim.

"I don't think this is the appropriate time to have this conversation," Mom says calmly, setting her cutlery down. Her meal is half-finished.

But it's too late for calm. "Well, no, because apparently, we were *already* supposed to have had this conversation." My voice cracks as I stare at my father. "Why are you talking about selling the clinic with *Jim* and *Liz*? They have nothing to do with it. *I'm* the one running it."

"Yeah, into the ground." Liz collects Jim's plate and sets it on top of hers. "I've seen the numbers, Marie. It's barely operational."

"Oh, no." Vicki pinches the bridge of her nose. Beside her, Oliver keeps his focus on his plate.

The idea that Liz has been scouring over the clinic's revenue ignites my anger and squashes all semblance of civility. "First of all, *my* business numbers are *my* business numbers." I scowl at Jim, my cheeks burning. "If my accountant can't respect confidentiality, I'll *fire* his ass. Secondly, the clinic brings in more money than it spends, which means it *is* profitable. But I guess someone who failed basic math *twice* might not understand that concept."

Tillie gapes at her mother. "You *failed* math?"

Liz's nostrils flare, and I know I've struck a chord. "Whose name is going to be on that loan for the new ultrasound?"

"That's none of your business. And *I'm* the one paying for it!"

"Who owns the home you live in, rent-free? Who owns *basically everything* you have, besides your truck? *Not you!* And I may not be as book smart as you are, Marie, but I've made smart choices for *my* life. Can you say that?"

I know it's a dig about Jonathan. "Having a husband who pays all your bills doesn't make you smart, Liz. It makes you dependent."

"Girls, we're not having this fight." My dad tries to cut in.

But it's too late. Angry words that have been simmering under the surface for years are spilling out with the boil.

"Oh, and you're *so* independent?" A wicked smile warps Liz's pretty face. "You want that clinic so bad? *Buy* it from them, then."

I grit my teeth. She knows I can't afford that. "Dad wanted me to run it. He wanted to keep it in the family."

"Well, maybe they want something different now. Maybe they don't want to spend their last years living off whatever meager monthly check you hand them. But you haven't thought about that, have you? No, because it's *always* about Marie. *Everything* is about *Marie!*"

My dad bangs the table with his fist. "Enough!"

Dead silence echoes through the house, his anger a rare and jarring spectacle.

A symphony begins—first Nicole's confused whimper, then Tillie's poorly stifled sobs.

Until finally Molly lets out a strangled wail from the other room.

———

I pause, my hands holding a pot in the sudsy sink, to watch the moose hover by the clinic door across the lawn. He's young. Probably a little over a year old, and he's standing there as if waiting for someone to unlock the front door and invite him in. Behind him, the evening sky glows with rich hues of orange. It's almost ten P.M., but in the season of the midnight sun, it's nowhere near ready to settle for the day.

"He's been coming around a lot," Mom says from behind me, reaching for a tea towel and then a pot from the drainer. "Your father is convinced the one that driver hit down the road a few weeks ago was his mother."

"I think he's right. They walked along the tree line during winter, but I haven't seen her lately." He hadn't begun to grow his first set of antlers yet. Now, they're blooming into a majestic crown atop his head.

I give the animal another moment of my attention and then finish scrubbing the last pot and set it to dry. The house is eerily quiet. Everyone decided it was best to go their separate ways soon after dinner. The girls even got away without finishing their broccoli. "I'm going to head home now, if there's nothing else to do here." I can't help but tack on, bitterness in my voice, "While it's still my home."

Mom sets a soothing hand on my shoulder. "Liz and Jim have *no* say in what we decide to do."

"Tell that to Liz."

"You know your sister. She always has an opinion to share. But you need to talk to him, Marie. Neither of you will sleep otherwise. Which means *I* won't sleep. So, *please*, sort it out."

She's right, and yet my feet feel leaden as I drag myself toward the living room.

My father is settled into his recliner, his cast-wrapped leg propped up with an extra pillow, Yukon sprawled on the floor beside him.

At the sound of my footsteps, Dad peers over his shoulder. "Everybody was in such a rush to get out of here. I thought you'd left, too." His voice weighs with weariness.

"I wasn't going to leave that mess for Mom to clean up on her own." Bentley lifts his head enough to acknowledge me stepping over him before he drops with a thud and a huff that usually makes me laugh.

Tonight, though, my heart is too heavy.

Dad swallows. "I'm sorry that unfolded the way it did."

"I don't understand. I'm running the clinic because you asked me to. You wanted to retire, and you didn't want to sell it or see it sitting there, empty. You've always said how much you love looking out the window and seeing the clinic running." He said it again only two weeks ago, up in Hatcher Pass. "When did you and Mom decide all this?"

"We haven't decided, and we don't *want* to sell. At least, not tomorrow. But it *is* something we've been talking about more." He picks at a loose thread on the blanket my mother draped over him. "Your mom and I put everything we had into this place. We talked about saving for retirement, but there was always something to spend money on. New equipment for the clinic, helping you with your tuition, cars. Remember that old beat-up Dodge you and Liz used to drive around?"

"The one that kept breaking down every time we stopped at a red light? How could I forget?"

Dad chuckles. "Anyway, I made decent money, but with three kids and a business with high overhead, I never did manage to put much away for down the road. We always assumed we'd sell this place if we needed to, even if it broke my heart. When you came home to work with me, I was *so* happy." He punctuates that with a smile. "I loved knowing one of my daughters would continue my life's work. And it still makes me happy." He pauses. "But I wonder now if I shouldn't have closed down."

"*Why?*"

"Because you worked so hard for so long. You could be operating in one of those big hospitals, doing the kind of complex surgeries you're trained to do, not vaccinating stray dogs in that rundown shack with *one* tech to support you. Even these other places in town have multiple veterinarians and techs, at least two receptionists—"

"I'm exactly where I want to be, Dad. I didn't take the job in Anchorage because I didn't want it. And I can do surgeries here. I have the equipment and the skill." While we may call ourselves a clinic, that little shack has seen as many emergencies and saved as many animal lives over the years as places that label themselves a hospital.

"But not necessarily the patients." He watches the dancing flames in the woodstove. "Your mother has always wanted to travel. She's never been to Europe, or to the Caribbean. We talked about that a lot over the years, thought we would be able to afford it."

"But you guys are going to Mexico this winter. You've been saving for it."

"We were going to. And then Vicki and Oliver's truck broke down, and you know they can't afford to fix it. Those two *really* have no money. That boy, he needs to think about a trade or something. Anyway, that's a topic for another day." He purses his lips. "Liz and Jim have that walkout basement apartment. They've offered it to us. Jim's never home, and Liz could use the help with the kids. It'd free up money and give us a chance to travel a bit while helping you all out." He shrugs. "Just a thought that I was gonna bring up with you while we were on the hike. And then I had to go and do *this*, and I got distracted." He gestures at his leg.

I think back to that day, to the conversation we were in the midst of before he fell. It was about money, about how I wasn't making enough. And maybe, though Dad would never bring it up, about how I couldn't pay them more. "If you increase my rent, will that help?"

"It's high enough." Dad waves his hand dismissively. "But that Jim ... I don't know how someone so smart can be so damn dense sometimes."

"It's not even Jim who's the problem. I mean, *yeah*, he's a dumbass. But it was Liz tonight. It's like she'd been waiting for years to unload. She made it sound like I'm some sort of failure, just because I don't make all my life decisions based on money and marriage."

"Yes, she could stand to focus a little less on the former. And *you* could stand to focus a bit more, Marie. It's not fun, being in this boat, where you have to make tough decisions like this. And your mother and I need to start thinking about how to leave what we have to you girls in a fair and equitable way."

"It sounds like the smartest thing for you and Mom to do is to sell this place." The anger I felt earlier is quickly evaporating. Though I don't want everything I've been building to flip over suddenly, I can't blame them for wanting to enjoy their waning years.

It just means I'll have to start making tough decisions of my own.

"I'm not ready to do that yet. Or to leave this place. This is still my home." He reaches blindly for Yukon, and the dog instantly meets him halfway, giving his hand a lick. "But life doesn't slow down any when you get old. *You* slow down. Boy, do you ever." He shakes his head. "But life just keeps speeding along. Lately, it's beginning to feel like some sort of super train. You know, the ones that go across Europe? Your mother's always talked about maybe trying one of those out." He chuckles. "Except this one is feeling like it has no stops. Yeah ... you start waking up in the mornings, realizing you've missed the view you've been waiting for while you were sleeping, and you can't go back."

"I don't want you to miss anything on my account."

"I still like the view I got, lookin' out that window and seeing the lights on next door. And it's too hot for me in Mexico, anyway. Plus, there're the sharks to worry about."

I laugh. "You don't even swim."

"Hey, I've always wondered, where do you suppose sharks go on vacation?"

We're switching out of this somber, depressing conversation and back into corny dad jokes, a far more comfortable area. "I have no idea."

"You should ask Tyler. I'll bet he knows, given he's from *Fin*land."

I frown. "Why would—" The answer hits me, and I groan.

CHAPTER FOURTEEN

My head is down when the front door to the clinic chimes.

"You're in early today," Cory says in a singsong voice.

"Yeah. Couldn't sleep, so I figured I'd do some housekeeping." I abandon the computer screen to watch her glide across the floor to the desk. I've always said she looks better in blue scrubs than anyone I've ever met. "And *you're* in an unusually good mood for a Monday morning. *Why?*"

"Oh, *no* reason." She props her chin on her palm.

The diamond on her ring finger shimmers for attention.

My jaw drops. "No way! Joe *finally* did it?" They've been dating for almost seven years.

Cory's round face bursts into a beaming smile.

I leap out of my chair and rush around to crash into her, my heart swelling, her excitement contagious. "Oh my God! Congratulations! When did he do it?"

"Yesterday morning!" she squeals.

"Where? How? Hold on! Let me pee first. I've had too much coffee already." I've been here for hours, replaying last night's family blowout and crunching numbers to try to prove to myself that Liz isn't right.

So far, I'm not sure I can.

"Fine, but hurry." She taps the sign I printed and taped to the counter, reading it out loud: "'All payments for services rendered are required same day. *No* exceptions.' This is new."

"And long overdue." Especially when I tallied the outstanding invoices. No wonder Jim has been on my case. Brad Garvis's bills are still unpaid, and he and his ferrets haven't been back. A copy of his outstanding bill is printed and ready for the mail, with interest tacked on that has always been part of my policy but I've never enforced. "We're going to run things a bit differently here from now on."

"Well, giddyup. You know *I'm* game." Cory stretches her arms in front of her, her entwined hands cracking at the knuckles.

———

"What did you feed him?" I can't help the accusatory tone. When Cory begged me to squeeze in her future brother-in-law today, I thought it was for a simple examination. Looking at the ball python on my table, its head and body riddled with vicious bite marks, it's clear a thawed mouse wasn't on the menu.

"A rat."

"A *rat.*"

"My friend down in Florida feeds his snakes rats all the time. I thought it was okay!" Ivan shrugs.

"Like, a feeder rat from the pet store?"

He hesitates.

"I need to know what happened, so I can help him."

With resignation, he admits, "I flew down to Juneau with a buddy in his plane so I could visit my mom, and she was complainin' about some rats in her shed, so I figured I'd catch them and bring them home for Benny." He shrugs a second time. "It's a free meal, right?"

"You brought *rats* home from Juneau and fed them to your

snake," I say slowly, my face surely a mask of dumbfounded shock. "Okay, there are a few issues with this, Ivan. First of all, what you caught are *wild* rats. They're not the same as a feeder rat your friend in Florida buys at the pet store. Wild rats do *this*—" I point to the snake in the container. "Secondly, bringing rats here is a *big* problem. They are highly invasive. You could get into *a lot* of trouble if people found out you did that."

The Anchorage area has so far avoided the kind of rodent problems that some of the islands and cities like Juneau can't seem to shake, and they've done it through stringent laws and vigilant measures. To have a rat-free port is unheard of, and yet Anchorage has worked hard to maintain it.

The twenty-two-year-old blanches. "Really?"

Cory warned me this guy is far from the smartest person I'll ever meet. "How many did you catch?"

"Three."

"And where are the ones you didn't try to feed to Benny? Tell me you didn't let them go?"

"Uh ... I *didn't* let them go?" he says slowly, unconvincingly.

Hopefully, a fox catches them. *And* they're both male. "Okay, Benny is going to need surgery." I haven't operated on a snake in years, but this is fairly straightforward. "Luckily, I have some time in my schedule today." Otherwise known as my lunch break. "But I don't think I'll be able to save his eye."

"Really?" He stares at his injured pet as he processes it. "*So ...* I'm gonna have a one-eyed snake?" A slow grin stretches across his face. It vanishes when he sees that my stony expression isn't breaking. "How much is this gonna cost me?"

"If you wait in the lobby, Cory will give you an estimate in a few minutes, but Ivan? A *whole lot* of frozen mice."

A curse slips from Ivan as he exits the exam room.

———

"If it were up to me, you wouldn't be getting the family discount. You deserve to pay every penny of this, dumbass." Cory delivers the insult to her future brother-in-law with a grin, saying to Ivan what I desperately want to.

"Yeah, I guess I do." He grimaces, his fingers twirling the shaggy hair at his nape. "Just fix him for me. Please."

I offer a sympathetic smile because the idiot genuinely didn't mean any harm. "I'll do what I can on my end, but you need to go home and disinfect *everything*. Especially his habitat. Wild rats carry diseases." Behind me, the bell on the clinic's door chimes as another customer walks in. "We'll give you a call when he's ready to be picked up."

"Thanks," he mumbles.

I'm still wearing the smile when I turn to greet the person who has come in.

It falls off at the sight of Tyler holding open the door for Ivan, who grunts his thanks.

With a curious look at the sullen guy's back, Tyler wanders into the clinic. He's off duty today, in a faded black concert T-shirt that hugs his body in all the right places without being tight, blue jeans, and a New York Yankees ball cap pulled low over his brow. He probably rolled out of bed and threw on the first thing he pulled from his dresser. How do men like him make such a casual outfit look *so* good? He didn't even bother to shave this morning, his stubble a fine dusting over his cut jaw.

Keys dangle from his fingers. I steal a glance behind him, to the lot, expecting to see the shiny new truck he won at the Iditarod. But instead, it's the forest green pickup that was buried under snow in his driveway the day I basically accused him of animal abuse.

"So, *this* is your clinic."

"It is."

"And that little cabin over there, where your truck is parked, is that where you live?"

"Yup."

"I like it." He pauses to scan the various certificates on the wall —my undergrad, my veterinarian license, and the one that proves I'm a board-certified surgeon. He stalls on that last one a moment before shifting to the wall of photos. He frowns at my picture.

"The police station was kind enough to send over Marie's mugshot the last time she was arrested," Cory calls out.

"She does have a habit of trespassing," he throws back without missing a beat.

I shoot Cory a glare, but she's not paying attention to me, her vivid blue eyes locked on Tyler's backside. "What are you doing here?"

"Just in the neighborhood. Thought I'd see how your dad is doing."

Was he really? We're west of Wasilla, and there's nothing to draw Tyler out this way unless he's driving to Trapper's Crossing, which has even less of a draw. "He's fine. Back home, in a cast. Pestering my mother."

Tyler's attention shifts around my tiny lobby as if searching for something.

"Hi, I'm Cory, Marie's vet tech and admin." She rounds the desk to offer him a broad smile. "And you look *awfully* familiar."

His smirk is coy, as if he knows she's feigning cluelessness but is willing to play along. "Do I?"

"This is Tyler Brady," I supplement, mainly because I don't want this exchange to drag on any longer than it needs to. "He won the Iditarod this year."

"*That's* why I know your face. It was plastered *all* over the local news."

Local? More like statewide, along with the major national outlets. And Cory spent several days buying up the various papers just so she could drool over the sport's new golden boy.

"I have a snake waiting for surgery, so if there's nothing else …" I'm already moving for the door to the back of my clinic.

"Wait." Tyler holds up a hand. "Can I have a minute or two of your time?" He pauses, steals a glance over his shoulder at Cory, still gawking shamelessly at him. "In private?"

My heart races. What does he have to say that needs privacy? "Cory, can you get the room prepped for surgery?"

"Sure thing, boss." She trots over to flip the In Surgery sign before disappearing into the back, mouthing "so hot" with dramatic flair at Tyler's back on her way past.

Despite everything, I struggle to suppress my laugh. "So? What do you need?"

He falters. "You're operating on a *snake?*"

"Apparently. The owner tried to feed his pet python a wild rat to save money."

"Ouch. The kid who just left?" He jabs a thumb toward the lot, though Ivan's long gone.

"Yup. And now I have to remove one of its eyes." While I've never been a fan of reptiles as pets, I don't relish seeing any living creature mutilated.

Tyler's cringe morphs and his hand goes to his face. He looks to be hiding his amusement.

"This is getting old, fast." I guarantee when I tell Jonah this story, he won't even bother to hide his deep bellow of laughter.

"Oh, man." He loses the battle, flashing a wide, honest smile that shows off those straight, white teeth my father was admiring. "Tell me the fool didn't make *that* joke." His chuckle is deep and soft, and I fight my own threatening smile, despite the morbid topic.

"It's *not* funny." And I can't allow myself to be drawn into Tyler's easy charm again. "Did you get in touch with Don?"

His laughter dies and he smooths his expression. "That's actually why I'm here. I don't want Don Childs, or Frank, or anyone else." He settles his steady gaze on me. "I want *you.*"

His words and that look make my breath hitch. They don't mean what I wish they did, but it's nice to hear all the same.

His throat bobs with a hard swallow. "For my dogs," he amends. "I want *you* to be my dogs' veterinarian. I guess I wasn't clear enough the other day."

"No, you *were*. I just …" What is my valid excuse for peddling another veterinarian on him, besides the truth, which I'm not about to spell out in painstaking, embarrassing detail?

"You just what?" he urges.

"You said you don't want to complicate your life. Well, neither do I." And my gut tells me that spending too much time with Tyler will complicate *everything* for me.

"Complicate it how? Because of *Harry*?"

"No." I laugh, though taking on Tyler would *definitely* complicate my relationship with the Hatchetts. But it already seems to be heading down that path. Harry grumbled at my monthly billing proposal and decided it best to keep things as they are, but he didn't seem happy about it. Where that will lead—if anywhere —I don't know. My father's convinced it'll go nowhere, and I hope he's right.

Tyler's forehead puckers. "Okay, then, is this because of what happened in the tent—"

"*No*." My cheeks burn. Not *just* the tent. It's about *everything* to do with this man, and how I find myself drawn to him. It's about him breaking the law and risking his reputation and career to spare a dog's life, and how he spends his summers watching over the parkland I love, how every time I find myself in Tyler's vicinity, I'm acutely aware of him, and when he's not around, he's in my thoughts more than I care to admit.

It's about how perfect he would be for me, if not for his unwavering devotion to his late wife. But even *that* is endearing.

Most of all, it's how I don't want to repeat past mistakes, how I need to guard my reckless heart.

"I don't understand, then. Are you too busy here?" He gestures around the clinic. "Do you have too many clients?"

He's handed me the perfect excuse. It would be so easy to lie, and yet I can't form the simple yes.

And so I stand silent, like a fool.

"I want—no, I *need*—the best veterinarian in the area, the one who's going to go the extra mile, who *really* cares about these dogs, who will tell me what I don't want to hear. I know that's you." There's a pleading quality to his tone that tugs at my heartstrings, and my ego appreciates the strokes. "I know you're not about the money, but I'll pay you extra if that's what it's going to take. I just want the best for them."

Owning the role of the Iditarod champion's kennel would be great for the clinic's reputation, and twenty-one more dogs to care for would pad my revenue. After Sunday's explosive dinner, turning Tyler away would be a stupid business move. It would prove that Liz is right, that I can't make smart choices.

I take a deep breath. This is silly. I'm thirty-eight years old. I need to accept this relationship for what it is—strictly professional—and move on. I *can* stand to be around an attractive man and not fall hopelessly in love with him. "I'll need to see your kennel before I commit to anything."

Tyler's mouth falls open, as if surprised that I bent so easily. "That's fine."

"And if I see something I don't like, you'll need to change it."

"You won't find anything. But okay." He punctuates that with a nod.

"And I charge for travel time. To and from your place."

"I wouldn't expect anything less."

It's a good thing he's not on civil terms with Harry, then. "Perfect."

I make a strangled sound. "Yeah, we'll see."

A curious look flickers across his face, but it vanishes just as quickly. "So, when can you make it out to my place?"

"I'll check my schedule and get back to you." Somewhere in

the deep recesses of my mind, I feel that buzz of anticipation that comes with knowing I have an excuse to see Tyler on the regular.

It's the same feeling I got when I was flying out to the villages with Jonah.

"Here, I'll give you my number." He leans over the front desk to grab a pen and scrap of paper. The move stretches his T-shirt across his body, pulling my attention to the cut of muscle across his back.

Which drags out memories of him pressed against me.

And so it begins.

He pats the paper once and then leaves it there. "I'm off today and tomorrow, so I can make any time work. You call and let me know."

"Cory does the scheduling. *She'll* let you know." She'll be more than happy to dial that number.

"Okay, well …" His gaze flitters over my scrubs before shifting to the mug shot on the wall. "I'll let you get back to your one-eyed snake."

I shake my head. "Why are guys *all* the same?"

His chuckles follow him out the door.

I take a few calming breaths.

I'm now Tyler Brady's veterinarian.

This is not how I saw today going.

I'm going to regret this.

Cory plows through the door from the back. "*What happened in the tent?*"

CHAPTER FIFTEEN

The last time I was at Tyler's, the air was bitterly cold, the property was blanketed in snow, and I was angry.

Today, a warm summer breeze blows through my truck's open window and across my cheek, the grass is green and freshly cut, and while I'm not angry, I'm certainly not at ease.

"Quick tour, in and out," I tell myself, pulling up behind the green truck parked by the woodshed. The doors to the barn sit wide open, and several dogs mill around freely.

I check my watch. I'm a few minutes early, but the sooner I get this done, the sooner I can move on to a schedule of castrations and lumpectomies.

I hop out and smooth a hand over the front of my shirt, reminding myself again that the blue jeans and plain black T-shirt I settled on after trying four different outfits is perfectly adequate for inspecting a kennel. What's more, this look says that I'm *not* trying to appeal to anyone. *Especially* not Tyler. I even skipped the mascara on my otherwise invisible blonde lashes.

I'm as plain as I can be without showing up in sweatpants.

Three dogs trot toward me, their tongues lolling. Two I recognize from the race, but the third, I—

Wait. "Nymeria? Is that you?" I ask, as if she might answer.

Her heterochromia and fur coloring give her away, but everything else about her is unrecognizable. She's put on ten pounds, the bite marks have healed, and her limp is gone.

I lean down to give her my hand, but she surprises me by jumping up, her front paws landing on my chest while she licks my cheek.

I laugh, even as I stumble back a step, the move unexpected.

Heavy boots dragging across gravel pulls my attention to the right, my breath hitching with excitement. But it's only Reed, strolling from the house with a bottle of water in hand. He's in head-to-toe navy, save for brown hiking boots that he doesn't fully lift off the ground with his steps. His clothes are streaked in dusty paw prints, and the curly black mop on his head is in disarray, as if he just rolled out of bed.

Now that I've seen pictures of Mila, I can see the family resemblance—the same dark hair, cow-brown eyes, and sharp jawline. He's a good-looking kid, albeit a bit gangly.

He flashes a sheepish smile, his cheeks flushing, before his attention shifts to the dog. "She remembers you."

As I'm sure he does, given our first meeting. "How are you, Reed?"

"I'm good." H reaches out for the black dog. It comes running toward him without a moment's hesitation.

"I'm here to see Tyler." I look around the property. "Do you know where he is?"

"In the barn, but ..." Reed frowns as he checks his watch.

"I'm a bit early, but he knows I'm coming this time." I chuckle. "He unlocked the gate for me and everything."

"Oh. Okay." Accepting that, he moves toward the barn without another word, his stride lazy, as if it's too much work to lift his feet.

I follow him, my curiosity brimming. "Tyler told me you moved here from Montana. How do you like Alaska so far?"

"Yeah, I like it." He steals a glance at me before his focus is back on the path ahead, his fingers weaving through his hair. A rhythmic beat of rock music carries from inside.

"You lived with your parents before?"

"Uh-huh."

I sense I'm going to have to pry answers from him. "How do you like living with Tyler?"

"It's more fun than living with my parents."

"I imagine it would be." Even out here, in the middle of nowhere.

He steals another glance, this time grinning shyly. He just seems so innocent. I have to remind myself again that he's twenty.

Tank trots out of the barn, and upon seeing me lets out an excited bark before speeding to greet me, sniffing my thigh.

"Do you guys normally let them run loose like this?" I scratch the lead dog behind the ear, wary of not standing too still after what happened last time I was here and he was off chain.

He shrugs. "Some of them, sometimes."

"Some of them, sometimes," I echo. That's about as vague an answer as a person can give.

Reed leads me into the barn where the music is exponentially louder, and it smells of clean hay and fresh-cut lumber. I don't know where to focus first. I'd never been to the Danson property, but it's obvious the barn has been restored and converted into a keep for the dogs, with rooms on the right to house equipment and supplies for mushing. On the left, the stalls have small cutouts in the exterior walls. A giant shelf holds an array of trophies and framed photos, including the one of Tyler at the Iditarod. It pays homage not only to their achievements but to their past. In the center is a large photo of Mila on her sled, dressed in a red as vibrant as that of the barn.

I stop for only a second before a soft grunt pulls my attention past the area to an open space in the back corner.

My steps falter as I take in Tyler's shirtless, dangling form, the muscles in his arms and back straining as he hoists his chin above the horizontal metal bar. Up and down he moves to the beat of the music, never breaking his stride, his skin coated in sweat, his track shorts hugging an ass that has clearly been hardened by countless squats and miles of jogging.

I realize with utter mortification that my mouth is hanging open.

And what's worse, Reed is watching me drool over his brother-in-law, an unabashed grin of understanding on his face.

The song ends, and Tyler drops to the dirt floor. He's reaching for his water bottle when he notices us standing there. "Marie." The startled look on his face probably matches mine, but for vastly different reasons. "What are you doing here?"

I clear my voice, feeling my cheeks burn. "We have an appointment, *remember*?" Did he *conveniently* forget, so I could be treated to *this* when I arrived? He's turned around and the front view is even more impressive than the back, taut from the muscle strain and damp from exertion, the peaks and ridges like that of a chiseled statue.

"Well, yeah, at nine." He checks his watch. "Couldn't wait to see me?"

"No. Cory booked us for *eight*." Early enough that I could get back for my morning appointments without rushing.

"I do my workouts at eight on my days off. I told her that." Tyler reaches for a towel that dangles from a bench press and wipes it across his forehead.

"Then there's obviously been a misunderstanding because my calendar says eight," I declare as I pull my phone out to prove myself right. "And she's *always* good with ..." My voice trails.

Eight A.M.: Tyler's workout. Hopefully shirtless.

Nine A.M.: Kennel check at Tyler's.

Cory must have revised my calendar moments ago. She's

added a smiley face and a "please don't fire me" to the eight A.M. time slot.

She has *never* messed with my schedule like this before. I don't know whether to be irritated or to laugh at her brazen attempt at forcing a connection that I already explained would *never* happen.

"What does it say?" Tyler is suddenly beside me, hovering over my shoulder.

I startle and slam my phone against my chest to hide the screen. "Doesn't matter. I'm here, so let's do this." I tuck it into my back pocket as I take a few steps away from him.

Tyler laughs, smoothing the towel over his chest. "Come on, I don't smell *that* bad."

He smells like clean sweat, not bad in the slightest, but I'm not about to admit that.

He looks past me. "Do I, Reed?"

I'd forgotten the kid was here, witnessing this entire mortifying debacle. "I have a busy day ahead of me, so are you ready?" I didn't intend the snippy tone, but it serves me well in this case.

Tyler reaches for a navy blue T-shirt hanging off the bench press. "I can be ready." He tugs it over his head, covering his impressive body. "Come on, let me show you around." He passes me with a secretive smile.

———

"This is all ..." I search for a word that doesn't make me look like a preening fool. I can't find one. "I've never seen such attention to dogs before." Not even the Hatchetts have a system like this in place, and Tyler designed and built it all, with Reed's help.

The seven-foot-tall fencing that Howie and I saw when we were here last encloses an area of more than an acre around the barn, creating a barrier against wildlife—particularly wolves and moose. Within that enclosure are the individual kennels and a robust agility course for the puppies. Along the outside of the barn are large pens with double kennels, suitable for housing two dogs per, so they can roam and play freely. Each has a name plate for the dog, giving it a personal touch. There are also dogs in individual kennels with lengthy running circle chains. As Tyler walked me through, he explained the two-system approach, and how they choose which living style fits best for each individual dog, based on personality and racing skill.

The wooden kennels themselves are well built, sitting on stable blocks with snug entrances to protect from inclement weather, shields to block the wind, wide roofs that the dogs can sunbathe on, and big overhangs to provide adequate shade.

The wall of clipboards I noticed coming into the barn houses thorough information on *everything*—medical charts that include not only the basics—age, weight, and vaccination dates—but also weekly checks with detailed notes on everything from massage needs and nail trimming to medications and pressure sores, running and training logs with specific mileage for each dog, bedding changes, molting hair collection, feeding maps, female cycle schedules, injuries, and past fights. There's also a comprehensive map coding every dog by character, and which dogs prefer their space versus the ones who want to be placed together.

"You track *everything*." He's a veterinarian's dream.

"We transfer all this information to our computer once a week. I can open up a spreadsheet and show you each dog's complete history from the time they were born, right down to how many miles they've run, every pound they've gained and lost, which muscle they've pulled, and how long it's taken for a boil to heal." There's pride in Tyler's voice. "It's a lot of work, but it's worth it. It's how Tero and Anja Rask run their kennel, and how Reed's father taught him. He takes care of this for me in the summer."

Mila's parents. He seems close with all of them. I watch the boy who sits in a lawn chair by the firepit, pulling a brush through Tank's fur.

"The kid is meticulous with detail. Way more than me. I'm the one who made *that* mistake." Tyler nods toward Nala, the now-pregnant lead husky lapping at her water bowl. An unintentional breeding when Tyler marked her cycle down in the wrong column and left her and Tank alone together.

But he owned up to it right away, rather than blame the kid. He's not one of those men who's too full of pride to admit his errors.

Another appealing quality that I don't want to know about.

"Didn't you say you wanted to breed Tank, anyway?"

"Yeah, but not with her, and not at that time." His eyebrows draw together with worry.

"So, what are you going to do, then? Sell the puppies?"

"Doubt it, but I don't have to make any decisions now." He shakes his head. "I'm getting phone calls from people who somehow got my number and letters in my mailbox from people who found my address. If I didn't have that gate, I'd have people driving up here daily. Linda Cogsby is looking for a new swing dog. Some Sam guy needs a few team dogs. And remember that guy at the checkpoint? Gary something?"

"Gary Seymore. Yeah."

"He called, wanting to know if I'd consider leasing some dogs so he could build a team to race the Iditarod himself. The guy couldn't operate a damn coffee maker. As if I'd ever trust him with any of my dogs, if I had any to spare. I wouldn't even loan him Pope for a five-mile Sunday tour."

The mushers' names are ringing alarms in my head. They're the same people Harry mentioned a few weeks ago when he was complaining about interested people ghosting his calls.

I'm beginning to see where they've gone.

Right next door, as Harry has feared all along.

"For these puppies"—I point to Nala—"you're either training

them to race or selling them to someone who will. They *need* to run. It's in their blood." No matter what reservations I have about the bad apples in the industry, I've seen these mushing dogs leaping with wild excitement the second someone holds up a line, and howl with dramatic protest that only a husky can deliver when they realize they're not going out that day.

"You're right. I *know* you're right. And my wife would want to know that her dogs are still out there running." A wistful look touches Tyler's face, and I can tell he's drifted somewhere else.

Somewhere far away from me, to another life where he was someone's husband and almost a father. I'm beginning to think Tyler spends a lot of time lingering with the dead. What must that do to a person?

"You bring the dogs into the barn on the very cold nights?" I ask, pulling him back to the land of the living.

He clears his throat. "Yeah, if it's really cold, especially the ones with the shorter hair. I kept the paddocks so we can separate them into smaller groups to avoid fighting. Most of them are pretty good, but every once in a while, we have an unexpected issue. We found out the hard way that Bella and Simone can't be together if Lasso is around, ever since they both had puppies with him." Tyler waves a hand at the black and white husky that saunters over in front of us to lie down on his back and show his belly. "This is Pope. He's decided he doesn't want to be a sled dog anymore. He'll run until he reaches twenty-four to twenty-six miles, and then he just stops."

"That's precise." And listening to Tyler speak so casually about his dogs, as if they're his children, makes me smile whether I want to or not.

"*Every* time. Shitty-ass sled dog, but the friendliest guy around. He's three and basically retired now. He and Sleet don't get along."

"Sleet's the swing dog under the tree?"

"Yeah. And he doesn't like lazy sled dogs, which Pope is. This one's good for chasing rabbits, eating more than his share, begging for belly scratches, and not much else." Tyler leans down to smooth his hand over Pope's thick midsection before pulling himself back up. "So, there's your full tour of my kennel." He folds his arms over his chest. "Anything you want me to change as the veterinarian on my payroll?" The tiny smirk tells me he knows I won't find one thing wrong.

"Actually, yes. The heat lamp you have set up in the treatment and birthing room, put it in the corner farthest from the door." It's a good idea, but it's also not critical, and yet I feel the need to poke holes in both Tyler's setup and his ego.

Tyler's lips twist, and I think he's going to question my demand. "Consider it done."

"Also, some sort of video feed, especially once you have puppies out here. And I want access to your full database." I've never had anything like that beyond the information that we collect at the clinic. Secretly, I'm a data nerd.

"I'll have a camera up by the end of the week, and I'll have you added to the database by the end of the day. So, does this mean you'll take me? I mean, *my dogs*?" he corrects, and a hint of color touches his cheeks that sparks my curiosity.

I set my jaw. "On one condition—that we keep this between us for now. I don't want whatever issues you and Harry have with each other to impact my clinic in any way." It's inevitable that the Hatchetts will find out soon enough, but the longer I can avoid Harry's resulting fit, the better.

He chuckles. "That's fine. I don't talk to that asshole, anyway."

"Okay, then." I check my watch. It's almost nine. I could easily spend the day here. "I should get going. Cory will send you an invoice for my time today," I say, already moving for my truck. "You can either e-transfer the payment or come in to pay within forty-eight hours. She'll include our regular operating hours in the email."

We walk back in an oddly comfortable silence. Tank, free of his grooming session, trots behind me.

"What'd you say that pregnant dog was at? Thirty days?"

"Thirty-two. Frank already did the X-rays. She's having six."

"So another month before she whelps." I can avoid Tyler until then, unless there's a fight requiring stitches. I climb into my truck and slam the door. "I'll have Cory send you a detailed fee list so you understand all my rates up front. And they're nonnegotiable." I hold my breath, waiting for him to ask if those will be discounted kennel rates.

Tyler settles an arm on my door where the window is rolled down. It's a strategic move. I can't pull away without possibly injuring him. "Why do I feel like you're trying to scare me away?"

"Maybe I am."

"I don't scare easily." His focus wanders ahead of us, over the trees, as if searching for something. "You going straight to your clinic?"

"Yeah. Why?"

Amusement dances in his eyes. "Might want to change." He nods toward my T-shirt.

I look down to find two muddy paw prints conveniently located on my chest, like well-placed handprints. Which explains why Tyler's gaze kept veering there all morning.

I sigh as I crank my engine. "At least I didn't get peed on again."

"And Marie?" He leans in a touch, as if sharing a secret, and my nose catches a faint but delightful mixture of clean sweat and spearmint gum. "Don't fire Cory. She meant well." With a wink and a pat against my door, he shifts away.

My cheeks burn as I drive off.

He *did* see my calendar.

I spend the long, bumpy driveway considering ways to punish my assistant for that stunt. By the time I've reached the end, I've decided she'll be taking on *all* anal gland secretion appointments for the foreseeable future, beginning with Gladys Burt's twelve-year-old pug this afternoon.

A familiar truck slows as I'm pulling out of Tyler's driveway. It's Bonnie Hatchett, her shriveled face angled toward me.

With a curse under my breath, I force a smile and wave on my way past, not slowing.

Well, that secret didn't last long.

CHAPTER SIXTEEN

The familiar clown horn honks outside the clinic at one minute to noon, pulling a chuckle from Cory. "You having lunch with your dad today?"

I peer out the window to see him sitting in the UTV, his splinted leg stretched out the open side—a maneuver I doubt his doctor would approve of. A picnic basket sits on the seat beside him. "I guess I am." We hadn't planned on it, but if my father is here with sandwiches, it means he wants to talk.

And I already know what it's about.

Harry called me yesterday to find out why his mother saw me pulling out of Tyler's driveway. I'd bet my professional license and a thousand dollars that Bonnie was standing opposite him, coaching him on what to say.

I didn't lie. I shouldn't have to.

But that set off a tirade, because Harry also happened to drive out to Linda Cogsby's kennel yesterday to get an answer, and he didn't like the one he got—she's holding out for a dog from Tyler Brady.

Harry delivered an ultimatum to me, I told him he would not

be dictating my clients and patients, and he informed me that the Hatchetts would no longer be clients of mine.

I haven't told anyone yet—not Cory, not my father—as I try to wrap my head around what this means for the clinic's bottom line. But my guess is, my father has already heard.

"Joe and I are going up to the ranch to pay a deposit." Cory collects her purse. "I *might* be a few minutes late, if that's okay?"

"Of course. Have fun." A part of me is envious of my assistant. I remember when Jonathan and I were going through the motions of planning a wedding. It was exciting for a time, despite how it all fell apart in the end. We visited locations around Anchorage, collected quotes, but I kept finding excuses for why none of them felt right. It turns out the location was never the issue. I needed a different groom.

"You want me to lock up?"

"It's fine. We won't go far." Dad still struggles on his crutches on smooth ground. I'd rather he stay put out here.

I flip the Closed sign on the clinic door and grab a light jacket as I walk out. It's sixty-five degrees Fahrenheit today—the warmest it's been all month, given the onslaught of rain we've had. But I don't mind, because more rain means less risk of the forest fires that have ravaged the state, year after year.

All three dogs followed my father here, but they're busy sniffing the bushes for various scents from clinic animals relieving themselves. "I can't believe Mom allowed this."

"I snuck out while she was distracted." He pats the basket. "I thought you'd like to watch me eat, if you've got time."

"I always have time for you."

He winks. "I knew I was your favorite."

With a chuckle, I climb into the passenger seat, stealing a glance inside the basket. "Pulled pork?" I was expecting turkey on rye—the healthy choice, and a staple in my father's diet.

"There's a lot going on, and your mother's been stress cooking all morning." He gives the UTV gas. It lurches toward the nearby picnic table.

"Are you still being difficult?"

"Not *me*. For once." He gives me a sideways glance. "I suppose you haven't talked to Vicki yet, have you?"

His question catches me off guard. "Not since I went over on Monday so she could cut my hair." A twinge of panic stirs in my stomach. "Why? What's wrong? Is Molly okay?"

"She's fine. They're all fine." His shoulders slump. "Vicki's pregnant."

I gasp. "*Again?*" Molly's only five months old!

"It's funny how biology works, huh?" He chuckles. "Clearly those two missed that day in school."

"She can't even get a night's sleep!"

"They definitely found something to do while they *weren't* sleeping."

My thoughts are spinning. "What were they thinking? How can they afford this?"

"They *weren't* thinking. And they *can't*." Dad shakes his head. "Hence, the pulled pork sandwiches and the apple pie baking as we speak."

———

"Bonnie Hatchett called me this morning."

"I was wondering when you'd bring that up," I mumble around the last of my sandwich. We've been too busy discussing Vicki and Oliver's carelessness that has now put them in a position of having to raise two babies on one meager income and a vehicle that is in the garage every other month.

And yet, despite the panic my sister is surely swirling in, there's that part of me that envies her for the things she has that seem to have slipped from my grasp.

"Bonnie was upset to learn that you'd throw away a four-decade relationship so easily."

Of course she'd blame me. "What'd you say?"

"What *could* I say? I didn't even know you were taking on Tyler Brady's kennel until she told me."

"I know. I should have mentioned something sooner. It all happened kind of fast, and I wasn't sure I'd agree until yesterday." That's not totally truthful. I knew, when Tyler was standing in my lobby, pleading with me, that I was a goner. Tyler transferred money to cover his bill within ten minutes of Cory sending it. That's a promising start. "It's good money for the clinic, and you should see the place, Dad. It makes the Hatchetts' look like a run-down circus show. He knows what he's doing. More than Harry does, that's for sure. Maybe even more than Earl did."

"I believe you. But you had to have known what might happen when you took him on. The repercussions of that."

"I did." Especially once Harry heard that all their prospective clients would rather be getting sled dogs from next door. "But they can't dictate which kennels I treat. They've gone too far."

He holds up his hands in surrender. "You're absolutely right. I'm not suggesting they can."

"They're the ones throwing away a four-decade relationship, all because Harry's a sore loser."

"Yup. There's no arguing that, either." Dad purses his lips. "Who was Tyler Brady with before?"

"Frank." Now that I know how tightly Tyler runs the day-to-day at his kennel, I can see why that relationship didn't work. Frank wouldn't see the value that I do in all those medical records and databases. Me? I'm a three-year-old tearing through presents on Christmas morning with that level of information.

Dad smooths a hand over his cheek in a slow, circular motion, his signature thinking tic. "I just know you and that Tyler fellow have had your differences in the past, and it seemed to me that day up in Hatcher Pass that they might not all be sorted out."

"They're sorted. It's fine. This is purely a business relationship."

"*Oh.*" Dad's bushy eyebrows arch. "I *see.* So there was a time when it might have been more than—"

"*No.* That was a misunderstanding that is now *crystal* clear. There is nothing else between Tyler and me." I'm saying that for my father's benefit, but it's also helpful to remind myself.

"I'm only bringing this up because I'd hate to see you lose *both* kennels if things don't work out with Tyler. That's *a lot* of money. And with this new baby on the way ..." His words drift, but his meaning is clear.

I can't afford to miss any rent payments to them, because some of that will inevitably be going toward helping my sister. I can already see that the extra cash I was planning on giving them to recoup their Mexico savings account will never get them there. They'll stick it in an envelope and leave it on Vicki and Oliver's kitchen counter without a word the next time they visit, to help ease this new burden. And how much can *I* say? They've done it for me once or twice while I was in school when money was especially tight.

"Tyler and I have worked out our issues, and he begged me to take him on, so I don't think he's going anywhere. And as far as the Hatchetts go, Harry's going to learn quickly how good he had it. I wouldn't be surprised if he comes crawling back." I say that with more confidence than I feel. "But Dad, you guys can't keep throwing money at Vicki." If my parents have made any mistakes with us, it's being generous to a fault. Other parents would not be so quick to try to solve their adult children's financial problems for them. "I know you think you're helping them, but you're not. They need to figure this out on their own."

"How's she gonna do that with two babies in tow and a husband who's always working? They're struggling to pay their rent for that apartment as it is."

"So, they move in here until Vicki finishes school and gets

established. The room in the attic is big enough, and Mom will help take care of Molly."

"We've offered. More than once. You know your mother loves having a house full of people, and Oliver wouldn't mind. Knowing Eleanor, she'd be sending him off to work with packed lunches every day. It's Vicki who doesn't want to move back in."

"It's not about what she *wants* at this point. It's about what she has to do, and as long as she knows you guys will cover them, she has options." I love my little sister fiercely, but her lack of responsibility and feeble work ethic infuriate me to no end, as does her ability to take our parents' money without showing a shred of guilt. "Maybe moving in with you will make her follow through with the hair design school thing." That I know my parents paid for, just like they paid for her semester in college and her real estate license.

What can I say? They fronted a giant chunk of my veterinarian college fees. My parents have never wanted their daughters to miss an education because of financial strain. But in Vicki's case, maybe they have been too open-handed.

He sighs. "We never have been good at the tough-love thing. I just can't sit back and watch my kids, *and* my grandkids, fall on hard times when I can help them. But maybe you're right. They could save their money rather than us handing them more. Vicki could finish school and start building a real career. Eventually, they might even buy a house."

"That won't ever happen if they don't start making smart decisions. And stop having babies they can't afford." And selfishly, I will admit, if Vicki moves back here, this idea that Mom and Dad sell and move to Eagle River will vanish, at least in the short term. Liz doesn't *need* help; Vicki genuinely does.

I'm going to have a frank conversation with my little sister about how this option makes the most sense for her family.

I check my watch and then the parking lot in the distance. Cory's not back yet, and my afternoon appointments will start rolling in soon. "I should get going. Sarah Mickle's coming in with Stitch."

"Oh, that feisty little dachshund. I remember when he was just a pup." Dad frowns. "He must be getting up there now?"

"Fifteen." I give my dad a look. There's nothing more I can do to ease Stitch's aches and pains, other than make his last moments as comfortable as possible. This is the part of my job that I will *never* get used to. It's going to be a long, draining afternoon.

Dad's frown grows deeper. I always knew the days when he had to put pets down. His shoulders would be sagging when he walked through the door. "Give her my condolences."

I climb from my seat at the picnic table as the dogs take off barking toward the house. My mother's hollers carry on the breeze. She's standing in the doorway, waving us over.

Dad scratches at his chin. "Wonder what that's about?"

"Maybe the pie's ready."

His eyes sparkle. "We should get over there, then, before she calms down and doesn't let me eat it."

Dad hobbles on his crutches toward the UTV, settles in, and cranks the engine, and I hop into the passenger seat. We coast along the narrow dirt lane.

The closer we get, the clearer my mother's shocked expression becomes. Her hands are busy wringing a tea towel.

"I don't think this is about pie," my dad mutters.

"I think you might have pushed her over the edge." I call out, "Is everything okay, Mom?"

"Yes, it's just ..." She has a bewildered look on her face. "We're going to be grandparents again."

"I know. Dad told me." And once her worry ebbs, she's going to be ecstatic. My mother lives for her grandchildren.

"No." She shakes her head. "I'm not talking about Vicki."

If not Vicki, then ...

"I just got off the phone with Liz. She's two months along."

My jaw hangs open for the second time in this lunch hour. "*Liz* is having another baby?" Liz, who has openly said she didn't want any more kids? Who booked and drove Jim to his vasectomy appointment? "With *whom?*"

My mother shoots me an exasperated look.

CHAPTER SEVENTEEN

"You guys have been busy."

"And you've been a ghost," Jonah counters with a pointed glare.

"I've been busy too." I take in the structure. When I last stopped in at Calla and Jonah's in early spring, Jonah was cutting down trees on this spot with his chainsaw. Now there's a two-story log cabin overlooking the lake, its tin roof and windows matching the green of their home across the water.

I guess it *has* been a bit too long since I've been by.

"Cute little place, though, huh?" Jonah pats the porch post. The sleeve of his blue T-shirt falls back to show off the scar he earned from the surgery to reset his bones last year. Aside from that, no one would know the arm had been broken, the muscle tone even with his other. "Two bedrooms, two baths. Not bad for a prefab. Took them no time to put it up."

"I can't believe it's already done."

His eyes drag across the overhang. "*Almost* done. The plumber and electrician are finished. Bathroom and kitchen are functioning. Floors are in. Now it's just a lot of finishing touches."

"Agnes must be getting excited?" I've known the Alaska Wild

office manager for as long as I've known Jonah. She is the kindest woman I've ever met—a soft-spoken Alaska Native without a judgmental bone in her body.

His smothered smirk reminds me of a boy trying to hide his delight—and failing. "I talked to Aggie this morning. Everything's sold or donated, their suitcases are packed. They're ready to go."

No matter how much Jonah loves Calla, I know he struggled with leaving Western Alaska. He built a full life there, with villagers who depended on him as a pilot, and friends who were like family. But then Calla came into the picture—a city girl visiting from Toronto, reconnecting with her estranged father—and that full life was suddenly empty without her.

Jonah had to make a choice, and he chose to build a new life, here with her. He chose Calla, but he *hated* leaving Agnes and her daughter, Mabel, who he's watched grow from a stumbling toddler to the fourteen-year-old she is now. He's been pushing them to move here for over a year. I honestly didn't think he'd convince Agnes, but as I look around at this perfect life they've assembled for themselves in Trapper's Crossing, with log cabins on a lake, the mountain peaks in the distance, the planes floating on standby, and the community that has welcomed them whole-heartedly, how could anyone say no?

"When are you flying out to Bangor to get them?"

"First thing tomorrow morning. That way we can get back ahead of the fish fry. You're coming to the Ale House tomorrow night, right?"

"Wouldn't miss it. Muriel and Teddy always throw a good party." The couple and their son, Toby, who I dated ever so briefly last summer, run a three-season fishing resort down the street, complete with cabin rentals and a lodge that serves fries and burgers and beer. Plenty of locals find themselves at the tavern on the weekends in the summer months.

The McGivneys have become more than neighbors to Calla and Jonah. In many ways, they're the family Jonah and Calla have come to love and depend upon as if they were blood relatives. Not that they had much choice. Muriel is a nosy busybody who rammed her way into their lives, dragging her jolly husband along for the ride.

"Goddamn it!" A loud clatter inside the cabin accompanies the familiar voice. "Son of a bitch!"

I lift my eyebrows in question.

"You good in there, Roy?" Jonah calls out.

"Yeah. My level's shot, though."

"Let me check the workshop. I'm pretty sure there's one in there."

"If it's Phil's, then it'll be a piece of shit."

Jonah sighs with exasperation. "Lemme look, anyway, and we'll go from there."

"He's in a good mood today," I whisper dryly.

"Eh, he's just pissed off that Calla decided to go with stock cabinets for the kitchen instead of letting him build custom." Jonah scratches absently at his beard. "But custom would have taken forever, and she didn't want him tying up his days. There's still a lot to do in there, and his family is flying up from Texas this month."

"Right. I forgot about that." The daughter that Roy hasn't seen since she was a baby and grandchildren he's only ever met over video calls. People that Calla has somehow befriended. I only know bits and pieces of the man's past. I don't think even Jonah knows the whole truth, but Calla and their ornery neighbor have an odd relationship that no one can understand. "He must be a bit off-kilter?" Though it doesn't take much to ruffle Roy's feathers.

Jonah grunts. "You don't know the half of it."

"And they're staying with you?"

"Yeah. Up at the house." He nods toward their place, a green-roofed log cabin on a peninsula that juts out into the lake. "Calla's been busy getting everything ready. Between that and this place, and all the stuff she's doing for the farmers' market, she's dog-tired. Can barely stay awake at night." There's a hint of reverence in his voice when he speaks about his wife.

Another clatter and curse sounds inside.

"I better go and get that level." Louder, Jonah hollers, "Be back in a minute, Roy."

A grumble is the only answer he gets.

"Take a look around inside if you want. Ignore him." Jonah hops on the ATV and takes off for the old shed next to the hangar.

I climb the porch steps and stroll through the open door, inhaling the scent of wood that permeates the air. Whereas my little log cabin in the woods is nothing more than a room divided into sections for living and sleeping and eating, with a bathroom carved into the back corner, this is a real *home*—all new and clean and fresh—with an eat-in kitchen on the left and living room on the right, and stairs behind the kitchen that lead up to the bedrooms.

It's not large, but I've been to Agnes's bungalow before, and it's more space than what they're leaving behind.

And it's currently occupied by a crusty old Texan wearing sawdust-coated jeans and a deep scowl while he chisels out the slots for door hinges. The pine door to the bathroom leans against the wall, waiting to be hung.

"Hey, Roy."

He pauses in his work to look up. The scowl softens a touch. "Oh. It's *you*. Hi, Marie."

That's as much enthusiasm as I'll get from the old grouch who Calla has dubbed the Curmudgeon, but it's more than what most receive.

I've always thought Roy an interesting fellow—a hermit with a southern twang who hides in the woods and has gone to great lengths to scare people away while he spends his days building stunning furniture and his nights whittling wood into artful collectibles. It's Calla of all people who has wormed a hole through his prickly exterior. He moans and he growls, and yet apparently he's making appearances here almost every day now, whether it's to work on one of the many buildings on the property or to trim their goat's hooves or use Calla's computer.

"This place is looking fantastic."

He juts his bearded chin toward the manufactured kitchen cabinets. "I told Calla not to hire those people, but she *never* listens to me. So? *This* is what she gets. Goddamn cheap, crooked cabinets."

The cabinets look straight to me, but I know better than to say that. Roy is a carpenter by trade, and fussy to a fault. "I'm sure you'll be able to fix it for them."

He mutters something under his breath that I don't catch, and it's probably for the best.

"So? Have you been building anything new and exciting in that shop of yours?"

"Bed frames for Agnes and the girl. Mabel." He adds after a moment, as if coaching himself to remember—and use—names. I suppose that's what happens when you spend decades shunning everyone. You have to relearn basic social graces.

"I'm sure they'll appreciate it." They're coming with nothing but their suitcases. It's not worth the cost of flying their furniture here, and there are no roads that connect the two sides. The place is already furnished with a few staple pieces to get Agnes and Mabel settled—a kitchen table and chairs, a soft gray couch, and a TV near the woodstove.

"As if I had a choice in the matter. You know Calla. Always gets what she wants, eventually."

"She does, doesn't she?" A spark of envy stirs inside me. As I look around this perfect life, she seems to have gotten everything she could've wanted, and a lot she never imagined.

I feel Roy's shrewd gaze on me. He's no fool. Thankfully, he keeps whatever thoughts inside his head to himself. "I was thinking I need to come by to see Oscar and Gus soon. They're due for their shots." More like overdue, but Roy isn't the type to bring his dogs in for regular checkups. I doubt those two had ever seen a veterinarian before last summer, when Calla called me in a panic because Oscar was caught in a trap. I was able to save his leg, but he'll forever walk with a limp.

"Whatever you say, Doc."

Roy also may not be the type to book appointments—he doesn't even have a phone—but we've fallen into an arrangement: He doesn't argue when I ignore his multitude of No Trespassing signs and show up to check on them, and I don't mention the fact that his dogs are more wolf than the malamutes he claims them to be, and those are illegal to own in the state of Alaska.

And he *always* pulls out the tin can with his money and pays, right down to the penny.

Roy toils away quietly while I mill around the cabin, testing the new stainless steel appliances and a few kitchen cabinet doors, stealing a peek upstairs at the cozy bedrooms—each with high-quality, Roy-built beds and dressers—until the familiar buzz of the ATV approaches.

Jonah is in the kitchen when I reach the landing. "From Calla." He holds up a quart-size basket of strawberries. "We've got them coming out our ass." There's another large basket on the table, next to a muffin, I assume for Roy, who is preoccupied with scowling at the level Jonah brought.

"No good?" Jonah asks.

"Why do you think every shelf in that house of yours was lopsided when you moved in?"

"'Cause Phil was always drunk?" Jonah answers glibly as he accepts the tool back. "Lemme run and grab a new one. You comin', Marie?"

"Where? To the hardware store?"

"Unless you want to hang out here with Chuckles?"

I check my watch. I don't have to be at the clinic until this afternoon.

He jerks his head toward the door. "Come on, Lehr. Let's go for a ride."

"Don't cheap out on the level, neither!" Roy barks after him.

———

"I haven't done this in a while."

"What? Bought a tool?" Jonah throws his truck into gear and pulls out of the hardware parking lot.

"Nothing. I haven't done *nothing* in a while." I stare out the window. It's one of those in-between days—overcast, but not raining, dull and gray, but with a warm breeze to trick you into thinking it's nicer than it is. At least it'll help dry up some of the rain from the past few days.

"What's botherin' you, Lehr?" Jonah steals a glance my way. "You seem down. Not yourself."

He always has been able to read me. I shrug. "Just stuff with work and home."

"Okay?" he prompts, and I know it's a push to elaborate.

"Harry Hatchett 'fired' me because I took on his neighbor's kennel, and they don't get along." I air-quote the word *fired*.

Jonah scowls. "He can't fucking fire you! You're not his damn employee!"

I smile at Jonah's outburst. I can always count on him to rage on my behalf. "That's what I said. Sort of."

"Well, fuck him. That arrogant little shit. Whatever. So you're trading one kennel for another. Don't give that idiot another second's thought."

"Tyler's is a lot smaller, though." And I've crunched the numbers. Without having a baseline for him, it's hard to calculate exactly how much I'm going to lose, but no doubt, it'll hurt.

"Still, you'll be fine. It's not like your parents can't cut you some slack on rent if it takes a couple months to catch up."

My laugh is awkward. "Right. About *that*." I fill him in on the talk around my parents cashing in the property.

"*Everything*? The clinic and all?"

"That was the plan, so they can move in with Liz and travel, but now with my sisters being pregnant—"

"Whoa. Wait a minute." Jonah holds up a hand. "Sisters?"

"Did I forget to mention that? They're pregnant. Both of them. The one who *just* had a baby and the one whose husband got snipped five years ago."

He snorts. "What're the odds of that happening?"

"Higher than you'd think, actually. Anyway, Vicki and Oliver are moving in with my parents to save money and so Vicki can finish her hours for her certification, which is a smart plan. Liz is beyond livid." She didn't even come to last Sunday's family dinner. She claimed morning sickness, but everyone knows she's pissed. "She was banking on her surprise pregnancy guaranteeing her my mom as a live-in nanny, but my mom will be tied up for the foreseeable future with two other kids."

It took an hour of frank conversation with Vicki to help her make the smart decision, but she's under the delusion that this'll only be for a few months, that they'll be in an apartment before the new baby's born. I'd bet money that a few months turns into a few years once she starts leaning on my mother for childcare that would otherwise be impossible to afford.

Liz has figured this out, too, and isn't happy about it. But Liz can afford a sitter for her Friday wine nights with her friends. She just has to clear the expenditure with her prudent husband.

Jonah shakes his head. "Too much family drama."

"Don't get me wrong, I'm happy for my sisters." More so Vicki than Liz, if I'm being honest, because I like her more and because, selfishly, her mistake is buying me some stability. "And I can't blame my parents if and when they do decide to sell. It's their money and their life, but it kind of feels like I'm in a holding pattern now, until mine is blown up." I'll lose my clinic *and* my home. I'll have to start over.

"Yeah, I know that feeling."

I offer him a sympathetic smile. "I know you do." Jonah put ten years in at Alaska Wild. He was Wren's right-hand man, running that place—a family business that had kept the villages connected for decades. Wren offered to sell it to Jonah when he knew the cancer was terminal, but Jonah couldn't afford it.

Just like me. I can't afford to buy my parents' property. In hindsight, maybe I *should* be farther along financially than I am, despite my student debt.

"Don't worry. It's just a building. It's *you* they're coming to see." He reaches over and pats my forearm. "It'll all work out."

"One way or another, right?" I sigh. "And is it just me, or does it feel like *everyone* around us is pregnant or just had a baby or is getting married?" Or otherwise moving forward with their lives. And here I am, in the same place I've been for years.

And if my parents end up selling the clinic in a few years' time and I have to work for someone else because I can't afford to open my own place, it'll feel like a giant step backward.

"Not *everyone*."

I steal a glance at Jonah to see if there's any animosity behind those words—I know he's desperate to start a family, too, the millisecond that Calla's ready—but he's focused on the bald man standing next to a red truck in the parking lot of the drive-thru coffee shop ahead, wiping a glob of ketchup off his shirt with a napkin. "Shit, that's Sam. I gotta stop and talk to him." Jonah barely slows as he veers into the pothole-riddled parking lot. "I'll only be a minute."

Any time Jonah gets into a conversation with another pilot, it's *never* just a minute. "It's fine. I think I need a coffee."

"Grab one for Calla, too. She's on a kick. What are those things called?" He snaps his fingers. "A fog something or other?"

"London Fog?"

"Yeah. With soy milk. And lavender."

I feel my face screw up. *"Lavender? Here?"* I throw my hand toward the little blue-and-green shack on the side of the road—a tourist landmark, its walls plastered with mushing-themed signs, the roof's ridge adorned by wooden sled dogs and a sled, and a Porta Potty next to the back entrance.

"I don't know?" He shrugs. "That's how she makes it at home."

I burst out with laughter, and it's a welcome reprieve from the weight I've been under. "I never thought I'd see the day."

"Yeah, yeah, I know." He grins. "Just get whatever they have. But make it soy."

I hop out of the truck and walk toward the shack. I stop at the vacant window, my hungry eyes drifting over the assortment of danishes and other treats on display.

The window slides open. "Marie Lehr! Is that you?" Charlotte tosses her long gray braid over her shoulder. "My God, it's been years!"

At least three since Micky, her cocker spaniel, passed. That's how I know everyone in the Mat-Su area—by their four-legged family members.

"What can I get you today?"

I put in the order for Calla and myself—a plain old black coffee for plain old Marie—along with an order of biscuits and gravy that I will regret in an hour and Jonah will complain about. And then I listen as Charlotte fills me in on the latest local gossip while toiling in her little kitchen shack.

When my food is up and the rumble of a truck behind me says there's another customer waiting in line, I quickly depart.

Jonah is still deep in conversation with Sam, so I head toward the picnic tables. I'm halfway there when I realize that I know the man sitting at one of them, leaning over to make faces at the baby in the car seat while a woman fumbles with a diaper bag, in a frantic search for something.

I stumble over my feet as I stop abruptly. Of all days … seeing my ex and his adorable little family is the *last* thing I'm in the mood for. Before I can make a sharp turn left toward Jonah's truck, Jonathan looks up and sees me.

His hand lifts halfway before he falters, as if suddenly recalling how badly I hurt him. I've heard through mutual friends that he still sometimes drops comments that hint at lingering resentment. Finally, he commits to the wave.

With my hands full and a clear, straight path toward them, I'm now stuck.

Deep breath in, I force a smile and close the distance. "It's been awhile. How are you?" I hover rather than taking a seat, silently hoping Jonah will rescue me soon.

My ex looks the same—clean-cut brown hair, lean build, head-to-toe Patagonia gear—but the dark circles under his eyes are new.

"Good, good. Actually, I'm *great*." He gestures at the plump baby watching us, as if presenting an artifact. "Meet Clancy. My son. *Our* son," he quickly corrects, turning toward the woman. "This is my fiancée Carrie. This is *Marie*." Nothing else. Just *Marie*.

"Nice to meet you." I nod toward the petite, dark-haired woman. I'm sure she's heard plenty of stories about me. "Congratulations."

"Thank you," she says, holding up a pacifier in the air. "Found it!" The diamond engagement ring catches my attention. It's far bigger than the one I handed back to him.

"Oh, thank God." Jonathan rubs his forehead. To me, he explains, "We're heading up to Talkeetna for the day, and Clancy screams in the car when he doesn't have it."

"He looks happy enough right now." I smile at the boy, and I get a toothless smile in return. "How old is he?"

"Almost three months?" He looks to Carrie for confirmation.

"*Four*," she corrects sternly.

"Right. Holy. I can't keep track anymore." Jonathan chuckles, massaging the back of his neck. He always did that when he was uncomfortable. "Between our son being born, and work taking off, and the upcoming wedding, the days are flying by. But *all* amazing things. Wouldn't have it any other way."

I'm sure it's not a dig at me, and yet I feel the shovel blade hit my back all the same.

Healthy baby, check.

Happy spouse, check.

Blooming career, check.

All things Marie doesn't have. Check, check.

Not that he would know that last part.

But would this have been Jonathan and I, had I stayed? Had I settled?

It's a discombobulating feeling—to stand across from a person who once knew your most intimate secrets and now is virtually a stranger with an entirely new life of his own.

"What's new with you, Marie? Still doin' the vet thing?"

"*Still* doing the vet thing."

"And where are you living now?"

"Same place."

His eyebrows arch. "With your parents?"

There's no mistaking the judgment in that tone. "In the cabin on the property," I correct with a shrug. "It's easy."

"Yeah. Of course. I just thought you'd be, I don't know ..." He lets that thought go unfinished. Maybe he truly doesn't know, or maybe he's just playing dumb. "And you're here, grabbing coffee for you and—" His eyes tally the cups in my hand and then searches the vicinity. I know the moment he sees Jonah, recognizes him, because his jaw tenses.

"Coffee for me and tea for Jonah's *wife*," I say, because I know where his assumption is headed, and I have no desire to hurt him more than I already did.

When we split up, I made the mistake of being too honest

with Jonathan about my feelings for the bush pilot. The truth that we weren't meant for each other fell by the wayside as Jonathan railed. First came the accusations of infidelity, and then the promises that I'd regret throwing away our future over a crush. And even with his son staring up at him and his soon-to-be wife listening intently, I can see Jonathan's ego still feels that sting.

"His wife," he repeats, and there's a moment of confusion, followed by understanding that suggests he hadn't heard.

But the smug little smile that touches his lips? That makes me wish I'd let him stew in false assumptions.

This was the last encounter I needed today when I've already been feeling so low.

"Just the person I was looking for," a familiar deep voice announces behind me.

I spin around to find Tyler strolling toward me, his uniform hugging his perfect form, his park ranger vehicle rumbling, the driver's side door propped open.

God, he looks good. But ...

Jonathan.

Jonah.

Tyler.

All in one parking lot.

"I'm in the twilight zone," I mutter.

Tyler tilts his head.

"Nothing," I say before he has a chance to ask. "What are you doing here?"

He holds up a coffee, as if that's explanation enough, and then takes a few casual steps closer, just within my personal space, and drops his voice to a whisper. "And you look like you might be stuck in something you'd rather not be stuck in. Am I right about that?" Gentle eyes search mine.

He was the truck that pulled in behind me. I never bothered to look back. He must've seen me falter, must've read the tension in my body. Am I that obvious? Or is he that perceptive? He is in law enforcement, after all, trained to spot conflict.

Can he see me at war with myself?

I feel my head bobbing without much thought.

Tyler slips his free hand around my waist. I feel the warmth of it through my jacket. "I hope you don't mind, but I need to steal this one away."

He's saving me. That's what he's doing.

I turn back toward Jonathan, watching curiously. Maybe it's rude to not introduce them, but I have no reason to. Jonathan is part of my past, and Tyler is … well, Tyler is just a client, but Jonathan doesn't know that. "It was good seeing you. Enjoy your day up in Talkeetna. And congratulations again on *everything.*"

Clancy lets out a screech that has Carrie darting around the picnic table, aiming the soother toward his mouth like a plug to stop a leak.

I allow myself a breath of relief as Tyler guides me away. Only where my stomach was coiling with discomfort before, now it's full of nervous flutters, the faint scent of cologne with notes of cedar and citrus peel drawing me in closer. "Thank you."

But Tyler doesn't answer, his gaze hanging off Jonathan and his crying son.

On his son.

My heart pangs for this man as I see the pain in his stony expression as clearly as if it were written on a page. How often does Tyler see his unborn child in the faces of these living ones? How often does he wonder how different his life would have been, had they survived?

"Tyler?" I call out softly. His hand is still curled around my waist.

He snaps out of whatever trance he was in with a sharp inhale. "Yeah?"

"Thank you," I repeat.

He slides his arm away from me. "What are friends for?" He mock frowns. "Oh, *wait* …"

He's back to his casual charming self, but I just caught a hint of what's hidden beneath the facade. "Were you actually looking for me? Is there something wrong with the dogs?" It's been two weeks since I visited his kennel.

"Nah. Dogs are all good. I saw you there and you seemed anxious." His eyes drift over my frame. "Your body language was off."

"You're an expert with body language?"

"With some things." He hides a smile behind a sip of his coffee.

We're heading back down this dangerous path again—where Tyler flirts shamelessly and I read too much into it, where I let false hope trick me into believing something that isn't true.

"Who's that guy?" he asks, nodding toward Jonathan.

"My ex."

"Serious?"

"Five years." I hesitate. "We were engaged."

He shifts his focus from Jonathan to Carrie to Clancy, as if itemizing possibilities. "What happened?"

"It wasn't meant to be. Long story." I check Jonah. He's still gabbing. "You're a bit out of the way for Hatcher Pass, aren't you?"

"I've been working at Nancy Lake this week."

"Anything exciting?" I find myself desperate to change topics, to keep this casual conversation going. It feels good to be with Tyler. When I'm with him, I'm not thinking about anything else.

"Besides the family of tourists who thought bear repellent worked the same as mosquito repellent and sprayed it all over themselves?"

An unexpected burst of laughter escapes.

"You like that one, huh?" Tyler grins. "It's not as good as the naked couple I found hiding in the trees yesterday."

My jaw drops. "You're lying!"

"Swear to God." He presses his free hand over his vest where his heart resides, under a thick pad of muscle. "They were camping and decided to go skinny-dipping in one of the lakes in the afternoon. When they got out of the water, their clothes were gone. Went back to their campground and *everything* there was gone too. They were trying to get to their car when I came across them."

"Naked and afraid."

He chuckles. "She had a few well-positioned tree branches but kept dropping them to swat at the mosquitoes. Man, that was a *long*, uncomfortable walk back to my truck for everyone."

If I had a free hand, it would be covering my hanging jaw. I'm not sure which would be worse—darting through the mosquito-infested forest bare-assed or being found that way by *this* man. My cheeks flush with the thought. "Did you figure out who stole their things?"

"The woman seemed convinced his *girlfriend* had something to do with it."

"*Oh.*"

"Yeah. If it was, I say good for her." He takes a long sip of his coffee.

I'm momentarily caught on his mouth and his jaw, and the way his Adam's apple bobs with his swallow. But mostly, I'm caught on how much I like being near Tyler.

He flashes another smile, this one showing off deep dimples, and a look that says he can somehow read my thoughts.

"Sorry 'bout that. Once you get Sam talkin' about his fire boss planes, there's no stopping him."

I jump at the sound of Jonah's deep voice behind me. "Yeah. No worries."

"Aw, man. You did *not*." He grimaces when he takes in the paper tray of biscuits and gravy. "How do you eat that stuff? It looks like cat vomit."

Exactly the reaction I knew I'd get from Jonah. "Cold cat vomit now, thanks to you."

He shakes his head with disgust, then points at the tray of drinks in my hand. "That's dairy-free, right? 'Cause Calla will murder me in my sleep if it's not."

I'm about to say yes when Tyler cuts in. "Hey, you were flying dogs out of White Mountain back in March, weren't you?"

"Dogs, straw, HEET, kibble, pork belly, you name it. *She* roped me in." He jerks his chin toward me.

"This is Tyler Brady," I introduce.

Jonah frowns as recognition slips in. "You won this year, didn't you?" He sticks his hand out. "Congratulations. Good to see you, man."

"I didn't know you and Marie were friends. What's that like? Did you have to fill out an application? Go for an interview?" Tyler is talking to Jonah, but he's grinning at me. "Did she tell you to fuck off a few times, too, before she gave you a chance?"

I'm shaking my head, but I'm laughing now. And my cheeks are flushed. *Again.* "Don't you have more naked people in the woods to rescue?"

"Oh man, I hope not." His eyes twinkle with laughter.

Jonah watches curiously as if trying to decipher the cryptic joke, before tapping my arm with his elbow. "We better get back with that level before Roy quits on me. He's on a super short fuse." His gaze darts between Tyler and me, and I see that look of determination settle into his jaw a second before he says, "Hey, listen, if you're around tomorrow night, you should come by the Ale House in Trapper's Crossing."

What is he doing? "Tyler lives too far away," I blurt, glaring at my best friend.

"Actually, I don't mind the drive. You going to be there, Marie?" Tyler is smiling. Is this a challenge? He must be able to sense my panic now as surely as he did earlier from across the lot.

"Yeah, she is," Jonah answers for me.

"Then maybe I'll make an appearance. Cheers." He holds up his paper cup, the blue ink paw prints almost comical in his large hand, and then heads back to his pickup.

The second we're in Jonah's truck, he turns in his seat to declare, "You hooked up with that guy."

"I didn't!" I falter. "Not exactly. It's a long story, and I don't want to get into it. And why did you invite him to the Ale House?" My hands free of the coffee tray, I smack his arm.

"I was tryin' to help you out! Come on, you two wanna jump each other."

"We don't."

"Yeah. Bullshit," he scoffs, cranking his engine. "I may be an idiot about a lot of things, but I can tell when two people are into each other."

"We're not. Or *he's* not. Believe me, he couldn't have been clearer."

Jonah cocks his head, waiting for an explanation.

He is not going to relent. "His wife died giving birth to his son. They both died." I watch the green-and-white ranger pickup truck sit at the main road, the little light blinking as Tyler waits to make his turn. "He's not interested in dating anyone."

Jonah's face twists. "Christ, Lehr, you're bringin' *a lot* of drama with you today. Poor guy, though. That's gotta be rough." He works his fingers through his beard in thought. "So, you wait. Get to know him. Be friends, and when he's ready—"

I burst out with mirthless laughter. "And when he's ready for a relationship, he'll decide that *I'm* the one for him? Gee, where have I heard this before?" Oh yeah, that was me, convincing myself of that brilliant plan for years. "No thanks. I'm thirty-eight. You think when he gets over her, he's not going to be looking for someone younger than him?" Someone who won't be in her sixties when their child is twenty? *If* she can even have a child by then? "I don't have time for the wait-and-see game. I've been there, done that, and I am *never* putting myself through it again."

The second the words are out, I regret them.

We've never openly addressed the elephant in the room. I don't think Jonah's ever seen it. At least, I've convinced myself of that because it's easier for my pride that way. But *I've* seen the elephant, stomping around with a trumpet affixed to its trunk, just in case it needed more attention.

Jonah takes a deep breath, as if preparing himself to unload words he was hoping he'd never have to say.

And I'm suddenly terrified that, above all else, I'm about to lose my best friend. That storm, I cannot weather. "Jonah, I—"

"No." He puts up a hand to stop me. "First off, plenty of women have babies in their forties, so stop thinkin' that you can't. And I know things may not have worked out how you saw them going." He swallows. "But I only ever want to see you as happy as *I* am with Calla."

"I truly am *so* glad you found her. You two are perfect for each other."

"We are, aren't we?" He smiles wistfully. "Honestly? I never thought I could be this happy. It's like she was made just for me."

I watch the truck pull onto the main road and speed off toward the entrance to Nancy Lake. In another world, I wonder if Tyler might have been made for me.

But in this world, it's beginning to feel like I'm on my own.

"Hey, you feel like going for a ride tomorrow? Just you and me. Hit up some villages for old times' sake? Play with some strays?"

I laugh. "Actually, I could use an escape from *everything* right about now."

For old times' sake.

CHAPTER EIGHTEEN

"You wanna borrow the cot in the back?"

I cap off my gaping yawn with a laugh. "I might. I'll let you know." We left Jonah's private airstrip at five A.M., the sun already high in a cloudless sky, the day promising to be unseasonably warm. After dropping Calla in Bangor and refueling, Jonah and I took off to a few villages along the river, stopping in to check with locals, as much to say hello to them as to treat their pets. It was nostalgic and therapeutic—and exactly what I needed.

We arrived back in Trapper's Crossing at six with Agnes and Mabel, giving me just enough time to get home to shower, try on everything in my meager closet, and consider canceling my appearance tonight.

Toby's face splits into a wide grin as he slides a bottle of Coors Light across the bar toward me. The sable-brown scruff that coated his jaw during the winter months is long gone, revealing a baby face that looks far younger than his thirty-six years. "Might have to wrestle Rich for it."

I search out the construction worker—a staple drunk around here—to find him leaning against the wall for support before letting my focus wander. The Ale House's interior of mismatched tables covered in vinyl clothes, kitschy signs, and dead animals mounted on the walls has enough charm to draw in a crowd on the regular, and it's filling up tonight, as the aroma of batter, hot oil, and fried fish lingers in the air.

Jonah and Calla are on the other side of the bar, mingling, Jonah's arm slung over Calla's shoulders in a way that's casual and yet protective.

Calla stands out as usual, her caramel-colored hair styled in beachy waves, her makeup impeccable, her simple outfit of jeans and a rich red-plaid shirt looking both effortless and carefully selected.

She catches me staring, and her smile transforms from amused to sympathetic. I don't know what reason Jonah gave her about my spontaneous tag along today, but since I arrived at their place this morning, she's been handling me with kid gloves, as if I might burst into tears at any moment.

She holds up her martini glass in a cross-the-room cheers. This place had never seen anything beyond a pint glass and beer bottle before she moved in. Now she has the McGivneys stocking their bar for her drinking tastes, and I doubt she ever asked them to. They just started doing it because they wanted to. It's a gift to have that kind of influence over people.

I return the gesture before shifting my focus to Agnes and Mabel, standing with them, Agnes's smile wide while Mabel absorbs the Ale House's rambunctious crowd with innocent curiosity. It's a different world here from the life they're accustomed to in the west, where booze may no longer be outright prohibited in Bangor, but it's still restricted due to high rates of alcoholism among the villages.

"Haven't seen it this busy in a while." I check the clock on the wall. It's after nine, and there's still no sign of Tyler.

Will he come?

"That's because you haven't been here in a while," Toby chides softly.

"I guess I haven't." Not since the wedding on New Year's Eve, when a team of ambitious women, led by Calla's mother, transformed this shabby place into a sophisticated reception hall that could rival any rustic-themed magazine spread, teeming with copper and crystal and flowers and candlelight. "I've been busy."

"As long as that's all it is." His gentle gray eyes leave the pint glass he's filling for just a second to meet mine, the unspoken question in them.

Toby and I went on two official dates last year, and then we didn't go on any more. There weren't any awkward conversations, any "it's not you, it's me" excuses. I'm not sure if Toby felt anything for me, but I didn't feel anything beyond friendship for him, and I think he figured that out when I deftly avoided a good-night kiss.

I think he also figured out where my heart loitered, struggling to let go.

But friends, we've remained, because I enjoy his easygoing demeanor.

"That's all it is. I promise."

The door creaks, and I swivel on my bar stool to check the newcomers. I don't recognize them. Fishermen, from the lower forty-eight, probably.

"Who are you expectin'?" Toby asks.

"No one."

"Is that why you look so nice tonight? For *no one*?"

"I look the same as I always do." Except with makeup and an attempt at loose waves and a casual black summer dress that I reserve for nights out—few and far between.

"And you keep lookin' at the door."

I suck back a gulp of beer to avoid answering, earning his chuckle.

Toby's father, Teddy, waddles over to this side of the bar, his thumbs hooked behind his orange suspenders, his frown aimed across the room. "How old is Agnes's girl again?"

As if part of a perfectly timed stage production, Muriel barrels through the saloon doors with a rack of freshly washed beer glasses in her grip, catching his question. "*Mabel* is fourteen, and she's gonna be puttin' some time in around here this summer, so learn her name, would ya?"

Fourteen, though she could easily pass for sixteen, with her tall, graceful figure and the sleek new bob that highlights an emerging angular jawline. As childhood gives way to adulthood, it's evident that she's inherited a flattering mix of both Agnes and her father, a pilot who died in a crash a few months before she was born.

"Around *here?*" Teddy threads his fingers through his long white beard, a core part of his costume when he plays Santa at the town Christmas party every year. "Doin' what?"

The glasses clang noisily as she drops them onto the counter. "Cleanin' rooms and stayin' out of trouble." And nothing in Muriel's tone suggests that's up for discussion. She's already decided.

I watch the trio behind the bar. I knew the McGivneys were my kind of people the moment I saw the All Dogs Welcome mat outside the front door. I realize now how much I've missed them.

This.

Maybe I *have* unintentionally made myself too scarce around here.

Muriel's shrewd gaze passes over me. "You look extra lovely tonight, Marie." As quickly as she swooped in, she strolls away, her wide hips swinging with each step.

Toby smirks knowingly at me.

"Oh, I remember the kind of trouble you teenagers were." Teddy waggles his finger at his son and warns, "Don't serve her. She's underage."

"I'll try my best not to." Toby shakes his head at his father's back, earning my chuckle. He leans his bulky frame over the bar.

"Hey, so I heard through the grapevine that the Hatchetts found themselves a new veterinarian."

I'm caught off guard. Sometimes I forget how small the mushing community is. And how loud a tiny woman like Bonnie Hatchett can be. I didn't want to talk about this tonight, but I've complained to Toby about that situation before. "Yup. A four-decade relationship down the toilet."

Toby whistles.

"And all because Harry's an entitled jerk who thinks he owns me."

A subtle cedar-and-citrus scent catches my nose a second before a deep male voice purrs, "I could have told you that about him," in my ear.

The fatigue that has weighed on me all night evaporates as I turn to find Tyler standing beside me.

"You look nice." He nods toward the empty bar stool. "You saving this for me?"

"No, but you can have it."

He sheds his black-and-tan plaid jacket and tosses it onto a hook before easing his jeans-clad bottom half beside me.

I do my best to ignore my racing heart and Toby's obnoxious grin.

"One of these, please." Tyler points to the local IPA on tap before shifting back to me. "What has Harry done now?" Those hazel eyes glow with liquid gold undertones against the color of his forest green shirt. Did he know they would when he dressed for tonight, or is it just a coincidence meant to torture me?

I clear my throat, struggling to maintain an aloof demeanor. "Doesn't matter." I don't want to start this night off making Tyler angry. "I'm surprised you made it."

"Why?" He swivels on the stool to get a better look, forcing his legs apart to make the turn. "Looks like my kind of place."

One of his thighs presses against mine, his jeans pleasantly rough against my bare skin. I allow it for a few beats, waiting to see if he'll pull away.

He doesn't.

And I'm enjoying it too much.

With a slow, calming breath, I shift, putting space between us.

Toby sets the pint down on a paper coaster. "Hey, you're Tyler Brady, aren't you?"

Tyler dips his head once.

"Good to have you here at the Ale House."

"This is Toby. His parents own this place. He runs the mechanics shop, if you ever need something fixed." I introduce them and then slip into the background while they talk, content to watch Tyler's attractive profile as he sips his beer, feeling the eyes on my back as whispers of the Iditarod winner's presence makes its way around the room.

His demeanor is relaxed as he asks Toby questions—how long they've been in the area, how many tourists they see in a season, what type of engines he works on. The conversation stays on Toby, and I can't tell if that's because Tyler's truly interested in what he can learn, or if it's a tactic to keep the dialogue and questions off himself. There's *still* so much I don't know about Tyler.

"I hear we've got a world-class champion in our midst!" Muriel appears behind us, her attention locked on Tyler.

I knew it was only a matter of time.

"Glad to see you finally makin' your way to us."

We do another round of introductions, and then she backs up. "Well? Come on, then. *Everyone* wants to meet ya."

"Uh …." Tyler falters on a suitable answer. He wasn't expecting the likes of Muriel. No one ever is.

"Here, let me top that up for you." Toby fills his glass to brimming. "On the house, seein' as you have to deal with my mother."

"If you're trying to avoid attention, you came to the wrong place." Despite my better judgment, I lean in to whisper, "It's best you just go with it, *champ*."

The tension in his jaw eases, and a crooked smile curls his lips. "You knew this was going to happen, didn't you?"

"Yes, I did. Have fun." I tap his full glass with my bottle and then swig from my beer.

The move draws his attention to my mouth—*not* my intention.

He collects his pint and rises, his thigh brushing against my hip. "Save my seat."

"I'll *try*." I watch him trail behind Muriel, admiring the shape of his shoulders and his tapered waist.

"So, is *that* why you've been busy?" Toby teases.

"No. We're just … friends." I falter over that last word. Despite my best intentions, it's happening, anyway. We've become friends. And I'm wildly attracted to him.

"Right." With a chuckle, Toby heads off to fill some orders.

And I watch as Muriel drags Tyler from group to group, introducing him as if he's a special guest for hire, coordinated by Muriel herself. I'll give him credit; even if he hates the attention, he smiles and laughs with the best of them.

And hides the profound sadness that I've caught glimpses of beneath it all.

A commotion stirs behind the bar.

"You forgot the alcohol!" Teddy slaps his son over the shoulder, and with a laugh retrieves the bottle of vodka from beneath the bar—the only hard liquor in this place, and it's been brought in solely for Calla. "Look at that. You haven't even opened it yet! Is your head not screwed on tonight?" Teddy cracks the seal on the lid and sets the bottle down on the counter in front of him with a heavy thud.

Toby and Calla share a pointed look. Beside her, Jonah leans against the bar, absently watching while in the midst of a conversation with someone else.

"There. Bet that'll be *a lot* stronger. Fix her a new one. A proper one," Teddy goads, patting the counter so Calla can trade in the drink Toby just handed her for one with alcohol.

She was drinking a martini earlier. This is her second drink—at least. There's no way she didn't notice the absence of vodka in the last one.

Unless …

She's dog-tired.

Can barely stay awake at night.

My breath hitches with the sinking realization.

Jonah has dismissed his conversation entirely and is frowning at his wife, and I can tell he's walking through the exact same thoughts.

His mouth hangs as he grasps what I just did.

"Calla …" He drops his hand on his wife's shoulder and leans in, eyebrows arched in a wordless question.

From this angle, I can only see her profile, but it's enough as she sets the glass down. With a rare shy smile, she nods.

Jonah covers his mouth with a palm as he absorbs the shock.

"Way to blow it, Dad!" Toby smacks Teddy in the arm, a rare bout of irritation twisting his features. "She wanted to tell him *later,* when they were *alone.*"

"Tell him what—*ooooh.*" Teddy's mouth forms a perfect O as he watches Jonah collect Calla in his arms and lift her into the air.

Toby was obviously in on this elaborate ruse. The *only* one in on it, I note, as I take in Agnes's and Mabel's faces, brimming with shock and unbridled excitement.

I plaster on what I hope is a matching mask to show my support, even as an odd, empty feeling settles over me.

This is *really* happening.

Jonah is going to be a father. He's having a baby with Calla.

I knew this day would come. It was only a matter of time. Though, we only just mentioned it yesterday in passing, and it still seemed like years away.

And I'm *thrilled* for him, for them.

So why am I suddenly overwhelmed by emotions that feel entirely unsuitable?

Jonah has set Calla down on the counter, knocking over a pint in his oblivious excitement as he presses his face into her stomach. She's beaming as she laughs, not a hint of the same trepidation she had when they had that pregnancy scare last year.

Panic swells as a painful lump forms in my throat, and I fear the worst—that I'm about to lose my composure in the middle of the Ale House. My hand is shaking as I down the rest of my beer in a giant gulp and slide off the stool, intent on stealing a moment for myself in the restroom, to deal with *whatever* this is in private. Only my legs keep going, carrying me past that little door and through the outer one.

The sun is still high in the sky as I head for my truck, parked in the farthest possible corner of the lot, closest to the tree line. My face is frozen with a smile to mask the ugliness beneath in case anyone is out here, until I crawl into the driver's seat and shut the door behind me.

That's when the first sob wrenches from me.

I try to swallow it.

"I'm happy for them."

"I'm happy for them."

"I'm happy for them," I chant over and over again.

And I *am* so happy for them.

But at this very moment, I'm *so* utterly unhappy for me, for the things I'm beginning to accept I may never have.

The pitiful tears win out, rolling down my cheeks in rivulets that feel like they may never end now that I've let them loose.

My passenger door opens, and Tyler climbs in, shutting the door behind him.

Oh God. An already horrendous situation has suddenly gotten ten times worse. The last thing I want is to have to explain myself to *anyone*, but especially to him.

I turn away before he can see my face, wiping my palms

against my cheeks as covertly as possible. "Finished meeting the entire bar already?" I force out, my voice strained as I struggle to suppress my tears.

With a heavy sigh, he slides across the bench seat.

"I'm fine." I'm clearly *not* fine, and he knows that.

I tense as his arm slips over my shoulders. "Come here, Marie." He's strong, but I don't resist when he angles me toward him, his other hand collecting my chin and gently guiding it into the crook of his neck, a hiding spot so I don't have to meet his gaze. I appreciate that.

"It's not what you think," I manage, my body stiff against his even as I absorb the pleasing scent of his skin.

"It doesn't matter what I think. But I'm not thinking anything." His fingers weave through my hair in tiny but calming strokes. It almost feels like a hug, the way he's wrapped around me. "I saw you leave, and I knew something was wrong."

His kind words are pushed aside as dread grips me. "Did anyone *else* notice me leave?" Jonah and Calla unintentionally announce their pregnancy, and I—his best friend—run out, ready to burst into tears?

"Nah. They were all pretty wrapped up in your friends. I only had a second to escape while people were distracted, so I took it." His hand has not stilled as he talks. "Did you know Thomas White needs hernia surgery? And Dylan something or other is divorcing the same woman a second time?"

Despite my abysmal mood, I offer a weak laugh. "You got the full Muriel experience, town gossip and all. Must mean she *really* likes you."

His responding chuckle is relaxing, and it allows me to focus on my breathing as we sit quietly in my truck.

"Thank you. I think I'm okay now." I start to pull away.

Tyler's arms tighten, holding me in place. My ears catch his hard swallow. "I remember when Mila told me she was pregnant." His voice has turned croaky, hollow. "I'd been out all night, helping search the dark for two teens who'd gone missing. Followed the tracks in the snow until the wind covered them. Then we had nothing to go by. Anyway, I got home feeling drained and defeated, and there she was, sitting at the kitchen table with a white plastic stick in her hand." There's another long pause. "I'll never forget the look on her face when she held it up to show me. She knew how much I wanted kids. How happy I would be."

Maybe I wasn't the only one needing a moment to myself after watching the accidental announcement unfold. This time, when I try to pull away from Tyler, he allows it, though he keeps his arm around my shoulders. I smooth my hands over my cheeks to catch any wayward tears. "I'm sorry you had to go through what you did."

His jaw is rigid as he swallows. His focus is on the tree line ahead as he asks, "So, if it's not what I think it is, then what is it?"

I shake my head. "I can't."

"You *can*." A thumb and index finger pinch my chin, turning my face toward his. The raw sincerity in his expression squeezes my heart and loosens my tongue.

I feel the words tumbling out. "Jonah's my best friend, but I used to be in love with him."

Tyler's eyebrow twitches, the only reaction to my confession.

"He was my pilot when I'd fly to the villages in the west. We met when I was engaged to someone else and became good friends instantly. But I saw us ending up as more one day. I *hoped* we would end up as more, and I misread things." I hesitate. "I left my fiancé for that possibility."

He nods slowly, as if pieces are beginning to make sense. "The guy at the coffee shop that you didn't want to be talking to."

"Yeah. He didn't take it well, obviously. Anyway, Jonah met Calla and fell in love with her, she moved here to be with him, they got married. And now they're having a baby, and that's that." It sounds so simple.

"And you're still in love with him?"

"No." I laugh. "I still love him, but not like that anymore. No, that started to fade when I realized that whatever I thought was there ... wasn't. I'm happy for him. Really, I am. Even though it might not look like it right now. He asked me to be his best man at their wedding, and I did because I wanted to. I was honored to be there. I just—" I falter as the lump flares and the tears burn again. "I'm lonely." Those words ... God, I hate admitting that out loud. It makes me feel pathetic.

"Everyone around me is moving forward with their lives. Getting married, having kids, and here *I* am, thirty-eight, alone and without *any* prospects." Liz's voice echoes in my mind. "I want children. *I want children. And* a husband. I want that in my life. And there's this clock ticking, and it's getting louder and louder every day, and it's scaring the shit out of me. The idea that someone will come along in time doesn't seem real anymore. What if Jonathan was it, and I blew it?" I'm rambling without any filter now. This is by far the most candid and vulnerable I've ever been with anyone, and I can't believe it's with *this guy*.

"You have enough friends," he whispers. "That's what you meant."

We're too far down the path of embarrassing truths for me to turn back now. "I thought we clicked. You know, during the race. Not so much *before* the race."

He snorts.

"But I guess I completely misread things, *again*."

He rubs my shoulder gently. "You didn't misread *any*thing." His eyes flip to my mouth before he averts his gaze. "You're the first woman I've kissed since Mila."

"And you thought I was her while you were doing it."

"Yeah. Not going to lie, that was a rough wake-up." He purses his lips. "There I was, running Mila's dogs, and kissing another woman. Ready to do a lot *more* than kiss. The whole back half of the race, I felt guilty."

"She wouldn't understand?"

"She would. She'd want me moving on by now. The problem is, it's been two years, and I still haven't figured out how this could ever have happened to us. How the hell do I figure out how to move on?"

It seems we're both showing our vulnerabilities in this truck tonight.

I hesitate but then take the leap and ask softly, "How did she die?"

"An amniotic fluid embolism. Very rare, the doctors told me. Very rare, but serious." The muscle in his jaw ticks. "Maybe if we'd gotten to the hospital sooner, at least my son would have survived. But I guess there's no point in dwelling on what can't be changed ..." Something pulls Tyler's attention behind me, through the back window. "I think he's looking for you."

"Who?" I check the side-view mirror to see Jonah's hulking frame wandering the crammed parking lot, scowling as he searches. For my truck, I'm sure. My stomach drops. "Oh God, he can't know I'm out here, crying. How bad is it?" I check the rearview mirror and gasp with dismay at the streaks of mascara. "He can't see me like this! This is, like, the happiest day of his life. What kind of friend am I?" Just the idea of the look on Jonah's face when he sees me has more tears—this time of horror—streaming down my cheeks.

"What do I do?" I look to Tyler in a panic, knowing there's *nothing* I can do to keep this nightmare from playing out.

"We can make it too awkward for him to come here." His eyes land on my mouth a second before his lips follow, parting mine gently. I can taste the beer he had before coming out as surely as he can taste mine, but it's far from unappealing. I respond, tangling my tongue with his.

It takes me a second to cut through my shock—Tyler is kissing me, while conscious—and clue in. He assumes Jonah will see this and change his mind about banging on my window to see where I ran off to. He doesn't know Jonah like I do, though.

"This isn't going to work. He can be a bit of an ox," I whisper against Tyler's mouth.

"No?" There's a pause and then Tyler hooks his hand around my thigh and hauls me onto his lap with startling strength, until I'm straddling his thighs, my hands settled on his muscular shoulders. "How about this?" There's no caution this time as he seizes the back of my head and pulls my face into his, his lips prying mine open. I feel a tug at the hem of my dress and then his other hand sneaks beneath. Calloused fingers skim over my bare skin along my thigh, sending a pulse of anticipation into my core.

The soft moan that escapes from the back of my throat is unintentional.

Tyler breaks away from the kiss suddenly to look up at me. His gaze is molten, his breathing shallow. A curse slips out under his breath, and then he's diving into me again. The hand that was on my hip shifts to the small of my back, and he pulls my body forward, flush to his, until I can feel his hard length pressed against the apex of my thighs. He rolls his hips into mine.

I don't know if this is all intended to be part of the act anymore, but this more aggressive, dominant version of Tyler is intoxicating, and I give myself over to the situation without thought for consequences, reveling in the feel of his strength and his warmth and his intensity, my fingertips trembling as they crawl across his stubbled jaw, along the rigid lines of his collarbones, down over the hard planes of his chest and stomach.

Down farther, slipping beneath my dress, my hand moving in between us, my palm smoothing over what makes him so utterly male.

With a sharp inhale, his hand is suddenly there between us, too, working its way into my panties. His fingers deftly push into me, and he curses again. It's been so long since I've let a man touch me like this, and I can't remember when I wanted anyone this much. The responding gasp would be embarrassing if I wasn't aching to feel the rest of him inside me. Right now.

I vaguely recall how this started, but the reason no longer matters, as Tyler's frantic mouth works over mine with skill, and I fumble with his belt and jeans, unfastening them in a rush, before either of us comes to our senses. He lifts his hips and pushes his own pants down.

Beneath the cover of my dress, I wrap my hand around his smooth, warm length. He groans as I stroke him, my thumb sliding over the bead of moisture pooling at his tip. If I'm the first woman he's kissed since Mila passed, then surely I'm also the first to touch him like this.

"Is anyone out here?" he whispers, his voice strained.

I break from his mouth to check the back window. "No. No one." The parking lot is full of vehicles and empty of people, and even if it isn't, unless someone is climbing into the adjacent truck, they're not likely to notice us here.

No one is heading this way.

Our breaths are heady and ragged, our chests heaving as we check each other's eyes. For signs of hesitancy, or insanity, I don't know, but I'm hit with an overwhelming sense that it's now or never.

"I need you." It slips out, goaded by the fact that the only thing between us right now is a thin slip of cotton underwear.

He smooths a hand over my cheek, and then he's kissing me again.

Kissing me while he pulls me onto my knees to work my panties down. I help by sliding them off one leg, freeing me to shift my body forward. His bare thighs are hot against mine as he reaches between us.

We moan in tandem as he pushes inside me, our lips stalling as our hips work against each other, the delicious stretch of my body pulling sounds I can't contain. My hands curl around his thick neck, my thumbs stroking his jawline as I slide on and off him in a steady rhythm, acutely aware that we don't have the luxury of time, chasing after that high building in my core.

Finally, I catch it, and a sweet throbbing pleasure erupts inside me moments before Tyler himself does. The cry that escapes him is deep and primal, and if there were anyone within ten car lengths, they would've heard that.

Tyler's breathing is as ragged as mine as he lets his head fall back and closes his eyes. "I think it's safe now."

I laugh, and the simple muscle spasm reminds me that he's still seated deeply inside me. The last thing I feel right now is *safe*. My body buzzes with adrenaline, the relief that I should be feeling over avoiding a confrontation with Jonah overshadowed by the fact that Tyler and I just had sex.

In the Ale House parking lot.

"Thank you." It stumbles out.

His soft chuckle fills the truck's interior with warmth. "I can't say I've ever been thanked for that before." He cracks his eyelids. "You look as shocked as I feel."

"I can't believe we just did that." I'm thirty-eight years old and I have a reputation to think about. What the hell came over me?

"It's been awhile for me. A bit relieved to know everything still works." He's made no move to shift me from his lap, though his grip on my hips has loosened.

"Right." I look down to where my dress is bunched between us. He came inside me. I didn't even consider needing a condom, didn't think about it once. How stupid can I be?

"I'm clean," he says, as if reading my mind.

"Me too." Unease pricks at my conscience. I'm the first woman Tyler's kissed since his wife, and now we've had sex. Unprotected sex. "Maybe we shouldn't have done this?"

He works his lips with an answer that he seems to struggle over. "That's what friends are for."

"The last I checked, that is *not* what friends are for."

"Yeah, well ..." A serious expression takes over his handsome face. He reaches up to stroke a wayward strand of hair that clings to my lip. "I think we understand each other better now, wouldn't you say?"

I understand that Tyler is attracted to me—a candid truth he's revealed that threatens to launch me into the clouds with the thrill it brings. And I understand that I am undeniably attracted to him in a way I can't remember being with *anyone* else, even Jonah. Probably because that was all in my head, and *whatever* this is between us, it's real.

But Tyler has made it clear he's emotionally unavailable, and I don't see that changing anytime soon. I'd be a fool to even hope for it.

Something tells me a fool is just what I'll be if I let myself get too close to him.

I slide off him and shift back to my spot behind the steering wheel, turning away so he has a moment of privacy to dress himself. Maybe it would have been better if Jonah had found out what a terrible friend I was, rather than complicate this situation with Tyler. My father's warning stumbles into my head, and my worry spikes. "You'll still want me as your veterinarian, right?"

"What?" Tyler chuckles. "I was a second from dropping to my knees to beg you to take my dogs on. I'm not letting you go anywhere over this." He frowns curiously. "Why would you think that?"

"Just needed to be sure."

Tyler studies his empty ring finger. Did he ever wear a wedding band? Surely, he must have. When did he take it off last and decide not to put it back on? "The dogs are all I have left of Mila, and I'll do whatever I can to give them the best. The best is you. I know that." His eyes search my face for a long moment, and it reminds me that I have makeup smeared all over it. "I think I'm going to call it a night."

"Yeah, me too." Go home and wash my face under a cold stream of water while I *don't* think of how Tyler feels inside me.

His hand stalls on the door handle. "If you want to keep this cover going, you should follow me out. Make it look like we're leaving together in case anyone's watching."

I hadn't thought of that. "God, I *hope* no one's watching."

He chuckles. "Have a good night, Marie."

While he heads for his truck, I clean up as best I can and fix my panties. I tell myself that there was no need to tell Tyler that I'm not on any sort of birth control. The timing's off, anyway.

In moments, I'm tailing his truck out of the Ale House's driveway, squinting against the glare of the glowing orange sun in my rearview mirror. I follow the forest green truck all the way to his turnoff, and a part of me—the physical part that aches to feel Tyler's hands on my bare skin again—hopes he'll continue past it and lead me back to my place.

To my disappointment, he hangs a left, sticks his arm out the window, and waves as he speeds off.

But it's better this way, I remind myself, and head home.

CHAPTER NINETEEN

"Is that it?" Mary Beck's voice is shaky, her hand stroking Eddie's head.

I will the lump in my throat to disperse as I press my stethoscope to the Cavalier King Charles Spaniel's chest to confirm the lack of a heartbeat. He was always vibrating with energy when he came in here. Now, his cancer-riddled body is lifeless on his favorite blanket, laid out on the metal table of my examination room. "Yes. He's gone."

She dabs at a single tear that trickles down her wrinkled cheek. "At least he's not suffering anymore."

"We did what we could for him, Mary," I say gently. It's the standard line, one that brings all the comfort and yet none.

"He's all I had left." More tears begin to stream, too many to dab at with her tissue. "Can I have another moment alone with him?" She's trying her hardest to keep it together—her lips pursed tightly—but I get it. She's going to fall apart, and she wants to do it in private.

I offer a sympathetic smile. "Take all the time you need." I duck into the back room, pushing the door closed firmly. It doesn't muffle the sobs that erupt behind the door.

Eddie wasn't my dog, but even *I* feel like crying. He was ten—too young. If not for the countless lumps throughout his body and the oozing sore on his face, he would've seemed fine. His tail was still wagging right to the very end when the sedative kicked in.

He's the third pet I've had to put down this week—an unusually high number for me. I used to keep count of the animals I euthanized, convincing myself it's a number I should know. Now I only keep a tally of the animals I've saved.

Unfortunately, this little guy was not one of them.

I let my body sag against the wall, willing this day—this week—to be over.

The door to the clinic lobby swings open, and Cory barrels through.

"She just needs a few more minutes with him—"

"I'm sorry, because I *know* you need some time to yourself after that, but you should come out here." Cory points behind her. "Like, *now*."

This is not standard Cory behavior.

Peeling myself off the wall, I follow her out.

Tyler is standing in my lobby.

I haven't seen or heard from him in a week, but that doesn't matter right now. What matters is that he's in my lobby, in his park ranger uniform, his arms flexing beneath the weight of a whimpering Bernese mountain dog. Blood drips from its front leg at a steady rate, despite the cloth tied around it, splattering on the lobby floor.

A young woman stands behind Tyler, streaks of mascara down her cheeks. Through the front window, a silver Mini pulls up next to Tyler's ranger vehicle, and another young woman jumps out, in a frantic rush to collect her purse and phone.

"Rachel, this is the veterinarian I told you about. Her name is Marie," he says, his voice calm, as I'm sure he's been trained to be for these situations.

I offer a quick, polite smile in response. "What happened?"

"Beau stepped in a trap while they were hiking. I got him out of it, but I thought it best we come here."

The fact that a park ranger hauled a hundred-pound dog and its owner straight to a vet tells me all I need to know about its seriousness. I've seen enough to know those traps can destroy an animal's leg. "Can he walk?"

"No."

And there's no way this tiny brunette, who likely matches her dog in weight, would be able to carry him. "Okay." My adrenaline kicks in. "Let's examine his leg first to see how bad it is—"

"Is he gonna live?" Rachel asks, her voice borderline hysterical.

The other woman—her friend, I presume—blows through the door in a panic. They can't be more than twenty, practically still kids. This is traumatizing for them.

I offer her what I hope is a reassuring smile. "I've seen my fair share of dogs caught in traps, and a lot of them live. Especially when it's this type of trap." Thank God it wasn't a conibear. "I'll have more information for you after I've examined him."

"The surgical room is already sterilized and prepped," Cory offers.

"Right." For a surgery on another patient. "I need you to bump the rest of my appointments. Tell them there was an emergency, and I have to reschedule." This is going to take hours to fix. Turning to Tyler, I point toward the rear door. "Can you carry him there for me?"

"I'll show you the way." Cory leads him back.

Well, this day has taken a turn, and I'm not sure if it's for the better or worse yet. "I'll be out with an update as soon as I can."

The brunette's head bobs, tears streaming freely again. "Okay. Thank you, Doctor. Marie." She frowns, as if she's not sure what to call me. I get that a lot. "Whatever you have to do to save him, *please* do it."

My guess is this girl has no idea what "whatever you have to do" might cost. "Do you have pet insurance?"

She shakes her head. "No, but I'll find the money."

Not that it matters if she doesn't, I accept with a resigned sigh. I'll do whatever I have to, regardless.

Maybe Liz is right. Maybe I *am* going to run this clinic into the ground.

———

Rachel and her friend are huddled next to each other, both typing furiously on their phones, when I step out, Tyler trailing behind me.

Her head snaps up right away. "How is he?"

I settle in the empty chair next to her. "I've stopped the bleeding, and Beau is going to be fine, but I can't save his leg."

"What does that mean, you can't save it?" She stumbles over her words. "You want to cut off his leg?"

"I don't *want* to amputate. I need to. The trap crushed his bones, and his tissue and nerves are torn up beyond repair. He was fighting to get out of it, wasn't he?"

Her head jerks up and down.

"That did even more damage. He's in *a lot* of pain right now, and it's not the kind of pain that will go away."

Rachel's bottom lip wobbles as she looks first to her friend, and then to Tyler, who hovers nearby, his ranger uniform stained with the dog's blood. "Are you sure?" She's asking *him*.

I guess I can't blame her. Tyler gave me the brief rundown of what happened—they were hiking on a trail in Nancy Lake when Beau wandered off and stepped in a trap. After a few frantic moments of struggling to release it from the thrashing dog, which neither of them had learned to do, Rachel's friend called the emergency line. Tyler, who's working the park this week, responded. One look told him it was bad enough to get them here, so he took over.

He's the knight in green armor.

He crouches in front of her. "I have twenty-one dogs, and I trust Marie with them. If she says it needs to be done, then it *needs* to be done."

She nods slowly, but she's reviewing my little lobby, and I already know what she's thinking—that I'm some sort of hack animal doctor operating out of a shack in the woods. "Maybe I should take him back to Anchorage to his regular vet?"

"Are they going to clear their schedule to fit him in as soon as you get there?" Tyler's voice remains steady.

"I don't know?"

"Well, you have one of the best surgeons in the state in front of you, and she already has."

Those are Wade's words. Tyler must have been talking to him.

"My guess is he'll be recovering before you even get through the other door. But he's your dog. If you want to put him in your car and drive all the way back to Anchorage to try to get him in today, that's your call. I just want to make sure he gets the help he needs as soon as possible. But I *can* promise you that Beau won't get better care anywhere than he will with Marie. They call her the Crusader because she saves animals all over Alaska. That's just what she does." His eyes shift to me, and there's an odd, unreadable look in them.

I almost groan at the nickname, but it's the confidence in his voice that amazes me. Aside from volunteering in the Iditarod, I've done little more than inspect his kennel. Where is all this faith coming from? It seems almost fraudulent, like he's lying to this girl.

And yet my heart swells with gratitude.

"The only thing I hate more than amputating a dog's leg is *not* doing it when it needs to be done. Another vet might tell you that they can try to save it. I've seen it happen before. But I can promise you'll end up right back in this position, after spending double the amount, and Beau will be suffering. The leg *has* to go." Sometimes I can be too bullish when it comes to sharing my opinion on an animal's care, something my father has cautioned me about.

I take a deep, calming breath. *Please don't be a fool, Rachel.* "It's a major surgery, but I am a surgeon. I have all the equipment here, and I've done these types of procedures before. I don't foresee any issues. *But,* if you prefer, we can call your clinic to see if they can fit you in. I can bandage him up, and we can help you get him into the car. I can even give him some pain meds to make him a bit more comfortable for the ride—"

"No, no … Do what you have to do." She nods with steely determination. "Just fix him."

"Good call, Rachel." Tyler's heavy sigh echoes my relief.

She falters. "But will he be able to walk?"

"Yes. He'll have three other legs to keep him going. He'll have to find his new balance, and for big dogs, it's a bit harder to lose a front leg than a back one, but you'll be surprised how quickly he adapts." I stand. "If you're good with this, then we're going to prep him for surgery, and I'll want to keep him overnight for observation. Cory will be out in a minute to get all your information and figure out a plan." That she hasn't asked how much it's going to cost yet—a question that normally comes up immediately—is surprising, but maybe she has resources. It's probably the bank of Mom and Dad.

Tyler is up now, too, answering a dispatch call on his radio with a quick code as he trails me. "I have to get a few details from them and then head back to the park to figure out who the hell set that trap and when." He asks quietly, "You good here? He's a big guy."

A hundred and two pounds, according to the scale. "Yeah. Cory and I can manage him." She's in the back, keeping Beau calm on the surgical table.

"Okay." He bites his bottom lip in thought.

The move drags my mind back to the Ale House parking lot. It's clear to me now that things between us have changed, at least from my perspective. Can he feel it, too? Did he go home, laden with regret for following me out to my truck? If he did, he must've worked through it already, because he's not giving off awkward vibes.

"Thank you." He reaches out to give my elbow a gentle squeeze.

Even such a simple, innocuous touch has my blood racing, my body craving more. But I don't have time for this. "Yeah, yeah, I have work to do," I mutter, trying to squash the distraction. "You'll see yourself out?"

The crooked grin he flashes, dimples and all, tugs at the corners of my mouth despite my efforts.

I feel his gaze on my back as I march to the surgical room, shifting my focus to the grim task ahead.

CHAPTER TWENTY

Molly's tired wail drifts over on the evening breeze as Vicki loads her into their truck. My sister has been next door every day this week, moving truckloads of belongings and readying the attic between bouts of vicious pregnancy sickness.

Their landlord let them out of their lease at the end of this month without any penalties. Oliver thinks it's because the man lives on the first floor of the duplex, and he can't handle Molly's crying anymore. He wants them out as soon as possible.

Whatever the reason, my parents have had a spring in their step—or in my father's case, in his crutches—that they'll have another daughter *and* a granddaughter back home soon.

On the off chance that Vicki checks her rearview mirror and sees me perched in my red Adirondack chair on my porch, where I often am in the evenings, I throw up a wave. A horn tuts in answer.

I smile through a sip of my Coke. I'd kill for a cold beer, or maybe something stronger after the day I've had, but a three-legged Bernese mountain dog is resting in the clinic. It's going to be a long night.

My task is mostly done. Rachel has a lot of work ahead of her.

I feel terrible for the girl. Her only error was allowing Beau off his leash, something *everyone* does from time to time. That could've just as easily happened to Bentley or Yukon. There should *never* have been a trap set anywhere near that trail and *especially* not in July.

My ears catch the sound of wheels rolling over gravel, and I assume it's Vicki, hopping over one driveway to say hello before she heads to pick up Oliver from work. But it's a familiar olive-green truck that rounds the bend in the trees and coasts forward, pulling up next to my vehicle.

My pulse quickens as Tyler slides from the driver's side. He's changed out of his uniform and into jeans and a long-sleeved shirt. A six-pack dangles from his fingers as he saunters toward my little screened-in porch.

I regret the oversized gray sweatpants and heavy plaid jacket I threw on, and the haphazard topknot I pulled my hair into, but it's too late to do anything now, so I hold my casual position, feet propped on a small table. "Twice in one day?"

The door opens with a creak as he ducks in and holds up the cans. Coors Light. "I won't judge you for your taste in beer if you'll let me have one of them."

That he remembers what I was drinking at the Ale House means he was paying attention—a rare occurrence for most men I've met. Even Jonah forgets how I take my coffee sometimes.

I try not to read too much into this as I smile and gesture toward the empty Adirondack chair opposite me. "Knock yourself out. I'm on duty until Cory gets here at midnight to take over."

"Just the two of you running this whole place, huh?"

"It's a small place. And it works most of the time."

Tyler sinks into the chair, his thighs falling apart as he yanks a can off the ring. The sound of the tab cracking cuts through an otherwise silent night.

Every nerve ending in my weary body has come alive. "So, how was the rest of *your* day?"

"Frustrating." He takes a long sip. "No tags or markers on the trap, and it was set maybe fifty feet off a main trail. On top of the long grass, not buried under it, so it couldn't have been put there too long ago. I think someone was trying to catch a dog."

"Asshole." My stomach clenches. It's hard to imagine someone doing something so cruel, but it happens, and his theory makes sense. Trapping and hunting is allowed in the recreation area, but not in July. The season for animals needing that size of trap doesn't start until November. "You call the trappers' association?"

"I called them, called Wildlife, called Fish and Game. I called everybody. Spent the evening on the phone and doing paperwork. I doubt we'll find the sick bastard who did it. Don't be shocked if you get a call from the paper once they catch wind of this, though."

"No doubt. It's a story." And more ammo for the anti-trappers. It's a never-ending battle, between those opposed to *all* trapping and those who see legal trapping as a right and a way of life. In this case, this trap was illegal, and *no one* will condone what happened. But still, there will be those who can't help but point their stubby fingers at Rachel for allowing Beau off his leash, and that will get plenty of dog lovers' backs up.

"How is he?" Tyler asks.

"Sleeping right now." I hold up the baby monitor screen on the clinic post-op room. "He's doing well. His surgery was straightforward."

Tyler adjusts his position, stretching his legs, setting his boot heels on the edge of the table, inches from my running shoes. "It's amazing, how you know how to do that."

"Yeah, it's amazing what eight years of school, a residency, and a few hundred grand can get you." Though, in truth, I started learning long before I ever sat down for my first lecture in veterinary school, all my free time spent in the clinic with my dad.

Tyler whistles. "Bet that's gonna take forever to pay off."

"And I'll end up giving this girl a discount because I feel so bad for her." Cory said Rachel's face paled when she gave her the estimate for the surgery, but then she nodded and reiterated that she'll get the money. "At this rate, I should be done paying off my loans by the time I die." Even with the help my parents provided.

"You won't need to give her a discount." He digs his phone out of his pocket, and hitting a few buttons, passes me his phone. His fingers graze mine.

I struggle to ignore the innocuous touch as I study the grid of aesthetic pictures that fill it. "'Beau the Bear-nese,'" I read out loud, checking the profile. "He has a *million* followers on Instagram? A million people have followed a *dog*?"

Tyler smirks. "And that's growing by the hour. Apparently, her TikTok profile is just as big."

"How'd you find this?"

"I'm good at getting information out of people. More than I need, usually."

He certainly got a lot out of me last weekend. It seems all he had to do was bat those long lashes my way, and now the man knows *all* my dirty laundry, my biggest vulnerabilities.

But I've seen another side to him, too, one he works hard to hide from everyone else.

I scroll through the pictures, scanning the quick and quippy captions. I assume Rachel has taken most of these pictures, save for the ones she's posing in with Beau, looking nothing like the sobbing, frightened kid in my clinic and everything like a confident, sensual woman. "Wow, she even has merchandise." T-shirts and beanies with caricatures of Beau.

"She's smart."

"I don't understand *any* of this world." Sure, I opened accounts, but I'm never on them. I don't even remember my passwords. "Jonah's wife is all over this sort of thing. She'd be impressed." Calla not only manages the plane charter business—

all the marketing and administrative paperwork, and a website she designed and built herself—and the cabin rental, which is booked well into next year, but she's also establishing herself as a marketing expert around the area. What started out as volunteering for the Winter Carnival and local farmers' market is turning into a marketing side hustle that she's now charging for.

On top of all that, she still keeps a personal blog alive, posting regularly about her life in Alaska with her yeti. The girl has more balls in the air than I could ever manage, and she hasn't dropped one yet.

Tyler nods toward the phone. "Did you see Rachel's latest post?"

"No." I scroll back up to the top. *Huh.* "She's set up a GoFundMe page for him." That has already earned enough to cover the surgery fees plus recovery appointments *and* therapy. I curse under my breath. "She wasn't kidding when she said she'd find the money."

"I wish I could cover *all* my vet bills like that."

"You can. It's called sponsorship."

"So I have to answer to someone else about my dogs? No fucking thanks." He sucks back a gulp of his beer, his gaze drifting over the meadow between my place and my parents'.

I skim through the post to read Rachel's description of Beau's tragic accident and her plea for help. "'Thanks to the *heroic* efforts of Park Ranger Tyler Brady, who went above and beyond by not only releasing a distressed Beau from the trap but carrying all one hundred pounds of our favorite bear to his truck and driving us to the veterinarian he swears by twenty minutes away. If not for him, I fear Beau might not have survived,'" I read out loud. "'He is a true hero.'"

"As if I had any other choice. The dog weighs more than she does." He studies the can in his grip with intense interest.

"Something tells me you would have done it no matter what."

To that, he says nothing, taking another sip.

"And in brackets, 'P.S. Why can't all park rangers look like him?'"

He groans, but the little smile says he's not bothered.

"'If I weren't so distraught, I would've gotten his number. Maybe I still can.' Man, this girl has guts." Something sharp pricks at my chest at the idea of another female chasing after Tyler ... and of one catching him. It's bound to happen, eventually. "She *is* pretty," I tease.

"I'm old enough to be her father," he mutters through a sip.

"Well, yeah, but then she could call you da—"

"*No.*"

I chuckle.

"I haven't been interested in girls her age since I was sixteen."

"*Sixteen?*"

He grins slyly. "I've always liked older women. More experienced."

"Especially in parking lots?"

Tyler, mid sip, chokes on his beer.

My cheeks heat. I don't know what compelled me to say that just now. Perhaps it's the fact that we both seem to be dancing around that night as if it didn't happen. "Make sure you let Rachel down gently."

He pinches the bridge of his nose as if in pain, and I laugh. It feels *so good* to sit out here with someone and laugh. I'm often alone on my porch. "You know this is going to be on the local news, especially when they make the connection." I click on the comments. "Oh look, someone already has. 'Is this the same Tyler Brady who won the Iditarod?'"

Tyler groans again.

"You're gonna have to do interviews—"

"I'm *not* doing any interviews—"

"Pose for pictures ..." I hand his phone back to him, earning myself another finger stroke that skitters all the way to my spine.

He watches me swallow a sip of my Coke. "Anyway, it looks like you don't have to worry about being paid."

"Yeah, not going to lie. That is a relief." I have to pay Cory for seven hours of tonight's overtime. I can skip paying myself, and I don't mind, if I'm spending my time sitting out here with Tyler. "How did you end up as a park ranger, anyway?"

"I've always been heading toward this. I spent years volunteering in the parks, and I knew how competitive it would be to get hired on, so I decided to go to college for a criminal justice degree. From there, I worked with Montana Highway Patrol for a few years, gaining experience, before getting hired on with the state parks."

"And then you went to Finland?"

"Then I met Mila. She was in Montana for a month in the summer, visiting her father." He smiles to himself. "She assumed it was just going to be a vacation fling, but I convinced her to give me a chance to prove it could work. We did the long-distance thing for about four months, and it was hard. I asked her to marry me. She said no at first, because she wouldn't leave her dogs. So I left everything in Montana and moved to her."

It feels awkward, hearing him talk about falling in love with her. But the conversation is important.

It's like going through your medical history with a new doctor before they take you on. Uncomfortable, but essential to share vital details that might make a big difference in the future. In this case, it helps me understand the kind of man Tyler is, what he's willing to give up for the right woman.

Everything.

"Their family business was too important for her to leave, and I was willing to do anything to be with her." He toys with the tab on his can. "That's the thing with me—when I'm in, I'm *all* in. It was tough, though. Most people there speak English, but I didn't speak the language, so getting hired in my field wasn't going to be easy. I started taking language lessons while helping out on the farm. That's what they call their kennel. That, or a homestead. It's nothing like this. It's a whole tourist attraction, with guided sled tours and snowshoeing, snowmobiling. I learned about mushing and fell in love with it. Ended up becoming a guide, taking people and dogs out for hours, sometimes days, all over the Arctic Circle. It's a pretty wild life."

He pauses. "After Mila passed, I stayed to help Tero and Anja. The dogs had been training hard with Mila for years, and Tero wanted to race them in the Finnmarksløpet in her honor but didn't think he had it in him. I needed something to keep me going. So, I decided I would do it. He helped get me to the start line." He pulls the metal tab off his can. "Mila got me to the finish."

"And your talent and commitment to these dogs got you there first."

His smile is sad.

"Then you decided to move to Alaska?"

"It was too hard to stay in Finland without her, so I started looking at moving back home, to Whitefish. I went for a visit. It was good to see family but moving back didn't appeal to me. Then I ran into Marshall Deeks in town, also visiting. I've known him since I was a kid, volunteering. He told me if I wanted a job up here, he'd make it happen. Even something seasonal, if I wanted to keep racing. Tero and Anja told me the dogs were mine to take wherever I wanted, as long as I cared for them the same way she had. Then Reed called me up, begging me to let him come help, my real estate agent found the farm, which was exactly what I was looking for, and it all kind of fell into place. It seemed like this is how I was meant to move on with my life."

And yet, Tyler hasn't moved on. He may have physically relocated, but his head and heart are still living four thousand miles away and two years ago.

I curl my arms around my chest to ward off the first hint of a chill. "Is this your plan for the long term, then? Ranger in the summers, musher in the winters?"

"Honestly, I'm still taking it one day at a time. Between my savings, Mila's life insurance, and a decent inheritance from my parents when they sold their property to developers, I have enough money to keep me going for a bit. I'll race this team until they can't race anymore. After that ..." He shakes his head. "Reed wants to compete, so maybe I'll help him get set up with a team and then I'll see about something more permanent for myself, up in Denali, working with the dogs there."

He's talking deep within the park. There is an expansive area that is only accessible by sled dogs in the winter, where anything motorized is banned.

He inhales deeply, as if that'll expel the weight of the topic. "How's our friend Harry doing, by the way?"

"Harry? I have no idea. I guess you haven't heard?" I assumed everyone would have by now.

Tyler frowns. "Heard what?"

"I'm no longer the Hatchett Kennels' veterinarian."

His eyebrows arch. "Are you kidding me? Since when?"

I hesitate.

Tyler's head falls back. "Since you took me on, and he found out." The muscles in his jaw clench. "What a little shithead."

"It was going to happen eventually." Tyler's rage reminds me of Jonah's, and it's oddly satisfying. "Things have not been going well for Harry, and he's looking for everyone else to blame so he doesn't have to take responsibility. Let him learn the hard way how good he had it." I just hope it's not at the dogs' expense.

"Do you know who he went to?"

I clear my throat. "From what I've heard ... Frank Hartley."

Tyler's bellow of laughter echoes through the night. Across the property, through the open windows, Yukon and Bentley howl in response.

"Shhh!" I give his boot a playful kick. "You'll wake my

parents." My dad has no doubt fallen asleep in his chair watching TV.

"It's been awhile since I've had to worry about that." Tyler shifts to peek through the window behind him. The curtains are open, and the lamp inside casts enough light to see most everything—the kitchenette, the couch, my bed in the back. "I meant to ask, whatever happened with your friend after last weekend?"

"Who, Jonah?" I shake my head. "Nothing." I dropped off flowers and nonalcoholic wine the next day, apologized for ducking out before I had a chance to congratulate them, Jonah pestered me about making out with Tyler in the parking lot—he obviously made a sharp turn back the way he came and missed the worst of it—and that was that. If he or Calla suspected there was more to it than some rush of hormones between Tyler and me, they never hinted at it. Besides, Jonah's too busy bouncing around their place and measuring one of the spare rooms for the nursery to think about anything else.

"So, it worked, then?"

"Seemed to." Too well, because all I've been thinking about all week is the feel of Tyler's mouth and hands on me, and him, inside me.

Wishing for an excuse to experience it again.

Right now would be ideal.

A heady mood settles over the space within my screened-in porch, intensifying with each passing moment. Is that why he's here?

It can't go that far, anyway, I remind myself. My period came yesterday morning. Still, I can think of a dozen ways I'd like to touch him.

I check the monitor for a distraction from my illicit thoughts.

Tyler must take that as his sign to leave because he eases out of his chair with a stretch. "I should get going. Reed's been home alone all day."

K.A. TUCKER

Disappointment bursts within me, but I tamp it down. "You need to bring him out more. He should make some friends."

"You try telling him that. The guy's not too keen on meeting new people. I think he'd honestly rather be out there in the woods alone with the dogs."

"Bring him around the Ale House on a weekend next time you go."

"I think that owner would send him into hiding for the next decade."

"Muriel?" I laugh. "Nah. She'd put him to work."

Tyler finishes the last of his beer and then sets the remaining cans on the table by my feet.

"For me? How sweet."

"It's the least I could do after showing up here and making you cut off a dog's leg."

"Not just a dog. The most famous dog I might ever meet. But at least I'll get paid in full." I've always hated thinking about my patients in terms of money, but everyone around me does. Maybe that's where I've gone wrong all these years.

Tyler moves for the door but then stalls, his brow furrowed. "I'm sorry about Harry. I know you said you needed the money from his kennel."

"He needs me more. He'll be back." I don't necessarily believe it, but if there's one thing I hate showing, it's vulnerability.

"Make him beg."

"More than I made *you* beg?" I wink to show that I'm teasing.

His eyes drift slowly over my face, over my plaid jacket and my oversized gray sweatpants, all the way down to my dust-covered running shoes. He hesitates for a long moment. "All that stuff you said in the truck last weekend … there's nothing wrong with wanting that in your life and being sad when you don't have it."

Or when you've lost it all, as in Tyler's case. I'm not sure what's worse. At least I'm only plagued by longing for something I've imagined but never experienced.

He's haunted by actual memories, by real loss.

My heart sinks, and the urge to wrap my arms around him for comfort, as he did for me last weekend, is overpowering.

I don't know how to respond, so I simply nod.

"And as far as your ex goes, you didn't make a mistake. You left him because deep down you knew he wasn't right for you. If he were, you wouldn't have cared about possibilities with someone else. It's as simple as that."

"Maybe you're right." I toy with a thread on my sleeve, unable to meet his gaze as I admit with embarrassment, "But I'm beginning to think there isn't anyone right for me." Friends have married and divorced, and remarried again, and here I am, choosing between deadbeat dads and blind dates set up by my family.

"There is. There's a person out there for everyone." He pats the door frame. "If we're lucky, maybe even two."

I watch Tyler's back as he walks slowly to his truck, his steps faltering … once … twice … as if he's reconsidering leaving. But that's just my wishful thinking. This is what I'm good at: getting caught up in fantasy.

He climbs into his truck and pulls away.

Was this impromptu visit a one-off? Or might it be something I'll be treated to again?

I hope for the latter.

Even if it's only as friends.

CHAPTER TWENTY-ONE

I give Dingo's long, velvety ears a gentle stroke. "I'll meet you out front with the prescription. It'll take about ten days to clear up the kennel cough and then bring him back for his Bordetella shot. It's the only way you can avoid this."

"You got it, Doc. Hey, before you go …" Scott Ponsford lifts his shirt to his neck with both hands, revealing a full chest of dark hair and a rash that stretches down over his round belly. "What do you think this is? It's itchy as hell."

"Um …" I clear my throat, caught off guard. "My guess would be an allergic reaction, but I highly recommend you go and see your doctor for a diagnosis. My expertise is with patients like Dingo here. Not humans."

"Yeah … What could I be allergic to, though?" He grimaces at his body. "And it goes down, past my belt—"

"Definitely something to ponder with your doctor. See you out front." With one last playful stroke over the beagle's ear, I slip out of the exam room to the back, my palm pressed over my mouth to muffle my laughter. It's not the first time a client has tried to hijack their pet's appointment, looking for medical advice. Normally, they're a bit subtler about it.

Ten minutes later, after Dingo and Scott (and Scott's rash) are gone, I'm in the lobby, checking the mail before I head out to Jed Carling's kennel to give his puppies their first set of shots and check on two dogs that got into a fight.

I set the utility bill in the To Pay folder behind the desk, freeing my hands to knead the sore muscle in my neck, earned after lugging Oliver and Vicki's furniture down and up flights of stairs all day yesterday. My entire body ached when I woke up this morning, and it's grown progressively worse as the day has gone on.

"That was the *fourth* new patient booked this morning. A Jack Russell named Jacqueline who hates men," Cory declares as she drops the phone receiver on its base. "Your calendar is filling up fast. Between new clients and a bunch of procedures, next week is going to be busy."

"That's good for us." I step into my rubber boots and haul my travel bag from behind the counter. "I'm heading out now." And looking forward to coming home and curling up in my bed. The forecast is calling for this heavy rain to continue into tomorrow.

"Marie, I've been attached to this phone all week. I hear it ring in my sleep. Some of these people want your full résumé. Others want a rundown of everything we do here before they move their pets over. If this keeps up, we're going to have to hire someone for the desk. At least part-time."

"Don't worry, it'll die down soon. But I already talked to my mom, and she said she'd help out if we need it—"

"We need it." Cory's holding the tail of her French braid in her fist—a sign that she's stressed—as she points to the newspaper sitting on the counter. "And it's because of *that*."

The Anchorage paper arrived yesterday, but I didn't have time to read it. I pause to unfold it now. Beau's lovable face fills the full-page cover story.

As expected, Rachel and Beau's tale has grabbed headlines, not just in the Mat-Su borough but all over the state, amplified by the unique details—Beau, being an internet celebrity and the park ranger hero being none other than this year's Iditarod champion. The call to ban trapping in Nancy Lake Recreation Area has already been made, a petition circulating to collect signatures growing each day, and the pro-trappers are already on the defensive, pointing out the obvious—that no ban would stop this from happening because whoever did it doesn't care about regulations.

Tyler has hidden behind the cover of his department head and the ongoing investigation to avoid dealing with reporters. Cory has passed the receiver over with more than one waiting on the line, looking to verify facts about Beau's medical condition. I've shared what Rachel has permitted me to share and nothing more.

But Rachel is not staying quiet. The twenty-one-year-old has a steel spine where her dog is concerned. She's been online nonstop, sharing every minute detail about Beau's misfortune. She even went back to the spot on the trail to record herself retelling the story in detail, bringing a friend to set a leghold trap and triggering it with a stick to amplify the horror of what Beau went through.

Beau himself has caught plenty of the limelight, with Rachel's friend Morgan video-documenting their reunion the morning after the surgery, and Beau's struggles to get from my clinic and into the car, aided by Cory and me and a heavy blanket to lift him. He's gained a few hundred thousand followers since, from all over the world. Even I've found myself checking the account daily for updates on his progress, cringing when I see myself captured in some of her posts. Those always come with her steadfast praise about the care and dedication "Marie the Crusader" has shown throughout this traumatic experience.

Honestly, I didn't expect to see Rachel or Beau again once they drove off, but she returned with him yesterday for a follow-up appointment and is booked to come back again in another week. I am now officially Beau's doctor, as declared on Instagram.

That, plus all the media swirl, has kicked up a cloud of pet owners who are either unhappy or apathetic toward their current veterinary care or are curious to learn more about "one of the most talented veterinary surgeons in the *country*, who's hiding out right here in the valley." My credentials are inflating by the day.

The phone rings as the clinic's doorbell chimes. I look up from the paper to see Calla and Mabel strolling in, their curious gazes roaming the clinic's little reception area.

"… So, you're saying you're *new* to us!" Cory gives me a wide look as she speaks to the caller. "Yes, we've had quite a few calls recently because of Beau's story."

I dismiss her as she jots down information and instead round the counter to greet our visitors. "What are you guys doing here?" My focus inadvertently drifts toward Calla's belly, looking for a hint of the baby growing inside, but it's far too soon. She's not due until March. "Is Bandit okay?"

"Oh yeah, he's fine." She waves off my concern, pausing on my framed mugshot, her perfectly shaped eyebrow arching. "We were on our way to Target, so we thought we'd stop. Mabel was hoping you might have some puppies running around."

"I'm sorry, we don't. Not for a while now." We've taken in rescue litters from time to time, keeping them in the clinic until they're adopted out. I shift my focus to Agnes's daughter. It stuns me how much she's grown in just a few years. She was an exuberant little girl when I met her, prattling nonstop and tailing Jonah around. Now, words need to be dragged from her. "How do you like living in Trapper's Crossing so far?"

"Yeah, it's fine, I guess." She tucks her hair behind her ear, doing her best to remain aloof as she drifts around the room.

"Muriel has been keeping her busy at the resort, cleaning cabins."

The sharp look Mabel shoots Calla says that part of moving to Trapper's Crossing has *not* been fine.

Calla's eyes sparkle with amusement. At least she's not taking teenager syndrome personally. "Jonah said everything went well yesterday with moving your sister in?"

"We got it done in half the time with his help." Frankly, we wouldn't have gotten it done at all. Vicki's bedroom furniture was far too heavy for me and Oliver, and Jim conveniently had to work. "I take it he told you all about Beau the Bear-nese?"

"*Yes!*" Calla exclaims. "I spent all night catching up online. I am *so* impressed."

I laugh. "I knew you would be."

"Sounds like it's helped drum up some business for you, though?" Calla's face pinches with concern. I have a feeling Jonah mentioned my financial woes. Is that why she's standing in my clinic's lobby for the first time since she moved here?

"It has. We'll see how long it lasts. How are you feeling?"

"I'm okay. Tired. More because I cut out caffeine than anything." Her lips twist with a sour expression. "You don't realize it's going to be the last time you have a cup of coffee for nine *months* until after you've had it. Hey, so, how old is this picture of you?" She points to the wall.

I school my expression, fighting my urge to laugh. She can't let it go. "A few years, maybe?"

"You know, it's always good to keep these things updated. I have a pretty good camera. I could come by and take a few new headshots for you. Something fresh and ..." She searches for the word.

"Less like she belongs on the six o'clock news for a meth-induced string of murders?" Cory chirps, ending her call.

Finally, Mabel's face cracks with a smile.

"It's okay." I laugh. "I know how bad it is. It's more a joke than anything at this point."

"Oh, thank God," Calla mutters under her breath, frowning at the framed picture. "But *still*, Marie. Okay, let's make plans. Soon." She hesitates. "And I was also thinking, I could update your website, if you want?" It's a tentative question, her nose wrinkling as if afraid she's overstepping. "I was skimming it last night and, I don't know, it could use some—"

"Yes, *please*," Cory pleads, nodding vigorously, first to Calla and then to me. "I meant to spend some time on it this summer, but I'm swamped with wedding plans, and now *this*"—she gestures at the phone—"we don't even have the right hours listed."

"It won't take me long."

Cory doesn't understand what Calla means when she says "update." "Thank you for the offer, but I can't sink money into that now." I looked into design costs once after flipping through Frank Hartley's professionally built website. I could stock my shelves with syringes and gauze for months with that amount.

She waves my words away. "Consider it payment for all the times you've come by to check on Bandit and Zeke. We owe you."

And I'm certain now that Jonah has told her *everything*.

She looks around my lobby. "You know, a plant might look nice in here. It doesn't have to be *real*."

She says plant, but she's already picturing different chairs and wall art. Probably new flooring, too. This is what Calla does when she walks into a neglected space, whether it's by passion or compulsion. She somehow even managed to get her creative hands past Muriel and on the Ale House, and now its wayward personality is stylized with some semblance of intention. Small details, like harmonizing vinyl tablecloths, frames to replace the thumbtacks on the photographs, lanterns on windowsills, and montages of kitschy signs rather than a clutter of them. It's still the same bucolic watering hole, just with more charm.

I will be the first to admit Calla's wildly talented, as I'll also admit my clinic lobby fits the profile of a neglected, zestless space. But I can't spend money on a remodel.

The clinic's phone rings.

"Ten bucks says it's a new patient," Cory drones as she reaches for it. "Lehr Animal Care, Cory speaking …" Cory frowns as she listens. "Yeah, she's here. Hold on a sec, okay?" She covers the receiver rather than putting it on hold. "Tyler's brother is on the phone? Sounds like there's something wrong at the kennel, and he can't get hold of Tyler."

———

The rain falls in sheets against my windshield as I slam my foot against the brakes. My truck skids to a halt in front of the gate blocking the driveway. I'd thought Reed would come out on his ATV to open it, but I realize now what a foolish expectation that was. With how frantic he sounded, there's no way he'd leave Nala's side. He probably didn't think about this obstacle.

I grip my steering wheel and consider my options. The driveway is a mile long. It'll take me at least ten minutes to jog it —likely more, with stops. That, plus the twenty-minute drive here, speeding along the dirt roads, and if I have to take her to the clinic to operate …

I could still call him and have him come out …

But all I can think about is Reed's shaky voice as he described the lodged puppy and how helpless he sounded, and how Tyler might react to one of his lead dogs—one of Mila's dogs—dying during labor if complications persist.

I throw my truck in Reverse and back down the road, and then, giving myself all of two seconds to reconsider, I jam my foot against the gas and grit my teeth.

The hinges on the aluminum farm gate snap on impact, the pieces flying out of the way. I speed down the driveway, hoping I'm not already too late.

———

Nala licks my fingertips and then dismisses me to lie on the fresh towels as five puppies burrow into her underbelly. The body of the sixth puppy—the first to be born and the one that got lodged sideways in the birth canal, prompting Reed to call me in a panic as Nala's struggle dragged on—is wrapped in a towel and set in a box until Tyler comes home and decides where he'd like to bury him.

It always pangs my heart to hold a lifeless creature in my palm, but all things considered, I'm content to sit in this little room in the barn, listening to the rain pelt the roof while I steep in my relief.

"That never happened with the other dogs." Reed sits across from me, his face grim, his arms tucked around his body. This experience has rattled him.

"You've seen a lot of puppies born?" Tyler mentioned Reed's parents—Mila's father and stepmother—being avid mushers themselves.

"Fair amount. They always just came out."

"I'm sure the dogs giving birth didn't think it was so easy. But you were right to call me." I reach out and gently scratch Nala's head again. She doesn't so much as twitch at my invasion of her space. "She'll be fine." Aside from the first pup, the others delivered without issue.

"You don't have to stay. I mean, I know you're busy with people and animals and stuff," he stammers. "I just mean, if you have to go, it's okay. I'm good now. I can take care of them from here."

"I know you can." I sense that Reed takes great pride in his responsibility for these dogs while Tyler is away. And Jed Carling *is* expecting me. But Cory's already warned him I'll be a few hours late. "Tyler's almost back, though, right? I might as well wait a bit longer." I mock cringe. "How mad do you think he'll be about the whole gate thing?"

Reed frowns, as if seriously considering this question. "He can replace the gate. He can't replace Nala," he says with a degree of finality that makes me smile.

"You're right." And if I know Tyler like I think I do, he won't value anything above these dogs.

"He should be home any minute." Reed checks his watch and brushes a hand through his mop of curly dark hair to sweep it away from his eyes. It's gotten long in the last few weeks and could use a cut. If I could get him to my place, I'll bet Vicki would love to take her scissors to it.

Reed's cheeks flush, and I realize I'm staring at the poor kid.

"Tyler told me this was your sister's team?"

He nods toward the exhausted new mother. "She was Mila's favorite. Her and Tank."

"Did you get to see Mila a lot, growing up?" How well did they know each other, living on different sides of the world, years apart, sharing nothing more than a father?

"Not a lot, no." Reed smiles then, and it's such a boyish, genuine grin, with a hint of a dimple in his left cheek. "She used to call me all the time, though. And I went to Finland to visit her once. Tero and Anja invited me. That was a good time." The words tumble from him now, that veil of timidity that normally holds him back lifting. But the smile slips away as easily as it came, replaced by a pensive look.

"I'll bet you miss her. I can't imagine losing either of my sisters like that." No matter how big a thorn in my side Liz may be, her absence would leave a gaping hole ten times larger, filling up with regret for all the ways we should have been better to each other.

He bobs his head, the move sending his hair falling into his eyes again. He pushes it away.

"Tyler told me you want a team to mush? Maybe these pups will end up on your team."

"Yeah, maybe." His lips purse, as if weighing the possibilities.

Ten minutes later, a truck door slams outside the barn, and a chorus of dogs howl in greeting. Footfalls approach in a rush.

My blood pulses in my ears just at the anticipation of seeing Tyler again.

The door creaks open, and he pokes his head in cautiously. His eyes go first to Nala and then to the suckling puppies, and then to me, on the floor, my legs stretched out, my rain boots crossed at the ankles. He's still in uniform, though missing the vest. His pant legs are soaked from the rain. An odd mix of relief and panic fills his face.

"Where's Reed?" he asks as he pushes the door farther open until it bumps into Reed's leg, matching my position but against the other wall. "There you are." He studies his brother-in-law's face a moment, and they seem to share unspoken words before he asks, "You good?"

Reed hesitates but then nods.

Nala hears Tyler's voice, and her tail swishes in greeting.

"Hey, girl." He eases in and shuts the door behind him, then settles between me and her.

I shift over to give him room, but there isn't much to give, and we end up sitting side by side, our shoulders pressed against each other.

"You did good," he murmurs.

She rests her cheek on his palm and watches him through tired eyes.

With a heavy sigh, he leans back against the wall beside me. "I was out looking for a lost hiker all day. I didn't get any of your messages until I drove to a signal spot."

"Did you find her? The hiker?" Reed asks.

"Yeah. She got chased off a trail by a bear and couldn't find her way back, but she's fine."

Reed hoists himself up. "I'm gonna go check on everyone else." He stalls at the door as he brushes his hair aside. "See you around, Marie."

"Soon enough, I'm sure." I smile at his retreating back until the door is shut tight, keeping the damp air out.

But Tyler's not smiling. "We knew when I left this morning that she was going to have them. I was going to call in sick, but Reed said he could manage it. I shouldn't have left him here alone like that. I'm an idiot." His jaw is taut with tension.

"He *did* manage it. He called me, which is *exactly* what he should have done." I'm not going to point out how panicked Reed sounded on the phone. "It's what *you* would have had to do even if you'd been here."

"Yeah, I guess. Still, I should've been there. He shouldn't have had to do that alone." He studies the small room we're in. "I'm starting to feel guilty about him being by himself like this all summer. It can't be good for him."

"It's only until you're off for the season. And then you'll be together for, what, seven months straight?" Minus the two weeks Tyler's running the Iditarod. As I study the man's handsome profile, I'm suddenly envious of a twenty-year-old boy.

"He'll be sick of me by the end." Tyler smirks. "I was thinking of hiring another handler. Give Reed a chance to make a friend or two. Maybe there's an eager kid who wants to earn some extra cash."

"I'll keep an ear out for someone like that." From the other side of the door, I hear a snuffling and then a soft whine.

"It's Tank," Tyler says. "He doesn't like being away from Nala for too long. But he can stay out there. He's already caused enough trouble." Tyler watches the puppies for a moment before his head falls back against the barn wall, angling toward me. "Thank you."

"Of course. It's what I'm here for, right?" Under the dim lights, amplified by a glow from the heat lamp, Tyler's features are somehow more alluring. I admire the shape of his lips and the cut of his jaw, the way his dark ash-brown hair rests in a slight wave.

He watches me studying him, and the sudden vulnerability in

his expression brings me back to those stolen, intimate moments in my truck at the Ale House. Will that ever happen again? For a guy who doesn't want to complicate his life, he has quite the track record of unintentional kissing.

And for a thirty-eight-year-old woman who doesn't want to get hung up on false hope again, I seem to keep wading in deeper.

"What's that look for?" he asks, his head tipped at just the perfect angle to lean in and kiss me.

I have to turn away before he reads my thoughts. Thoughts that don't fit the label of friendship or business under any circumstance. "I should get going. I was supposed to be at Jed Carling's place hours ago."

"By the way, I'd say you've topped your first visit here with your entrance."

I struggle to keep from smiling.

"Did you hesitate at all or just plow right through?" There's a playfulness in his voice that confirms he's not angry.

"I *did* stop." I meet his gaze again, marveling at the golden flecks in his irises. We're sitting shoulder to shoulder. He's so close.

His left eyebrow arches with amusement. "You did?"

"Yeah. And then I reversed so I could take a good run at it."

His chuckle is deep and contagious, and I feel it dance along my spine as I laugh alongside him. "I'm trying to picture that, and I can't—no, wait. Actually, I can. You were probably biting the side of your bottom lip like you do when you're determined to get your way."

"I do *not* do that."

His laughter only grows. "Yeah, okay."

Despite my best efforts, my eyes drift to his mouth. "I didn't have a choice. I didn't know how bad it might be, and I couldn't let something happen to her. I know how much that would hurt you."

"So you raced over here and crashed through my gate to protect me—is that what you're saying?"

And suddenly neither of us are laughing anymore as his words seem to pluck the humor from the air.

Tyler falters, then leans in to press his lips against mine. A shaky sigh escapes him, as if he's been holding his breath until now.

There's no excuse for it this time—no sleepy confusion, no ruse to avoid a confrontation. Tyler is kissing me because he's chosen to, and realizing that drives me forward, leaning into him, teasing him with the tip of my tongue. He responds in kind, the taste of mint taunting my taste buds as we explore each other's mouths, his cradling hand leaving Nala to curl around the back of my head, pulling my face in closer.

"Hey, Ty?"

Tyler breaks away with lightning speed.

Reed stands in the doorway. I didn't hear the door creak. "You left the windows open in the truck." He studies his boots. "The seat's getting wet."

A few beats pass before a curse slips out under Tyler's breath. He fishes his keys out of his pocket. "I'll go out and close it." He pulls himself off the barn floor. "You have all your things, Marie?"

I tap the open black leather bag with my foot. "Almost." I don't trust my voice with more than that.

"Okay. I'll meet you outside." His gaze passes over mine, and the heat and playfulness I saw only moments ago is now shuttered. He ducks out, pulling the door shut behind him.

Leaving me reeling in a swirl of confusion and regret.

I shouldn't have let that happen. Despite my resistance, we have become friends, and he's already told me—twice—that it won't go further than that.

And yet, he just kissed me.

I do one final check on Nala, sterilize my stethoscope and thermometer, and pack up the portable ultrasound I brought with me. Finished here, my boots splash through puddles as I trudge toward my truck. Aside from a few scratches on the hood, I don't see much in the way of damage from plowing through the gate, the grille guard doing its job. But my truck is the furthest thing from my thoughts.

Reed was still in the barn when I left, grooming one of the dogs while several others lounged in the straw. He was quiet—but he always is. Still, I felt him watching me as I strolled away. What's going on in that head of his? Does it bother him to see Tyler kissing another woman? Does he think it's too soon?

Is two *years* too soon?

By Tyler's reaction in the barn, what Reed thinks matters. But that's not a surprise. Reed is Mila's brother—a piece of his late wife—and Tyler is still living for her. I can't allow myself to get caught up in a heady swirl of hormones and emotions and forget that.

And still, as these thoughts solidify in my mind, I refuse to dismiss the feeling that this isn't just friendship for Tyler, either, despite his earlier words.

Tyler's head is bowed against the rain as he marches toward me from the house, his uniform replaced by sweatpants and a pullover that'll be soaked soon. He reaches my truck just as I'm starting the engine. I open my window, my stomach a knot of anxiety and anticipation. "I can come by on Monday to check on her if you want."

"That'd be great. Cory'll send me the bill for today?"

So smoothly we've switched to business. "Yeah. Let me know what I owe for the gate—"

"Nothing. You don't owe me anything for that." He scowls as if my offer is preposterous. "You did what you had to do to get here to help Reed, and I appreciate it."

An awkward silence lingers as he rests his forearms on my door, keeping me there, as he peers over his shoulder toward the barn. "You know what's freaky? They have the exact same big, brown eyes. Sometimes, for like a split second, it feels like Mila's watching me." He turns back on a deep inhale. "I got caught up in the moment, and I didn't think." He shifts his stance, leans in a little more, his head resting against the door frame, his voice softening as he says, "It's just that, when I'm with you, I forget about everything else. You make me feel like myself again." He studies my mouth like he wants to kiss me again.

And I would allow it, I silently accept, watching raindrops cling to the ends of his hair. "You're getting soaked. You should get in my truck so we can talk."

His crooked smile is roguish. "If I get in your truck, you and I both know we *won't* be talking."

Blood rushes to my ears as I hear the promise in those words and weigh their truth. He's right, and we both know it, and I won't bother denying it.

Tank comes trotting out of the barn, his head on a swivel as if searching for Tyler. Seeing him, he barks and speeds up. Nymeria follows closely.

"Look at that. They're coming to keep me in line." With a pat against my door, Tyler takes a wide step back. "You should get to that appointment. I don't want you to lose anyone else on my account."

"Jed's not going anywhere." He's one of the most easygoing men I've ever met, an Iditarod musher who's happy just to cross the finish line, no matter which place. He's earned himself two Red Lanterns over the years—the award that goes to the last musher to pass under the Burled Arch.

Tank reaches Tyler, and rather than stopping at his side, he leaps into the air, his paws landing on Tyler's shoulders. Tyler was ready for the move and holds the amorous husky against his body.

Reed pokes his head out the barn door and upon seeing me still in the driveway, ducks back in.

A thought strikes me. "Hey, if you're serious about hiring help,

I might know of someone. Her name's Mabel. She doesn't have any kennel experience, but she loves dogs." She's fascinated by Roy's wolf dogs when they come lurking around. "She's fourteen, so she shouldn't be too intimidating for Reed. And I'm guessing she'll do anything to avoid working for Muriel."

Tyler grunts with understanding as he releases Tank to the ground. "Let me know."

"I will. I'll see you on Monday." I ease down the driveway in my truck, my attention constantly flipping to my rearview mirror as my mind hangs tightly on to his words and the feel of his lips.

Is it possible? Could Tyler finally be looking toward the future, instead of lingering in his past?

Or am I just a child toying with a lighter in a room full of kindling?

CHAPTER TWENTY-TWO

"Dad, not so much! She just had those tubes put in!" Vicki scolds as our father bounces Molly on his good leg.

"It's been a week. She's *fine*. But are you sure they gave you the right kid back? This one's *way* more fun. Aren't you, *Milly Molly?*" He caps it off with a silly singsong voice that has her screeching with delight.

I smile as I set plates out for Sunday dinner. He's not wrong. Whether it's the ear tubes or the move here, or that she's finally settling into life, it's like a switch has flipped in that child.

"Were you expecting someone, Marie?" Mom's focus is out the kitchen window.

"I wasn't, but maybe someone is hoping I'm open?"

"I don't think it's for the clinic."

My heart skips a few beats as I spot the familiar green truck parked next to mine and the figure standing inside my porch. I'm driving out to Tyler's kennel tomorrow evening after his shift, an appointment I've been looking forward to *all* weekend. Maybe something has happened with Nala or the puppies. But he would've called, and my phone has been with me all afternoon.

"I better go see what that's about." Setting the rest of the dishes aside, I promise, "I'll be back in a minute." I rush for my boots and the door, yanking my hair free from the topknot I threw it into while preparing the potatoes.

By the time I reach the mowed path that connects the two sides of the property, Tyler is almost back to his truck. "Hey!" I holler, my hands cupped around my mouth, hoping my voice will reach him as I trudge forward. The worst of the rain is over, but a thick blanket of cloud still smothers any glimpse of the sun. "Tyler!" My boots sink into the soft ground, collecting mud with each hurried step.

His head swivels.

Today's bleakness can't dampen the energy that surges through my limbs as I watch his sleek figure move toward me, clad in blue jeans and a soft gray shirt that stretches across his chest and shoulders, the collar framing his columnar neck.

When I'm with you, I forget about everything else. You make me feel like myself again.

The closer he gets, the harder my heart beats. I haven't been able to dismiss his words, and they've kindled a heady anticipation that now burns inside me, no matter how hard I try to douse it. "Hey. I saw you through the window." My breathing is a touch ragged by the time our paths meet. "Is something wrong?"

His eyes glow with soft amusement. "You always ask me that when you see me."

"That's because when we see each other, something usually *is* wrong." If I rifle back through our run-ins—a heated accusation of animal neglect, a downed musher, an unexpected encounter with a bitter ex, a maimed dog, a pregnant dog in peril—every single one has been marked with trouble.

"Fair enough. Nothing's wrong this time." His attention roves over my joggers and sweatshirt, and I silently curse myself for not dressing better today.

Car doors slam behind me. I turn to see Jim and Tillie heading hand-in-hand for the front door, Tillie skipping beside him. She is a daddy's girl, through and through. Meanwhile, Liz is helping Nicole down from the back seat of their new extended cab pickup. Jim may be frugal, but ironically, he's always eager to open his wallet when the purchase involves a motor. In this case, he rationalized it because, with the baby coming, they needed a bigger vehicle. The baby's not due for many months, and an SUV or minivan would have made *far* more sense for three children, but he'll find an argument to counter that logic.

My sister is hiding her bloated belly behind a bulky sweater and leggings.

"Looks like I came at a bad time?"

"No, it's fine. That's just my sister and her family. We get together on Sundays for dinner." And Liz, still annoyed with my part in convincing Vicki and Oliver to move home, mostly ignores me, aside from a subtle dig here and there.

"*Every* Sunday?"

"Pretty much."

A pensive expression touches his striking face. "I just came here to give you this." Digging into his jeans pocket, he produces a key and holds it out for me. "It's for the lock on the new gate. I figure it's cheaper if I give you access to my property."

I laugh as I accept it from him, his thumb grazing mine in the process. "This could have waited until tomorrow."

"It could have." He bites his bottom lip. I wish I could read the thoughts behind that look.

You make me feel like myself again.

Is that why he's here, now?

I'm about to ask how Reed is when a clown horn blasts, breaking the staring contest.

We shift our attention to the UTV puttering down the path, my white-haired father behind the wheel, his cast-wrapped leg sticking out the open door. All three dogs trot alongside him.

Tyler smiles. "Good to see that leg isn't slowing him any."

"His doctor wouldn't agree." Dad must have moved quickly

after I left, to have made his way out the door and into that seat. What kind of mischief is the stubborn old man up to now?

I guess I'm about to find out.

"This is what I call service, the park ranger coming to check on his rescue," Dad bellows. "Hello there, Tyler Brady!"

Tyler breaks into a wide grin, accentuated by two dimples deep in his cheeks. "Good to see you, sir."

"Don't 'sir' me. Call me Sidney. Or Sid. Or Dr. Lehr."

Yukon and Bentley reach Tyler at the same time and set to sniffing his jeans, no doubt picking up the scent of his kennel on his clothes. As usual, Aurora hangs back, watching warily from a distance.

Tyler gives each of them a hand to sniff before weaving his fingers through their fur coats. "I wanted to drop something off for Marie. I didn't mean to interrupt your family time."

"You're not! In fact, I came out to ask you to join us."

I spear my father with a stare.

But he continues, deftly ignoring me. "Normally, we have pot roast on Sundays, but we've got two pregnant women in there. The smell of beef is turning Vicki's stomach right now, and Liz says she can't handle pork, so honestly, I'm not sure what the hell we're eating tonight."

"Mom made *chicken*, Dad," I say dryly.

"Is that what that was?" His brows draw together. It's all part of the act, though. "Well, you're welcome to it, Tyler. Any *friend* of Marie's is a friend of ours." He gives the UTV gas and steers it back toward the house, hollering over his shoulder, "Oh, and I *will* be offended if you don't take me up on the offer!" With a sharp whistle, all three dogs chase after him.

"He's just kidding."

"About inviting me to dinner?"

"No, about being offended. Don't worry, you're not obligated to come."

Tyler frowns. "Are you saying you *don't* want me there?"

"No, I didn't say that—"

"Good, because I think I want to take him up on it."

I glare at him. "You're kidding, right?"

"No." He punctuates that with a head shake. "I actually *really* want to sit down with the Lehr family."

I laugh it off. "Yeah, I *really* don't think you do."

A smile tugs at the corner of his mouth, and it would be downright sexy if not for my dread. "Why not?"

"Because things have been weirdly volatile, with clinic stuff and the pregnancies and … and …" I stumble over my excuses. "We don't bring *friends* to Sunday dinner." Or emotionally unavailable men we have sex with in parking lots. None of us have ever brought a guy to Sunday dinner who we weren't dating. Jonathan was the only man I ever invited. I never even invited Jonah, afraid someone might betray me and reveal my true feelings.

Tyler shrugs. "There's a first time for everything." But there's that look of determination on his face, much like the day Jonah invited him to the Ale House.

"Well, okay, you've already met my father, so you know what *he* can be like. My nieces are fine. They're picky eaters and they're loud, but cute. Vicki will spend the entire dinner trying to set us up. Liz will spend it judging me. Oliver isn't here, which is too bad because he's a good buffer for my lazy and obnoxious brother-in-law, Jim, who thinks he has a say in how I run my clinic. It will be one of the worst nights you've had in a long time."

His frown grows deeper, more thoughtful as he considers that. "So, it's *this way*, right?" He starts moving toward my parents' house.

I grab onto his forearm, stalling him. I'm still not sure if he's being serious or if this is all a game to unsettle me, but he needs to understand. "I don't know what kind of questions they're going to ask you about your *life*." I give him a pointed look.

"I'm not as fragile as you think, Marie. You don't have to protect me." His voice is soft, warm.

"I know. I just …" My eyes drift to his mouth. *I just want you to kiss me again.* "What are you doing here, Tyler?" Besides confusing me.

He swallows. "Remember when you said maybe we could grab a coffee or dinner sometime?"

"Yeah?" All those months ago, back when I put myself out there, and he promptly shut me down.

"So then, let's do that."

Is he saying what I think he is? "You want to complicate your life?"

He reaches up to gently stroke a wayward strand of hair off my face. "I think that's happening, whether I want it or not. Wouldn't you agree?"

"I'm honestly not sure what's happening."

He jerks his head toward the house. "Come on … I don't want to miss your horrible family dinner." Giving my forearm a gentle squeeze, he leads me the way I came with backward steps and a mischievous smirk.

"Don't say I didn't warn you." I trail after him, my boots caked in mud.

And my heart soaring with new possibilities.

———

"*Quit* playing with your food," Liz warns Tillie.

"I don't like bones in my chicken," the nine-year-old grumbles, her chin resting on her propped arm as she stabs at the meat with her fork. "Why can't we have beef?"

"Because the smell of it makes your aunt Vicki want to throw up," Vicki says from the end of the table, shoveling spoonfuls of pureed carrots into an impatient Molly's gaping mouth, her own plate of food growing cold.

"I don't like bony chicken, either!" Nicole whines.

"Eat everything on your plates or no dessert," Liz hisses. Her temper is unusually short today, and I can't tell if it's the physical strain from the first trimester or the mental strain from missing the glass of wine she normally has with dinner. Probably both.

"I get twenty-two miles per gallon in that truck," Jim announces around a forkful of chicken, having tuned out his children and wife.

"Is that good?" My mom feigns interest.

"Not as good as if they'd bought that truck used. May as well have flushed fifteen grand down the toilet as soon as they drove it off the lot," my dad counters while Jim's mouth is too full to respond.

Beside me, Tyler sits, eating and watching and answering the odd question thrown at him about the Iditarod and his seasonal park ranger position.

"Have more chicken, Tyler." Mom gestures toward the platter in front of him.

"I'm good for now. Thanks, Eleanor." Tyler smiles politely at my mom. "I still have a piece."

"What about green beans?" She holds up the casserole dish. "Or carrots?"

His smile widens. "Still got some of those, too. Thanks."

She pauses a beat. "Potatoes?"

"*Jesus*, Eleanor. The man hasn't even finished his plate!" My dad gives my mom an exasperated look.

"*Jee*-sus!" Nicole echoes, bursting with laughter as if my father's made a joke.

"*Don't* say that!" Liz scowls at my dad. "*Either* of you!"

Dad winces at his granddaughter. "Sorry, Tyler, it's been a few years since we've had someone new at the table. Well, a new male grown-up. Not these little urchins." He casts a wink toward Tillie and Nicole. "My one son-in-law, the one who's at work right now, eats like he has a hollow leg, and this one has no problem helping himself to thirds."

"Don't mind if I do, actually." Jim reaches across the table and grabs a thigh by the end with his fingers, dropping it unceremoniously on his plate.

"I mean, not that I'm looking to add you to my collection of sons-in-law," my father continues.

I groan. "Dad."

Beside me, Tyler chuckles.

"So, where did you two meet again?" Vicki asks as she wipes a smear of carrot off Molly's chubby cheek.

"At the race," I lie, at the same time that Tyler answers with, "On my property, when Marie trespassed to accuse me of neglecting my dogs."

I give the side of his leg a swift kick.

"*This* is the one you were talking about that night?" Liz stares at me, genuinely surprised. As am I. I didn't think she was listening.

"You've been talking about me with your family? All good things, I hope." He smirks as he carves into his chicken. But beneath the table, he gently nudges his knee against mine.

The simple contact makes me falter. "That was a misunderstanding that we cleared up *during the race*. Now I'm his veterinarian."

"Funny, I don't remember Harry ever coming to dinner," Vicki quips, flashing a wry smile my way that says she doesn't buy the emphasized *just a friend* label I threw on when I introduced Tyler to a kitchen full of curious stares.

As if waiting for her mother's fleeting distraction, Molly throws her bowl, splattering pureed carrots all over the floor and nearby walls. She shrieks with delight as Yukon and Bentley dive in for the cleanup.

"No one can say those dogs don't eat well." My mom laughs,

climbing out of her chair and heading for the cupboard for a fresh bowl. "You eat, Vicki. I'll finish feeding her."

"It's the new game around here this week." Dad grunts as Vicki cradles her forehead in her hands in frustration. "So, Tyler, how's the off-season training going? Must be tough to handle, with your day job."

"It's busy. My handler works on commands with them through the day, and I take them out for short runs on their harnesses with the ATV at night, when it's cool enough. Between work and the dogs, I don't have much time for anything else."

And yet he's here now, having dinner with my family, I think with a bubble of satisfaction.

"Earl Hatchett used to love takin' his dogs out under a midnight sun." My dad waggles a finger at Nicole and Tillie. "Girls, that's how these mushers keep these dogs in shape when there's no snow. They have them run ahead of the ATVs."

"*I know.*" Tillie's eyes flick upward to the ceiling.

"Oh, of course you do. I forgot you're nine years old and you already know *everything*. Tyler, you gonna do tours?"

"Nah."

"Not interested, huh. Yeah, don't blame you. Dealin' with all those people traipsing all over your property. Besides, you already have an off-season income. I heard Harry's been pushing those kennel tours hard this summer."

"I'd believe it. I've seen quite a few cars heading into his place." If Tyler is annoyed by the traffic, he doesn't let on.

"Anything to save that kennel. I hope for Earl's sake, he can. His father and I were good friends."

"You're good friends with *everyone*, Dad," I tease.

"Can't help being such a likable guy." He winks. "Which reminds me ... I was tellin' my *good* friend Bill Compton all about your kennel, Tyler. Marie was raving about it. He would love to do a piece on you. Come out, ask you a bunch of questions.

Maybe spend the day. Thinks it would be good for the sport. The bad apples have been getting way too much attention."

I should've known there was an ulterior motive here. "Dad …" I give him a look. "Tyler doesn't like doing interviews." Something both he and Bill have learned already.

He shrugs. "Was worth a shot. I guess he can go to Harry. Lord knows that guy likes to talk about himself."

"Hey, what happened with the Hatchetts, by the way?" Jim tears off a chunk of meat from the bone. "Sid says you lost their business?"

His choice of words and the very fact that he's asking stiffens my spine. "Harry thought he had a say in how I run things, but he doesn't. *Nobody* does," I say pointedly.

"Still, that's *a lot* of revenue gone." Jim shakes his head as if in disapproval.

I grit my teeth against the urge to tell him to fuck off.

Even my father is annoyed. "Mind your business before she finds a new accountant, Jim."

But my brother-in-law, as obtuse as usual, doesn't take the hint. "Just pointing out the obvious, Sid. Especially now that you've got all these people to feed under this roof."

"Tyler, you *must* want another beer," my mom declares suddenly. "Marie, why don't you grab your guest another from the fridge."

I know what she's doing—trying to fend off an explosive argument. For Tyler's sake, I appreciate it.

But before I can even set down my cutlery, Tyler is on his feet, his palm resting on my shoulder to keep me in place. "I've got it. I'll get you one, too. Can I grab anyone else anything?"

My dad waves his drained bottle in the air.

With a quick stroke of his thumb against my collarbone, Tyler collects the empties from the table and heads for the fridge.

I track his sleek, easy movements the entire way.

"Take notes, Jim," Vicki murmurs under her breath, but loud enough for everyone to hear.

I snort, and the simple act helps alleviate some of my anger. Tyler's lingering touch is also working its magic, a pleasant warmth that's spreading through my chest and down into my lower belly. He may have meant it as an innocent move, for reassurance, for comfort. But to me, it's also a promise of how good his hands would feel all over my body.

Liz's gaze narrows as she cuts off the rest of Nicole's meat for her. She knows her husband's a lazy sack, but she always acts offended when anyone else points it out. "So, Vicki, *are* you actually going to finish your school hours this time?"

Vicki takes a deep breath, but I can almost hear her teeth grinding. "I've already spoken to my instructors about coming back."

"Good. Because you won't have time once the baby's born. You think Molly is hard? Just *wait* until you have two." Her laugh drips with a patronizing tone, her words a careless dismissal of our youngest sister's struggles.

Vicki smiles sweetly. "But just imagine how hard it'll be with *three*."

I would be ecstatic with one, I acknowledge silently as Tyler returns with the beers and takes his seat next to me again, his thigh bumping against mine when he shifts in. "What are you going to school for, Vicki?" If the undercurrent of tension flowing through our dining room bothers him, he doesn't let on.

"Hair design. I want to run my own place at home, in a garage or a back room. Somewhere I can take clients at my own pace while being able to raise my kids."

I nudge Tyler's side with my elbow. "I was thinking Vicki should come out to your place and cut Reed's hair."

He chuckles. "If she can pin him down long enough."

"You know"—Jim taps the air with his fork, his attention on

my dad—"you could convert that cabin into a salon for Vicki, and she can work out of there."

The cabin. But ... "I *live* in that cabin." I stare at Jim with disbelief.

"Well, *yeah,* but how much longer are you gonna do that for?" He shrugs, as if he's not suggesting evicting me from my home for the past decade. To my father, he says, "Vicki can pay you rent. That way you have two business income streams on the property."

Jim's *always* looking for ways to save or make money.

"I live there," I repeat, the edge of my fork digging into my thumb as I squeeze it.

"Realistically, it's the *only* way Vicki'll ever be able to afford her own place on the kind of money those two make."

"*I* think it's a great idea," Liz announces.

"Of course, you do."

She purses her lips. "Vicki has kids to think about. Remember? That's why you convinced her to move back in here?"

She's *still* angry about that.

I brace myself. When Liz is angry, she gets mean.

"Dad *already* gave you the clinic. Just because you're the oldest doesn't mean you can claim *everything* on this property."

"Nobody's *claimed anything!*" Dad sets his fork and knife on the table, his voice rising a notch. "What is going on under this roof? Can we *not* just have a normal dinner anymore?" He glares at Jim, who stirred the pot. Again.

Tyler's hand slips under the table to give my thigh a gentle rub. "Hey, girls, why don't you two show me that game you were playing in the living room before dinner."

Nicole and Tillie scramble out of their seats and run toward the doorway before their mother can check their plates and hold them back.

Tyler is up quickly after them, aiming for the high chair.

"Why don't I take this one off your hands, too? She looks finished."

"Oh, I don't know if she'll go with you ..." Mom's voice fades as Tyler deftly unbuckles the belt keeping Molly in place and hoists her out with two strong hands around her waist, as if he's done this a thousand times before.

He lifts her little body high in the air above him before tucking her against his side. "Molly and me will be just fine, won't we?"

The dimpled smile he treats her to seems to disarm any wariness she might have over the stranger. Her puree-covered hand reaches for his nose to test it with a gurgle of interest, earning his laughter.

I watch in awe as the two of them disappear down the hall, and a swirl of emotions surges in my chest.

Tyler would have made a good father to his son.

He *will* make a good father.

"Okay, if I weren't already pregnant, I think watching that would have knocked me up." Vicki turns her dazed eyes to me. "He is *perfect* for you, Marie. He loves dogs and babies, and he's *so* hot."

My pulse races. *I know.* But others see it, too. "We're just friends." Dare I hope for more?

From the living room, a sharp whistle cuts through the air, and Yukon and Bentley bolt out of the kitchen.

"See?" Dad holds up his finger in the air. "Dogs *always* know."

———

"I hope that wasn't the *worst* dinner you've ever had." My mom wrings her hands as she walks us to the door. I'll bet she's as relieved as I am that it ended without a cataclysmic screaming match, but she's suitably embarrassed, regardless.

Tyler's unexpected and swift removal of the children seemed

to disarm the bomb about to detonate, allowing everyone a moment to calm down and reevaluate words that likely would've caused lasting damage once they were spoken. Jim and Liz left soon after, citing Jim's workload and Liz's condition for their speedy departure. Vicki escaped upstairs to bathe Molly and ready her for bed. Tyler tried to find a spot next to me at the sink, but my mother chased him off, so he ended up parked on the couch where my father regaled him with countless stories about Earl Hatchett and other mushers who became more than just clients.

When I emerged from the kitchen, Aurora's chin was resting on Tyler's knee as his fingers moved in a slow, circular pattern over her forehead. I've never seen her get that close to anyone besides my mother.

"Actually, Marie specifically promised me a horrible dinner, and didn't deliver on it."

"Oh." My mom laugh-snorts and shakes her head. "Did she mean my cooking or the company?"

Tyler's eyes sparkle as he towers over my tiny mother and charms her. "Both were enjoyable, Eleanor. Thank you for the invitation."

"You're welcome!" my father hollers from the depths of the house, where he's settled into his chair. "See you again, if you're crazy enough to return."

Tyler chuckles and then, with a pensive look, hollers back, "Tell Bill Compton that I'll give him that interview, but *only* if Marie's involved."

I stare at him. Is he serious? Where did that come from?

"She'll do it! I'll let him know!"

"Stop hollering! Vicki's trying to put Molly to bed," my mother hisses in the direction of the living room before reaching for my wrist, giving it an affectionate squeeze.

I smile. "You sure you're okay with helping out at the clinic this week?" It's been years since she sat at that desk.

She waves away my concern. "It's like riding a bike. Plus, I could use the break from this madhouse." She peeks around me to confirm that Tyler has already reached the bottom of the steps. "I *really* like him," she whispers. "But I don't think this one is just a friend."

Warmth swells in my chest. I can't tell if it's wishful thinking or if she sees something I want to see. Either way, I hope she's right. She knows well enough the heartache that's woven into my history with Jonah. "Good night, Mom."

I rejoin Tyler on the grassy path, my steps buoyed with hope as we walk toward my cabin in the gloomy dusk. The chill in the damp air prompts me to pull the front of my jacket closed.

Without a word, Tyler slips his arm around my shoulders, fitting me against his side, much like he did that night in the truck when he was offering me comfort.

Now, he's offering me warmth.

Butterflies stir in my stomach as I try to relax against him, but this is all so new. I keep my pace slow, not wanting this part of the night to end.

Tyler's chest rises and falls with a sigh. Is he as happy as I am at this moment?

"So, will you admit now that we should have started with coffee?" I ask into the quiet.

"And miss that shit show? No way."

I shake my head, but I'm laughing. "I don't know what's going on lately. If it's the pregnancy hormones or money worries ... We're not normally *that* bad." Clearly, there's animosity fermenting beneath Liz's skin, and I seem to be the catalyst. "My sister has *always* had an issue with my dad handing over the family clinic to me. She thinks I have it too easy."

He chuckles. "You did *how* many years of school again?"

"She thinks I should have started from scratch after I got out," I amend. "Built up my own clientele. That, or paid Dad outright for his. She doesn't see that technically, I *am* paying for it monthly. It's kind of a rent-to-own business." Except I'll never own the physical structure. "Anyway, I hope that wasn't too painful. Even though I *did* warn you."

"Honestly, I'm not fazed by that sort of stuff. Every family has its own dynamic, and the best of them are messy sometimes. Mila and her mother argued a lot, about *everything*. And I'm the youngest of six."

I mouth, *Wow.*

"Yeah. Three boys and three girls. I was the youngest and an accident. But I remember *a lot* of fights at our table. Now both my parents are gone, and everyone's busy with their own lives and their own families. Some of my nieces and nephews are in their late teens and twenties. I remember them being babies."

"Is that why you're so comfortable with Molly?"

"I guess. It's been awhile though." A soft smile tugs at his lips. "She's adorable."

"So were you, when you carried her out." Adorable isn't the right word. I can't decide what is. Sexy. Potent. Intoxicating.

His cheeks flush. "I can't tell you the last time all of us were in one house. What you have back there?" He nods toward my parents' place. "Still getting together every week? That's special. You'll miss it when it's gone. Even the nights you want to stab Jim with your fork."

My deep laugh drifts through the still night. "You noticed that, huh?"

"It was pretty hard to miss." He pulls me tighter against him, his thumb stroking my shoulder. "And I don't blame you. I'll bet that guy tells himself he's the smartest person in any room he walks into."

"He's a pain in the ass, but he usually means well. I think he's always doing stuff like that because he wants to prove his value to my father."

"I can understand that. Your dad seems like the anchor in the family."

"Yeah, I guess he is. We're all a bunch of daddy's girls, me being the worst of all. Our family would be lost without him." *Will be* lost without him one day, I'm afraid. "But it's my mom who's the glue. She's the one who insists on these weekly dinners. She's always trying to keep the peace. Always bending to accommodate. Too much, sometimes."

"Sounds like someone else I know," he murmurs, his arm around me squeezing.

I laugh. "You don't know me well enough to start poking at my shortcomings."

"That's the thing I like about getting older. It takes way less time to figure people out." Even at our slow pace, we've reached my porch too soon.

"So, this is the place Jim wants to evict you from?"

"It is." I hesitate, but a yawning need aches inside me. "Do you want to come inside?"

He seems to consider that. "It's better I don't. Things will get out of hand too fast."

Would that be so bad? I'm not ready to say good night yet. "By the way, the interview? With Bill?"

"Your dad is a hard man to say no to." He slips his arm off me, turning to lean against my porch post, his hands sliding into his pockets. "But he's right. The sport could use some positive attention, and I think my kennel and my dogs can do that. With your help, because I *hate* anything to do with the media."

"I'm not sure you want me there."

"Why wouldn't I? You're my vet, *and* an Iditarod trail vet."

"*And* I have a lot of issues with the industry, with the laws, and all the money tied to the sport." I guess this conversation needs to happen, eventually. I just don't know how Tyler will react, given how firmly entrenched he is in this world. "I may have grown up in Alaska, around all this, but I struggle with it. I see dogs like yours, who are cared for better than a lot of the house pets that come into my clinic, and I feel the energy and excitement of the dogs on the trail. But then I see dogs like Aurora, and Nymeria who was *owned* by a champion musher—"

"I already know where your head's at, Marie. I knew that first day when you showed up at my place. And we share the same issues. Haven't you figured that out yet? Hell, I snuck onto a man's property and stole his dog. I would have taken them all if I could." His chuckle is without mirth. "Before I met Mila, I didn't know much about this world, besides what I'd seen on the news. Then I moved to Finland and started living in it, and I saw a whole other side.

"That first snowfall, when I bust out the sled?" He shakes his head. "*No one* can see how those dogs react and actually believe they're not living their best lives. But I'm no idiot, and I don't have blinders on, and I'm not going to pretend there aren't shitty people out there and things that don't need to change. People like Zed Snyder shouldn't be *anywhere* near this sport or these dogs. You can say whatever the hell you want during that interview, and I'll back you up." He frowns, and I sense disappointment. "I'm surprised you'd even doubt that."

"It's not that I doubted it. It's just ..." I guess I needed to hear it. "How do you always say the right things to me?"

He smiles. "Do I?"

They're the things that pull me in deeper every time. Deeper, and closer to admitting that I'm falling in love with this man who casually leans against my little cabin as if he hasn't so thoroughly invaded my life and my thoughts.

Can he see that as plainly as I can?

Slipping a hand from his pocket, he holds it out, palm up.

Beckoning me.

I slide mine into it without hesitation, allowing him to pull me closer.

His expression softens as his eyes roam my face, lingering on my mouth. "You know, I never expected this to happen."

"Neither did I." I'd all but given up on it.

I'm waiting for him to lean in to kiss me, but he reaches for the screen door instead, leading me inside.

The surge of expectation in the air is palpable as I step out of my muddy boots and into my little home. I pull the chain on a nearby lamp for some light. "It's a bit of a mess." I wasn't expecting company. There are dishes in the sink and a hamper of laundry that I hauled to and from my parents' earlier.

He surveys the cozy space, his attention slowing on my bed. At least I washed the sheets and remade it. "It's just like you."

"Are you calling me an old, messy shack in the woods, Tyler?"

He's about four inches taller than I am, but it seems like more as he closes the distance, herding me until my back settles against the wall. An oddly somber expression comes over his face.

My heart pounds as he reaches up to stroke a strand of hair off my cheek, tucking it behind my ear, the touch sending a shiver skittering over my skin.

"It's honest, unpretentious, practical ..." His words drift into a kiss that feels much like the one yesterday in the barn—gentle, and yet needy.

I part my lips for him, allowing him inside, our tongues toying with each other as if testing boundaries for the night. In my head, there are none. We've already crossed lines I never expected us to even approach. The fact that he changed his mind about coming in tells me he knew where this would lead, and he made the conscious choice to let it happen.

That night in the parking lot was frantic and rushed and desperate, our bodies mostly covered as we satisfied each other. Tonight, I want to see *all* of him, I want to *feel* all of him, every inch of bare skin against me.

I press my palms against his stomach, sliding them upward, over his shapely chest, over his collarbones, up to scrape my fingertips across his bristly jaw, admiring every masculine inch of him.

His lips leave mine to skate across my jaw and along my neck.

Shivers dance along my spine as his hands slip beneath the hem of my shirt, splayed around my rib cage as they climb upward, until they reach my cotton sports bra. It was a choice for comfort rather than style that I vaguely regretted before, but now I see the benefit, as Tyler's thumbs easily edge beneath, pushing up the material. I moan softly as he fills his palms with my breasts.

I've never enjoyed anyone's hands on me like his.

I've never wanted anyone's hands on me more.

Tugging my top over my head, I toss it to the floor. My sweatpants follow immediately after until I'm standing in front of him in nothing but plain white panties that aren't in the least bit sexy.

But the way Tyler's eyes heat as they rake shamelessly over my body sets my blood on fire, and nothing else matters. With a hard look of determination, he yanks off his shirt, uncovering a torso that, while lean and athletic, is sculpted with seasoned muscle.

With eager anticipation, I loop my finger through his buckle and unfasten his belt. In seconds, I have his jeans undone and pulled open, exposing the ridge that I ache to feel inside me again.

Strong, calloused hands grasp my thighs as he hoists me into the air and pins me against the wall, his mouth landing on mine, this time with that uncontrollable hunger that sent us spiraling last time. Maybe fast and furious is our only speed.

My fingers curl around his biceps, memorizing their curves and firmness, acutely aware of the hard length pressing against me where our bodies meet and the way my body responds.

His eager mouth leaves mine to drift over my jawline, along my neck, and down to seize a nipple.

My head falls back against the wall, reveling in the delicious sensation and expertise in which he uses his tongue to tease until my breathing is labored and my fists are grasping at his hair and the building ache where his hips are nestled against me is almost unbearable.

A wave of adrenaline rushes through as he lifts me off the wall and carries me toward my bed. But he stalls at the small wooden dining table, setting me on it. "Shit. Sorry." He quickly sheds his shoes.

I couldn't care less if my entire place was covered in Tyler's muddy footprints.

My mouth goes dry as I trace the cut of his body, his jeans sitting low, exposing the sharp V at his hips.

His palms slide over my bare thighs. "Marie, when you look at me like that ..." His words trail, his eyes wild as they search every inch of me.

I reach up to drag the soft pad of my thumb over his bottom lip. His mouth closes over it, his dark, heated stare locked on mine. The moment feels like the calm before an unyielding storm.

I welcome the storm, arching my back instinctively.

With a soft curse, his frantic lips land on mine again, his hands hooked around my thighs. I'm expecting him to carry me the rest of the way to my bed, but he tips me backward instead, until I'm splayed across my table and he's guiding my panties off my hips and down my legs. His lips are a whisper against my ankle as he tosses the last of my clothing away.

"Tyler ..." I whisper, my voice thick with need. I peer up at him and am treated to a crooked smirk, as if he knows how utterly consumed I am by him.

"I was waiting for you to say my name like that." His gaze is molten as it touches me everywhere a second before his finger-tips do, trailing the length of my body from my jaw down, over the swell of my breasts, along my rib cage, over my hip bones, between my legs. My body responds, undulating as he teases me with gentle but expert strokes.

And then he drops to his knees, fitting his shoulders between my thighs. His mouth takes over for his hands, and the sounds that escape me are raw and deep and uninhibited, my fingers grasping handfuls of his hair. The scratch of his soft stubble against sensitive flesh has me lifting my body into him, and words that I shouldn't dare say yet cling to my tongue, ready to slip free.

A deep, heady pulse erupts in my spine, sending my body into a wave of euphoria.

Somewhere in the hazy moments right after, I hear him shucking his jeans, and then he's standing before me, giving me my first uninhibited view of his body. I admire his size as he lines his powerful thighs up with mine, his palms hot and forceful as they seize my hips.

Only when he pushes into me, when my body stretches around him, welcoming him, and his hips are already moving, do I *finally* remember.

"Wait." My God. Why can't I seem to think straight when I'm with him? "Did you bring anything with you?" The only condoms in my drawer are surely expired.

"It's a bit late for that, isn't it?"

If diseases were the concern, yes. I hesitate, not wanting to ruin the moment. "I'm not on any birth control."

His hips stall, his focus drifting from my face down to our current predicament.

I search for a hint of annoyance in Tyler's expression, but I see only curiosity. "There was no risk the last time." Unlike Vicki, I've always been aware of my cycle and able to tell the signs. "I haven't been on it in years." All the Lehr women have struggled with hampering side effects. I relied on an IUD while I was with Jonathan, but never replaced it with a new one when the old one was removed. There was no need.

"And now?"

"It's pretty risky," I admit sheepishly.

His mood is unreadable as he studies my face for a long moment, his chest heaving with shallow breaths.

And then he leans down to kiss me again, his lips supple and affectionate as they pry mine open. I prepare for him to slip out, but instead he whispers, "Do you want me to stop?"

"Well, *no*." I laugh, my hands smoothing over his jaw, the moment oddly intimate, even on my dining table. "I *never* want you to stop this." If I can feel like this every day for the rest of my life, I'd die happy.

His lips catch the corner of mine in a teasing caress.

And then his hips start moving again, a slow grind.

"Tyler." My warning is weak as my hips curl into him.

"I can pull out right before."

I chuckle. "And if that foolproof method doesn't work?"

He sets his forehead against mine. "Then it doesn't work."

I push his face back to get a good look, to make sure I understand him, and make sure he understood me.

He seems to be searching for the same answer in mine. "Tell me that's not what you want, Marie. Tell me you don't want that with me." Vulnerability shines in his gaze.

I open my mouth to say … what? Every day that I spend with this man, every detail I learn about him, I fall harder. In my gut, I already know I want this—*all* of it. Tyler, sitting beside me at the dinner table; Tyler, stripping me down the moment we step inside our home; Tyler, next to me when I wake, whether it's in my bed or in the frigid Alaskan tundra.

Tyler, loving me.

And, fate willing, a chance at what I've started believing I would never experience.

Tyler knows all my secrets, he knows what I want, and he's not shying away from *any* of it.

At this moment, I know there is *nothing* I want more than him. All of him.

"Then it doesn't work," I echo, granting permission of sorts.

In seconds, he's collected me in his arms and lifted me off the table to carry me to my bed. My body feels like it's about to erupt beneath his weight and his hot skin as he climbs on top of me, even as my mind grapples with what's happening, with what I've agreed to.

Tyler completely takes over, pinning my arms above my head, his hips thrusting against mine without any hesitation. Soon, I've dismissed any concerns that dare poke at my conscience, and I'm rocking my hips to meet his, our bodies moving together in an erotic dance full of unspoken promises, our lips never breaking, all the way to the end.

Our cries meld in the quiet night.

I welcome each pulse of Tyler inside me.

CHAPTER TWENTY-THREE

I note the red Honda Civic in the parking lot as I push through the clinic's front door.

"See? Click there." Mom and Cory are behind the desk, Mom squinting at the computer screen through her thick-rimmed bifocals while Cory hovers over her shoulder, explaining the booking system we installed years ago.

A plate of home-baked muffins sits on the desk counter, as it always did on Monday mornings when Mom sat behind that desk. The scene brings a wave of nostalgia. "Morning," I call out in a singsong voice that's very unlike me. But the high I've been floating on since my eyelids cracked this morning shows no sign of abating.

I can still feel Tyler's weight on my body, his hands all over me.

Him, so deep inside.

I struggle to clear thoughts of what we did last night as I focus on a day at work. "Hey, Cory, did you get a new car?"

"No. Joe dropped me off. But Mrs. Perkins is here." She nods to the lobby chair tucked in the corner where a woman sits, a Jack Russell on her lap.

I double-check the clock on the wall in case I somehow lost track of time while getting dressed. But no, we don't open for another half hour.

"I know I'm a bit early," the woman calls out in a reedy voice.

"That's okay." I shift my focus to her young terrier, its tail wagging. "This must be Jacqueline?" I let her sniff my hand in greeting.

"Yes! Jackie, for short." Mrs. Perkins's clouded blue gaze lights up with a mix of surprise and delight. "But I needed to talk to you." Slowly, she lifts herself out of her chair and sets the dog on it with a soft command of stay, and then leads me a few feet away. "Your receptionist already said there were no men working here." She speaks in a hush, as if afraid her dog might overhear. "It's just that Jackie gets *very* stressed around male doctors and techs. Any men, really. I had such problems at the last clinic, with her shaking and vomiting and biting. The place was just too big, and they weren't very accommodating." Her wrinkled face furrows, as if with unpleasant memories.

I remember Cory mentioning the dog's hatred of men. I resist the urge to ask who they went to. "As you can see, this is a very small clinic. It's usually just Cory and me. My mother's helping out this week because I have a lot of procedures. *Occasionally,* my father does help out, but only if I'm unreachable and there's an emergency. He's a retired veterinarian and lives next door, so he can get here pretty fast. But honestly? Other than the two weeks in March when I'm volunteering for the Iditarod, or a few days here and there when I'm out west helping in the villages, I'm always around."

"Oh." She frowns as she considers this. "Well, if, God forbid, something *were* to happen and we needed his help while you were away, do you think he would mind wearing this?" She checks over her shoulder once at the dog and then reaches into her purse to pull out a lengthy blond wig. "Bob wears it when he comes to fix things around the house and check on me. Bob's a neighbor. He was good friends with my husband. Anyway, it's been working. She even let him hold her!" She shrugs as if to say, *who knew?*

On the spectrum of pet owners, from people who shouldn't be trusted with keeping so much as a snail alive to those who name their pets in their will, Mrs. Perkins is clearly on the end that I will go out of my way to accommodate. "Mom? What do you think?" I already know the answer. Dad always got a kick out of strange requests owners made on behalf of their pets. To this day, I think his favorite story to tell is about the man who insisted my father speak directly to his dog and the man would translate the dog's responses. Though, in that case, it had nothing to do with meeting the animal's needs.

"Oh, my Sidney would be *more* than happy to oblige, I'm sure." My mom nods her approval, her grin broad and genuine.

"Yeah, the only problem you might have is getting the wig back from him after."

"That's a relief to hear." Mrs. Perkins's shoulders sink as she tucks the wig back into her purse.

"So, Jackie's pregnant? That's why you're here?" I steal a glance at the Jack Russell, sitting quietly in the chair, her midsection bulging and likely the only reason she isn't investigating every corner. She looks young—less than a year old—and ready to deliver any day.

"They said there's three in there. Her first veterinarian wanted to wait a cycle before he fixed her. I agreed, because what do I know? I've never owned a dog before. I got her after Ned passed. Anyway, it's just me at home, my son's living in California, and I've taken to chucking her into my neighbor's yard to burn off some of that energy with Dax, their husky." She shakes her head, her face a mask of bewilderment. "No one told me he wasn't neutered! Imagine my shock when I saw what he was doin' to my sweet Jackie that day!"

I stifle my laughter.

She peers at her dog, her face a mix of adoration and concern. "I'm eighty-three years old. What on earth am I going to do with a litter of puppies?"

The struggle in her voice tugs at my heart. "We can help you find homes for them, if you'd like."

"Vets do that?"

"*I* do that. Sometimes." When it's warranted, and in just a few minutes, I've learned more than enough about Mrs. Perkins to know that she can barely manage little Jackie, let alone the energy of three Husky Jacks. I gesture toward the first door. "Why don't you two head into exam room one. I'll be there in a minute." Cory squeezed this appointment in before a morning of surgeries, and we have several patients coming in to be prepped for surgery soon, so the sooner I can shuttle Mrs. Perkins and Jackie out, the better for all.

With a smile, she leads the pregnant dog into the room.

"Tell me I didn't just earn myself three new dogs?" my mom whispers, and I can't get a read on her tone, whether it's humor or panic. Maybe it's both.

"Relax. Puppies are way easier to place than old sled dogs. We'll figure it out," I promise around a sip of coffee from my travel mug, reaching down to test a leaf on the fake plant Calla dropped off while I was delivering Nala's puppies. "What all's on the schedule for today again?"

"*Well*, you have an appointment at six tonight at *Tyler's*."

"Yeah, I remember—"

"I'll bet you do." Cory leans against the desk, chin propped in her hand. "*So?*"

Beside her, my mother adjusts her glasses and feigns deep concentration on the computer screen. Clearly, they've been gossiping. I don't doubt that my mother hovered at the kitchen window, noting when Tyler's truck pulled away just before eleven, much to my dismay.

"*So*, what?" I try to play clueless, but it lasts all of three seconds before the foolish grin stretches across my face.

"I *knew* it!" Cory explodes. "I *knew* it was only a matter of time!"

My mom's face lights up. "Will he be coming to Sunday dinner again?"

Shaking my head, I leave the two of them to their squeals as I head for the exam room, my hope riding on a cloud.

———

I hum to the song on the radio as I coast up Tyler's driveway, hoping the simple act will allay the nervous flutters in my stomach. Last night was unexpected, and I'm still reeling from it. But I don't regret it or the possibilities that might transpire.

What Tyler does to my heart …

This is happening, and in the most unconventional way.

So many people find the start of a relationship exciting, but I've always found it more unsettling than anything. If you get past the first few dates and decide you want more, you're in an all-consuming testing stage—uncovering delightful secrets that make you fall harder while discovering flaws that will endear or annoy you, or both, catching glimpses of troublesome things that you downplay or pretend don't exist because you're focused on the here and now. You might faintly wonder about five, ten, twenty years down the road, but you can't see it. You make your decisions for your future based on what you want to see.

When I met Jonathan in my late twenties, I was still figuring out who *I* was, revealing the best parts of myself and hoping that when my flaws and insecurities exposed themselves in the months and years to come, he'd be in too deep to be scared away. I fell for Jonathan's sense of humor, his work ethic, and the stability he gave my life. I convinced myself that he didn't understand my love of animals because he didn't grow up in a house like mine. I outright ignored the fact that our nights in bed were often lacking the passion I'd found with others.

And then I met Jonah, and everything I thought I knew—about myself, about men, about what I wanted in life—blew up.

Now, here I am, a year and a half to forty, and I don't have the time or patience for *any* of it anymore. But nothing about this thing with Tyler has been conventional, from the first day we met to now, seven months later, as I pull up behind his green truck, wondering how long I should wait before I buy a pregnancy test.

It's insane and reckless.

And I desperately want this to be real.

I hop out of the driver's seat, smoothing my hands over my favorite jeans and adjusting my flowing green top. I spent far too much time after my shower deciding what to wear for a post-birth examination.

The barn doors are open, so I collect my black bag and head toward the raucous barking. It's as if all the dogs have congregated in one post.

When I stroll through to the other side of the barn and the farthest set of open doors, I see that they have. The entire team, minus Nala, are untethered and trotting in circles within the expansive enclosure, barking and playfully nipping at each other. Even Sleet is there and tolerating Pope.

And in the middle of them is Tyler, his back to me, his cargo pants already covered in streaks of mud, his stance wide as he tosses out names and warnings, like a schoolyard supervisor watching children.

Now that I know the feel of his body far more intimately, the pull to him is much more potent.

The dogs notice me before Tyler does, and several charge forward. The rush would be daunting, had I not grown up around this, had I not already met each of them personally at the race. I laugh as they all greet me at once, nipping at my fingers, brushing past, several jumping, leaving muddy paw prints on my legs and waist, reminding me why I don't dress nicely when I visit kennels.

"Airi," Tyler calls out, his voice calm but his tone warning as the black swing dog tests the leather handle on my bag with his teeth.

"They're excited today."

"They know I'm taking them to the creek."

There's a strained note in Tyler's voice that prickles my senses. I've heard that in his voice before—when he was preparing to leave the Cripple checkpoint. And when he turns, when I see the dark circles that line his eyes, as if he didn't sleep last night after he went home, I know something is wrong.

"You got them?" he asks Reed as he walks my way.

Reed pauses in his attempt to harness Nymeria with a gray husky nipping at his hands, stealing a glance my way before he nods.

"What's going on?" I ask.

Tyler's hand slips over the small of my back to guide me toward the barn, but even that simple touch feels off compared to how his hands felt on me last night.

I hold my breath to calm the dread already building along my spine as he pulls the barn door shut to keep the dogs from following.

And when his Adam's apple bobs with a hard swallow …

I know, before the words have even left his mouth.

"I thought I was ready. But I'm not." Hazel eyes plead with me to understand.

I absorb those words like a hard punch to my chest.

"I'm so sorry, Marie."

"I just … What does that even mean?" I can't help the sharpness in my voice. We both know what we did last night. And when he left me, he seemed to do so reluctantly, turning back three times for another kiss. So, what happened between then and now?

I'm afraid I already know the answer.

When I'm with you, I forget about everything else.

But then Tyler went home, and he remembered.

"I didn't think about them once all night, Marie. Not once while I was with you. It's as if I was ready to replace him, just like that." His voice grows hoarse, his lengthy eyelashes blinking against the sheen materializing.

Him. He must be talking about his son.

My heart pangs with sorrow as I reach for him. "Tyler, that's not what that was—"

"I know. But it's how I feel right now." He swallows again. "I'm not ready to move on. God, Marie, you are incredible. I love *everything* about you ... and when I'm with you, I fool myself into believing that I'm ready, but I'm not." He shakes his head with resolution. "I don't know how to love two women at the same time."

I'm not sure what that means—is Tyler admitting that he loves me? Or that he won't be able to—but it confirms what I *always* knew would be a problem.

A snarl sounds outside. Too many dogs left waiting for too long.

"They're getting impatient." Tyler reaches for the handle but stalls. "I'll stand by whatever you decide to do. You know, if it comes to that."

He means if I'm pregnant. It feels like another punch, this time to my stomach. "How considerate."

"Marie—"

"*No.* Just ... no." I spin and rush away, needing distance to process this.

Rolling in behind the nauseating wave of hurt and disappointment is resentment. At Tyler, for leading me so far down this path only to leave me stranded, but mostly at myself, for being so damn stupid. I knew Tyler was still very much in love with someone else. A woman he still reaches for in the night, who he races a thousand miles across the Alaskan tundra for while wearing her name on his sleeve.

I knew all this, and still I let myself fall for him.

I'm halfway through the barn before I remember why I came here. As much as I want to head straight for my truck and drive off, I veer toward the birthing room, gritting my teeth to keep my tears at bay.

When I emerge, Tyler and the dogs are long gone, and the kennel is quiet.

CHAPTER TWENTY-FOUR

"Okay, *so* … what do you think about *this?*" Calla pauses for dramatic effect before spinning her laptop around on the clinic's counter, revealing a home page of earthy greens and golden yellows against a white birch-patterned background, with bold buttons and scrolling pictures and tabs that shift to pages full of information—the clinic's history, my credentials, our services. Content that was sparse on the old site is now paragraphs long.

I blink in disbelief. "How did you do all this?" And so fast.

"I've been doing this sort of thing for years." She shrugs. "I've gotten good at it."

"Yes, but …" I scroll through pictures of myself at eight years old, wearing my father's stethoscope and attempting to check a puppy's heartbeat as it gnawed on my fingers. I flip through the tabs, stalling on the one that details the clinic's history in the valley, and smile at the pictures of my father in his white coat, standing outside the clinic's front doors the day it opened for the first time. My mother is next to him, her belly swollen with me. "Where did you get these?"

"Cory. She went through some of your parents' old albums."

The only "albums" my mom has are a dozen shoeboxes tucked

away in the back of their closet, with no rhyme or reason for how pictures are sorted.

"That girl is too good for me." As is Calla. I was doing inventory when she messaged to see if she could swing by. I don't know what I expected to see, but it wasn't this.

"That summer when I came to visit my dad, I tried to help him with Alaska Wild by building a website for him. You know, because that would've fixed *all* his problems." She chuckles softly to herself. "The whole thing turned out to be pointless, but I did learn about my grandparents and their lives while running it, and my dad's life. There was a lot of family history there. Like this place." Her curious gaze drifts around the lobby. "I thought it might be helpful for people to see that. It's what a lot of the other clinics around here don't have."

I sink into my desk chair. The effort, the personal detail, even the nature-inspired design.

It's as if Calla knows me.

Or is *trying* to get to know me.

"This is amazing. Honestly. Thank you."

Her smile is genuine. "I need to make a few more tweaks to header sizes and then I can transfer it over. Which leads to my next thing ..." She holds up a finger and then darts out the front door to her Jeep. Thirty seconds later, she's rushing in with a large roll tucked under her arm.

To anyone who doesn't know Calla, there's still no visible evidence to hint at the human growing inside her. But I can see how her athletic body is already changing—a thickening midsection, her swelling breasts. "I saw this at the store and thought of you. It's actually what gave me the idea for the site design." She stretches the wallpaper out to show me the black-and-white illustrated birch trees. "This would make a great accent wall, don't you think?"

I groan.

"It's just wallpaper!" She bites her bottom lip. "And maybe some new chairs?"

I laugh, even as I pinch the bridge of my nose. I'm dealing with someone who could live off the interest she's earning on her inheritance from Wren. The real world has slipped through her grasp. "I lost my biggest kennel, and yeah, we've been getting some new business, but it won't make up for it." Especially once race season kicks off. I hesitate. "And I think I might have lost another important kennel."

Calla frowns. "Why?"

"Because I broke my rule about dating clients." Not that Tyler and I were even dating. We were a complicated string of encounters that somehow culminated in a reckless night that had me heading to the pharmacy for emergency contraception.

A pill that I stared at for hours that night but didn't take.

And in the following days and weeks, I convinced myself that this all happened for a reason.

It's all moot now. My period arrived yesterday morning, like clockwork. And along with the surge of relief came far more disappointment than I'd expected.

I could have done it on my own. I *would* have. It would have been the one good thing that came out of that mistake.

She nods with understanding. "That Tyler guy."

I swallow against the prickle in my throat. "He said he doesn't know how to love two women. Whatever that means."

Cory emailed the bill for Nala's checkup and Tyler promptly paid it, but I haven't heard from him since. The puppies will need deworming soon. If he's found a new veterinarian, he hasn't informed me yet, but I wouldn't be surprised if he simply stops calling us.

If I could afford to drop Tyler as a client and simplify both our lives, I would. But I've crunched the numbers, and losing that income isn't an option if I can help it. So I go about my days while pretending nothing ever happened between us.

Calla's brow furrows as she searches for the right answer to a problem she doesn't fully understand. She gets all her Marie-related gossip secondhand through Jonah, but I haven't given him the more explicit details, or how far down this gorge I've tumbled. Despite everything, I don't want him hating Tyler.

I don't hate Tyler. I won't make excuses for how he hurt me, but my heart does ache for him, for how he still struggles. Maybe that's foolish. But *I* let things move too fast and go too far with him, blinded in my attempt to catch what I was beginning to think was a fable.

For just one day, *everything* that I wanted seemed to be aligning.

For just one day, I truly believed I could have it all.

And yet, there's also that voice in my head, a jaded voice that whispers what I don't want to hear—that a woman will come along, and Tyler will make room for her in his heart, that it's me —*I'm* just not meant for Tyler. Just as I wasn't meant for Jonah.

All these years, all these mistakes I keep making, and I haven't learned a damn thing.

"It's okay. I'm a big girl. I'll survive." I offer Calla a smile that is wide and fake. Surely, she doesn't buy it. We've done the whole forced pleasantries song and dance before, so we know when the other is being genuine. At least this time, our phoniness isn't directed at each other.

"Well …" She taps her painted fingernails on my counter. "It will cost almost *nothing* to freshen up this place."

"Calla," I groan.

She continues, rushing her words. "Agnes loves to paint, and I'll get everything from the thrift shop. In fact, I've already found the perfect frames for all your degrees. I'm going to spray-paint them gold to match the yellow on the website. Come on, let me do this. *Please.* Your clients will appreciate the change, and I think you *need* a change. And I need to keep myself busy. You know how summers are. Jonah's out flying every day. And when he's not, he's driving me insane about the baby. This will be fun for me. *I* need it. You'd be doing *me* a favor."

Her pleas are wearing me down if for no other reason than to serve as a suitable distraction. "It would have to be *super* cheap. I'm talking a few hundred bucks max."

"It will be. I swear. This?" She gestures at the wallpaper. "This was free."

I snort. "It was *not* free—"

"It was! They gave it to me."

"They did not just *give*—"

"Fine. I stole it."

She says it so deadpan, I almost believe her. My cackle of laughter echoes through the clinic.

———

I scrub the stench of latex off my hands and dry them with a paper towel before tossing it in the trash next to the surgical gloves. I've always hated that smell. "Holler at me when she wakes." Cory answers with a thumbs-up, her attention on the monitor for freshly spayed Mrs. Whiskers.

I smooth my palm over the never-ending ache in my neck as I push through the door and head into the lobby, where my mother sits behind the desk, Molly on her knee.

"… we'll see you next week. Okay, then. Okay …" Mom is attempting to end the call while angling her head and glasses away from Molly's grasping hands. She sets the receiver on the base just as Molly shrieks with frustration. "You can't have those! You can't!" Mom laughs and collects her granddaughter's hands in hers and pretends to nibble on her stubby fingers.

I smile as I watch the two of them. "You okay out here?" Vicki's at school today, and my parents have split babysitting duty. Mom's on watch now so my father can have his afternoon nap.

She sets her glasses on the desk. Without them on, the wrinkles around her eyes are far more noticeable. "I don't know how I did this job while chasing you and Liz around here all those years ago. I suppose I *am* almost forty years older."

Forty years older, with arthritis working its way through her joints and a slight hunch in her back. Sometimes I worry that we're asking too much of her, even putting in just a few hours a day behind the desk. "Have you heard from Mrs. Perkins?"

"Yes! Just now. The puppies were born, and she wants to bring them in for a checkup."

"How's she handling it?"

"Okay, I think. All three lived. She's got some help from her neighbor's kids, and *Bob* in his wig"—she snickers—"but she's already asking how soon we can find homes for them, so take that for what it's worth. Now, who else, let me see …" She slides her glasses back on.

Molly dives for them again.

"Come here *you*." I collect my niece off Mom's lap and tuck her against my side, flashing her an exaggerated smile that earns one in return. She's warm and soft and smells of a freshly changed diaper and the rice crackers she's been gnawing on. Drool trickles over her bottom lip to collect on her bib. "Here, what's this?" I press the end of my stethoscope against her chest, drawing her attention to it for the moment.

Mom reads through her handwritten notes that she'll transfer to the computer—it's faster this way, she insists. They're mostly old clients with new puppies, which is always exciting for me. Nothing critical. No euthanasia.

She slides off her glasses to look at me, her expression tempered with concern. "Tyler called."

My chest tightens. "And?" I brace for the inevitable.

"The puppies need deworming, Airi might have sprained his hind leg, and"—she squints at her sheet—"Pope got into a fight with Sleet. He needs a few stitches."

"Oh." I guess I'm still his veterinarian after all. A surge of emotions erupts—dread, longing, annoyance.

Mom's brow furrows. She was the first to figure out something wasn't right. I gave her the standard "we're just friends" line that I've given everyone, though we're not even that anymore, and went about my day. Thankfully, Mom has never been one to push too hard for information. But I've also been conveniently busy with "emergencies" over the last two Sunday dinners, knowing that a single wrong word from Jim or Liz might break me.

"Honey, I don't know what happened between you two, but—"

"Did you book the appointment?" I pull the end of my stethoscope away from Molly's mouth just before she has a chance to soothe her sore gums on it.

"I said I'd have to check with you first, but that you might be able to come out tonight, if it wasn't an emergency, and he said that would be fine."

"Okay. Confirm with him. Thank you." I shift my focus to the baby in my arms, seeking comfort in her innocence for another moment, before shuttling her to my mother and getting back to work.

————

Tyler's truck is absent when I pull up to his place.

It's both a relief and a frustration. I don't have to swallow my feelings and put up a front for the sake of professionalism, but at the same time, part of me aches for a confrontation.

Nymeria and Tank trot out of the barn to meet me. Reed appears moments later, dragging his boots in his typical lazy walk, poly rope dangling from his hand.

I smile despite my unfriendly mood. "You have Nymeria in a harness."

"Yeah. Ty said to try her out." He pushes his hair to the side with his free hand. "I've been doing some training with her. She's takin' to it."

"How are the pups?"

"Bigger." He nods toward a paddock. "I got Pope in there."

"When did it happen?"

"This morning. He's walkin' fine and I cleaned him up, but his leg looks pretty bad." He shakes his head. "I turned around for one minute and the dumb dog wandered over. He knows better than to mess with Sleet. Lucky it didn't end up worse."

"We'll get him fixed up." Hopefully without needing to bring him to the clinic.

"Yeah." But Reed worries his bottom lip. I'll bet he hates that this happened on his watch. Tyler did say he takes his role here seriously.

"You know, I've met a lot of handlers over the years, but I've never met one as good as you." I keep my focus ahead as Reed walks alongside me deeper into the barn, but from the corner of my eye, I catch his grin of satisfaction.

"Ty's still at work, but he said to do whatever you think Sleet needs."

I don't care.

I don't care.

I don't care.

"How is Tyler doing?" How much does Reed know about what happened?

He shrugs. "Lookin' forward to the racing season."

"Right." It is what he lives for, after all. "Come on, let's fix those dogs."

———

I'm halfway down the driveway when I spot the truck approaching from the other direction.

The tension in my body intensifies as the distance closes and Tyler's handsome face comes into focus. The lane is too narrow to pass one another like strangers on the road. We'll each have to maneuver along the edges to squeeze by. And because I'm an adult and here on business, I open my window.

Both trucks crawl to a stop, our doors aligning perfectly, our side-view mirrors inches from colliding. I note how Tyler's chest rises with a deep inhale, as if he's preparing himself for an uncomfortable conversation.

I let my eyes touch his for a brief second before I have to look away, the pain too raw. "I'm pretty sure Airi just has a mild sprain. I left some anti-inflammatories. If it doesn't get better within the week, you'll need to bring him in for an X-ray." In my attempt to sound professional, I end up sounding robotic. "I stitched up a jagged tear on Pope's leg. The rest just needs to be kept clean and monitored for any abscess. I've left antibiotics and painkillers, and Reed knows what he's doing." The benefit of having a living spreadsheet of information on every dog—I knew how to mix the prescriptions ahead of time.

"Thank you."

"That's what I'm here for, isn't it?" I hate that mixed in with my swirl of disappointment, hurt, and anger is foolish yearning. Why do I keep doing this to myself? I know better. "Cory will send you the bill tomorrow morning."

"Marie—"

"I'm not pregnant," I blurt out. "In case you were wondering." With that, I lift my foot off the brake and begin rolling forward.

"Wait, Marie. *Please.*"

The pleading quality in his tone slips past my defenses, softening a heart I've never learned how to harden. I hesitate for two seconds before I let my foot fall on the brake.

A high-pitched squeak sounds as Tyler backs up his truck until our windows are aligned again. "I'm sorry."

"Yeah, you already told me that." My anger is solidifying in my throat, forming a prickly lump.

"Can you at least look at me?"

After a beat, I meet his eyes, and the golden pools that shine with regret make my chest ache.

"I swear, this is the *last* thing I was looking for when I moved here. But then I kept running into you, and I couldn't get you out of my head. I still can't."

A twinge of satisfaction stirs inside me, knowing I'm not the only one struggling.

"I didn't think I'd ever feel anything for another woman. Definitely not so soon." His voice bleeds with sincerity. "That night at your place? I wanted to give you *everything* you want."

"I don't want a sperm donor, Tyler."

He flinches. "Come on, Marie, you were there. That's not what that was."

A single tear slips down my cheek as countless intimate touches and sighs and cries flitter inside my head. "I don't know what it was anymore. Besides a huge mistake." Born from desperation and desire, on both our parts.

He smooths a hand over his bristly face. "If I'd met you ten years ago ..."

Before he met his wife is what he's saying.

But would I have been enough, even then? This is what happens when someone hurts you—you begin to doubt *everything* they say.

His throat bobs with a hard swallow. "I have a lot of things to work through still, and it's not fair to you if I can't be all in. I see that now, and I understand if you don't want to wait around for that day."

How long will it take for Tyler to make enough room in his heart for someone else to stay?

It could be *years*.

It could be never.

It could be tomorrow, with someone who isn't me.

And I know myself too well.

I take a deep breath, knowing what I have to do. "Call Don Childs. He might not be as flexible as I am, but he's good—"

"No, Marie." Tyler's face twists with unhappiness. "I still want you as my vet."

"It's not going to work." I can't go down this road again. "And this friendship of yours, Tyler? I don't want it, either." This time when I take my foot off the brake, he doesn't call after me.

I keep the tears from spilling until I've tucked his gate key into his mailbox and climbed back into my truck, and then I don't hold them back any longer. The sooner I let myself break, the sooner I can start putting myself back together again.

I'm halfway home when my phone rings. I intend to ignore it, but my parents' home number appears, and I can never ignore that. "Hi." I hope whoever's calling can't hear my misery through the receiver.

"Oh, hi, Marie, I wasn't sure if you'd be finished with your appointment." My mom's voice sounds off.

My unease swells. "What's up?"

"I'm at the hospital with Vicki." There's a long pause. "She lost the baby."

CHAPTER TWENTY-FIVE

"You get more than she does because you're bigger." Liz emphasizes her point with another scoop of carrots on Tillie's plate.

I pass the bowl of mashed potatoes past my squabbling nieces and across to Vicki. "How much longer until you're done?"

"A few weeks, and then I'm starting at the salon full-time— Ollie, stop that! This is why she won't take food from anyone else now!" Vicki scolds.

Next to her, Oliver mimics a plane landing as he brings a spoonful of food in toward Molly, complete with hyperbolic sound effects. "But we can't help having so much fun, can we?" He makes a silly face at his daughter, and she squeals with glee.

"It's not fun when you're at work and I'm trying to feed her." Vicki glares his way before setting the potatoes in the open space in front of Liz.

"Good thing the season's over and I'll be here to feed her every night, then, huh?" He leans in to peck his wife's cheek while deftly snatching three slices of beef from the platter.

The week after the miscarriage was difficult around here. We all took turns helping with Molly while Vicki recovered, both physically and emotionally. Even Liz came by, bringing a collection of vegetable-laced cakes and, for once, none of her harsh opinions.

Vicki has mostly recovered, embracing the philosophy that it wasn't meant to be, but I don't miss her solemn expression whenever her blue eyes touch Liz's growing belly. Unplanned or not, she *wanted* that baby, had imagined an entire life with it already.

"That's right. Oliver will be feeding babies and cutting firewood *all winter long*, right?" my dad says around a swallow, and I catch the hint of annoyance in his tone.

"Oliver with an ax. That sounds like a great idea." I wink at my brother-in-law. The first snowfall blanketed the valley on the fall equinox, a thin layer that lasted just long enough to shrivel the late-blooming flowers. Since then, it's been falling steadily and staying, the temperatures hovering at freezing, answering many winter adventurists' prayers.

It's also enticed Oliver to keep the woodstove stoked far more than necessary. I had to peel off a layer when I came in today, and the dogs have been scratching at the door every hour on the hour to get out so they can cool off. "You know, you and Terry, one of the trail vets, would get along well."

"Speaking of the race ..." Dad waves his empty fork. "Bonnie Hatchett called me. Harry's in the market for a new vet."

"What's wrong, Frank didn't agree to cut his fees in half?" I say dryly.

"There definitely was some squabble about money. So then Harry went to Don Childs, but Don's heard what a royal pain in the ass he is, so he said no. Plus, he said he's too busy with Tyler's kennel now."

I feel everyone watching me, looking for my reaction to the mention of that name. I wash my food down with drink. Much like Vicki, I've used the "it just wasn't meant to be" line more than once. And much like Vicki, no one is fooled by my brush-off.

"So then, she started fishin' around to see if you'd consider taking the kennel on again. Didn't come right out and say it, but I've known that woman long enough to read her."

"If Harry wants me back for his dogs, he can come ask me himself." What my answer will be, I can't say. But I do miss the dogs.

"That's basically what I told her. Oh! And Bill was askin' if you're still gonna jump in for that interview with Tyler. He's been trying to nail him down, but he doesn't seem so willing anymore—"

"*Dad!*" Liz spears him with a bewildered look.

I'm equal parts stunned and appreciative that she would come to my aid like that.

He winces, as if just clueing in.

"So, how has working at Wade's hospital been, Marie?" Mom deftly steers the conversation to safe territory.

"Feels like being back in my residency. Except I'm getting paid. And Wade's been very accommodating." After leaving Tyler's that day, knowing the clinic would take another financial hit, I called my old mentor and asked if he would be interested in having me in his operating room once a week. He jumped at the chance. It means closing the clinic on Mondays and a long, exhausting day, but the income is good and the scenic commute to Anchorage—the snowcapped mountains towering over a kaleidoscope of autumn-tinged trees—reminds me how much I love this valley.

"Well, that's positive. Do you think you'll do more days there?"

"It's an option."

I catch the fleeting look she gives my father, and I sense this is more than just casual interest. No one has mentioned real estate agents or land value lately, but Oliver has strapped a plow to the front of their truck and is clearing driveways for the winter, banking as much money as he can so they can move out of our parents' attic by spring. That must sadden my parents, given how happy they've seemed these past few months, having children in the house. And I overheard Liz mentioning the contractor they hired to update a few things in their basement apartment. If Liz and Vicki could stand to be around each other for more than an hour, it'd be a perfect arrangement for them.

But I'm no fool, and Liz will soon have a house with three grandchildren to watch. That *has* to be more exciting than seeing the lights still on in the clinic, forty years later.

My father is wearing a walking cast to get around, and progress with physical therapy has proved far slower than the doctor hoped. Each day, my mother makes a comment about the ache in her arthritic bones, and how this place is getting to be too much work. With every year that passes, their aging bodies will only rebel more.

Maybe the clinic is tying them down from experiencing new, better things.

Vicki clears her throat and then casts a look at Oliver, her elbow not so subtly jabbing into his ribs.

His eyes widen with understanding. "*So*, Marie, Steve called me today about something. Remember? My boss? Anyway, he asked if you were still single. Now that the season is basically done and he's not working so much, he was wondering if—"

"Sure. Give him my number."

Oliver falters. "Really?"

"Yeah, why not?" I shrug. "It's just a date, right?"

But more importantly, it's closing a chapter and moving on.

———

The brown-and-white puppy bounds toward Mabel, stumbling several times in its unbalanced rush. Her giggles border on hysterical as she watches it. It's an unbridled sound that hints at the little girl I used to know who chased chickens and rambled nonsense.

"They're all so cute." Her face pinches. "I can't pick!"

I smile. "You have another hour to decide before your mom comes back." It's Sunday afternoon, and we've parked ourselves on the floor in the clinic lobby, each leaning against a wall as Mrs. Perkins's three Husky Jack puppies run in circles. She surrendered them to me on Friday—a week earlier than I'd prefer to take puppies from their mother, but they were taxing the old woman. Having spent the past two nights with them, I understand why.

"Which one do you think she should take, Roy?" I ask.

He holds his level against the shelving unit he spent the morning installing. "The least annoying one."

At the sound of his voice, the all-white female puppy, smaller than the other two and with shaggier fur, darts to him, tripping over his boot in her attempt to sniff his pant leg. Roy pauses in his tinkering to watch her tug at his bootlace, and the corner of his mouth twitches.

"Maybe that one?"

Roy realizes I'm watching him, and he sets back to his task, ignoring the pup. "How'd you get roped into this, anyway?"

"One of my older clients needed help." And when Jonah mentioned that Agnes was thinking about getting a dog, inspiration struck. "How'd *you* get roped into *that*?" I nod toward the unit he's been securing to the wall studs. It's different from his usual craftsmanship—an industrial feel, with rustic pine boards and black pipes—but it looks far nicer than the gray metal shelves that used to line that wall for dry food goods.

"Trust me, I'm still askin' myself that same question."

"How much am I going to owe you?"

His chuckle is deep, grating sound. "That's between you and Calla. I'm just the jackass pullin' the cart."

I can already guess the answer. She'll tell me the wood was going to be burned and the pipe was salvaged from the dump, or something along those lines. The girl is so resourceful, sometimes I don't know whether to believe her.

But she was right. I take in my neglected little lobby's face-lift. It's like her website design breathed air and came to life. The bright splashes of yellow mixed with earthy greens and crisp whites have completely transformed the space and the mood. It didn't take much. A weekend of painting and wallpapering, and another to change out the light figures and move in small details that add personality and charm, including several fake plants to add texture, and sleek new chairs in forest green.

But I think my favorite change is the full gallery wall of ornate, golden-yellow frames, showcasing the history of our little clinic in the woods, along with fresh pictures of Cory and me, and even my father.

None of the alterations are earth-shattering—to do that, we'd have to tear down this building and replace it with a new one—and yet the change was good. I feel a bit more pride as clients walk in and remark on the improvements.

"Here." I toss a ball to Mabel, who tosses it back. All three puppies give chase. Back and forth we go, playing a game of keep-away, the gray one faster than the other two. Even Roy struggles to hold his scowl, but I can't tell if it's because of the puppies or the jarring way that Mabel's face takes on Agnes's mannerisms when she laughs.

He shakes his head, as if catching himself watching her. "Muriel and Teddy are havin' their annual big wing night next week."

"I swear, is there any food group they don't throw a party or a competition for?" The annual fish fry, the annual chili cook-off, the annual rib "rub-off" that has me chuckling and Toby's face turning red every time his mother mentions it.

"Right?" Roy snorts. "You gonna be there for that?"

"Depends on what the guy I'm seeing wants to do." Steve loves microbreweries and hates my taste in beer and is determined to expand my horizons. Since he called, we've been on four dates, all of them landing in local breweries. He doesn't mind driving, and I don't mind his company. He's kind and handsome and doesn't pressure me to do anything beyond trying his favorite lagers. He's kissed me good-night a few times, and I haven't minded that, either.

It's been easy.

It's been ... nice.

I frown. "Why are you asking? Are *you* going?"

"Maybe."

"I thought you hated people." I smile to soften the jeer. I think I've figured out how to talk to Roy, but with a man like him, whose mood for the day dictates whether he laughs or bites, you never can be too sure.

"I do, but I love chicken wings more."

A knock sounds on the door a moment before it swings open.

"Is Agnes back al—" The air feels like it's been sucked out of my lungs as Tyler steps through, stomping his boots on the doormat to shed the snow.

He can't seem to decide where to look first—at the puppies rushing for him, at Mabel and me sitting on the floor, our legs splayed in a badly formed corral, or at the old man installing shelves.

In the end, the puppies win. He crouches to greet them, his deep chuckle soft and genuine as they paw at his knees.

Finally, he shifts his focus to me. "Hey."

"Hi." I hadn't forgotten how pretty his eyes are but seeing them now reminds me what it's like when they're on me. Like nothing else in the world matters.

It feels like just yesterday and yet forever ago that I saw him last. He looks much the same, except with a short and tidy ash-brown beard that coats his jaw, giving a more rugged look.

Because he wasn't attractive enough.

I shutter the memories of that night before they can escape

the box that I sealed them in and remind myself that Tyler is a mess of unresolved feelings for another woman.

That helps douse the simmering flames, but only a touch.

He scratches behind the brown-and-white one's ears. "What are you doing with these guys?"

"Looking for homes for them. Mabel's going to take one. She's not sure which one yet."

"*This* is Mabel?" Tyler looks to her. "The one working for that Ale House lady?"

Mabel lets out a low groan of despair, which makes Roy bark with laughter and me chuckle.

"Mabel, this is Tyler. He won the Iditarod this year. He was looking at hiring another person to help out at his kennel in the summer, and I mentioned you." But that was before our relationship fell apart.

"To do what?" she asks curiously.

"Play with dogs?" He smirks. "Basically, what you're doing now, except with big dogs, too. I'm there for the season now, but we could still use an extra hand, keeping them cared for and entertained. If you're interested, let Marie know."

"I don't know anything about mushing, though," she says warily.

"Yeah, that's okay. My brother-in-law, Reed, is pretty patient when it comes to anything involving dogs."

Her gaze darts to me, and I can't get a read on whether there's interest or reluctance there.

Tyler collects the gray puppy in his other hand. "What mix are these?"

"Husky Jacks."

"High energy." He holds it up to study its face.

"He's *way* faster than the other two," Mabel says.

"Yeah?" He smiles at her. "Bet this one could run in a team?"

She giggles. "I don't know. Maybe."

This all feels too normal, too casual. "What are you doing

here, Tyler?"

He sets the puppy down and it bounds away, its attention on the ball again. "Was in the area. Thought I'd come and see you."

"Why?" It's only one word—one vague question—and yet it seems to thicken the air in the room.

"You know, Mabel, why don't we take these things outside before they piss all over the floor?" Roy sets his drill on the shelf, collects his winter coat off the chair where he haphazardly threw it and his trapper hat, and scoops up two of the puppies, leaving Mabel to chase after the last and follow him out.

Tyler ventures farther in. "Looks good in here."

I contemplate staying where I am, sprawled on the floor, my back propped against the wall, but drag myself up. "It was time for a change."

He slows on the new picture of me, perched on the picnic table my father and I sometimes lunch at, Bentley, Yukon, and Aurora sitting prim at my feet. Vicki even did my hair. "How's your family?"

"They're fine." I hesitate. "Except Vicki lost the baby."

His frown is deep. "I'm sorry."

"Yeah. Well … between Molly and finishing up school, she's keeping busy."

Silence lingers as I watch him appraise the new details. Or maybe it's so he can choose his words. God, I miss him. Seeing him now soothes a relentless ache in my chest, and it shouldn't.

"I know you aren't treating my team anymore," he begins slowly, "but I was hoping you would come out and see them run, like you said you did for Hatchett. I'm trying something different this year." He bites his bottom lip. "A different matchup. Dryland training went well, but now that we have snow on the ground and I'm starting to build up their endurance, I was hoping you'd come out."

"I don't know good matchups. I'm not a musher."

"But you know dogs. And I trust you."

"You've got Don—"

"Not for this. I don't want Don for this. I want you."

This is all feeling too personal. Even having him in the room with me now, the pull that sunk me in the first place tugs at me once again. "Tyler, I—"

"Please?" He peers at me earnestly. "There's no one's opinion I value more on this, and I just ... I need your opinion. I don't want to make a mistake that any of these dogs pay for."

He knows what to say to wear me down.

My gaze ventures outside to where Mabel packs snow into balls and tosses them for the puppies to chase while Roy watches, chuckling. "When?"

"Next Saturday, if that works for you. It's actually Reed's twenty-first birthday. He was saying how much he'd love to see you."

I laugh, despite my tension. "Reed did *not* say that."

Tyler grins. "He was *definitely* thinking it, though."

I shake my head. How am I back here again? "Fine. What time?"

"Eight A.M.?"

Déjà vu hits me. "With or without your shirt on?" My tone is dry.

He laughs and holds up his hands in surrender. "I'll be fully clothed this time. I swear. It's too cold for chin-ups in the barn, anyway."

"I'll have to check my schedule and let you know. But I'm sure I can make something work."

His shoulders sink with relief. "Great. Thanks." He opens his mouth to say something else but then hesitates, as if thinking better of it. "Okay. I'll see you then."

I watch from the window as his green truck disappears, an uncomfortable swirl of emotions churning within. Why am I such a glutton for punishment?

"I'm taking this one," Mabel declares as she and Roy push

through the door, holding up the brown-and-white puppy. Her grin is a wide mirror of her mother's as she adds, "And Roy's taking the white one."

He harrumphs.

But doesn't argue.

CHAPTER TWENTY-SIX

The gate is already open when I turn into Tyler's freshly plowed driveway, the snow crunching beneath my tires.

"So, this Reed guy knows I don't know *anything* about sled dogs, right? Like, he's not going to be annoyed with me for asking stupid questions?" Mabel fidgets with the heat dial, adjusting it down. Between that and my radio, she's been playing with the truck's buttons and vents since I picked her up outside her house. I can't tell if it's nerves or just a subtle reminder that there's still a kid in there.

"I highly doubt it. But he's *really* shy, so if he doesn't say much, don't take it personally, okay? You can check things out, and if you want to work here on the weekends, I'll let Tyler know."

Smoke swirls from the chimney of the small, ranch-style house as I pull up behind the green truck. Reed sits by the barn next to a blazing fire in the outdoor firepit, stitching a gangline, his curly mop of hair covered in the same trapper hat he wore the first time I met him.

"That's him?" Mabel frowns. "I thought he'd be older."

"He's twenty-one. Today, actually. Hence, *this* guy." I pluck the gray puppy from Mabel's clutches and tuck him inside my coat before hopping out of the truck, my arms wrapped around me to keep him secure. Still, the puppy squirms as we walk toward the barn, and I struggle not to laugh as I try to keep him contained.

Only Pope is running loose this morning, but the dogs howl and bark from their little houses, wanting to know who's arrived.

"You're up early!" I holler as we approach.

Reed's big brown eyes dart between me and Mabel before frowning at the moving bulge in my chest.

"Got you something for your birthday." I hoist the puppy out, adjusting the blue bow I fastened to its collar.

He drops the line and collects the writhing pup from my grip. He's grinning, his dimples on display. "How old is he?"

"Only a few weeks younger than Nala's puppies."

Reeds lift him in the air, studying his face, much like Tyler did. As if he can see something that the rest of us can't.

"I figured you can train them all together. See how he does. Maybe he'll be a good runner." Pope rolls over to show us his belly and waits for a scratch. "Or maybe he'll be like *him*." But either way, I know this dog will live a good life.

Reed's mouth gapes as he searches for something to say. "Does Ty know?"

"He's not Tyler's dog. He's *yours*." And I may be an asshole for springing a puppy on them, but if there's a place and people built for this kind of surprise, it's here with these two.

"I have his brother," Mabel offers. An attempt to forge a connection, perhaps, and she's never been shy.

I tug off my glove and lean down to grant Pope's wishes. His belly is warm beneath my bare fingertips. "Is Tyler in the barn?"

"No. He's in the … house." Reed pauses in his study of his birthday gift. "He said for you to meet him in there. I mean, in the house."

"Really?" For all the times I've been here, I've only ever been in the barn. But … "Okay."

Reed smiles as he ducks his head, his attention back on the new addition to the kennel.

I leave Mabel there and walk to the side door that the two of them always use. It creaks as I step into a galley kitchen with terra-cotta tiles and rustic wooden walls covered in cast-iron pans of various sizes. Beyond is a long, narrow table against the bank of windows overlooking the property, and a corner closed off by gates, where I assume Nala and her puppies sleep at night. I smile at the collection of large dog beds that litter the floor, creating an obstacle course. The dogs may have their homes outside, but it's clear they have one in here, too.

I'm about to announce myself when Tyler's deep voice calls out from another room in the house.

"Hey, come here for a sec?"

My stomach tenses at the sound of his beckon. I take a calming breath while I shed my snow-covered boots and then weave through the kitchen and around to the living room. Hardwood scratched up by countless paws groans beneath my socked feet.

"Marie should be here soon. I haven't told her about—"

Tyler freezes midsentence when he looks up to find me standing at the threshold, my mouth gaping as he slides on a pair of briefs. The towel he dropped is heaped on the floor, the couch covered with spilled laundry that he's obviously washed but not folded.

Surprise is painted across his face. "I thought you were Reed."

"Clearly." My face burns, but my gaze can't stay off his body, still as perfectly sculpted as the last time I saw it in its entirety. "He sent me in here."

"Really?" Tyler frowns. "He knew I was in the shower." Understanding fills his face at the same time as it dawns on me.

That little smile. Reed pulled a Cory. I'm not sure whether to laugh or scream.

By Tyler's smirk and head shake, he's thinking along the same line.

I try to ignore the way my blood races and my body flushes, memories I've been struggling to suppress dragged to the surface. "What haven't you—actually, you know what? I'll meet you in the barn once you're dressed." I rush for my boots and push out the door, welcoming the frigid cold across my cheeks.

Reed and Mabel are standing by the trophy case, watching the puppy investigate its new home. I stab the air with my index finger, pointing at Reed. "*Not* funny." My cheeks burn anew.

I get an unabashed grin in return.

Five minutes later, as Mabel and I are stealing heat from the bonfire, Tyler makes his way down, dressed and donning his mushing jacket and a black beanie. But the fresh image of everything beneath still blazes in my mind. "Where is he?"

I nod toward the barn.

Tyler passes me. Through the open door, I hear his chuckle and, "I don't care if it's your birthday. You're gonna pay for that one later, man. Swear to God."

"Bring it on," Reed chirps back, hinting at a playfulness between the two of them that he hides from the rest of us.

Despite everything, I smile.

"What happened?" Mabel whispers, but I only shake my head, still listening.

Waiting.

"Why is that dog here? *And why does it have a bow?*"

———

I check Tyler's expression to see if he's joking. "You want to race her."

"Yeah."

"In the *Iditarod.*"

"Yes." He crouches in front of Nymeria, his hand weaving

through her thick coat as he strokes her neck. She sits on her haunches, accepting the affection with an occasional contented whine. "Reed's been working with her all summer, but she already knew all the commands. And she kept up with the dryland training. She loved it."

I can't help but look at this dog and still see the frail and wounded one dangling from Harry's arms. "You think she can handle a hundred miles a day?"

"Not yet, but none of them can, yet. Not even Tank. They're all out of shape. But she's keeping up. And she and Tank seem to be a good match—"

"Match. *Wait*, you want to run her as a *lead dog*?" A position that is typically earned after years of running.

Tyler chuckles at the gobsmacked look on my face. "I *know*. But I'm telling you she's done this before. Zed said she'd been a team dog for a few years before he started breeding her. She knows what she's doing. And I have a good feeling about her, Marie."

"What about Nala?"

"Nala doesn't want to run. We pull out the harness, and the enthusiasm isn't there. She'd rather stay close to her puppies." He shrugs. "I can't force her."

"So then you *need* Nymeria for the Iditarod." Unless he leases a dog from someone like Harry.

He leans back against the barn wall, resting his arms on his bent knees. "I can run with one lead dog if I have to. Tank is strong-willed enough for two. But if she wants to do this, then why wouldn't we give her a chance? After what she's been through, she deserves another shot at being happy." He reaches for her, and she tilts against his leg, lifting her chin to give him her jowls for attention.

"There're other ways for her to be happy. Smaller races. It doesn't have to be the Iditarod."

"But what if she wants it?"

"Maybe it's not worth the struggle."

"Maybe it is." Tyler frowns, but whatever is on his mind, he keeps to himself. "I *am* going to start her off in smaller races. There's one out of Cantwell next month, and one in Paxson in January."

"It sounds like you've already decided, so what do you want from me?"

"You know her full history. Things I can't tell Don or anyone else. Come out with me and watch. Tell me if you think I'm crazy. That's all I ask."

I peer through the far door to where Mabel observes Reed harnessing the team.

With a heavy sigh, I climb to my feet.

———

"Gee." Tyler's voice is barely above conversational level and yet the dogs veer right on the groomed path ahead, working in tandem. There's nothing to hear but the soft crunch beneath the sled's runners and forty paws as the ten dogs run the trail through trees and brush, and we glide across the snow.

I look up from my seat in the sled's basket to find Tyler standing over me, grinning smugly.

Despite the turmoil churning inside me, this moment is oddly peaceful.

"Whoa," he calls out, dropping the snow hook to stop the dogs and anchor us. The team is happy for the pause so they can test their lines and pee on the nearby brush.

I climb out to stretch my legs. My cheeks and nose are numb from the cold air, and I wish I'd worn a different scarf. We haven't gone far—maybe a mile or two—but we're deep within the trees of Tyler's property. Ahead is the river, and beyond that the mountain range. Somewhere to the right of us are Harry's seventy-five dogs.

But out here, it feels like we're alone.

"So? What do you think?" Tyler asks, watching me as I edge along the path toward the front.

Dropping to my knees beside Nymeria, I tuck my gloves inside my coat to keep from Tank's nipping teeth. I check her joints and muscles with my fingers, searching for any tenderness or other warning signs. I can't find anything.

"Hey, girl. You want to do this?" I murmur.

She answers with a hot lick across my cheek.

I settle on my haunches. "Officially, I think you're nuts, Tyler. You do realize how risky this is, right? You want to race a stolen dog in the Iditarod. As the returning champion. There will be pictures of her all over the paper and the news." Which Zed will surely see, as will his nephew Jody and countless others.

He cocks his head. "Come on, Marie. She's a beautiful dog, but she's not *that* distinctive."

I mock gasp and playfully cover her ears. "Don't listen to him!" But he's right. Heterochromia is common in huskies. And Zed is likely arrogant enough to believe that if she wouldn't run for him, she'd *never* run for anyone else.

Tyler chuckles as he helps two of the dogs untangle themselves from their line. "Seriously, though, she wasn't chipped before, so there's no proof that way. And you have to admit—she's a different dog from the one you met last January."

I stroke her fur. "She is."

She's a different dog.

He's a different man.

What am I, besides the same old Marie?

I stand and move back toward the sled. "It's hard to see her gait from the basket when she's up front." Harry always took me out in a tour sled that could accommodate two people standing. "But she obviously has the enthusiasm and the drive, and the temperament. If you can get her physically ready, then ... I don't see why she can't do it, if she wants to." I steal another glance to see Nymeria and Tank brush up against each other. She seems happy.

Tyler lets out a deep exhale, as if he's been waiting for my verdict. "Well, wait, if you can't see her like that, then you should stand." He hooks his hand on my elbow and gently tugs me toward him. "Come on, we can both fit."

"I don't know—"

"Trust me. I used to do this with Mila all the time."

It has nothing to do with trusting Tyler and everything to do with being this close to him again. Unable to find an excuse I'm comfortable using, I step onto the footboards and take hold of the handlebar with gloved hands. Tyler settles in behind me, his toes at my heels, his body snug behind mine.

He cages me in with his arms as he seizes the handlebar. "You ready?"

He's asking me, but the dogs hear the command and begin to bark and tug against their lines, earning his chuckle. He releases the hook, and we take off in a jolt. Tyler's muscles tense to hold us in place. After a moment, he leans in and whispers into my ear, "See? I told you it would work."

A shiver runs down my spine.

I do my best to focus on the gaits of the dogs ahead and ignore the strong, hard torso pressed against my back, the way his beard scratches my skin every so often as our bodies bump and his jaw brushes across my cheek.

We follow the trail around a loop in silence and then meet up with our tracks from earlier, hinting that we're already heading back toward the house.

"By the way, how is everything going at the clinic?"

I know what he's *really* asking: How is everything at the clinic now that I've lost the income from both Harry and Tyler's business?

I *should* answer with a dismissive lie, but the moment I open my mouth, the truth tumbles out. I tell him everything—working in Anchorage for Wade, my parents selling the property, my growing sense that I'm holding them back, this feeling that my entire life is in limbo. Talking to Tyler has always been so easy.

"What happened to opening up a hair salon in your cabin?"

"That was a half-baked option Jim threw out. It wouldn't work, anyway. Vicki doesn't want to live there. She wants to be on her own." But the issues Liz raised are fair. The clinic and cabin aren't mine. There are three of us, and short of me buying them out one day, tough decisions will have to be made.

Will I still feel the same desire to live on that property and walk through that clinic door and look at the house across the field once my parents are gone? Once Sunday dinners and the blare of the clown horn are nothing but a memory?

I remember Jonah in those weeks and months after Wren's death. He said everything had changed. Everything felt hollow.

Maybe I'm dwelling too much on something that won't happen for another ten or fifteen years.

But what if it happens tomorrow?

"I'm beginning to think they *should* sell now. Go to Mexico or Europe or wherever else they want. Enjoy life while they still can. But I don't think my father will make that call. *I* have to make the decision for him." I worry my bottom lip. "It's hard, pulling the plug like that. Making such a big change that you *don't* want." Letting go of the clinic, the house. My childhood. My life as I've always known it, up until now.

"Yeah, I know what you mean." A soft sigh slips from him. "But in the end, it's just a building. It's replaceable. The people in it aren't. *You* aren't. You can set up a new clinic anywhere, and people will come to you."

I smile. "That's what Jonah said."

"It's true. Have you ever looked into one of those mobile vet clinic trailers? They had one on a show I was watching, and it made me think of you. You're always coming out to kennels, anyway, so why not drive your clinic there?"

I laugh. "Do you have *any idea* how much those cost?" I *have* looked into it. "Plus, then I'd need somewhere to park it."

"You could park it here."

"What? No. I'm not parking a clinic here."

"Why not? Look at all the land I've got, Marie. And I have a third bedroom we don't use. You're always welcome to it."

I don't know where these offers are coming from, but I assume they're empty. "I saw enough this morning about how you guys live around here to pass on that, but thanks, anyway."

He chuckles. "Didn't appreciate that one, huh?"

"I didn't say that." I'm sure I'll be dwelling on it late into the night.

"Haw," he calls out, directing the dogs to the left. I brace for the turn as they propel us forward.

"So, you *did*? Is that what you're saying?" There's a hint of something in his voice, and I sense him leaning closer into me, that familiar and intoxicating scent of cedar and citrus teasing my nostrils.

We're falling back into dangerous territory where he flirts, and I flirt back, and we both forget that he's going to hurt me. "I'll make sure to meet you in the barn from now on," I say in a more even tone, adding, "With more puppies, if you ever ask me to do this again."

He snorts. "I can't believe you did that."

"He needed a home, and really? You don't know me very well, then. I have no boundaries when it comes to dogs, remember?"

"I may not know everything about you, but I *know* you, Marie." His breath skates across my cheek. "And I miss you."

The longing in his voice tugs at my heart. "I miss you, too," I admit in a whisper before I can talk myself out of it.

His arms tighten around me, and he leans in to press his bristly cheek against mine, the corners of our mouths lined up perfectly. Just the tiniest turn from me, and our lips would find each other.

I shouldn't allow any of this, and yet I can't pull away, my eyes closing as I absorb this feeling, wishing this moment could last forever.

We slide home in silence.

————

"Happy birthday again!" I holler over my shoulder.

Mabel waves, and without hesitation, Reed waves back, his furry gift tucked beneath his arm as they disappear inside the barn.

Tyler is jogging from the house on a path toward us, and I instinctively slow my pace, allowing him to meet us just as we reach my truck.

"So, Mabel, what do you think? You interested in a part-time job here?" He holds her door open for her.

"Yeah, I think so." She matches her words with a nod. "This was fun." She holds up her torn gloves—one, care of Tank, and the other, Airi. "Except for this."

Tyler chuckles. "Yeah, I have a box full just like those in the house. Okay, come next Saturday at the same time?" With Mabel seated inside, he rounds the front of my truck to meet me on my side. "I think that's going to work out well."

"Yeah, they seemed to get along." Reed taught her how to unharness the dogs and water them when we returned. She took to the tasks naturally.

"Hey, I heard there was something going on at the Ale House tonight." His voice has shifted a notch to a softer, more inquisitive tone. "I'm going to take Reed. If he wants to get serious about competitive mushing next year, he needs to get out of this place and start meeting people."

"Those nights are usually fun."

"I'm sure he'd love it if you came." He hesitates. "So would I."

Thoughts of the last time Tyler and I met at the Ale House burn in my mind.

Why is he inviting me out again? Why is he saying these things to me? Is this still his attempt at friendship or has something changed? Has …

No, Marie, you can't go down this road again. "I'm sorry, I have plans tonight."

He bites his bottom lip, shifting his focus to nudging at the snow with his boot. "Are they legit plans? Or 'I'm being polite but drop dead, Tyler' plans?" His face cracks with a sexy, crooked smile. "Just for my own understanding."

There's humor in his tone, but I sense him holding his breath for my answer.

"Legit." I hesitate. "I'm seeing someone, and we're doing something tonight." Taking a trip up to Talkeetna to meet his friend at the brew house.

Tyler's brow furrows and I instantly regret being so truthful. "Right. Well, have a good night, then." With a gentle pat on my hood, he backs up. "And thanks again for coming out."

Nausea roils in my stomach as I climb into my truck and crank the engine.

Mabel frowns. "What's wrong?"

I force a smile. "Nothing."

And everything.

CHAPTER TWENTY-SEVEN

The faint, sweet scent of tobacco is in the air when I climb into Steve's truck. Lingering, I assume, from the package of cigars near the heat vent. I don't mind those as much as I mind cigarettes. Besides, he said he only smokes them occasionally.

"You look nice tonight." His blue eyes crinkle as he leans across the console to greet me with a spearmint gum–laced kiss, his lips lingering longer than usual. The first time he kissed me, it was at my porch door at the end of our first date, and he asked beforehand. Since then, he's grown bolder, and the lip locks have lasted longer. And I've been willing.

Now, though, I pull away.

"Hard day?" Steve deftly navigates his truck along my driveway and out to the road.

"*Long day.*" Spent lost in conflicted thoughts, battling the urge to cancel this date. I *should* have canceled, but then I'd be sitting at home, battling the urge to show up at the Ale House. I unfurl the knit scarf from around my neck. The truck is warm, and the drive to Talkeetna is almost an hour from my place. I may as well get comfortable.

"So … plans have changed," he announces. "A bunch of my

friends are meeting up in Trapper's Crossing. There's a big wing night happening out there, and I think it'll be a good time. Plus, it's a lot closer, and I've been up since four. I'm beat." Steve reaches over to collect my hand. His skin is calloused, his thumb wrapped in a bandage to hide a gnarly cut—one that *should* have seen stitches. "You're good with that, right?"

My stomach sinks. There's only one place in Trapper's Crossing he could be talking about. Am I good with showing up on one man's arm while the man who's dominating my thoughts sits across the room? No, of course I'm not good with this! But what am I supposed to say? What excuse do I give that doesn't trigger questions?

"Marie?" Steve's gaze darts between the road and me, his hand giving mine a squeeze.

"Yeah." I clear the strain from my voice. "I'm good."

If I'm lucky, maybe Tyler will have changed his mind about coming.

———

The blazing firepit to the right of the Ale House's front entrance is new, and a popular addition judging by the ring of people huddled around it, savoring pints. Above them, festive strands of colorful Christmas lights hang in the canopy. They match the ones lining the long, narrow building's roof that Muriel keeps up year round.

I try to be inconspicuous in my scan of the parking lot as we walk toward the hum of casual conversation. But it's dark, and there are several green trucks. I don't see any familiar ones.

"You've been here before, right?" Steve loops his arm around my waist, and I try not to stiffen. "It's a good place. Fun atmosphere. And Muriel and Teddy have owned it forever."

"You know them? Wait, of course you would." It only makes sense. They're all in the fishing industry.

I catch a familiar, deep laugh a moment before a bellow of "Marie!" carries. I couldn't see Jonah standing among the group before, with it being dark and me wrapped in growing dread. But there he is, Calla beside him. His presence is a life preserver thrown into deep waters, and some of the tension slips from my shoulders.

I check the other people in the circle. Some, I recognize. Locals who always make it out for the McGivneys' more festive nights. None are Tyler or Reed.

Maybe I've lucked out tonight.

I turn to Steve. "I'll meet you inside?"

A funny look skitters across his face, but it's quickly gone. "Sure. I'll grab you a beer." He kisses my cheek and then diverts his path.

And all I can think about is how that kiss doesn't stir an ounce of the desire that Tyler's bristly cheek pressed against mine earlier today did.

Jonah ropes his free arm around my shoulders and pulls me into a side hug. "I thought you weren't comin' tonight."

"Yeah, neither did I, but plans changed."

He watches Steve slip through the door. "Who's that guy?"

I smile at the wariness in his voice. "Just a guy." That maybe I *should* have introduced to my best friend. I nod toward the rectangular structure and the propane-fueled flames that dance over its surface. "This is fancy."

The diversion works. "Yeah. This was Calla's brainchild. Muriel actually listened."

I shift over to offer her a hug. Her hair smells like strawberries and cream. "How are you feeling?"

"I'm good! This trimester is *way* easier."

"Show her," Jonah goads, holding open Calla's coat.

I bark with laughter at her sweatshirt and the "future yeti" slogan printed across her adorable pregnant belly. "Did you change your mind about finding out what it is?"

K.A. TUCKER

Jonah's firm head shake answers that.

Calla rolls her eyes at him and then shifts away, her rapt attention on me. "So, *just* a guy?"

"We've been on a few dates." I shrug. "He's nice."

She lowers her voice to a whisper, "In case you care, Tyler's inside."

Nerves flutter in my stomach just hearing his name. "I knew he might be coming."

Her brow pinches with worry. "Are you going to be okay?"

"Honestly?" The fact that I'm standing here, talking about my trepidation concerning a man with *Calla* of all people, isn't lost on me. I could continue the lie, but she'll see right through me. "How long do you think I can hide out here before I'm a complete asshole?"

She winces and smooths her palm over my arm in a simple but comforting gesture. "Not long enough, I'm afraid."

We last another five minutes around the fire before Calla's teeth start chattering, and Jonah herds us both toward the door and into peak unease for me.

Outside was calm and casual and chilly. In here, it's loud and boisterous and toasty, the woodstove blazing with an orange glow. Music plays in the background, but the conversations are too loud for anyone to decipher the song. A medley of spices permeates the air, drifting over from the far side of the room where Muriel and Teddy man a row of tables lined with a dozen chafing dishes.

"I ain't never seen *anyone* drop a snow hook and run into the woods with a roll of shit tickets so fast in my life as Earl did!" A man with a straggly beard roars, slapping his hand across Harry Hatchett's shoulder. The entire group gathered in the center of the Ale House erupts with laughter.

They must be trading old musher stories. There are plenty of them here tonight, some long since retired, but many I recognize from the Iditarod, both mushers and volunteers alike.

Despite my trepidation, the moment I spot Tyler, my heart begins to race. He and Reed are seated at a table, gripping their pints and chuckling at the tales. They haven't noticed me yet, but this place isn't that big. It's only a matter of time.

"I was just about to come out to you." Steve appears then, holding a pint. "Local IPA. One of my favorites. I think you'll like it."

I remember tasting it on Tyler's tongue the last time I was here, and I loved it.

I smile politely as I accept it and then introduce Steve to Jonah and Calla. The conversation doesn't last long before someone's pulling Jonah aside, wanting to know about his planes. It's inevitable.

"Well, the sergeant is waving me down, so ... come see me when you're hungry. Or for *any reason*." With one last knowing look, Calla ambles toward Muriel, shedding her coat along the way.

"My friends are over there." Steve points toward the corner where a group sits, his hand settling on the small of my back, goading me that way.

But my focus quickly snags elsewhere, on the set of hazel eyes locked on me. Tyler's seen me, and there's not much I can do but cast a tentative wave.

He returns it with a lazy salute, but his face is stony.

I feel sick, as if I'm doing something wrong when I know I'm not. *He's* the one who isn't ready. Not me. I was ready for *everything*.

"Are you okay?"

I nod, hoping it hides my inner turmoil. "You know what? I'll be there in a minute. There's someone at the bar I need to say hello to first." I don't wait for Steve's response, rushing to the other side of the room, hoping to find temporary haven in Toby.

Only, Harry Hatchett cuts me off.

I stifle my groan.

"Hey, Marie! I was going to come into your clinic next week, but here you are. Man, it's been awhile, huh?" He smooths a hand through his blond hair.

"Since you tried to tell me how to run my business and then set fire to a four-decade relationship between our families? A few months, yeah." I am in no mood to be exchanging false pleasantries. I step to the side to go around him.

He moves with me. "I'm sorry." His face is a mask of sincere apology. "I was an idiot, and I was wrong."

His blunt admission takes me by surprise.

"The last few years have been hard. It may seem like I know what I'm doing, but half the time, I think I should quit." He pauses, as if waiting for me to counter his frank words.

I allow the awkward break in conversation to drag on until Harry begins to fidget. "I appreciate your apology. Is there something else you want?" Bonnie must have relayed my father's advice.

"Okay, what I mean to say is, you and Sid have always been good to us. *Too* good. You are the best vet I could ever hope for, and I was hoping you'd come back. At least consider it," he adds quickly. "The dogs would love to see you."

I know Harry is quickly running out of veterinarians, but I sense remorse in his voice. Taking on his kennel again would alleviate financial worries—that he aggravated in the first place. But I'm not in the right frame of mind to be making commitments to him. "I'll consider it."

His shoulders sag with relief.

Seated at Harry's table is a young woman twirling locks of auburn hair while scrolling through her phone, looking out of place surrounded by a pack of weathered mushers. "You should get back to your date. I'll let you know what I decide next week." Let him sweat for a few days.

With that, I head for the bar.

Toby sees me approaching, and his scruffy face splits with a wide smile. "Didn't know you were coming." He frowns at the pint in my hand. "Changing things up?"

"Don't ask." I set the drink on the counter.

Roy is on the stool next to me, gnawing on a chicken wing. In front of him is a full bottle of beer that will still be full at the end of the night.

"Good wings?"

He grunts in response.

I shrug off my coat and hang it next to his cowboy hat on the wall. "How's Lucky?" That's what Mabel's been calling the white puppy after Roy refused to name it. Agnes and Mabel are keeping her at their place for now, until she gets bigger, and he gets used to the idea of owning another dog.

"Still alive and annoying."

And wearing a pink collar that Roy drove into town to buy for her, from what I've heard.

"Marie!" Agnes saunters through the swinging tavern-style door, holding a tray of clean glasses. Around her hips is a bar apron with several beer bottle openers holstered in the pockets.

"*Agnes*? You work here now?"

"I'm helpin' out. Pouring drinks and giving people advice." She grins as she carefully positions a pint glass to the draft tap, dispensing the beer with the skill of a person just learning how. "I always wanted to be a bartender, ever since I saw *Cocktail*. What do you think? Do I look like Tom Cruise?"

"Just your hair." Roy tosses a meatless bone onto his plate and then pauses mid reach for another one. For as long as I've known Agnes, her dark hair has been cropped short and always uneven, as if she cuts it herself. "It suits you better," he offers after a moment.

I hide my smile behind a sip of my beer. Was it the wings or the bartender that drew the old grouch to the Ale House tonight?

"Was that a new fella I saw you with over there, Marie?" she asks.

"Yeah. We've been on a few dates."

"You think it might be serious?" Her dark eyes flicker from the pour to my face. I don't miss the hopefulness in that look. She was never blind to my feelings for Jonah.

"Not while she's in love with *that* other one over there." Roy waves his wing in Tyler's direction.

My mouth gapes. "I'm *not* in—"

"*Who?*" Agnes follows his direction, leaning over the bar and searching the faces.

"Black and tan flannel. Tyler somethin'."

"The musher who just hired Mabel at his kennel?"

"You should have seen those two at her vet place last week." Roy takes another bite.

"Oh, *that* one," she whispers conspiratorially, as if the two of them have been gossiping, before seeking Tyler out again.

My stomach drops. He's watching us with a curious frown. "Would you two stop it?" I hiss.

"What?" Roy scowls. "All you young folk think I don't know what's what around here."

In my peripheral vision, I see Tyler climbing out of his chair. He's on his way over.

Excitement and panic compete for my attention.

"Hey." The word drifts out on Tyler's sigh. "Didn't think you were coming."

"Yeah, neither did I." And that line is getting stale.

His focus flitters from me to the pint—he frowns—to Roy and his half-eaten plate of wings, then to Agnes behind the bar, as if he's trying to figure out how we all fit, and more importantly, why we were talking about him just now.

"Tyler, you met Roy." *Kind of.* I gesture across the bar. "This is Mabel's mom, Agnes."

Agnes smiles wide. "My daughter's excited for her new job. She's always loved dogs."

"That's great. We're looking forward to having her there." He bites his bottom lip in thought and then his expression turns somber. "Marie, can I talk to you for a minute? Outside?"

I guess we're going to do this now.

I check the back corner where Steve is occupied with his friends. "Yeah, sure." I reach around Roy to collect my coat again, the cold still clinging to the material.

"It's because she knows when to not give up," Roy murmurs quietly.

I frown. "What?"

"Calla. She always gets what she wants because she knows when to *not* give up." Roy peers over his shoulder, his shrewd eyes meeting mine. "Maybe you should take a page out of her book this time."

His words trigger my memory of our conversation back in the summer when Roy was cursing crooked cabinets, and I was envious of Calla's full and perfect life.

I guess he's not wrong. She didn't give up on Jonah or on Alaska. She certainly didn't give up on this prickly man, when I hazard most others have, and now I don't think there's a single thing he wouldn't do for her if she asked. And even if she didn't.

With an appreciative smile, I pull on my jacket.

Steve notices me heading out and flashes a questioning look.

I hold up my hand, palm out, and mouth, *Five minutes*, and then dismiss him from my thoughts as I walk out the door. A few people linger around the firepit, including Jonah. He pauses in his conversation, lifting his chin as if to ask what's going on.

I shrug and trail Tyler who leads me across the lot toward the shadows of a snow-laden spruce. The cold air is a welcome relief.

"Hatchett asked you to come back, didn't he?"

"Yeah. I told him I'd think about it." The last thing I want to talk about is Harry Hatchett. "Tyler, I—"

"Is it serious?" He faces me. "This guy. Is it serious between you and him?"

I falter at his pained stare and the stress in his tone. "We've been on a few dates. He's nice. I like him."

"But you don't want to be with him."

"I don't?"

"You stiffened when he put his hand on your back."

He noticed that. *Of course* he did. "That was because you're here," I admit.

His mouth twitches with a tiny smirk of satisfaction before he smooths his expression. "*Is it serious?*" he asks again, slowly this time.

I hesitate. Why is it so hard to give him an answer? "You know it's not."

He exhales heavily. "Then end it."

"What?" My laugh is hollow.

"I know it's not fair for me to ask, after everything." Tyler steps closer, his throat bobbing with a hard swallow. "But I *need* you to end it. You can't be with someone else."

"Tyler—"

"No, just listen for a minute. Please." He hangs his head, as if trying to gather his thoughts. "My old life is gone. I've always known that, but I'm finally starting to see it, if that makes any sense. I can run that team across Alaska a hundred times, and it won't change a thing. She won't ever be there at the finish line." He collects my face in his hands. "But you will be. I *want* you to be. I *can't* lose you, too."

A rush of warmth radiates throughout my body. "I don't know what you want from me." My voice sounds weak, helpless. He's saying all the right things, everything I want to hear, but that has never been his problem.

His thumb strokes my cheek. "Give me another chance."

"So you can hurt me again?"

"I promise, it won't happen again. *I* won't do that again. *Ever.*" Sincerity shines in his bright gaze as he shakes his head firmly. "I wasn't ready before."

My pulse races. "Are you saying you're ready now?" For what, exactly?

"I *will* be. It just might take me some time, but I want you here with me while I get to that place. I *need* you with me. I want to give you *everything* you want. I'm in love with you." He leans in to press his forehead against mine, his mouth inches away. "Please don't give up on me yet."

His words are an echo of what Roy just said inside, and coupled with his declaration, they pierce through all doubts and reservations.

"Marie?"

I startle and break away from Tyler, my guilt surging.

Steve stands over on the cleared path, twenty feet away. Maybe too far to hear what was said but surely close enough to see that this is far more than a platonic chat. The look on his face says as much.

Reed has ventured outside and is at the firepit next to Jonah, who watches us intently, looking ready to involve himself if needed.

Tyler smooths his palm over his beard. He has the decency to offer Steve a murmured *sorry* before he turns back to me. The question in his stare is clear, even within the shadows.

I swallow. "I need time to think." Time away from this heady vacuum I always get sucked into when I'm around Tyler, where nothing else matters.

His chest lifts with a deep inhale. "Reed and I are going to head home now." His eyes touch my lips. I know that look well. He wants to kiss me. If Steve weren't standing right here, I would let him. "You know where to find me, if you decide you want to." With that, he nods at Reed and then moves deeper into the parking lot for their truck.

And I slowly walk toward the man who doesn't deserve any of this. "I'm so sorry."

"Oliver mentioned that there was another guy." Steve watches Tyler's truck pull onto the road. "I take it that's him?"

"Yeah. I guess we still have some unresolved issues to work through." Namely, that I'm madly in love with him, and it sounds like the feeling is mutual. I allow that reality sink in for just a moment and a rush of adrenaline washes over me. "You're a great guy. Under different circumstances ..." I let the words drift because I know firsthand how much it doesn't help to hear them.

And if I'd never met Tyler, I wouldn't hesitate to invite Steve to Sunday dinner. Maybe I would've already invited him into my home, into my bed.

Maybe I'd be thinking about a future with him.

But the only future I'm able to see anymore has a hazel-eyed man with a crooked smirk in it.

"Well, if you guys decide you can't resolve your issues, give me a call." He smiles, but it lacks its usual warmth, and I can't say I blame him. He looks to the Ale House, to where his friends are. "I guess I'll give you a ride home, unless you wanted to stay longer?"

The last thing I want to do is go back into the Ale House, especially now that Tyler is gone. But the fifteen-minute ride home with Steve after this sounds even less appealing.

"I've got ya, Lehr," Jonah hollers, keys dangling from his fingers.

And my shoulders slump with relief.

Steve hesitates.

"It's okay. Go back and see your friends."

After another moment's hesitation and a lingering look—I'm sure this is not how he saw the night ending—Steve casts a wave and heads back inside.

Five minutes later, once Jonah's told Calla that he's driving me home, I'm climbing into the passenger's seat of his truck.

"Marie ..." He shakes his head as he cranks the engine and throws the truck into gear.

I chuckle. "Let me guess. I'm too much drama."

"What are you gonna do?"

"I don't know." I curl my arms around myself for comfort. "I know what I *want* to do."

"But you're scared of getting hurt."

"I'm scared of getting hurt *again*."

And again.

And again.

What does Tyler even expect? He said he *will* be ready. Does that mean I'm supposed to sit home alone and wait for his call?

The truck's powerful engine roars along the dark highway toward my house. Jonah's only ever had one speed for as long as I've known him: fast. "Remember after Calla flew back to Toronto? She told me she couldn't stay, and I accepted it, and I was fucking miserable. For months. And then you sent me the flight information to Toronto and told me to get on the plane already?"

I smile. "Yeah. I remember." The hardest—and best—thing I could have done for him both as his friend and someone who loved him dearly.

"If you hadn't given me that kick in the ass that I needed ..." He grimaces as he watches the road ahead.

"You would have gone, eventually." Jonah has never been afraid of taking a chance.

"Maybe." He drums the steering wheel with his thumbs—a tell that means he's in deep thought. "I don't know what all happened with you two because you haven't been talking to me—" He shoots a glare my way. "But it's pretty damn obvious you both want this to work, and you just don't know how. Don't waste your time with guys like *Steve*. I know you, Mare. I know what you want, and he ain't it."

"I guess not." Steve was convenient and easy, but he wasn't *it*. I want it all. Consuming passion and camaraderie, laughter and strength, hope and comfort.

It exists. I've seen it every time I look at Jonah and Calla.

And maybe I can have it for myself, too.

My heart flutters with the thought.

"Okay, so, this is *me* now, telling *you* to grow a spine and get on the fucking plane already. Because what I saw back there? That was a guy who meant whatever he was saying to you. And if he dicks you around again?" He gives me a serious look. "I know *all* the best spots to drop a body where it'll never be found."

I study Jonah's profile within the shadows of the truck, and my heart aches, not with longing for what I wish I'd had with him, but with pure gratitude for what I *do* have—loyal and uncompromising friendship. "I am *so* happy for you."

"I know you are." His eyes dart from the road for a split second, long enough to meet mine. He reaches across the console to squeeze my hand. "Now, do something that will make *me* happy for *you*. Go and get your dog man."

Our deep laughter fills his truck.

———

My fists curl tightly around my steering wheel, not because the road ahead is pitch-black beyond my headlights, and not because my tires catch the odd icy patch.

And definitely not because I'm doubting this decision.

In my gut and my heart and my head, I know Tyler is the one for me, even if our path here hasn't been simple. Even if the path forward proves bumpy.

I ease up to Tyler's driveway and consider the gate across it, pulled closed. It's late, but they couldn't have made it home too long ago. I reach for my phone but pause.

With a grin, I throw my truck in reverse.

And then slam my foot on the gas pedal.

The barn is nothing more than a shadow in the darkness when I reach the house, but the door is propped open, and a dark silhouette stands within it.

Tyler.

My blood pounds in my ears as I hop out of my truck and into the frigid night.

"How bad is it this time?" Humor laces his voice as he walks toward me.

"It's still hanging on by the hinges. The chain snapped." Kind of like me—clinging to hope, unwilling to let go. I trudge through the deep snow, my pace picking up the closer I get until I'm running. Running toward Tyler and whatever this is between us, unable to get to him fast enough.

But I'm not the only one this time, as he rushes my way.

We collide somewhere in the middle.

CHAPTER TWENTY-EIGHT

March

I pull the cowl of my coat tighter around my face. It's three A.M., minus ten degrees Fahrenheit, and my nose hairs are clinging together, but the growing cheers as Tyler approaches the Burled Arch for his second Iditarod win give me the warmth I need.

"They look good," Reed says, and I know his big brown eyes are on Nymeria, trotting alongside Tank, their mouths parted as they pant. He never experienced this last year, but Tero and Anja Rask came in from Finland again, and stayed at the kennel to care for Nala and the puppies. Jonah reluctantly agreed to leave Calla and two-week-old Wren at home to fly Reed up to Nome.

I give the dogs a quick glance as they close in and then my attention shifts to the man coasting in behind them. I haven't seen Tyler in six days, not since his twenty-four-hour rest at the Ophir checkpoint where I was working. It's the longest I've gone without seeing him, even during his lengthy training runs, preparing for this. He looks exhausted and cold and in need of a long, hot shower that I will gladly join him for back at the inn.

"Come on." With a hand against Reed's back, together we weave through the crowd to where the sled and team have come to a stop. By the time we reach it, Tyler is handing out frozen treats for the dogs and officials are rooting through his sled.

The dogs start howling at Reed who gives Tyler a brief hug before dismissing him entirely and dropping to the snow-covered ground to greet his canine companions.

Tyler dives for me, collecting me in his arms while simultaneously leaning into me as if for support. "God, I missed your face. It's all I've pictured for the last two hundred miles."

I ignore the reality that there are cameras on us and kiss him. "You did it. Again."

His forehead presses against mine. Ice pellets cling to his short but scruffy beard. "Reed can take them next year."

I chuckle. "I'll believe that when I see it." Tyler may have started this adventure in honor of Mila, but there's an innate drive in him. I've watched him for months now, dedicated to this journey he began after she died—day after day of abandoning a warm bed with me in it for a regimented day of conditioning himself and the dogs, leaving for days and sleeping on straw alongside them on the winter highway between Cantwell and Paxson.

He always returns to me with an unwavering heart.

"So?" He pulls away far enough to meet my eyes, eagerness in his. I see his burning question, begging for an answer.

I've learned that same drive laces through every facet of Tyler's life, the same determination to succeed. He once said that when he's in, he's all in, and that wasn't an exaggeration.

I think we both had intentions of wading into this relationship slowly when we reunited.

And we both figured out quickly—within five minutes of stepping into an empty paddock in the barn—that it would be impossible.

Since then, I've grown comfortable in Tyler's home, spending every night there when he wasn't out training and I didn't have an overnight patient, and even some nights when he was away. I've discovered Reed's competitive streak with the help of his PlayStation, and there have been several late nights of trash-talk while he pulverizes me at his video game of choice.

My little cabin in the woods beside the clinic has grown lonely over the months.

But it won't be lonely for much longer.

It's been a month since I sat my father down at the table with an apple pie and two bottles of beer and told him that it's time to sell. Tyler was on a training run, and Liz had just given birth to her third daughter, so my mother was at their place with the older girls. It was just the two of us.

He didn't argue.

Too much.

We have work ahead of us to get the property ready for the market in the spring. And I have *a lot* to figure out with how best to continue helping all the animals I've come to know and love, including Harry Hatchett's kennel. But what I do know, without a shadow of doubt, is that there's no one else I would rather make these decisions with than the man before me, as I begin this next chapter of my life.

"I took the test yesterday morning."

"*And?*" There's urgency in his voice and hope in his eyes. It's as if the crowd, the cameras, the waiting officials, none of them exist as he holds his breath and waits for an answer. I think he may want this even more than I do. He's certainly earned top marks for his effort these past few months, when we decided we would let whatever is meant to happen, happen.

I smile. "Did I forget to tell you that we Lehr women only have girls?"

ACKNOWLEDGMENTS

This was a fun but tough book to write. I always knew Marie would be an interesting character once I took the time to explore her. She's a woman who knows who she is and what she wants, but still grapples with how to get it. I really enjoyed getting to know her, as well as seeing Jonah and Calla from her point of view. This book is much subtler and softer than Calla and Jonah's story of plane crashes and tragic death, but I felt that subtle and soft is how Marie's tale should unfold—with competitive siblings and aging parents and real-life worries. I hope you enjoyed this different experience within this world.

As much as I've lived in this fictional world since 2017, when I sat down to write, I had to learn a lot about an industry that has proven controversial, especially in recent years. I wanted to recognize the real—fair—concerns while also respecting the sport, the history, and the good people who still embrace dogsledding today. There are *a lot* of opinions on both sides, and some things, I'm wary to believe. But I did have the opportunity to visit one of these kennels during my trip to Alaska in the fall. The dogs were *very* happy and seemed eager to run. They also loved to steal gloves and we were warned they might pee on us if we stood long enough (I kept moving.) I knew that had to make it in.

In case you were wondering about timelines, Marie's "today" starts in January, 2020. I couldn't bring myself to type out that year though, as it has brought such turmoil to every part of the world, including Alaska and the Iditarod race world. It would have been impossible to incorporate that real-life situation without losing the entire story. Within these pages, COVID does not exist.

I will continue to say an immense thank you to my readers. The Simple Wild released in 2018 and your positive energy for this fictional world has grown exponentially.

Hang Le, for your incomparable cover design talent.

Jenn Sommersby, for your editing prowess, your kind words, and your wisdom.

Chanpreet Singh, for lending your shrewd eyeballs to this manuscript in search of the mistakes I missed.

Nina Grinstead and the team at Valentine PR, for helping to shine a light on this book and for all the behind-the-scenes legwork getting copies of this story into eager hands.

Stacey Donaghy of Donaghy Literary Group, for nine years of support, negotiations, and combing through contracts. But also for the laughs.

My family, who has finally (mostly) embraced the Do Not Disturb sign on my office door, and still care to ask what I'm writing next.

ABOUT THE AUTHOR

K.A. Tucker writes captivating stories with an edge.

She is the internationally bestselling author of the Ten Tiny Breaths, Burying Water and The Simple Wild series, He Will Be My Ruin, Until It Fades, Keep Her Safe, Be the Girl, Say You Still Love Me, and A Fate of Wrath & Flame. Her books have been featured in national publications including USA Today, Globe & Mail, Suspense Magazine, Publisher's Weekly, Oprah Mag, and First for Women.

K.A. Tucker currently resides in a quaint town outside of Toronto.

Learn more about K.A. Tucker and her books at katuckerbooks.com